Paper Edition

of

Greatlander

by

Michael Bruce-Lockhart

ISBN 978-0-9864815-2-9

Publisher:
Cool Pond Publishing
www.coolpond.ca
236 bennett's rd.,
portugal cove, nl,
canada A1M 1Y5

1st paper edition, August. 2010
Also available as:
Kindle edition ISBN 978-0-986415-1-2
Smashwords edition ISBN 978-0-986415-0-5

for **Mona Alwine Ivy Bruce-Lockhart**
Who taught me how to read
And so opened the world

Table of Contents

Map of The Land

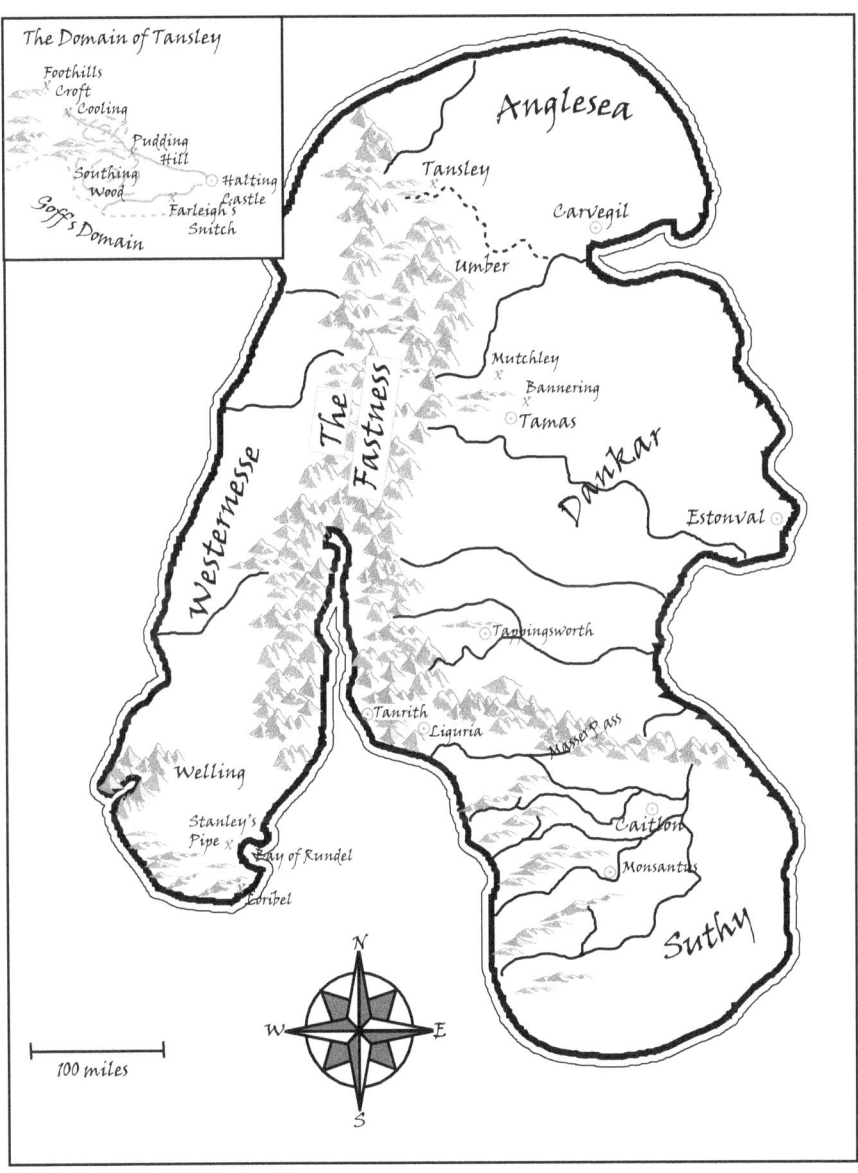

The Domain of Tansley

Foothills
Croft
Cooling
Pudding Hill
Southing Wood
Halting Castle
Farleigh's Snitch
Goff's Domain

Anglesea

Tansley

Carvegil

Umber

Westernesse

The Fastness

Mutchley

Bannering

Tamas

Dankar

Estonval

Tappingsworth

Tanrith

Liguria

Masser Pass

Welling

Stanley's Pipe

Bay of Rundel

Loribel

Caitlon

Monsantus

Suthy

N
W   E
S

100 miles

Prologue

The trap was subtle. Carefully, Damon moved his head, trying to define it. Fourth level? No, just below that, deep hidden, its full extent not clear. Nonetheless he was sure it was there. *Joshua Trap.* Damon kept his eyes locked on the center of the maze even as his head slid sideways, trying to hide his exultation. It was seldom that he saw them until too late. Just for once he was ahead of the game. His motion flicked the pieces in and out, occluding and emerging, establishing the crucial boundaries of the pattern. Automatically, he kept up his stream of routine orders, pressing forward as if nothing had occurred. *Keep the detection undetected,* he thought, forcing the attack down and right, sliding his forces past the trap as if he hadn't seen it. *Must flow smoothly to the trip point.* All the time he looked for his chance to cut back against the grain. *There!* One more second and he could veer, taking the scout on the pattern's flank. The rest of it would collapse around that crucial point.

Instead, wildly to starboard, it was the ship that veered. Joshua screamed, a long wailing cry unlike any Damon had ever heard him make. Sheer inertia hurled him across the cabin smashing him heavily into the port bulkhead. Rebounding, he grabbed desperately at the back of the settee as he went past. The support pad tore half away before he managed to bring himself into some kind of equilibrium. Fire coursed down his left arm. Somewhere in the back of his mind he registered his shoulder had dislocated.

Above the wardroom table the game maze had completely disappeared, as if Damon's passage through it had somehow shattered it. He shook his head at that impossibility. Joshua must have shut the projectors down when he veered the ship. For a moment Damon wondered if Josh hadn't realized that he'd discovered the trap and had decided to abort the game rather than lose it. He'd been a little shirty about *upstart mannequins* the only other time he'd lost.

Only time Damon corrected himself. The game had been far from over. Josh hadn't lost yet and there was no way he would put the safety of the ship, or Damon (*In that order,* he said to himself ruefully), at risk out of pique. It was a blank impossibility for personality modules to override the purpose of the base computer.

Even as he recognized the unworthiness of his thought, the silence in the cabin clamored for his attention. *Josh should already have reported.* Opening his mouth to break it himself, Damon was stilled as all the lights went out. Appallingly, he found himself in absolute blackness, absolute stillness, as if someone had hurled him into a coffin, ready made in the earth.

Panic welled inside him, thick and viscous, utterly debilitating. Blindly, he scrabbled at the bulkhead, searching for a porthole seal, a switch, a protrusion, anything to get himself light. Within seconds, he stopped abruptly, sweating and panting. "Easy," he muttered to himself, "Easy." Panic, he knew, could kill him just as dead as anything else. Deliberately, he turned around, feeling the edges of the settee, and sat down. As his panting slowed, he listened carefully, finally picking out the soft hum of the ventilator fans. Some power, then. Air. He tried to think through why the lights were out. Any power should mean plenty of power, for even if the reactor were down, Josh always kept the accumulators fully charged. *So if it wasn't power, it had to be control.* That didn't parse either. In the event of a complete control failure, the fail-safe condition was to put the emergency lights on, which they manifestly were not.

"Which means," said Damon out loud, "This is deliberate! Josh. Josh! Are you there?"

For several seconds, there was no answer. Then, just as Damon was about to call out again, a light came on. Not a conventional light. Not even one of the emergency units. Just a dim white glow that the spacer couldn't place, coming from the far corner of the cabin. He was practically on top of it before he recognized it as the screen on Josh's console. Josh had activated it, then, something that he only did for their annual equipment check, at which time all the cabin lights were on.

Tentatively, the man called out, "Josh... Josh. Are you there?"

No answer. Whatever the reason, Josh couldn't talk. Probably, since the screen remained empty of all except the blinking cursor, he couldn't even hear. Reaching back across the years to his basic training, Damon put hands to the unfamiliar keys. Laboriously, he began to type.

"j o s h . A r yu t h e r e?"

"You mean 'Are you there?', Oh man. Yes, I've turned off my verbal circuitry."

"Never mind the lesun." Damon swore, but it wasn't so satisfying with no one listening. He banged at the keys again, "I havent ritten since scool. Why?"

"School, Damon; with an 'h' and 'written', with a 'w'."

"C U T T H A T O U T !" Damon slammed the letters down. "What hapened?   Report!"

The font shifted. In his head Damon could hear the slight prissiness that crept into Joshua's voice whenever he deemed himself annoyed, "*I veered to avoid a micro meteor, small enough to escape detection until the last moment, energetic enough to do us real damage. The maneuver badly stressed the reactor and the main regulator blew.*"

"Thats crazy!!" typed Damon. "The sheeld would have handeled the problem."

"No, man. The meteor was aimed right at the generator coils, at the one spot where the lines are perpendicular to the hull. The energy was sufficient to give it a thirty percent chance of actually penetrating."

"One in a million!", Damon muttered to himself.

The screen scrolled on. "The odds against that precise event appear to be one in thirteen million, taken over the expected lifetime of a typical vessel of this class, presuming of course that it always operated in this region of space."

"What the hell!", roared Damon. "Josh, why am I making a fool of myself typing if you can hear me?"

The screen remained obstinately blank. "W H Y A R E Y O U M A K I N G M E T Y P E?", hammered Damon, banging the keys again for emphasis.

"I have shut down all unnecessary circuits to conserve power, oh mannequin, including my hearing and normal vision systems. I merely speculated that you would say 'one in a million', as I hypothesize you did from the damage you are seeking to do to my keys. It is your usual response to unlikely events."

"Yor heering and speech sistems only consume a smal fraction of yor power," objected the man.

"True. But the rest of me must go at full speed to keep up with them. Currently I am running on only one cycle in a hundred, cutting my power requirements by close to that same factor, but rendering me incapable of keeping up with those systems."

For the first time since the lights went out, Damon felt himself becoming genuinely alarmed. "Why the panic?", he typed, then winced at the irony and cursed anew the inadequacy of the keyboard.

"Damon, I think the regulator is damaged past all repair. It is not a matter of replacing a few components. The entire unit is fused past recognition. It can only be repaired by a major depot."

"Which puts us in the soup, for fair," muttered the human. He sat back from the keyboard, rubbing his chin thoughtfully. If Josh was right, they were beyond help. There simply wasn't enough power in the accumulators to get them back to a port. As far as they were from the regular lanes stars would die before anyone stumbled upon them.

"Lite the enjin room," he typed, "AND THE COMPANEUNWAY and Ill go check."

It was more than an hour until he returned. Five minutes in the engine room had been all he needed to ascertain that Josh was right. There was no hope for the unit. Nevertheless, he was a careful man and went over it minutely, seeing what, if anything, could be salvaged. Nothing could, nor could he see a way to lash together another. Not with the spares and tools he had. The damage was too great. For twenty more minutes, he took stock, mulling over his options, trying to find some way out of the bind before slowly making his way back to the terminal.

"Josh," he typed. "Why did yu turn so vilently?"

There was a long pause before the screen began to scroll again. "Boss," replied Josh, "It's hard to let you know how—SHEEPISH—I feel, using a screen. I had laid a little trap for you, down in the fourth level of the maze, well disguised. For an instant I thought you might have detected it, but I was unsure. So I turned up the gain and concentrated all the attention I could on you, trying to tell from your expression or your actions whether you knew or not."

Reading that, Damon stirred uneasily. Sometimes Josh was so human it scared him. He shook his head and continued.

"It was only for a few seconds, but it was enough to let the meteor in under my guard. I detected it late and reacted too violently. I'm afraid I called for far more power than was needed, and so overstressed the regulator."

"Blew it apart, more like. You were rite—it can't be repared." He paused for a moment, then typed, "What are our opshuns?"

"At the risk of pedantry, Oh man, I will summarize…

"Item We have blown the main reactor past all hope of repair.

"Item We have enough power in the accumulators to continue on our present trajectory in comfort for 2.3 years. This could be eked out to 7.5 years with careful rationing.

"Item Although we are 2 years from the nearest rescue center, there are no relay beacons at the last two gates we came through so it will take 140.3 years for our SOS to get to them.

"Item There are no useful planets within the region we find ourselves in.

"Item There is inadequate power for us to return to the last gate and boost through it.

"Item There is enough power to reach the gate we were headed for, jump through it, and proceed at standard speed for a further two months.

"Item No survey ship has ever been out even this far. We have no knowledge of where that gate leads, whether there are any star systems close to its exit, or whether they have any useful planets."

Damon considered the list for a minute and shook his head. Finally he typed, "Josh, I want to TALK to yu. Too important for this dam aneshunt tecknology!!"

There was a long pause. Then the screen switched off, plunging the cabin back into darkness.

"I am here, O mannequin."

"A light, Josh." His tone brooked no argument, "At least one."

Joshua sighed audibly, and turned on one lamp, very low, perhaps one tenth normal power.

"Thanks, Josh. Now, look, did you compute a normal solution, with all systems functional?"

"No, Damon. I assumed stringent power rationing. Which," he added with some asperity, "Assumption may have to be revised somewhat in view of our differing ideas on what stringent means."

"I understand that. But you did assume all necessary systems functioning, continuous monitoring and continuous control?"

"Yes, oh man. How else can we operate?"

"Ballistically, Joshua. Take aim, fire the engines, and then travel free, like a shell from an ancient cannon."

"I see, oh man. A clever solution. We can extend the search radius on the other side of the gate by about three percent. Not much, but every bit helps."

"So little," said Damon, crestfallen.

"You see," Joshua added apologetically, "The energy gains in the ballistic method are largely offset by the longer time taken to get there."

"You still don't get it, you bucket of bolts. I ought to have you checked for advanced electromigration in your calculating circuits! Look, I'm going to have to get into the medicom unit for at least forty-eight hours to get my shoulder fixed. Why not just leave me there and turn everything off that's not needed."

"The oxygen savings would be significant, but they don't take much power. And I hadn't intended to give you much lighting..."

"Heat, you electronic twit! You can let the ship go ambient, heating only the medicom. And I can strip some of the outside insulation to increase its R factor quite a bit."

There was a distinct electronic pause. "I calculate at least five times, Damon," Joshua said at last. He sounded almost humble. "Maybe you had better get my circuits checked. Since ninety point three percent of the power is required to get through the gate, we can increase our operational radius on the far side by a factor of three point four."

Damon got up and paced back and forth down the length of the cabin. At length he said quietly, "OK, Josh. This is really the reason I insisted we talk. If you get through the other side and find no…" and he hesitated briefly, "Useful planet within striking distance, you are to wake me." He faced the central control panel as he always did when engaged in serious conversation with Josh, even though he knew it made no difference. "I don't just want to go down in the dark. I'd rather live less time trying to take another game off you and end up with a hell of a party!" He finished up, "Is that absolutely clear?"

There was a moment's pause, then "Clear, boss!"

"Good. To work."

An hour or so later, Damon completed the jury-rig on the insulation and stood back while Josh measured the result. "A thirty-seven point four fold increase," he announced shortly, "Yielding a three point eight six factor increase in operational radius. Good work, boss." Reopening the cover, he waited while Damon climbed in, then closed it again and sealed it down. "Still three point eight six," he whispered in Damon's left ear.

Damon heard the whish as the anesthetic gases hissed in. Wondering whether he should save his only bottle of Hyperion whiskey for one big blowout or spread it out over the last few weeks, he was hauled down into the black and the cold.

Part I
The Boy

Chapter 1

I was born in the seven hundred and sixty-seventh year of the coming, an auspicious year, according to the priest though my mother put little stock in that. All her faith was for the god and she'd not much left over for priests. *Of the coming.* 'Twas an old style, even then, but she never could give a date without it so I got used to it and still think of the year of my birth that way. For her the coming was a shining time—I heard a thousand tellings of the old tales at her knee: of the five enormous boats that left the great land and pushed off to sea, leaving its evil behind; how they, one by one, were lost in storms and in the distance, in the endless, marching waves; how the remaining boat, guided by the god, had made it at last to the land, finding it empty and clean and free.

Whatever skill I have with words I got from her. She could make me see those waves, rolling on, not just for miles but for days and weeks and months. When I was small she would conjure them up before my drowsy eyes and send me rocking off to sleep upon their endless crests. I used to wake up believing I had arrived at last in the land with the people. Then the morning chill would get through and I'd know it wasn't so, but I wondered, sometimes, what it would be like to come new to a place, to be one with the god and with the people. Old bones you will say, but I was a farmer's lad, the barest trembling step above a serf, and this was magic to me. The more so as I knew from the few times I had played with other children that they'd only the vaguest notion of the tales. It made me feel special.

'Tis easy now to talk of us as almost-serfs but that trembling step which separated us from all the rest, was the sheerest cliff, impossibly high, which somehow my father still managed to climb. He resisted the notion that made him better. In his quiet way he managed to convey I was privileged, but in the old sense, meaning at the bottom I was no different from anybody else, just luckier. Beyond those two things, I felt no particular call. We lived remote in Anglesea, on the marches with Umbria. The domain of Tansley was all my world, and most of that only by repute. An I'd thought about it, which I did not, I would have said my life was a single thread somewhere out on the edges of a small and unimportant tapestry.

I have seen the mothers hush their children and point, whispering of the great lord, Nicodemus. I have been called enchanter and conduit of the god, the king's eyes and boy and harper. Though the god bumped the weaving so my thread lies not at the edge but somehow wormed its way into the very heart of the central hanging in the land, its color is not the brighter for that. Whatever the mothers say, I am not a great man for having been in the center of great events.

Sa. I spend most of my time before the fire now. In part, these old bones like its heat more than that of the hypocaust. 'Tis the basking heat of sunshine, of springtime and of youth and not the dry rasping of old age. But more, my eyes grow dim, hide it as I may. 'Tis only in the flames' dance that I find a few ghosts of what I once could see. There, and in my dreams, where the colors are as bright as ever they once were and my limbs as straight as childhood. I wonder sometimes whether the colors of memory are not brighter, made shiny mayhap by much handling. Most things fade from use, but memory is a jewel that, buffed, throws back the light. Alas! 'Tis split now into a myriad of fragments, each burnished still and bright, but broken from the others at the edges. The shape of the whole is there, the pieces clear but not the fit. Life reduced in the end to a dance of splinters.

They turn now before me, in the fire's flicker: old friends and enemies, great deeds and small remembrances, weaving in and out together. But always I see in the pattern, like a gifted dancer that stands out against the common swirl, that one, extraordinary sunset. At the time, it seemed a gift to cap a day of gifts, come straight from the god. There! Almost, I can touch it, the colors bright in the air, paling the poor fire behind. Time's polishings, mayhap, but it marked both the end and the beginning for me. Little wonder an the glow has grown with age…

§

I was late. No little matter, for my father was a stern master and we both knew the day had been gifted. Such grants came seldom and my father was not the man to be taken advantage of. Even so, he was just. My excuse would put no smile on his lips, yet an I spoke fair of the cause and looked him straight, he would accept it. There was little enough of beauty in our lives. Though he'd never have stopped himself, the certainty that my mother would should be enough.

It had been a rare day, the first real day of spring after a hard winter, which is why my father had gifted me it. The god knows, there was work enough and more for me on our croft. Since the snows had been in retreat we had worked through the lengthening days clawing the land back from the winter— repairing walls and drains torn apart by the frosts, plowing the stony soil. Hard labor for a lad of only twelve summers, but I was used to it; it was all the life I knew and I'd no complaint. We were free, after all, and not bound to the land. Though we worked harder than serfs, what we could wrest from the soil was ours to keep or sell as we chose. My father made much of this. As a young man, he'd saved the Baron's life, standing over him when he fell during a raid and holding off two trained men-at-arms with the Baron's own sword until help arrived. For this he'd been freed from the land and saved from starvation, the usual lot of free men, by the grant of the use, without obligation, of an abandoned croft on the marches of the domain. He was also given my mother, a sign of great favor as she was my lady's tirewoman. *Like so much baggage!* my mother was wont to say, but she would smile as she did so. They never said much, my father being a man of great reserve so that my mother saved most of her talk for me; but their love ran deep. That was a small miracle though I didn't know it then. I was to learn it soon enough.

Though the ground was soft enough to work with the plow, it had been a sullen spring, with little warmth. The farmers muttered on those few occasions they saw one another. At last there came a dawn with no clouds and as my father and I stamped towards the stone shed that served as our barn, our morning breath steaming visibly past our shoulders, he stopped and turned sudden.

"Nicodemus, 'twill be fair all day. Do you take your sling and see an you can't get some rabbits in the hills." I stared, barely believing my ears. "Go on with you, boy, we need ta meat. I'll start ta new wall for ta kitchen garden, should please your mother." He looked at the sky, "Ta weather will hold. We can plow ta north field tomorrow."

At once, he turned back to the barn where we kept our tools, expecting no reply. One gives no thanks for orders, but we both knew it as a gift. To be free of drudgery on such a day as this promised! To be able to roam the land and only a few conies to pay the toll at the end. I turned and ran for my sling and was shortly moving briskly up the track to the hills.

The day was more than was promised, an the god was trying to roll up all the days of spring we'd missed and put them into one. By the second hour the sun had steamed the dew to mist then burned that off so the air was clear and the grass, newly green, completely dry. The upland meadows were stitched by wildflowers into tapestries as rich and warm as any that ever hung on the old lord's walls. By the third hour, there was heat enough for the bees to be about and the meadows began to grumble with their buzz. Of conies, I saw little sign, but so full was I of the day and all its joys that I paid it little heed. So little that when I finally started one, it caught me unawares and my stone was late away. To my dismay it thumped hollow into the thickets long after the flash of disappearing rump.

Thereafter, I paid attention, writhing at the thought of betraying my father's trust by coming home with an empty bag. On the best of trips, rabbit starts were seldom enough and should not be wasted. As it happened, as far as rabbits went, it seemed the worst of trips, though the day was everything else that a boy could want. So it fell out that I went further than was my wont and stayed out longer, getting but two in the long afternoon. In no measure did this spoil my enjoyment. I think I felt that on such a day the god would be with me, an only I did my part. Why else would he send it? At last, with the sun westering, on ground new to me, I started three in quick succession, knocking down all and turning for home with heart and bag both full. Though I had come to the ground haphazardly, I went home direct, taking my path from the sun. I meant to mark it well so I could return to the place. An approving, the god sent me a final rabbit half way back and again my stone was true. I had to sling the furry creature from my belt for there was no room left in my game bag. Shortly after, coming over a rise and seeing the western sky off to my right, clear for once of trees, I stopped and after a few moments, sat down on a nearby rock. I don't really know why I did it. Six rabbits was more than I'd ever brought before and I felt fulfilled, a man coming home with his full contribution for the table. The day had begun with a promise, amply fulfilled, and here it appeared about to end with another.

As the sun fell below the horizon, seeming, as he always does, to be in so much more of a hurry than during the rest of the day, the lower sky caught fire. First it made northing and southing from the middle, where the sun had gone, creeping outwards into a great semicircle until it almost seemed as if it would come round behind me. Then it slipped upwards, deepening as it went, finally touching the low clouds of evening, just forming in the West. From there it seemed to leap from cloud to cloud, as a fire will, blushing them first pink, then red then purple, deeper, deeper until they smoldered, dark coals etched against the fire's glow behind. I hugged my knees against my chest and watched until at last the glow died down and the coals disappeared, lost in the dark of the nighttime sky.

Coming to with a start, I scrambled to my feet, felt around for the precious bag, and started off along the path again. In the dark, I must needs go carefully. Even so, I stumbled often, not knowing the way, but I held my tongue. The sight had been worth a barked shin or two and I did not think it meet to complain, so soon after the god had granted it. At last, the path slanted in to a familiar trail. Stopping, I fixed the spot in my mind so I could find my back track, night or day, and thus the new rabbit ground. Satisfied, I turned to hurry on in good earnest, hoping to come home before supper was fully done. I'd no fear of going without, my mother would see to that; but while both would wait up 'til I came home, an I caught them at table they would listen to my tale of the day as they would not once my father were up and restless for his bed.

As I approached our croft, the sunset glow seemed to rise once more in the sky and I remember thinking, just for a heartbeat, that truly the god was near, to kindle the sun again. Before the awe could properly take hold, I smelled the smoke and realized the glow was not in the West, to my right, where it should be, but straight ahead. Heedless of the dark or the branches that lashed at my face or the roots that reached for my ankles, I tore down the track, firm in the grip of the croftholder's terror—fire in the thatches. It could not be else, there was too much color and smoke in the sky. Barn or cottage, it must be one or the other. As I ran, I prayed it was the cottage. There would have been time for my parents to get out, as there would not be to get the animals safe away from the barn. Stone and thatch could be replaced, it simply meant more labor, but a family's wealth was its animals. Panting over the swell of the north pasture I staggered and stopped, swaying at what was simply beyond my grasp.

Not one, but both, thatch long gone, the timbers burned half through and the cottage collapsed at one end, where the gable stonework had cracked from the heat. Even the privy was gone, reduced to a pile of rubble and ashes. A disaster of such scale was beyond my young experience, though fire on the farms was common enough. Barns and cottages, where both existed, were spaced to keep fires from spreading in anything less than a gale and no such had blown that day. Weeping, I tried to make sense of what I saw, looking frantically for my parents. They could not have been caught inside, not both of them, not awake, in the day. Then my blurring eyes found what I had missed and I began once again to run, lurching down the slope, the rising from my stomach burning in the back of my throat.

That the agency of our ruin might be human had not been in my mind but, terribly, as I ran, the two bundles tumbled untidy on the ground became my parents. Yet not my parents. Stumbling into the kitchen garden where they lay, they turned monstrously into things. The thing that had been my father was doubled over, the hands wrapped around the great slash in its belly crusted over with dark blood, the face writhed in agony. Desperately, I tried to undo death's work, not to bring it to life but simply to make the hulk he'd left behind seem more like my father. I could straighten the limbs but no amount of smoothing would take the snarl from its face. The thing that had been my mother was worse. The dress was about its head, the undergarments torn and pulled aside, exposing the parts but no other mark I could see. Kneeling, wanting my mother's warmth, always so ready in my life, I flung my arms around the waist and found it fled already. I shivered then pulled down the dress beneath my hands, wanting at least to give her back her modesty. Smoothing it to the ankles, I found it sticky at the hem and turned to find the throat cut. 'Twas a single stroke clear across, a carcass slaughtered like a pig or a goat.

It was too much for me. I whirled and ran, away from the embers, away from the light of the nether world, away from the awful things it lit which once had been my parents. I ran to the swallowing dark, safe, no signposts, no love, no hope, the black without reaching to join the black that rose within until the two joined and gobbled me up. I have no more memories of that night, it falls on the edges. I know not how or where I spent it, whether I stumbled about or lay down or even slept.

I remember coming back to myself in the dawn, my grief somehow inside of me now instead of me inside of it. It felt like a great black lump that pressed inside my chest, making even breathing hard, but it was an entity, separate from me. For a moment what little of the child there was left to me fought against that, wanting to climb back inside and pull it over and so lose myself in my misery. Better than to face the world. I pushed it down, and so banished, an only I had known it, all childhood from my life. The lump is still there, dwindled now through all the years to a pebble, one of many in a sack of griefs. Yet I can find it. I know intimately the contours of each.

§

It was a gray dawn, slow and sullen. Of life, there was no sign at all, even the fires had died, but I thought little of it until a pair of kites flapped heavily down into the garden. That roused me and I reached for a stone and moved close enough to shy it at them. Protesting shrilly, they fled to the gable still standing and regarded me balefully, shifting from foot to foot. However little the bundles in the garden resembled my parents, I could not allow the kites to have them nor would stones serve to keep them off for long. I went in search of tools.

Looking, I realized there was no livestock left of any kind— not so much as a cock to crow the awful dawn. The ground was covered with the marks of horses' hooves, bespeaking not outlaws as I had supposed, but a sizable war party, mounted and armored an I read the tracks aright. When I forced myself to face the barn, I found no burnt carcasses. All the animals, down to the last chicken, had been taken. The tools, wooden as they were, were all ashes but the iron plowshare, my father's pride, had gone the way of the chickens and pigs. At last I found in the wreckage of the barn a plank that might be used to dig a grave in the earth of the garden. Grimly I returned and worked doggedly in the lower corner of the garden. I kept my back to the corpses which I could not bear to face before I had to, but close enough to keep off the kites. It took most of the day and even so I could not go very deep, the ground was too hard and stony. At last I had a hole that would decently hold both and, unable to put it off any longer, I turned and went to my parents. I had thought to be gentle but it was all I could do to drag them and tumble them in. My ruined reverence was mocked by the foul creatures behind, now grown to a good size flock. Defiantly, I arranged them as best as I could, getting at least their arms about one another and turning my mother half down to hide his wound and most of hers. They disappeared behind my tears long before I could get the dirt back over them.

When I had done at last, I stood there panting, knowing it was not enough. Their grave was too shallow to lie long undisturbed. Then I thought of the gable, built with my father's own hands, now pulled down by the fire. He had built the cottage for my mother, the prettiest one in Lord Cromart's domains, showing in the stone the love for her he could never say. She had told me of it when he wasn't there to hear, taking pride in his stonework and what it meant. It seemed fitting. I mined it carefully, taking only the best stones still left. One by one I piled them over the grave, placing each with a prayer. When I had done, I dressed the plank with my knife, then carved the god's symbol on it and wedged it down between the stones. It marked them for the god's as they would want.

Chapter 2

I awoke wet and shivering from the dew. The sky was clear and the day promised fine but the morning chill ran down to my bones and cramps grappled at my stomach. Fearing sudden that the well had been poisoned, I began to retch. I had heard of such things, around a winter's fire, when iron men on horseback putting torches to farmers' crofts were simply tales for children. Exhausted, driven by the need of my body, I had drunk deep from the well the night before without thinking, then gone in search of food. I'd not been able to face the rabbits, raw, without a fire, but I'd found the root cellar untouched and had made a meal from the meager store of withered apples and wrinkled yellow turnips. Eating them raw in the gathering dark, I could think only of my mother's soup and never of poisoned water.

Rubbing my stomach, looking at the ruins of our croft about me, I found myself desperately wanting to be able to reach out and touch it with a finger and put it all back: the walls, the timbers and the thatch; the fire in the hearth and the sound of the hens outside; my father's boots ringing his return on the stones from his morning chores, coming for my mother's pottage and cheese and eggs. *Pull yourself together, Nikki.*

I jumped, my father's voice, tolling deep within me. Blinking back tears, I knew it for what he would have said. The knot in my belly eased and I recognized it as just the effects of raw food together with a night spent huddled in the lee of a tumbled wall, safe from the wind but little else. My hands hurt, made ragged by my makeshift spade, and I could feel the stone pressing against my chest, but that was all was really wrong with me.

I shivered again and shook myself, trying to see the world as it was and reaching for my father. See what you've got, Nicodemus he would say, and what you've got to do. Think about it a bit, hard an you have to, but not too long. For ta purpose of thinking is to make ta doing easier, but in t' end 'tis ta doing as must be done!

So I knew he was not wholly gone, nor ever would be. He was there, deep and slow and my mother, laughing, both gentle, both there an I needed them. My part was to hold fast to what they were and had tried to make me.

I stood up, for the first time with some purpose. A fire first, now or later I would need one. The one in the starter pot had long since burned out but my father had taught me how to build one from naught. His tools should have survived the blaze. Sure enough I found them in their nook by the hearth and set out to look for fuel. 'Twas a small enough thing in the midst of all the other ruin, but I discovered the woodpile gone, a year's worth of cutting and hauling, stacking and splitting, reduced to ashes. It had stood separate, so must have been fired on purpose. Sudden numbness gave way to blazing anger. I had been proud of that pile, it had been my special charge, and now it was gone in the single backwards toss of a torch. Disaster wrought small, that I could comprehend. In my mind they merged into one, the arc of a torch to wood and the sweep of the sword to flesh. Our lives, our labor, 'twas all one to them, equally cheap.

Staring at the ashes, I knew sudden through my rage that there was nothing for me here. An I somehow could cobble together a hut from the leavings, I had no hope of running the croft. There were no animals, the seed for the spring sowing was gone with the barn, the plow was taken. Even had I all that was necessary, I could not do the work myself. My father I might carry with me, but that didn't give me his inches or his thews. Striding to the barn, I pulled loose several of the planks that had survived the blaze. There was no reason now not to use them for fuel.

Dry and warm, with a rabbit roasting on the spit above the blackened hearth, I stared into the flames, seeking what I should do. I found that the thought of leaving the croft did not worry me unduly. It had been my parents' dream, my father's in truth, my mother going to it freely for love of him and finding there a contentment she'd never looked for in the land. She'd loved her garden, her herbs and vegetables that found such fine expression in her pots, and more than them, her flowers. *A man can't eat flowers!* my father would growl, but he kept a cloth in his pocket to wrap the soil to the roots of anything new he found for her. Yet it was not the land itself, as she told me once.

"'Tis the freedom, Nikki, to do as we will with it. So long as the croft is kept up, Lord Cromart will not interfere. It is ours to do as seems good to us. That is what's precious, a rare thing and a mark of the high favor the lord holds for your father."

Though they loved the land, each in their own way, they had made it plain they wanted more for me. My mother had her letters and had taught them to me, by the fire at winter while my father mended harness. Sometimes, when I was slow or my mind on other things she would scold me.

"Nikki, you must learn your letters, 'tis the only key you can have to unlock your life."

An I protested, my unlettered father would look up from his work and growl, "Go to, boy. When you go before ta lord he must find you fitting!"

"Why must I go before the Baron? What's the matter with the farm?"

Usually, he would just grunt at this and the worry in my mother's eyes would keep me quiet, but once I had pushed it. My father put down the harness he was mending.

"Cromart's one thing, his son is another. 'Tis to Edgar you'd end up beholden and ta boy's plain bad." He spat on the floor, a thing he never did inside, then, in deference to my mother, scraped over it with his sole. "There's too many ways for a baron to put screws to a croftholder, Nikki. With that one, you'd end up a serf. Or worse."

They were of one accord on this. I gathered my mother had made the actual arrangements for me to see the Baron, through his Lady. She'd never said the reason of course, just that she wanted better for me. More they would not say, except that it would be up to me when the time came.

Sa. Since my father could not take me I would just have to take myself. That it must be before time could not be helped but no other course presented itself. There was nothing for me at the croft, nor could I find more than temporary refuge at any other crofts in the domain. Even were a family willing to feed an extra mouth for more than a day or two, at best I could only stay until the bailiff found the count did not jump with his tally, when I'd be hailed before the lord anyway. Mulling this over as well as the road I must take, I remembered that my father had an old friend who was headman at Pudding Hill, along the way. More, he had told me once that an ever aught were to befall he and my mother, I should seek out this Brychan who would help me.

"Don't be turned from this, Nicodemus," he had said, gripping me by the shoulders, "Brychan is an old comrade and knows what's in my mind. We have spoken of it. He will stand for me and not fail you."

Rising, I swung the spit from the fire then left the coney to cool while I gathered what I could for my journey. It was little enough. My father's lapping tools and his best knife, found in the barn, the precious fund of coppers buried beneath a stone before the hearth. The fire had consumed all clothing, I could not find so much as a scrap of cloth from which to make a bundle, so I passed over my pewter drinking cup and even the smallest of my mother's pots. Breakfasting on the coney I tried to think what small thing I might take of hers. Her two broaches had been melted into a single lump and her ring I'd buried with her. I'd found the trowel she used with her plants, but it seemed a poor keepsake, unhandy to take and carry.

They say that in the end all the god's waters flow the same way. Perhaps the trowel had been shown me as the means and not the end. Tossing the bones into the fire I took it up and started sifting carefully through the cottage ashes. For a time, the little I found was not to the purpose, being of general use and often much damaged besides. At last, where the table had been, I found a spoon, twisted but recognizable and, taking it as a sign, began to dig more carefully. Sure enough, beneath a piece of blackened, broken pottery that was probably my mother's plate I found her silver fork, misshapen only slightly. The soot washed off at the well, leaving the metal undamaged and I felt my labors and the damage to my only clothes well rewarded. The fork had belonged to my mother's grandmother and she had cherished it. More, she'd known how to use it and had taught me the art, quietly, when my father was not about.

"It might stand you in good stead, Nikki, one day; but I'd not want your father to think I was giving myself airs." She'd not used it for years, not wanting to remark on the differences between them, until he'd found her with it one day. It had been at the table since, my father unworried. "I like to watch you wield it", he'd say. "Good tools was meant to be used by them that knows how."

As best I could I washed at the well the soot from my hands and clothes. Then I went and kneeled at their grave and was silent, listening to the sound of the wind across the high moors and hearing in the distance a beerbird, calling for his stoup. At length, I said a prayer to the god to keep them fast in this peace and, making the sign, stood and turned and took the track. I did not mean to look back but as I crested the edge of the bowl in which the croft lay I could not help myself. The buildings were ruined and blackened, but the sun sparkled from the meadows and I could see the primroses at the end of the standing gable end nodding close to where the grave must be. Then they disappeared in a rush of unbidden tears and I plunged quickly down the track before I should turn back.

§

I ran for mayhap an hour, flopping finally by a brook where I cooled my face and drank. After a few moments rest, I pulled myself to my feet with a sigh and settled down to a steady walk. Running was no use, it would simply exhaust me. A steady walk I could keep up all day and all night if I had to. It had used to take my father all day with the ox cart to reach Pudding Hill and another to the castle where he went for the great harvest fair each year but I'd no very clear idea of how long he journeyed each day or whether he arrived early or late. That I would outrange the cart, even over a day, I was sure but by how much I'd no way of knowing. Starting late as I had, it was bound to be a long walk yet to Pudding Hill.

So thinking, I drew near to the hamlet of Cooling, where the track to our croft split off from the main road that ran from Halting Castle to the marches and beyond. With the breeze in my face, I smelt the place before I saw it, a sickly-sweet stench laid on the top of the odor of old burning. Before I knew quite what it was, I came round the bend in the road and saw the little village burnt to the ground, even the green of the common motley with black. Several corpses lay about, one tiny, a baby just outside the reach of its dead mother. The dogs and the kites had been at them and I saw the gleam of bones amidst the rotting flesh. A gust brought the smell anew, so powerful it hit me like a physical thing and I gasped and held my hand to my nose and mouth.

I could force myself no closer, but hurried round to the upwind side where at least I could breathe. Shielded from the worst sights by a cottage wall still standing, the smell reduced by the wind, I was able to creep in quite close. Lying still for minutes, listening closely, I could here no human sound, only the cry of a kite still at the bodies. At last, I hallooed and listened for a return and again and yet again. None came. I did not expect one. The raiders had burnt our croft nigh on to sunset so they must have burnt the village first. They'd been long gone so any who'd survived would be about now, an they'd not fled already. The breeze died down and the stench crept back around me like a choking mist and I made haste to leave. As I turned, I caught sight of circle scratched on a gable end, standing as at our croft, a circle with a crude bolt of lightning inside it.

My breath sucked in, was instantly regretted and I flung my hand again to my face and hastened back. I'd seen the sign a time or two before and knew it for Lord Goff's, from across the marches in Umber. Had I missed it at our croft or had they simply not bothered? Until then I'd assumed we'd been attacked by outlaws, but the mark made it plain there was more going on than that. The borders were never easy but the last such raid had been before my birth, when my father made himself by saving his high lord's life. The counter raid had been carried out by Cromart himself, my father in his train. Afterwards, my father told me, the two high lords had treated and made between them a pact that kept peace on the borders ever since.

"'Twas no profit in it for them, Nikki, you see, but only loss. So, having each other's measure they agreed to stand down and leave t'other be. They were proud of their word, those two," he added, "Though not all the lords be that way, the peace should last for their lives and, ta god willing, their sons as well, who have been brought up in it."

I'd never thought much about it. The enemies we'd fought had always been frost and flood and drought and though we could never win, we held our own most years. To me they were real adversaries while war and famine and plague were the stuff of stories. They'd been real enough to my father, but I think he must have regarded them like the weather. What came, came. There was no point worrying about it.

Leaving the village smoldering behind me, I pondered the meaning of my discovery but could make no real sense of it. Scratching the crest of Goff in the stone would have taken some time and I could not see the sense of that on a raid. Could it be misdirection? Where outlaws would raid and run, Goff's men might yet be about. I decided to keep to the verge, close to cover in case I encountered anyone on the road.

From Cooling, the track ran through the Eastings Wood for several miles. The verge was harder work than the road so that I did not emerge from the wood until much before sunset. At that point I left the track completely, slipping through the meadows, working my way southeastwards to a height of land. The road ran round the height and I though it best to spy what lay before me rather than walk straight into trouble. Lying at the peak in the fading light, I saw a village below, bigger than Cooling. The cottages lay calmly in the twilight, smoke curling up from the cooking fires within. Not a soul was in sight without, but I could see figures through unshuttered windows, moving against the firelight. Pudding Hill, to my relief, blessedly complete, its folk at their evening meal and not in hiding. My vantage point must be the very hill whose shape had given the village its name.

One house was larger than the rest, with a separate outbuilding, likely Brychan's an he were the headman. I marked it before the dark should swallow it, and made my way down. Square to the road, I had to slip across a sideyard. Before I'd fairly gained the track an awful cackle of geese arose from behind the fence so that one by one the doors popped open. In heartbeats I was seized, my arms twisted around behind me until I cried out, then forced to my knees.

"A t'ief!" The voice was rough and sharp and I received a clout to my ear that snapped forward my head.

"Nay, I'm no thief," I gasped, but my captor did not seem disposed to listen. Frantically I tried to duck away from the blow I could feel coming.

"'Old, Ned, you fool!" said a new voice, and I felt the bang of a wrist against my head as the descending fist was blocked. "Ye'll find not'ing from him, t'at way," said the voice. "Time enough for a beating when we knows 'tis warranted."

"Ach, we need no lies from 'im. 'e come in the night, as a t'ief, and not by the road, neither, as honest folk do. Only for my geese 'e'd 'ave robbed us blind! I saw 'im! Come t'rough t'e back, 'e did, from t'e Puddin'. 'Ee's been spying on us!"

"Be that so? An 'ee'd no honest purpose, seems ee'd have waited until we all 'ad gone to bed," observed my rescuer. He pulled my head round to the light from one of the doorways, framing his from behind in the process. I couldn't see much except that he was huge and bushy, black hair and brows and beard all in measure far greater than I'd seen on any man before. Or since, an it comes to that.

"Why 'tis just a boy!"

"I am Nicodemus, son of Jarn, and I am seeking Brychan, who is headman here."

He stared at me a long moment from under those brows, searching my face so that I knew he was the man himself. "And why would ta son of Jarn want to spy on us?"

"I was not spying *on* you. I was trying to see an it was safe." The words tumbled out of me, "Cooling's burnt, and our croft! All the people killed, my parents as well. I was away hunting rabbits in the hills."

There was much consternation in the crowd that had gathered and I could hear no little fear in the exclamations that my announcement brought. A man thrust forward and demanded, "How does 'ee know t'ey're all dead in Cooling? Maybe t'ere were others got to t'e 'ills."

"I was there this morning and nothing moved except the kites though I called out. It is two days since the attack, yet the dead had not been tended. Surely any who survived would see to their kin." There was a wail behind him and he turned back and gathered a woman in his arms. It died to a racking sob. Behind I could here her joined by others.

My rescuer had been pulling at his beard. "'Tis 'ard news you bring, boy, t'ough I need not tell you t'at. Many 'ere 'ave kin in Cooling. An ta raiding spreads like we'm not be safe even 'ere at Pudding 'Ill." He turned and spat. "'Tis little enough poor folk can do when Barons ride to war!" Then he pulled me to my feet and said, kindly enough, "I be Brychan, boy. Your father was a good friend. I will do what I can for his son, t'ough t'at be little enough. 'Ot food and a warm corner to curl up in, for a start, while I takes counsel what must be done."

He rapped out several names and when the man who questioned me started forward he shook his head and nodded at his woman, "Best stay with Ebeta, Tom. T'ere'll be nout to do tonight, any road. T' wind 'as gone round to ta southeast, so t'ere'll be rain and no moonlight."

Turning, bidding me follow, he walked off to the cottage I'd marked at the end of the street. Inside, I saw he was much older than I'd taken him in the dark, the black of his hair and beard dappled with gray. His woman was by the fire and she rose with a bowl as we came in, as fair as he was black and almost as tall, but slender, as he was broad. "You 'eard?" was all he said, and she nodded, her eyes bright with tears. He put his hand upon my shoulder, "Nicodemus. T'is be Annie, my wife. She'll take good care of 'ee while I 'old counsel, t'en we'll talk."

She took me to the back in a corner behind the hearth, warm from the fire, and gave me a bowl of stew and some new made scones and a small mug of ale. Drawing several larger mugs, she took them to the men who'd gathered in the front, then returned and gave my arm a squeeze and asked if there was aught else I wanted. I shook my head, mouth full of bread and stew, and she whispered, taking off her apron and hanging it on a hook by the fire, "I'm off to sit in t'en, and speak for ta women. When 'ee be done, t'ere's fresh straw and a good wool blanket in ta corner."

I meant to stay awake until the council was over, but when I had eaten I crawled into the straw and pulled the blanket round me for warmth. I could make nothing out, only a deep murmur of voices. They quickly put me to sleep.

Chapter 3

I was wakened in the dark by a hand shaking my shoulder. Seeing it was Brychan I asked as I sat up, rubbing my eyes, "Is the council over?" He rumbled with laughter and replied, "'Ours agone, Nicodemus. 'Tis almost dawn. Time we should talk." He drew up a stool and sat beside my pallet, pulling a pipe from a vast pocket as he did so. "Stay where you are, lad. As well be comfortable." I pulled the blanket back around me against the morning chill and hugged my knees, watching him go about the business of lighting the pipe and getting it to draw. Behind him I could see Annie alternately blowing up the fire and kneading the morning cakes. It felt so like home I had to bite my lip and look down to cover the quick flush of tears. An Brychan saw, he took no notice but attended to his pipe until I could look up again.

"Well, lad, I've 'ad a chance to 'ave a long think, while 'ee slept. 'Tis best 'ee go to the castle." He blew out a great cloud of smoke. "'Tis my duty to send a message to Lord Cromart at first light, soon as a man can see his way. By rights, should 'ave gone last night but the clouds 'id the moonlight. Now I think t'was a blessing. Most 'ere 'ave kin in Cooling and someone must deal with ta dead. And as many again must go to keep watch, lest ta raiders return." He blew another cloud and watched it swirl for a moment. "We can't 'ope to fight 'em, we've not ta weapons nor ta training. But an we keep proper watch we'm be in the hills before they arrive. So I'm for Cooling with most of ta menfolk."

"'Twill not be pleasant, sir. I could not get close for the smell, and I could see the bones where the dogs and the crows were at them."

He shrugged. "They're our people. No one else will take care of 'em." His face twisted, "Ta priest won't 'aul 'imself from 'Alting 'til they be buried. What of your folk?"

"I buried them myself, sir, and raised a cairn and a marker. It should keep them."

He looked at me keenly from beneath his great bushy brows, then nodded. "When finally I gets ta good brother down to Cooling will I 'ave 'im up to ta croft to say a few words?"

"They would like that, sir, an he would."

He grunted, "Most like 'e wouldn't, but a word to 'is lordship should see 'im there all right. Cromart wouldn't think of it 'imself, but 'e won't stand for slacked rituals. Not ta amount 'e feeds Brother Belfus." He knocked the pipe absent-mindedly into his hand then looked crossly for somewhere to put the ashes. At length, he went and threw them into the hearth and returned to his stool anew.

"T'any rate, Nicodemus, must I take most of ta men to Cooling. T'others I needs here to keep watch and to help ta babes and women away in case of trouble. So I can fairly claim you'm ta best messenger, ta more so since you've seen more than anyone 'ere, anyway."

"Claim, sir?"

"By rights, should send ta fastest man, as I would 'ave last night. But 'tis you I wants to take ta news to Cromart."

"Why, sir?"

"Ach, lad! Don't be calling me 'sir' - 'tisn't fitting. Brychan is good enough for me, I'm not free born. But," he said, putting his empty pipe back into his mouth, "You are." He leaned forward, his big hands between his knees. "Did your father ever tell you that you were to go before Lord Cromart?"

"Why yes, si... Brychan," I corrected, "He mistrusted Lord Edgar to let me keep the croft."

The great face darkened, "'Twill be 'ard times in Tansley when that one takes over!" He paused, lost in melancholy, then shook his head. "There be more to it than that, Nicodemus." He drew at the pipe so it whistled emptily while he gathered his thoughts.

"Your mother and 'e both wanted a boyhood free of worrying about 'ow ta world was made." He paused, "Land, but 'tis 'ard to explain! 'Ow much do you know of your parents?"

"Only that my father was born a serf, but saved Lord Cromart during a raid. In return he was given his freedom and the croft. He always said my mother was part of the bargain but it seemed a joke between them so I never really knew the truth of that."

"In a way, she was. The tale is true, as far as it goes, but there's more. Your father and I were boys together in 'Alting and an 'eedless, 'arum-scarum pair we were. 'Arvests were good and though we both came from large families, there was food for all and 'ands enough to leave a little time to spare. Danson was Baron then, ta god rest 'is soul, and Cromart 'is only son. We were all three of an age so when we were small were suffered to play together as Cromart had no other companions. As we grew older we were separated, though Cromart would slip away from time to time and join us on some romp or other. Eventually he was found out and even that stopped and your father and I were forbidden the castle. Two years later, Baron Danson died suddenly."

"Now, thinking Cromart was young and not ta man 'is father 'ad been, Goff started raiding into the domain. 'Appen 'e was wrong but the trouble was Cromart's own knights were unsure of 'im, too. Oh, they'd sworn fealty to 'im at his father's death, right enough, but they were older. They were uneasy with so young and untried an 'and at the 'elm in troubled waters. They 'eld back and forced 'im to take counsel with them. While ta parleying went on back and forth, Cromart decided to add to 'is own garrison from ta young men among ta serfs. 'E forced no man, but offered families relief from all other feudal duties that year in exchange for armed duty. 'Twas not usual and 'e took good care to keep it quiet from 'is knights, but a round score volunteered, your father and I amongst them."

"When we arrived at the courtyard, 'e drew us aside and warned us we could expect no different treatment for 'aving been companions in our youth. 'E offered to let us change our minds but we thought no worse of 'im for that and stayed. 'E armed us and 'ad us trained, often leading the practices 'imself." He smiled at the memory. "Well, 'e found you can't turn farmers into men-at-arms overnight. Only your father could fairly be said to 'ave learned 'ow to 'andle a sword in a real fight. Still, most mastered ta crossbow and…" I followed his gaze to the wall, "…I managed with a mace."

'Twas a wicked looking thing, three and a half feet long, with a head knobbed of iron. Strange to see it hanging on the wall of a farmer's cottage. As if reading my thoughts he added "Cromart gave it me 'imself, though that was later. 'Asn't been down in years, though I guess I'd best take it along to Cooling." He looked grim again and I shivered, thinking I'd not like to meet him with anger in his heart and that in his great hands. He stared for a moment then took up the tale again.

"Fell out, most of 'is knights came on side for a simple raid so 'e took only a few of the new recruits, and those just as scouts. Your father was one and 'e found Goff in ambush and got back to warn Cromart who turned ta tables on Goff. 'E did it right neat, nobbled most of 'is force, 'cepting Goff who escaped. Goff 'ad to ransom 'em back which cost 'im stiff and kept 'im quiet for a while. Cromart's knights stopped being so shy so 'e sent us back to ta crofts."

"Did Lord Cromart keep his bargain with you?"

"Aye, 'e was always a man of 'is word, even to serfs. But your father stayed on."

"I thought he was freed for saving Cromart's life."

"That came after. 'E was still serf, just served at ta castle instead of in ta fields. 'E was a scout, not a man-of-arms. Ta regulars would never have put up with that."

"They put up with all of you, before."

He shook his head. "Cromart was just using us to whip 'em into line. We were kept separate, dossed down in the stables and not the barracks, and they made sure we knew our place."

"How could my father stay on, with all that hatred around him?"

"Serfs don't get much choice. 'Sides, 'twasn't hatred. So's 'e kept 'is place 'e was all right, they even came to value 'im in the end. I doubt me it chafed 'im much, 'twas all 'e'd known." He looked at my face. "You don't really know what it is to be serf do you boy?" I just shook my head, wordless.

"We runs with ta land, like barns and wells. 'Alf of what we grows goes to ta lord, another tenth for ta temple. Then there's ta corvée—thirty days a year for ta lords own fields and ten more each for ta road and ta castle. Extra levies at ta lord's call, though neither Cromart nor 'is father 'ave been ones to abuse 'em." As he spoke, he ticked off the obligations on his fingers. Now he started on his second hand.

"Serf are not to marry without ta say so of ta lord, nor to build nor to travel, even to ta annual fair. We'm never to sit or eat in a noble's presence, nor even look 'im in the eye, saving 'e talks to us. We can lose an 'and just for being in ta 'unting ground and be 'ung for a chicken or even an egg. And if the land changes hands, we go with it." He stared at me a moment, then sighed. "Understand me, Nicodemus. Most of these don't 'appen here. Cromart's a good overlord, as 'is father was before." He blew out his cheeks. "Ta son's another matter. Ta god willing, 'twill be many years before that one takes over." He leaned forward, suddenly intense, "Good lord or bad, ta power's still *there,* and no serf forgets it for a moment. T'is why 'as been kept from you. They were such a part of your father's growing that 'e wanted t'em to be no part of yours."

"Cakes are done," Annie called softly. I became aware that the cottage had warmed and that it had filled with the smell of fresh oat cakes. Brychan motioned and we moved to table. As we sat down there was a knock at the door and a young man stepped in.

"I be ready, Brychan. There's light enough."

"Well thank 'ee, Robbie, but I've a mind to send the lad. There'll be work for you in Cooling, I'm thinking."

Robbie looked anxious. "Aye, that's so. But will my lord not expect a man to be away as soon as you can?"

Brychan put a finger alongside his nose then very deliberately broke in half the oat cake he was holding. Robbie grinned and vanished and Brychan looked at me and said, "There's not a serf born can't go slow when 'e's a mind to." He popped one of the pieces in his mouth and chewed it carefully, as if to make the point.

"Brychan!" protested Annie.

"Aye, lass, I know. Best not to push the game too far. We've a deal to tell the lad yet, so I'll get on." He switched his gaze to me, "What know you of your mother?"

"Only that she was, in some wise, born to a higher station than my father. She was my lady's tirewoman and knew her letters."

"Tirewoman!" snorted Annie fiercely, "She was a lady 'erself, for all ta good it did her. Be glad that you're a man, Nicodemus, or will be. Women of your station are no much better off than serfs!"

She relapsed as suddenly as she began and Brychan took up the tale again, building in blunt strokes a picture of the troubles, raids back and forth, the castle constantly ready for war, the marches watched. Young men, himself among them, had to serve with the border watch, this time with no relief of other duties. Cromart tried to distribute the burden as best he could, but war is a costly business and money comes from the land and so from the serfs. There were extra tithes and the work was constantly disturbed, so times got very lean. Though men-at-arms died sometimes in the fighting, it was the serfs got the worst of that as well. Goff would steal stock during a raid, for cattle graze where they are put. Serfs, however, he considered to have loyalties so he cut them down or burned them in their homes. Constant levies moved people outwards from safe havens like Halting which is how Brychan had ended up at Pudding Hill.

"Almost were Cooling," he added heavily, looking fiercely over at Annie, then sighed.

"Any road, your da' got ta watch running so smooth it got so Goff couldn't move without 'e was seen. 'Is losses went up, then Cromart stepped up ta raids against 'im and 'e sued for peace. 'E's a bloody man, is Goff, but 'e kept 'is sworn word." He finished darkly, "Don't know why ta peace should be broken now."

Torn between pride in my father and a rising sickness at how we were treated by the lords I managed only a weak, "I never knew."

"No, your parents kept it from you. Ta god knows whether they were right. But now you sees what it means to be born to ta land." He reached for another oat cake and broke it, gathering his thoughts.

"Ta watch was Cromart's idea but 'twas your da' that made it work. Folk 'ave not forgotten that. Jarn's son be welcome in any cottage in Tansley." He looked at me, "Still, best you go to ta castle. Cromart was expectin' you one of these days. 'E'll see you right."

I felt the heat of the cottage wrap me about and saw Annie, bright as a bird, watching me. The castle seemed far and foreign and cold and I wondered if *any cottage in Tansley* included this one. I forced the thought away, reaching instead for something that had nagged at me.

"What happened to the watch? I remember my father being gone for times when I was young, but not for years. And we were caught unawares."

Brychan pursed his lips. "T'elders. Ta duty was still extra and they kept at Cromart. I voted against but..." he shrugged eloquently. "Five years ago, 'e bowed to their complaints. Ta watch was disbanded and there was naught your father could do. 'E didn't even 'ave a vote." He rose from the table. "Best I get ready. For what 'tis worth, Jordan o' Cooling was loudest against the watch."

There was nothing to say to that. An my parents had paid for his mistake so had he and all his people. Instead I thanked Brychan, "I'm glad to know he was a captain of men. Somehow I knew he was different from the other farmers, but I never knew why."

The headman snorted from beneath the old tunic he was pulling on, "T'other farmers were serfs, boy, and 'e'd grown beyond that. But it would be like 'im to call them farmers." He paused, pulling the tunic down, then asked, almost shyly, "What said 'e of me?"

"That you were headman at Pudding Hill and an old companion from the troubles."

"Well, 'e'd a knack of seeing men as men and never mind their station. I think that's 'ow 'e won your mother." He looked troubled and pulled at his beard.

"Achh, men!", exclaimed Annie. "Ye're quick enough to make use of a woman when it suits ye, but ye're not so keen to talk about it."

"Annie!", he protested.

"Ah, go on wi' ye, Brychan! I know ye nivver made free yerself, no nor your father neither, Nikki, who was a rare good man."

Her accent was strange, I'd never heard it before. Seeing my puzzlement, Brychan volunteered, "Annie's from ta Fastness."

"And what's that to the purpose?" she demanded. "The short of it is, Nikki, that your mother was noble born, the daughter of a knight. She was taken in a raid whilst on her way to her weddin'. They killed her people and were about to make free with her when Cromart came upon them, your da' in his train. They'd most of the clothes off her but hadn'a done the deed, she fought like her father's son. Cromart hung the raiders and sent her back with your da' to the castle. He was the only man he could trust, after they'd seen her half naked!" she added, scornfully. "Hold, lad, what's the matter?"

I doubled over, thinking to be sick, but only choked. "'Twas long ago, lad, and it never touched 'er." Brychan said softly. Then, angry now, "'Ere, lad, if it didn't bother your father, there's no reason for you to 'old it against 'er!"

I could see Annie's face, outraged, and shook my head. "'Tis not that," I gasped, seeing her body before me, her dress pulled up and her parts exposed. I had not thought of that, perhaps I'd not wanted to or perhaps it was just the blindness of the young to such things. "I had not realized ..." I wailed, "They must have had their way with her before she died ... her dress was up and there was blood!"

Annie's arms were around me in an instant and she rocked me back and forth, clutched fiercely to her bony bosom, until my sobs died down and I was able to draw a great, shuddering breath. "I'm sorry," I said at last.

"Faith, 'tis I should be sorry," she said briskly. "I was blaming you when I should have known. 'Tis the way of men at war to use women like a cloth to clean a sword. One wipe, and then discarded!" she added grimly and lapsed back into silence.

Brychan broke it eventually. "Despite she was untouched, your mother was tossed aside just the same. Sir Ranald, 'er bridegroom, would 'ave naught to do with 'er, 'e claimed it touched 'is 'onor." By the door now, he opened it and carefully spat his opinion of knights. "Cromart was greatly wrath but, overlord or no, 'e couldn't overbear ta man in this. So 'e sent 'er to 'is lady and a message to 'er family. By the time 'e returned, word was there before 'im that she'd dis'onored the family name and they'd 'ave no more to do with 'er. Cromart could 'ave turned 'er out, after that, but my lady took to 'er and they let 'er stay."

"She's a good woman, my lady," added Annie. "But sair lonely. I was a maid at the castle and used to see her staring oot over the walls when her lord was away. Your mother and she became good friends. They tried to arrange another marriage, even to giving a wee dowry, but the story was known and the gentry were too fine to have her! In the end, she stayed five years and I think your father was the only friend she had in the castle besides my lord and my lady. She took to staying away from feasts when the gentry came to call and even the men-at-arms made sly jibes behind her back."

"She was ta only person, besides Cromart, your da' would talk lordtalk to," said Brychan. "Even to my lady 'e'd speak plain." Seeing my look he explained, "'Twas a game we'm played as youngsters, when we ran with Cromart. Ta three of us could slip back and forth at will. *The knack stays with you, Nicodemus!*" he looked a little sheepish, "Sa. May'ap it gets rusty. Any road your da' didn't like to. 'e'd use it with Cromart when they were alone, but not else, 'ceptin' when your mother came along. 'e said 'e used lordtalk when 'e took her to ta castle, never thinking to do else."

"He fell in love with your mither then," Annie added, "But he hadn'a hope. He forbore plain speaking so as not to add to her distress. Her attackers had talked plain."

"I knew he could do it." I smiled at the memory, good to reach through the hurt for the little things, "He always used plain speech with me but I heard him shift over sometimes, at night, talking to my mother."

"'E dealt with plain folk and 'ad no use for trying to rise above ta common touch. But 'e wanted you to 'ave both."

"He insisted always that I speak 'proper' and that I learn my letters."

"Aye, but you can drop back at need?"

"Ach, so I can, though it was t'back of t'and an' I did!"

Both of them grinned at that.

They told me that my mother hadn't even known my father was serf born until she got to the castle. Shocked at first, as her own kind turned against her she remembered him kindly and, in the end, had come to love him. Having married for love herself and not out of policy, Cromart's lady was kindly disposed and took my mother's side. When my father saved Cromart's life, she had pressed her case and, as Brychan put it, "Got 'im manumitted, dowered and wed all in a week." He got up and strode to the door and looked out.

"We've not much time. 'Tis you or Robbie must be away on the nonce or there'll be a new 'eadman at Pudding 'Ill."

Sitting down again, he pulled his stool around and faced me square. "Look you, Nicodemus, it comes to this. Foot'ills Croft is done. Whiles I could fix it with Cromart to 'ave you stay, aye and you'd be more than welcome…" at this Annie nodded, her eyes bright, "… 'tis not what your parents wanted for you. Or us either, in truth," he added and Annie looked at me and nodded again, more deliberately.

"The thing is, you're free. But you only remains so an you leave the land. Stay and sooner or later, you, or your children, will be bound back to it. You must do as free men do and move off ta land."

"And how do I do that?"

"Go before Cromart. Remind him who you are. For your father's sake and ta Lady Beatrice who will stand your friend, 'e will find out for what you're suited and help you to it. But 'e 'as not much time and will not waste it. You must put your best foot forward." He stood up with finality, "Can you wield a sword?"

"My father never taught me. Only husbandry, which I knew he never intended I follow, though I didn't know why until now, and my letters. They came from my mother but they were one on learning them."

"'Tis well. As a soldier you would have ended preying on your own kind. A priest, then?"

I laughed. "I doubt it. They put as little store in the brothers as you seem to. He preferred to talk to the god in his own way and taught me to do the same."

Brychan pulled his beard. "Well, letters are rare enough. I believe there be clerks and such who make a living at it. You must leave that with Lord Cromart. T'is your best chance to see 'im. Will you take the message?"

I knew he was risking Cromart's displeasure by sending me in place of the far swifter Robbie. That they were willing to keep me I was sure. Annie's face told that tale, plain enough. My future at the castle seemed vague, my parents' plan unclear. Reality was the fire behind me and Annie's oatcakes and the cold, wet dawn outside; but they say the god turns the wheel but once. I answered slowly, "I think I must. Else I turn my back on what they stood for."

"Good lad!" he said, with what seemed like forced cheerfulness. Quickly, he gave me directions to the castle and how to proceed once I was there. When he had done, Annie brought me a packet and a cloak.

"'Tis cakes and cheese for your journey, Nikki," she said. "The cloak is fra' a neighbor's whose last lad has grown and she was proud to have it go to the son of Jarn." I thanked her and she hugged me again and pushed me to the door where Brychan waited. "May the god keep ye!", she said and abruptly turned back to her hearth.

Brychan said nothing, but led me down the street to the edge of the village. The rain had stopped, but it was cold and damp, with a bitter breeze tearing at the curtain of morning mist. Though old, the cloak was serviceable and I was grateful for its warmth.

"Don't mind Annie," he said, at length. "We'd never a child and it frets 'er still. She knows ye canna stay but that doesna' mean she doesna' want it." He looked away and pointed down the road. "There's your way, lad. It runs straight to ta castle, so you can't miss it. Ta god go with you."

He shook my hand an I were a man and turned back to the village. At that moment, I knew 'twas not only Annie was fretted. He would welcome me as much as her.

Chapter 4

I came to the castle in the middle of the afternoon after a cold and wet but uneventful journey. There were other hamlets along the way, but mostly set aside from the main road so I passed unremarked. There were few folk about in the weather and they disinclined for a chat.

The castle itself was set on a knoll in the middle of a large plain, visible, as I later found out, from miles away on a clear day. All I could see was gray—gray road, gray fields and gray rain and though the cloak helped, by midday I was soaked clear through. I would have felt mightily sorry for myself except for the thought that Brychan and the villagers would be having a far worse time of it trying to put the dead away into such wet ground.

I arrived abruptly, practically banging into it, finding it far larger than imagination, a great stone cliff towering above me, dark and sinister in the drifting rain. Too wet and cold to be frightened, I looked for how I might enter and found it easy enough. The road ran round the walls, outside a noisome ditch, to a lowered drawbridge around the corner with a wide open gate behind it.

From my father's tales, I expected to find all barred or guarded but there was no one at the gate and the courtyard beyond was deserted. In the end I made my halloo, not once, but several times, until finally an old man stuck his head around a door let into the walls. He looked me up and down for several seconds before inquiring scornfully, "And what does you want?"

"I'm here to see Lord Cromart."

He scowled, "Oh you is, is you? And what do you think 'is lordship would want with a bedraggled little brat like you? Be off with you!" With that, he slammed the door.

I felt like a beaten dog in the rain but I remembered Brychan's instructions and went and banged on the door as hard as I could. It popped open immediately and the graybeard came halfway out this time. "I be warnin' you!" he snarled, his fist up-raised. I stood my ground.

"I'm Nicodemus, son of Jarn, and I bring word to Lord Cromart from Foothills Croft."

"Never 'eard of it." He chewed his lip. "Jarn, is it? And how'm I to know that?"

Taking care to stay beyond what I deemed the range of his fist, I said, "That's for the steward to decide. My lord will not be pleased an the message be blocked."

He lowered his fist and said, more respectfully, "You don't talk like a beggar's brat." Then, peering closely at me, "Nor not like Jarn's son, either." I held my peace, trusting that the puzzle was enough to make him pass me along to the steward. He stared at me grudgingly a few more heartbeats, then asked, "Dost 'ta know ta castle?" I shook my head and he pointed a twisted finger across the courtyard. "There. Second door, left down ta passage, and ask for Granzy. And ta god help you if you're lyin'!" Before I could reply he banged the door shut again. It made no odds. I knew from Brychan that Granzy was the steward. Plodding down the passage, I went over his instructions.

"You must get past 'is steward. Granzy will want to take ta message 'imself. Keep it from 'im without telling 'im any lies, no, nor don't let 'im know 'tis from me. An 'e thinks I 'ad the news first, 'e'll be wild for it."

I took a breath and knocked boldly on the door. *No use doing a thing timid* my father would say. I was a long time waiting. Screwing up my courage for a second knock, I at last reached for the door again when it swung smoothly open. The man behind it was gaunt, with hollowed cheeks bare of any beard they would have been the better for, and spare gray hair. A pale, pinched man except for his clothes which appeared to me to be quite wonderful. I stared, awed by the fineness of the cloth more like my mother's dress than the homespun I was used to. I felt a sorry drab, a feeling he plainly shared.

"How did you get past the gate? Old Rufus at his pots again?" He swore feelingly. "Hi, Rufus!"

I held my ground. "He let me in, sir. I have news for Lord Cromart."

"You?" he jeered, glaring at the water dripping on his floor.

"I am Nicodemus, son of Jarn, of Foothills Croft."

He gave me a long, appraising look. "Out with it then," he said at last, "What is the news?"

But I minded Brychan's advice and said carefully, "I'm sorry, sir, but I was told 'twas for the lord's ear alone."

Brychan had said he knew Jarn. Let him think my father had told me. He worried at it like a dog but I held fast, thinking of my parents and what people like this had put them through. This earned me some black looks but in the end he gave up, just as Brychan had said he would. He didn't dare hold up a message for Cromart.

"Well," he drawled, civilly enough, "You're bold enough to be Jarn's seed. But, look you, boy. An you're lying, were better to tell me now and be put back out in the rain for your troubles, than be found out by Lord Cromart."

"I'm being most careful of the truth, sir."

He raised his brows at that, but contented himself with calling in a servant. "Wring out this young wretch as swiftly as you may and bring him back." I was conducted to a bare little chamber where my clothes were stripped from me without ceremony and I was given a rough towel. While I dried off, the servant wrung out my clothes and handed them back to me, urging me to hurry. I got back no warmer than I left, but at least I didn't drip, which was all Granzy cared. He got up from his scrolls and bade me follow him, leaving the room on such long strides that I must run to keep up. We twisted down passageways and over staircases until I wondered an he was trying to lose me, but never a word he said. At length he came to a doorway like a dozen others, held up a finger to wait, knocked and stepped through.

In formal tones I heard him announce, "My Lord. Nicodemus, son of Jarn, of Foothills Croft, with a message for your lordship!" One long hand emerged from the doorway and waved me forward. Thinking he'd taken his revenge, making it sound an a baron were calling, I hung back, afraid to show the ragged boy. I found out later that was a disservice. An you were to be announced, then he did it properly.

Now he hissed, "Step forward, boy, and make your bow." With all the dignity I could gather, I stepped out of the passageway, advanced the prescribed three paces, and bowed as I'd been taught by my father, to my waist, no lower. I was free and no serf.

There was silence for a fist of heartbeats, broken finally by a deep voice, "Straighten up, boy, and let me see you." As I did so, he moved from the shadows at the back of the room, allowing me to see him clearly as I'd not when I came in. Somehow I'd expected a man larger than life, bigger than Brychan or my father, the largest men I knew, but he was not. Instead, I beheld a small man, lithe and quick of step, with a bald egg for a head and a small black beard, trimmed to a point. My disappointment quickened when I saw his clothes were no better than his steward's, except for his shoes which were pointed and of red leather. Nowhere could I see a weapon, not so much as a dagger let alone a great sword. He looked for all the land like a clerk instead of the haut baron I'd heard of all my life and I thought it a trick played by Granzy to get my news after all.

I was about to protest when I looked into his eyes. The clerk dissolved in an instant. They were a clear, cool gray, and while not precisely hard, there was no doubt that here was a man used to command and being obeyed. I swallowed, appalled by the indiscretion I had come so close to committing, and tried my best to look him back evenly. He stopped in front of me and grasping my chin between thumb and finger turned my face this way and that, regarding it.

"Well, brat, you have something of Jarn's look. Comes this message from your father?"

"Nay, lord, he is dead. Am my own messenger."

"How is this, then?"

So I told him my story, obeying Brychan's stricture, omitting nothing except Brychan's advice and my own vague expectations. Calmly, closely he questioned me. He could drag out detail I didn't know I had. He placed the raiding party at a score simply by having me describe the width of the attacking path which I hadn't noticed but could recall. He was interested in the crest and when I commented that it seemed peculiar to take the time to do, he answered, "Shrewdly observed, Nicodemus, and true enough an 'twere Goff. He died two months agone." He took a turn about the room, arms folded and chin down to his chest, "It seems his cub would tweak my nose."

Another pace or two and his head snapped up abruptly, "Granzy, best fetch my lady, then send outriders, one to each manor in the fief. I want all knights here by sundown, tomorrow, with half their muster." As the steward turned to go, he added, "And Granzy…" The steward turned, "…I'll tell the Lady Beatrice myself." The gaunt retainer bowed, inscrutable, and disappeared.

Cromart looked sudden gentle. "I'm sorry about your parents, lad. Your father was a good man. He'll be sore missed with trouble along the border. Brychan will have told you I let the serfs talk me out of the border watch. 'Tis a mistake I'll not repeat. They'll be quick enough to see it restored now. Still, it won't be the same without Jarn to lead it." He took another turn about the room. "Why did Brychan take such care to send you as messenger?"

"I told you, my lord, there were dead to bury at Cooling and he wanted watchers to make sure they were not taken unawares and men to leave at Pudding Hill to clear the people if they had to."

"Aye, that will serve and Brychan knows it. But an I know him, there's more than that, or he'd have sent a man anyway. Out with it, youngster, what else did he say?" Before I could answer there was a sound at the door and a lady, gray and grave and beautiful, moved through it, inclined her head and said, "My lord?"

"Leave us," said Cromart. "Await my call without."

I huddled in the passageway, and through the closed door heard just their murmur as they talked. Shortly there was a cry and then I thought I heard the sound of weeping. Eventually it faded to long silence that hung behind the great oak door like a cloud. At last, the voices took up again and then the door creaked. As it opened, I heard her say quite clearly, "I believe I can."

Cromart called me in and I stood before them. She was composed but her face confirmed what my ears had told. Otherwise, she was imposing, as Cromart, an you missed his eyes, was not. I made my bow, and when I rose I could see she was as tall as he.

"Nicodemus," said Cromart, "It is important to establish that you are who you claim to be. Have you proof?"

"None, my lord, but who else should I be?"

The lady intervened quickly. "That doesn't matter, so long as you can establish who you are. The proof should be in your head. May I?" Cromart nodded and she continued, "If you be Nicodemus, son of Jarn, what was your mother's name?"

"Constance, my lady."

"Common enough knowledge" interjected Cromart. She ignored him and looked fixedly at me and added, "And her other name?"

I hesitated a heartbeat, for it was rare to have a second name and my mother had disliked hers and did not countenance its use. "Amalia, my lady. She did not like it."

"Indeed, she did not. My lord," she turned to Cromart, "So little did my sweet Constance like that name that only her son would know it. I am satisfied that this is Nicodemus, son of Jarn and Constance." Cromart looked a bit disgruntled, perhaps expecting something a little more concrete, but he acceded with tolerable grace. "Good," she said. "Let us get him warmed and fed."

Before I knew it, a servant was called and I was whisked off to a bathhouse down by the kitchens. A tub was filled with steaming water by a laughing maid and I was scrubbed all over. I protested I could do it myself and after much persuasion she withdrew still laughing, leaving me to wallow in the heat. She returned a time or two to check on me. As I was lost beneath the suds we were both content, I with my modesty intact and she that I was getting clean as ordered. At length, the man returned with a towel and fresh clothes, old but warm and finer than anything that I had ever owned. As I belted the jerkin, a bell rang and I heard a bustle in from the kitchens.

We entered as a stream of servants staggered out laden with platters or baskets or pitchers. He waved down the same maid and had a word in her ear, then disappeared weaving through the stream. She took me to a table set in an alcove, near the great roasting fires, banged down her basket and grabbed a great hunk of bread from within.

"'Ere, dearie. Should keep you 'till we've sorted out that lot above!"

She was as good as her word, bringing me severally, a jug of small beer, a savory pie, several chunks of roasted meat with potatoes and a mess of boiled greens. It was the sort of meal I'd only had on major feastdays and I wondered whether they had one at the castle I knew not. When I asked, she only laughed.

"Castle folk always eats like this." I could see some of the other servants look sideways at me as they went past, but no word was said, and they otherwise avoided me. Even when they returned for their own meal it was to other tables, set apart from mine. My girl was the last one back. Even so, she asked first an I wanted more. When I shook my head, all she said was, "Well, then," and moved across to join the others, slumping gratefully on the bench.

Shortly after, the manservant returned, picking his teeth, and took me away to a little room with a pallet. "You're to sleep, here," he said. "My lady will see you on the morrow, after she's broken her fast."

Chapter 5

The next morning I was taken to a different chamber, the Lady's own, full of women's things, bottles and jars and fabrics. The morning sun streamed in through a window and the air was drifted with lavender layered with complex other scents I did not know. She waited, seated in a chair, as great to my young eyes as a throne. As I drew close I saw she was clothed, not in a simple dress such as my mother wore, but in a robe of softest white with ties and falls and cutaways through which peeped the startling, silken blue of her undertunic. The dove gray hair shone in the sun, not old and tired, but young somehow, though she must have been of my parents' age.

"Come, Nicodemus." From beneath the flowing sleeve a hand flashed slender white at a stool at her feet. "Talk to me of your mother." Was there sadness there? 'Twas hard to tell, the face schooled in unreadability.

So I told her, answering the occasional question, mostly following my head. I talked of her garden with its myriad of flowers, of her herbs and soups and pottages, of her teaching, plants and their uses in the upland meadows and woods, letters around the fire. Strangely, as I talked, I felt no urge to cry, but only the warmth of her flooding through me like the sun from the window.

"It sounds as though she was happy." The voice came from a distance, the face turned aside, staring out the window, naked, just for a moment.

The face swung back and I considered an I had not seen. 'Twas not something I'd ever thought about. "I believe she was, my Lady."

Beatrice still seemed far away. "She taught you your letters?" I nodded. She smiled, bemused. "Her letters," she murmured. "When she first came to Tansley, I was in awe of her because of her letters. We were both just girls then. The first time I first saw her, at the godsday feast, she was sitting aside while the adults talked, reading a scroll." She laughed at the memory, "I thought she was pretending and taxed her with it. Instead of taking offense, she read aloud to me, 'The Lay of Sir Hengist' an I remember aright."

I started, "She would recite that sometimes, what she still knew. She had no scrolls."

"She must have hated that." She paused a moment, hesitating, "What do you know of her past?"

I repeated what Brychan and Annie had told me. She frowned when I came to how she had been treated at the castle but said nothing, waiting until I had done.

"I knew about how she was treated but she was too proud to complain. I ached for her, but even as chatelaine, I was powerless to interfere." She regarded me a long moment, her blue eyes almost as penetrating as her lord's still gray ones. Then she appeared to make a decision.

"You should know it all. 'Tis your heritage, you have the right, though the god knows an I do you a favor."

"I became friends with your mother from that first meeting," she began, picking her way. "'Twas natural enough. We were the only two girls of an age in Tansley. Her father, your grandfather, was Sir Geoffrey of Benson, a proud name in Anglesea, and a high one, despite he was only a knight. The Benson's have held the high post of Right Knee to the king since time out of mind and Sir Geoffrey was no different.

"Besides his position in battle, whence the name comes, the Right Knee is an important advisor. 'Twas in that role that Sir Geoffrey fell foul of the king, why it doesn't matter. Suffice it to say he was lucky not to lose his head. Instead, he was rusticated…" her mouth twisted into a wry smile, "…to Tansley."

She sighed, "He was out of place in these parts, not least because he believed that children, sons or daughters, should have their letters." Her eyes came back to me, "I tell you this to show you we were equal once. Indeed, I felt her my better, though not through any word or look of hers. Time turns. I became lady of all these lands while she…," she faltered, seeing my face. "Well, you know the story."

I nodded, silent, and she picked at a thread. "She was not bitter, you know, though she was sore hard done by. She was used to say that though men set much store by their estate she had learned from her father that estate could come and go like the wind, that it was the person inside that mattered."

"He was quick enough to change hers and for no fault of her own," I retorted.

"He was not the man cast her out! He died two years before and his wife and lands were given over to a younger knight. She'd little choice, women seldom do." She sighed. "It was my dear lord who did it but, in truth, he'd little choice himself. Goff was a wolf at the door and he needed a proven man who would come to the marches. Sir Randalf was a good campaigner in the troubles, but he's a hard man. He'd little use for your grandmother, who was a gentle soul. She soon died, I think to get away from him. He's been through another wife since and now..." her lip curled, "Contents himself with the scullery maids."

I said nothing, lost in the wonder that my grandfather had been a famous knight. Annie had said my mother was gently born but I had not expected this. I tried to imagine what possibilities it might open. Beatrice gently cleared her throat.

Sympathy lurked in her eyes. "You must understand, Nicodemus," she said gently, "That your birth poses something of a problem. It has been kept from you but the murder of your parents has thrust it upon us before time." She rose and took a turn around the room, restless as Cromart, her robe sweeping the floor so it threw up little puffs of dust. "When Sir Geoffrey died, the king had Benson Manor plowed under so no one else could hold that name."

I puzzled at that. Not on my account. I wasn't born yet. "Did the king hate the name so much?"

"Nay, he respected your grandsire too much to ever let one not of his blood take the name."

"Respect!" I objected. "To take his lands and banish him and plow his manor under!"

"Banish, yes. The rest only after he'd died without male issue. Love and hate are often consorts, Nicodemus, especially with kings."

"You are saying, of course, that I am not male issue." I knew the answer but bitterness was in my mouth. I could not forbear.

"Nicodemus," she gathered up my hands and pulled me to her, sitting again as she did so. "You must understand. You are going to have to deal with the world as it is and not as you want it." She took a breath, then said fiercely, "You are the grandson of Geoffrey of Benson and deep inside you, through your mother, his spirit and those of all the Bensons before him are in you. But that is all you have of him. You cannot even have his name. In law and in custom the chain is broken, not once but at many links." She ticked them off on her fingers, "By the king's action, by your grandfather's death and your grandmother's remarriage, by the disowning of your mother by Sir Randalf and by her marriage to your father. Four links broken and a fifth, that you are a generation removed. One link might be reforged but never five. And never," she'd recaptured my hands by this time, and looked me straight and gentle, "Never the marriage to your father."

I tried to pull away, but she would not have it and I soon gave up the struggle as unseemly. "Nikki, your mother fought for her marriage. I set my face against her. How else? It was unthinkable, your father was naught but a serf even though Cromart had freed him. Yet she had nowhere else to go. She saw something in your father that in the end she made me see. I took up her case and Cromart at last agreed." She released my hands and sat back, "Do you know why we settled them at Foothills?"

I answered slowly, "So my father could watch the borders."

"That came later. So they could go where station didn't matter. Your mother was my friend, yet I could no longer receive her as that. She knew what she was giving up to marry your father yet she was willing. Her only concern was that she had to give it up for her children as well. You are the grandson of Sir Geoffrey of Benson, Right Knee to the King, but you are also the son of Jarn, freedman, born serf of Tansley."

And captain of the border watch," I added.

"And captain of the border watch," she smiled. "I see the second's as proud as the first for you; perhaps that's just as well for it bars the first forever. No herald would allow your claim to the name of Benson."

I stared at the flagstones, following idly the lines between them, trying to puzzle it all out. When I looked up she was watching me gravely.

"Prouder," I said, a little defiantly. "Jarn was captain in his own right while Geoffrey was born to the king's knee and let it from his grasp."

"Cockerel," she said, smiling, "Blood will always out. I can hear your mother talking and your father too, for that matter." She lifted a finger and sudden, 'twas an a darkness had entered the room, "Don't be so feisty on the subject of kings. They are slippery beasts to keep ahold and are not concerned to grease themselves with the blood of common men."

"Why tell me this, my lady. I'm not like to ride at the king's knee as you've been at pains to show me."

"I scarcely know, Nicodemus." She frowned, "I'd not intended it." The blue eyes swiveled back at me, "You've a feeling about you, like your mother, that is almost ... fey."

I started, "Do you mean she was a witch?"

"No. Just that she'd a stillness about her so that sometimes you'd think she wasn't really there and she could see farther than anyone else."

I remembered the stillness and my father saying she was out and would be back shortly. But I didn't voice that, objecting instead, "She always had to get close to see a thing clearly."

She laughed, a sound that was almost girlish. "I meant into affairs. Cromart would to the court and come back and she could always see better than he who'd been there what would be the outcome. He'd never say so, but he even rode to the foothills once to take her counsel. Did she never tell you?"

"Not as such." I thought about it, "I suppose she taught me rules of affairs. To listen and talk last, for the most effect. To give way in small things and so hold to what mattered. There were many others I can't recall, but they seemed all common place and not so very useful."

"Not common, and very useful, in the right place." She sighed. "Whether you will ever get to such a place, the god only knows. Getting you anywhere is the problem." I waited, knowing we were at the crux of the interview. She waved at the window, "My lord and I often walk the battlements on the keep where we can compass half of Tansley in a single circuit. From there, the fields are woven into patterns, each neatly in its place. I've been to the king's seat at Carvigal and seen the bustle and the throng and come home knowing my lord was just a country baron and I a country lady." She shook her head. "I would not change. Country folk are like country fields. Each has a place in the pattern and mine is a comfortable one. But you," she continued.

"Have no place," I finished for her.

"Have no place," she agreed gravely. "I'm sorry, Nicodemus. The tapestry was laid long ago and we cannot change its plan. We can but weave our piece. Save for the men-at-arms and one or two others, all else here are serf or gentle. Your parents understood that. We'd planned to move you on, when you were older."

"How?"

She shrugged. "Mayhap as an apprentice to a tradesman in one of the great seats. Merchant, by preference, an one could be found to take you. They have their guilds which they keep for their sons or one another's but your letters and my lord's influence might crack the doors. Mayhap as an understeward at another castle."

It all sounded bleak and very far away. I screwed up my courage, "Could I be understeward here?" and blushed that my voice squeaked.

She didn't seem to notice. Instead a shadow flitted across her face, "No!" she said too quickly, then closed her eyes, before slowly opening them again. "Believe me, Nikki," she said quietly, "It wouldn't work. 'Tis not you. There's just too much…history. Best you start anew, somewhere else." There was more, she wasn't saying, but I believed her when she said it wasn't me.

She went on, "You are here before time and no arrangements have been made. With the troubles breaking out again it may be a while yet so we must make dispositions." Sudden, she was the chatelaine again, remote, "You may keep the alcove assigned to you for sleeping but 'tis best you eat in the kitchens. An I sat you in the hall I would have to declare your place which would cause the kind of trouble I'd as soon avoid. Best you go unnoticed, as much as you can."

And so it was. Fighting flared across the border throughout the summer and into the harvest season and I was left to my own devices, trying, as I was bid, to stay out of people's way. I had the run of the place and soon learned where I could go and where not to cause no comment. The free men, soldiers mostly and touchy of their status, I avoided, though it made me ponder the point of being free. The Lady Beatrice contributed by never recognizing me publicly and seeing me but seldom in private. It met her purpose but it sorely multiplied my loneliness.

When we did meet, in the lulls of the castle's routine, it was to talk of my mother, each of us eager to hear what the other knew. She seemed to enjoy these sessions but there was an edge of sadness there not due to my mother's death. I got the feeling that she envied her old friend, despite all her troubles and her brutal death. We never spoke of those anyway, but only her life, and then, 'twas an a shadow stood at the Lady Beatrice' shoulder. I saw it clearest when once she said, *Constance was blessed in you, Nicodemus.* She schooled herself directly and passed on, but 'twas strangely said, so I wondered, *does she not feel herself blessed in Edgar?* Neither my father nor Brychan had liked him, I knew, but I had hardly expected their unease to extend to his mother.

I looked forward to these exchanges, but they were contained, directed backwards. What I remember mostly is the sound of the door closing firmly behind me as I left her chamber.

I have few clear other memories of the castle abovestairs. I felt like a coney on a vast cliff, dodging between endless holes. In the end, it looked all the same: a dank, blank warren of stone, dappled in darks, with stray arrows of light which too often blinded rather than lit. Years later, returning, I found it dwindled, though most of the walls still stood. To my surprise it cast shadows of a past that was pleasant rather than melancholy: the seat of a country baron built as much for comfort as defense. A child's memory—and I was still a child for all childhood had been forced behind me—is like a drawing. It never captures the reality of a place but only how it projects upon oneself.

Looking at the ruins I realized then that it must have been as pleasant a place to live as any of its kind could ever be. Pleasant for the lord and his lady, for the bailiff, constantly chiming his keys or the steward with his pots and parchments; even, perhaps, the maid in her scullery with her bended back and her raw, red hands. All of them belonged. Each had a place in the castle, a job to do that mattered, menial or not. More important, each had a place at the table. As Lady Beatrice made plain I did not.

I felt most at home in the kitchens. The servants soon found out who I was and accorded me a rough respect, on account of my father, tempered with a natural tendency to push me about, because of my years. It was a busy time and I was used to working; but they would accept no help, accounting it beneath me. They meant it for the best, knowing the Lady's designs as they seemed to know everything else. They wanted to help me along, but it stretched out time where I would fain compress.

Cromart was tied up with *the troubles* as they were called by the folk at the castle, though the most of the trouble for them was simply extra work. In my innocence I had thought that he would beard Goff's son, Lord Blanchard, at his castle. 'Twas with a high heart I watched as he rode out with his knights and soldiers two days after my arrival. The elation turned to ashes as the men in armor washed back and forth beneath the gates over the ensuing weeks. War was on the borders, but it was not directed at Blanchard's castle. It was fought, an that's what you could call it, against his crofts. Men returned dirty and weary, but never wounded, loud in their demands for food or drink, or baths an they were knightly. Often I saw them in the kitchens. They would ride in at odd times and would come down, swaggering before the serving wenches like heroes from the tales, demanding to be served immediately. The wenches made much of them and the compliment was oft returned as swelling bellies soon gave witness. An the Lady Beatrice thought of Tansley as a tapestry, unmarried mothers were unraveled threads. A flurry of marriages were arranged, some in the castle, most back to the crofts, as she deftly wove the loose ends back in again. The crofts needed it. 'Twas they that bore the brunt.

Cromart revived the border watch, under Brychan now, and by keeping half his men at a time in the field was able to secure the domain while raiding into Chandlebrook with impunity. For the castle servants, serfs all, with ties to every hamlet and manor in the domain, it was almost a festive time, the extra work notwithstanding. Worry about family and friends in border areas was quickly set to rest, food poured in from a grateful domain, and there were heroes to care for.

I was the only one, it seemed, who cared that the war was visited on innocents and not on those who started it. When I voiced my cares to Kat, the laughing maid who'd fed me first and came the nearest to a friend, she stared and told me they were none of ours.

"Besides, Lord Cromart will no suffer children or women to be touched, " she said, in her laughing way, "Which is why the men come back so randy!"

"And how will they fare with farms burnt and the menfolk slain?" I shot back. Her laughter died.

"Aye, they say Goff was a hard lord and Blanchard is worse," was all she would say. She turned away and would speak of it no more so I held my peace. But my dreams were black with burning crofts and iron men slashed with the red of flames and blood pooled in ashes. Nor could I stand to stay in the kitchens when the men came in and started their boasting. Despite my antecedents, I think I despised all knights and within a month I found the castle more than I could bear. I was close to suing Lady Beatrice to going back to Brychan and to Annie.

§

Turning this over in my mind, one day, I sought refuge, away from the clash of pots in the kitchen and arms in the yard. Plunging deeper into the warren than I yet had been, for once I was grateful for the dark, encompassing stone. 'Tis said you can hear the god call when he wants you, but I did not. I simply passed through a pair of great, carved doors and, sudden, the presence was there.

It pressed upon me, like water when you dive down deep, calm and cool. Looking around in a kind of wonder, I found myself in a chapel, small but beautifully wrought, built like great temples I since have seen, but all in miniature. Mayhap the presence was a trick of the builder's art for the chapel exceeded by far the simple whitewashed walls I knew from Cooling. Sometimes, I remembered, I'd fancied the presence there, faintly in summer with the windows open, echoing through the bees' drone or the wind talking to the trees. Then it had risen and fell with the sounds leaving me unsure whether it was really so or simply seemed.

I closed my eyes and the presence squeezed the more and I felt despair float up and out and so disperse. I moved forward and knelt and prayed, not in the rote of the brothers but directly to the god as my father taught. I paused and looked for an answer but the presence only waited. I did it again and yet again and still it loomed, unchanging and unsaying. And then it vanished with a pop that I could almost hear except I heard instead—

"What are you doing here?"

A banty little brother, fat and wattled red in the face, was advancing down the aisle. I realized the presence had just removed itself and wondered that the god would flee a priest. *Unclean,* I thought, rising to face him and grinned inwardly, looking at the state of his robe, *in more ways than one.* I said nothing, however, just looked him calmly in the face. For once I was sure of my place. An the god would stay for me and not for him I'd no doubt of who had the better right to be there. He stopped in front of me, disconcerted by my manner, his conviction greatly lessened.

"I said what are you doing here?" The voice was querulous.

"Praying," I replied, looking up at him, though not so very far, "As the Lady said I might." No such explicit permission had been given, but he could hardly complain that I'd been praying in the chapel. Instinctively, I felt he wouldn't push it. He said no more, but moved to the altar and fussed ostentatiously with the candles. Amused, I left and, sure enough, I heard no more about it. It didn't matter. I had my answer. As I had waited out the little brother, so had I been waited out and that very patience was the message. I was certain now that the sunset had been sent to stay me from the raid, the god only knew why. There was anguish for my parents, that they could not be included, but I'd always known that death was all around us. We are all tools to the god's use. All their lives they had played their parts and I could do no less. I would wait, making patience my study.

I had ample chance to practice it. Cromart's measures quickly gave him the upper hand but the troubles flared well into autumn. The festive air died with the summer and the mood grew grim as the frosts approached and folk thought on all the resources turned to war. I returned to the chapel from time to time, making certain always that Brother Belfus was occupied on other matters. The god was gone, the presence missing but it didn't matter. I could feel its echo in the silent, patient walls. They were all that was needed to remind me of my purpose. Still, patience is a hard discipline for the young, particularly when compounded with loneliness, and its mastery was a hard task. Determination I could take from the walls but nothing to fill the void. The gloom that settled in autumn, coupled with an unmarked entry to my thirteenth year, weighed heavily upon me.

At last, Cromart gambled and struck deep into Chandlebrook, knowing Blanchard to be the harder pressed. It worked. Blanchard sued for peace to the great relief of both domains. Even the god smiled on the endeavor for there came, just when the farmers looked for frosts and an end to the harvest, a second summer longer than any in memory, that stretched the crops and filled the storehouses depleted by war. When at last it was all in, Cromart declared a great feast of thanksgiving at the castle, asking not only his knights and their men, but even the scouts from the hamlets. They could not be seated in the hall, of course, but he had a byre cleaned out and chinked, close by the kitchens, and tables made, the whole inspected by himself and his lady and not left to the steward. It was a handsome gesture and the castle was abuzz, which was only heightened when he let a hint abroad that there might be something special in the way of entertainment. Though Lady Beatrice had just warned me that

Cromart did not trust Blanchard enough to journey to Carvigal that year, so there would be no meetings with the guildmasters at least until spring, I caught the mood. Brychan would be there with Annie. I longed to see her kindly face.

Chapter 6

I saw him first in the kitchen, sitting at *my* table, as I had come to think of it. Not so, of course. 'Twas called the groom's table, reserved for visitors who could not be seated in the hall. It was handy, well placed in the kitchen, and though I had shared it with many of the groomly calling, as well as Brychan a time or two, it was often used by any who could call for food away from meals, even Cromart himself.

He was a man well up in his prime, with a beard gone even gray like pewter. 'Twas clear he fed as well as Brother Belfus but, as he shifted on the bench, talking to Kat, I could see the iron in the frame beneath. Surprisingly in one so large his hands, wrapped comfortably around a tankard, were slender, strong and shapely, unmarred by any labor.

Lacking status of my own and with little to do, it had become a game with me to place strangers. I had become good at it, but him I could not fit. He'd the manner of a man who was his own but he seemed neither warrior nor priest and too fine, clothes and hands and mien, to be a wandering tradesman. Hearing my tread, he turned to face me full, blue eyes dancing even as they dug.

"Who's this, then?" he asked. Deep inside me I felt something stir.

"Nicodemus," I answered, giving him look for look, and then I added, "Son of Jarn." He regarded me for a few moments more so I wondered whether he laughed at me.

"Welcome, son of Jarn," he said, gravely, an the kitchen were his kingdom. "I am Bellarus. Won't you join me?"

The feast was to be in a fist of days and the thought came to me as I sat that here was Cromart's special entertainment. "Are you, perhaps, the entertainer the Lord Cromart has been hinting at?"

He roared with laughter. "Do I look like a juggler, boy? Can you see me on a high rope? Faith, it would be no trick to walk it if you could find one wide enough to hold the likes of me!" The laughter fell away and he scowled at me, "But who is the son of Jarn that he taxes a stranger with being no better than a common mountebank?"

I was all confusion at that and at the edge of a silly reply when I realized he was watching me close, without seeming to. My game was being played by two, with he the more expert. He could no more fit me than I him nor was his answer an answer. I inclined my head, striving for dignity, "One who has been taught to apologize for offense taken even when none was intended."

At that, he flung up a hand. "A hit!" he laughed, "Well done, young sir!" and drank off a great draught of his ale. Then he turned us to the troubles, listening as Kat and I talked, and others of the servants as they drifted in and out, saying little but steering things where he would. He'd a deft hand upon the tiller, so you'd never know it was there; but I noticed him drawing out details and, always, turning the talk back from him to them. When at length he'd left, all we'd gleaned was that he was a guest of Cromart's who knew him of old, there for the feast because he was in the neighborhood. There was a lot of speculation with some having it he was a knight, others a merchant; all thought him from one of the seats that Cromart visited, though none could say which because he hadn't said. Not one but thought well of him for his ease of manner.

The demands of work put an end to their talk and they soon forgot him in the press of other arrivals. I was not so sure of their conclusions, recalling how he'd turned me, and so kept an eye on him. He spent much of his time with the men at arms, and later the knights as they arrived, seeming to have a deep interest in things military. A knight would be no help to me, even a strange one, who brought no servants, but I could not break the puzzle and wondered an there was one. The slow chorus of the chapel walls beat on unchanged so I composed myself as best I could. He saw me watching a time or two, but that was as close as we got before the feast.

Annie and Brychan arrived the night before and were quick to seek me out. They were staying with friends in Halting, below the castle, and I slipped down to join them at their request. Annie had brought a cake and they made a fuss of my birthday.

"I know it's weeks agone," she said, "Though I don't know verra precisely the day. But I'd thought they'd no make any show for ye there in the castle." I was moved afresh to make them my people but the chapel had put me past that and I knew that I could not, that something in me had changed. Annie remarked it, saying I was "No the boy that left the cottage!" She left it at that, afraid I think to spoil the evening. We had a gay time of it, the kind that only simple folk can make and I left warm in the thought of such friends. As I walked up to the castle I felt sadness leak through. Whatever came, they were like to be permanently behind me.

Feast day dawned cool and clear or at least was so by the time that I got up. The feast itself did not get under way until early evening so I held to my bed as long as I could knowing that elsewhere I would just be underfoot. When I arose at last the castle throbbed. It was all I could do to cadge an apple from Kat to break my fast. Strolling around, watching as always, feeling keenly again that I had no part, I was suddenly struck with what a tapestry my lady could make of this.

Here a knight, from outlying parts no doubt, strutting on the battlements with his lady, showing her the sights with great sweeps of his hand. Here the men-at-arms polishing their pieces and there the steward, pounding the dust from his clothes as he emerges from inspecting the cellars, servants rolling the barrels behind him. The kitchens, of course, with sweating cooks and roaring ovens and spit boys crouching, the march of foods in steady cadence through the day, breads leading as always, hot from the ovens before ever I got up, followed by pies and pasties and then, at last, the joints and haunches, rolling and smoking on their spits.

The scenes would all be set against a twining ground of servants, figures running in dun, with pots and baskets and brushes and clothes and ewers of steaming water and scores of other needed objects. It was a pleasant conceit and passed time that would have otherwise hung heavy. 'Twas only when it was done that I noticed Bellarus had no part in it. I hadn't seen him once all day, though I'd been about most of the castle, adding pieces. I wondered an he was ill. For the week he'd been there he'd always been in the thick of things but no one I asked seemed to know, so I left it.

Feast time found me at my table, alone, for grooms were at the serf's hall. I'd thought of joining Annie and Brychan there, but that would undo all the Lady Beatrice's caution so I held my place. It did not matter. All were invited to the great hall after the food was done so I'd not miss out on the evening's entertainment and one was never stinted in the kitchens. When the time came, I trooped up the stairs with the kitchen staff and joined the flow from the serf's hall. 'Twas a cheerful jostle with many faces flushed and no few who leaned on the shoulders of their friends. I saw Brychan's bulk across the crowd and Annie smiled beside him and signed to see me after before they were swept in through the great doors to the hall beyond. My coming was slower, the entrance now a squeeze, but the small can wriggle an they can stand a buffet or two. Once close in they are generally thrust to the front by some good-natured soul. By the time the crowd was settling I'd a clear view of the entire hall.

The knights and their ladies were all seated at the high table, at the opposite end, with Cromart and the Lady Beatrice presiding. Beside her was a face I did not know, a young man just possessed, I judged, of all his inches. The knights were seated strictly by age, there being no other degree between them, the eldest by Cromart going out to the youngest at either end of the table, so he was not of their number. His position indicated a high station so I asked the nearest man, "Is that Cromart's son, back for the feast?"

"Aye, that's Lord Edgar, ta god rot him. Back for good, they say, and ta worse 'twill be for us!"

"Why? What's he like?" The man turned then whitened when he saw who had asked.

"You talk with ta Lady!" he said, "I've been drinking. I didn'a mean it!" His fear was visceral, twisting in his gut like a knife. I wondered that Edgar, two years gone, could leave so deep a mark.

"Don't worry, friend, my father was Jarn the serf. I tell no tales on my own." He seemed easier at that but I would get no more from him and I left it, thinking to ask Kat. Then I wondered that I knew so little of Edgar, beyond the bare facts of his existence and his absence at Castle Sanderling where he served as a squire. In all the kitchen gossip there'd been no talk of him. 'Twas just as if there were a black pool about his name that swallowed his very mention, leaving it to sink without a ripple. I studied him, but could get no closer to the mystery, seeing only a young man, with something of the look of both his parents, conversing at his ease with those around him. I gave it over and looked at the rest of the company.

The tables at the side seated the commoners, mostly men-at-arms and their wives, an they had them, with the steward, Granzy, presiding on the left and Brother Belfus heading the one on the right. With a start I realized I could not see Bellarus, nor did a careful sweep reveal his presence, but only an empty place at the high table at the end below the knights. So I'd been right, he must have been ill after all. Briefly, I felt sorry for him, to come so far to a feast and then have to miss it.

Then Cromart stood and the hall fell silent. He looked steadily about the crowd, stretching out the expectation until I tensed to hear it snap. At last he relented with a smile.

"Has been years since we had a harper…" A gasp breathed through the crowd and he smiled, "So I got a master to make up for the wait. Many of you have met him, without knowing who he was, so let me introduce him now. Bellarus, of Suthy, Master Harper!"

I'd been closer than I knew when I guessed he was our entertainment, but the thought of a harper had never occurred to me. I felt cheated in my game. To the people of Tansley, harpers might just as well be kings, known to exist, but never seen, rare and exalted, the stuff of stories. Yet everyone knew they wore the green. I'd not seen so much as a stain of that color in Bellarus' clothes.

He stepped from a serving recess, his identity revealed, waved forward by Cromart who sat down with a smile like a triumphant conjurer. In the light I saw indeed that the puffed sleeves of his jupon and his great flowing mantle were rich grass green, *harper green* my mother had called it. I was swept along in the applause with the rest, with a only a moment to consider that he hadn't talked like a man from two kingdom's away.

'Twas a magic evening. He played for hours, how many I never knew. He gave us all the old stuff, songs of the heroes, complete in all their glory, not like the snatches we knew from our mother's knees. He gave us love songs and songs of the chase and drinking songs. Knight or maiden at will, he'd a hundred voices, tender or funny or bawdy by turns, making us laugh or weep as he would. And always the harp, like rippling water flowing about his voice as he sung, so he seemed to swim in it, or sometimes to converse with it, throwing the liquid back and forth between his throat and the strings. Time was something he held in his fingers and it went as fast or slow as he liked. In the end I could not tell how much had gone, nor did I care.

I remember wishing I could take the moments and wrap them around me like a blanket and so hold onto them forever. I heard the voice of the god in the music. An I could not hold the moment yet 'twas born in me of a sudden, I must reach for the voice. At last he made an end and bowed and thanked the company for their attention and so turned to leave. The roar of protest doubled back and back from the walls, folding in upon itself and piling higher like a pastry, until it was painful to the ears.

He turned back, an surprised. Then he held up a hand for quiet and when he had got it said, "One more then." As he sat back to the harp he nodded at the steward and all the torches along the wall were doused leaving only one behind him and another behind Cromart. The effect was to strand those two in pools of light and the crowd stilled as if snuffed out by the dark. He started with the harp, slow and sad, staring at the floor an in thought and I saw sudden that this was to be a special song, done for the occasion. I'd have to add to my tapestry, away from all eyes in a corner, the harpist, untouched by all the bustle, composing his song in honor of his host; for that, of course, is what it was.

For the most part it was what you'd expect. His talks with the knights had been to some purpose letting him sing of the fighting so dear to noble hearts, with at least one verse for each of the knights and several about Cromart. He did it nicely, praising their valor without trying to make more of it than there was. All very conventional stuff, but it pleased them and I could see the old knight on Cromart's left in the edge of the light, pattering off his verse to himself so he shouldn't lose it. No doubt some of the verses clattered about the manor houses of Tansley for a few years after, but the song entire is long forgotten. Bellarus himself scorned to keep it. He was used to say such guest songs were the harper's chaff and should be blown to the winds.

But there was wheat. Not at the end, as at a winnowing, but right at the start, the very opening. 'Twas a lament by one of the serfs to set the scene for his theme, which was of stewardship and not really of war. It was strikingly simple and moved the audience immediately, common, serf and noble; it still can be heard in the north, though the names are often changed. The strings were a prelude and the first lines set up the hair on the back of my neck.

Serf's Lament

They ha' slain Jarn of the Foothills
And his lady, hand in hand.

Ma sister's dead in Cooling,
Her wee babies and her man.

They are burning house and byre
And smoke darkens all the land.

Is there nane to make them stay their bluidy hand?

They burn the golden wheat fields
And churn them to black mud

Wind is all that stirs in Cooling
Over cobbles stained wi' blood.

Death by sword or death by starving
Is there nane to stay the flood?

And who will keep ma babies safe from harm?

He sang it sad and slow and haunting, so that by the end mine was not the only face was wet. At the last line, he turned his face round and up at Cromart and held the pose, letting the sound die away through the hall. It was magnificently done, setting Cromart up as the protector of his people, while showing it was the serfs who always suffered. More subtle yet, he didn't name Blanchard as the source of the troubles, but just said *they*, echoing the farmer's feelings that the politics didn't matter much. One noble's sword killed just as dead as another's.

After twice two fists of heartbeats, he slowly held up a hand and a torch was kindled at the back of the hall. At that, he swung into standard ballad form and gave them verse after verse of conventional stuff, well metered and pitched to please, which of course it did. Every few verses his hand went up to light another torch. By the end, he had a full paean going to Cromart, all torches lit and the crowd rollicking along. On the last chord he sprang up and the torches doused again, except that above Cromart's head. The applause was thunderous, but when the room was lit again, Bellarus was found to have disappeared, harp and all. The cheering turned to Cromart which was, I think, the intention. When finally it settled, he gave a speech, short but gracious, and then gently dismissed the serfs. I went with them.

Annie and Brychan were just outside the doors, waiting for me in a backwash of the happy, chattering throng that streamed away down the stairs and into the courtyard beyond.

"Ah but that was a bonnie treat," she said, giving me a hug, "I've never heard a harper before. 'Twas a rare lament he made for your parents and our folk in Cooling. I wisht I'd thought to keep it in ma haid but I was so busy listening I forgot to remember. I've not the half of it."

"There'll be some as got it, Annie," Brychan said. "I've no head for words myself but I'll get it from ta kitchens when next I'm at ta castle."

"No need, " I said. "I have it all. You can take it with you now an you want, Annie." She hugged me again and I gave it to her whole, but it was only the first part she needed. Once more of that and she had it all, so perhaps I had something to do with its preservation. I doubt it for others must have got it or pieced it back between them, but one never knows the way the god works. At any rate, she was pleased to take it with her, warm, as it were, to the village.

"For we're goin' at first light, laddie, and must to bed. We just wanted to say goodbye and the god go with you."

I was about to protest that no provision had been made and that I was like to be at the castle for a long time yet when I stopped. Whatever the logic of the situation, the feeling was strong in me that this was goodbye. Somehow she felt it too. I stammered my thanks as best I could but was too young to be able to tell them what they'd meant to me. In the little time we'd had they had given me much and it gnawed at me for years that I did not show it. Now I know they had the wisdom of age and hope to think they could see through the awkwardness to what was in the heart beneath.

They were not long gone. I was in the kitchen, looking for company to ward the emptiness they left, when a servant rushed down from the hall. The news ran round like water. There'd been hard words at the high table, between Cromart and his son. The upshot of it was the harper had been locked in the tower.

Chapter 7

Rumor's a horse that runs wild without news to curb its bit. With no more of the matter forthcoming that night, speculation galloped through the castle, rounding on itself a dozen times, coming back in different shapes and colors. Yet always it was a horse in the dark, with no rider and no direction. What offense a harper could commit to make Cromart bend the rules of hospitality so far was beyond even the lowest imagination. In the end the wild gallop shuddered to a halt and I went to bed in disgust.

Heartsick, I couldn't sleep, but tossed until a rider clattered out with the dawn. Rising, I saw from my narrow window Cromart and his knights follow after, accoutered all for hunting. The plan had been for three days chase at Dimwiddy, in the Southing Wood, and was apparently being hewed to. I saw little of pleasure in Cromart's face as they silently filed past.

In the kitchens the news was that the rider had been sent to the King with word of the harper, who was being held in the King's name. What the King wanted with him or what Edgar had to do with it was still not known, but you could feel the tension ease even at that. To hold a harper, sacred to the god, was a bitter thing. They would rather it were King Cantor's doing than Cromart's who, it seemed, was wroth at the need. All reports had Bellarus being well treated, denied only his liberty. There was some hope the god would not blame Tansley for the crochets of a distant and elderly monarch.

Leaving the kitchen, I was accosted quietly by one of my lady's maids, an elderly soul whose disapproval I'd always been sure of. There was no sign of it then, but only a serious face and a discreet request to see the Lady Beatrice *as soon as you might slip away*. She stared at me intently, her whole demeanor shrieking caution, then gathered up her skirts and disappeared as softly as she'd come.

I wandered awhile, to see an I was watched, then took another route upstairs. Knocking, I was admitted at once to my

Lady's chamber. She sat in her chair, a carven queen upon a throne, serene and seemingly untouched by the event the night before.

"Ah Nicodemus, do come in."

She stretched out a hand to kiss which, while unremarkable, was quite unlike her manner of before. As I took it in my hand and knelt to kiss, I felt her fingernail move against my palm, three times, sharp in warning.

"My lady."

I looked up and could see no sign in her face and realized with a shock she was playing to her maids around her. I felt myself tauten, like the harper's strings, and wondered what tune she would play.

"Welcome, Nicodemus. How go your riding lessons?"

Had she belched, my surprise could not be more complete. I'd never been on a horse in my life. I fought for composure.

"W…well, my lady."

"And the mare we gave you? Is she as sweet as was promised?"

The dance was still obscure but I had the measure. Her lead was strong so I followed readily enough, "Aye, my lady, sweeter, an that were possible."

She laughed, gay and easy. "Come you must tell me more. I remember well how it first felt to own a horse." She turned to her three maids, "You may go," and they trooped obediently out. Firmly she closed the door behind them.

"Oh well done, Nikki!" Momentarily, her eyes sparkled, "Have you ever even been on a horse?"

"How could I, my lady? We'd not the means."

Her visage darkened. "Your mother's wretched stepfather! Did you know she was a wonderful rider?"

I watched her carefully. Though there was nothing I could put my finger on it seemed the shadow at her shoulder was blacker than ever. *How not, with a harper, a guest, locked up in her own castle?* But I knew that wasn't it. The shadow was for the mother and not the chatelaine. It was the first time I was to think of him as black Edgar. "She never mentioned it, my lady."

"She would never pine at what could not be mended." She twisted idly at the tassel at her waist, a rare lapse, "Did she mention your grandfather as a great breeder of horses?" I shook my head. "Aye, and he shared his skills, improving not only his but all the stock in Tansley. That upped our income in no small measure. It seems only just that one of his breed come down to his grandson, and that he be taught to ride like his forefathers."

"Since it seems I've been riding for a time, I'll have to work to catch up."

She laughed again, "You've your mother's quickness!" but her eyes were haunted. "You will, indeed. You start when you leave this room. I've a man I can trust to teach you and you'll learn it all. Not only to ride a horse, but to care for one and to gentle it and, of course," she looked meaningfully at me, "To saddle it."

It was not like her to weave such a tangled knot. I could see the surface strands—I was to learn to ride and quickly— but the twists and turns that lay beneath were beyond my understanding. I felt the tingle in my palm where her nail had been, and composed myself to wait, trusting in time and her to show me her design.

"You must practice all you can. To that end, I've given orders that you may saddle up night or day. So as not to disturb the other animals," she continued, "I've had the mare we gave you for your birthday moved to the outer stable, beside the…harper's."

My heart grew large in my chest and I thought, *Here is the warp of the matter,* but ventured just, "Bellarus?"

"You know him?" I nodded. "I thought so. Your face in the hall last night seemed to say he'd touched you beyond the common thrall. Did I read it aright?"

I told her what I could. Knowing the presence was not just a glow I could use to bask in other's admiration, I left out the sunset and the chapel. I just told her I'd heard the voice of the god in the harp and wanted to follow it. That seemed to satisfy her, an only because it ran with her need.

"What are they saying downstairs?"

"My lady?"

"Come, Nikki, don't play the serf with me. I'm not asking for tales, but only the thrust of the kitchen talk, which you must know."

"That Bellarus is well treated, that he is held for the King, and that Lord Cromart seems as unhappy about it as they," I replied.

"And what say they of Edgar?" She asked it lightly but went very still, watching me closely for my reply.

"Little, madam. They seldom do." She seemed on the point of interruption, then quivered her head in slight denial and went still again. "But they blame him, knowing he argued bitter with his father and that the harper was held direct."

"Edgar is..." she sifted words, "...ambitious. He heard at Sanderling the King's writ stands in Carvigal against a master harper and last night saw it must be Bellarus." She took a slow turn about the room, marshaling, I think, her words. "The writ is not yet here and 'tis only chance that Edgar knows of it. Hosting a harper is a sacred duty. He could be gone today and none to say we've failed the King, but Edgar sees only advancement and not the shame falls on our house." She sat down at her chair again and shook her head. "I don't know why I tell all this to you," she said. "It can do no good. We must hold him against the coming of the King's officers."

She looked me straight from beneath her eyebrows and gave her next word the slightest emphasis, *"Our* hands are bound, mine and my lord's." At that, she paused, then added lightly, "Well, you should go to your lesson. Baldric expects you in the stable. See no one else!" and stooped in dismissal to pick up her needlework.

It did not take the god to see she looked to me to get Bellarus away, but how a lad of thirteen summers was to do that and why she couldn't just instruct me in my role passed my understanding. It must have shown on my face, for she added, "An you would like to see Bellarus, why not take him his supper after your ride? You can tell him of your new horse."

§

My mood rose with each step I took down to the stables. The prospect of a horse, so far outside my expectations, put all else aside. I was not even daunted that it was Baldric to be my teacher. I knew him to nod to, a sour man, stooped, with little to say unless it were of horses. When I turned up at the stables, he seemed sourer still, disposed to blame me where he could not blame the lady. By the time we reached the mare neither was pleased with the other.

She was a beauty, small but compact, unmarked, without blaze or patch to mar the perfect chestnut of her coat. Instinctively, I raised my hand, palm outstretched, and she whickered softly as she nuzzled it. Gently, I stroked her, enthralled that such a creature could actually be mine. Across her nose I caught sight of Baldric's face, changed completely as he smiled.

"You just might be alra' at that. Her name be Megan."

So each had done disservice to each other. Yet he was a hard teacher and I left the shed that served as Megan's stable so sore I wondered an I would not rather walk. Before the riding, he'd shown me how to saddle her. Twice more he made me do it and then again on the other occupant of the stable, which must belong to Bellarus though he said it not.

Only, "Ta see what differs in ta gear and what's ta same," and then discoursed on other straps and buckles I might meet.

Satisfied with that, he had me lead her out and through a postern gate hard by the shed. He took good care that I could handle both the mare and the bar myself, then had me put her through her paces for hours without the castle. In the end, he had me walk her down to cool her, then brush and feed and stall her, joking me on my tender walk.

At last he dismissed me til the morrow with a final, "You'll be alra'" which left me feeling pleased.

§

My backside chafed me still as I climbed the stairs from the kitchen with Bellarus' tray, but I didn't mind. I still had the clean smell of her in my nostrils and the sound of sweetly flying hooves in my ears.

"Going somewhere, bastard?" The voice was cold but the eyes held that which chilled far deeper.

"Lord Edgar," I bowed as best I could with the tray and felt it sudden dashed from my hands and tumbled down the steps.

"You are careless, serf," he sneered.

My face ran hot, but I answered him as evenly as I may, "I am free born."

He answered lightly, "Oh yes, my father freed Jarn before your birth." He considered me, then said in words dropped one by one, like stones into a well, "Why...my...mother...should...keep...a...bastard...like...you ..."

I spaced my own words, an to instruct a child. "My...parents...were...married."

His dagger was beneath my chin, so I must needs stand upon my toes. "You are insolent! Well let me give you some instruction. Your mother, having given herself to some common soldiers, was happy enough to," and here he spat the word out, "*Marry* a serf, freed or not. For a lady, even a whore, to link herself to a serf can be no marriage," and he pricked the dagger up a little harder, breaking the skin, "You're nothing but a bastard."

Abruptly he withdrew his dagger and stepped back, going to the balls of his feet as he went, the blade before him. The provocation was such an outrageous twisting of the truth that, while any part would have inflamed me, the whole was just too much. Somehow it left me colder than when he started, which was as well. He was much a man to fear so I gave him no answer but only looked at him. Were his father dead and he the Baron, I could not doubt his would be the only truth in the domain. I shivered at the thought, thinking of Brychan and Annie.

He mistook me, lowered his dagger, reversed it to its sheath and sneered out, "Coward!" before disappearing as silently as he came.

Returning to the kitchen with the ruins of the tray, I got the shakes for real. Leaning weakly against a wall I felt sick, the warm trickle of blood down my throat telling me just how close I had really been to death. Wretchedly I wondered that he could see cowardice in thirteen summers, unarmed, refusing combat with seventeen, trained and with a blade. A figure towered over me and I started, but it was only an undercook, angry at my tray.

"Edgar!" was all I need say. Wordlessly, he fixed me another tray.

§

Bellarus was on his stool where he must have been staring out the window, though his face was turned as I entered.

"You've blood on your chin, son of Jarn."

I waved Edgar's name at him, like a perverted talisman, and he grunted, "An I knew not better, I'd say Cromart had a changeling. I wish him joy of him."

"'Tis not Cromart will catch the worst cold of him."

He sighed, "I'm afraid you've the right of that," then his eyes narrowed. "How comes it that you bear my tray? I'd heard there were strict instructions you were not to serve."

"The Lady Beatrice thought I might like to talk to you."

"Did she now?" He pulled himself to his supper and settled in, "Now why did she think that?"

So I told him the whole of it, the strange interview with the Lady Beatrice first, then my own story, this time leaving nothing out. An it was truly he I'd been waiting for, then he had a right to know. What I found difficult to say to him was how I felt about the music. I ended badly.

He pursed his lips, "Forgive me, but this all seems a little opportune."

I hung my head at that, then picked it up again and looked at him. "Mayhap 'tis the hand of the god."

We regarded each other for several heartbeats before he said, "Mayhap. You appear to think so, at all events, which is really all that matters." He paused for a time, staring at me still but beyond me, an I wasn't there, the way that people do when thinking deeply. At last he reached conclusion and his eyes refocused.

"Do you understand what's going on?"

I shook my head, "Not really. Not what's beneath the surface."

"I cannot tell you all, not now. Suffice it to say that I knew your grandfather. When King Cantor, the god bless his narrow little mind, broke the house of Benson and sent your grandfather into exile, I left Anglesea under a cloud myself. I doubt me he was pleased when I returned to Carvigal but I was circumspect and largely left alone. When I heard that Cromart's agent was looking for entertainment, I contracted to come, hoping to find Sir Geoffrey alive, though I knew he would be old. The agent was pleased to get a harper to come to these parts. My name meant nothing to him, though it did to Cromart, too late to stop me coming. Someone must have been poking under stones, for after I left Carvigal, there was shortly issued a writ for my arrest."

"Twenty-three years for a man as old as my grandfather seems a slender hope to come all this way!"

"Aye, I'd other reasons I'm not free to talk of. But the hope was real enough. I would have liked to see Sir Geoffrey once again. He was a rare man for harpers and many there were who'd rather play at Benson that at the palace." He looked at me keenly, "King Cantor thinks I work against him, which is not true but sometimes is a difficult thing to tell to kings, as Sir Geoffrey found out. A commoner like me is apt to be walking loosely or missing bits before a king gets round to believing him." He dropped into Annie's Fastness speech, "I'm unco' attached to ma bits and not quite ready to depart wi' them."

He was a natural fool, but I could not laugh, only gasp, "They would not harm a harper!"

"No one takes rank to the chamber." He looked at my face and said, "Never mind, 'tis a long way yet. But 'tis why the lady wants me away from here. I knew Cromart of old. Though there's nothing in it, she knows that truth pops on the rack along with joints and the chamber breeds strange tales. Edgar has not the wit to see that. Or, given what you've told me, maybe he does and seeks to hasten his accession."

"And why comes the Lady Beatrice so oblique?"

"I think she finds it hard to lie and this will let her say she entered in no plot but you helped me on your own." He jumped up, grasping my shoulders, "I make assumptions. Tell me plain, Nicodemus, are you willing to help? 'Twill be mortal dangerous for you an Edgar finds out."

I took a breath, finding that courage is needed for more than fighting with a knife. Much had the god wrought to bring me to this and it was not for me to let it slip. "I would go with you as your apprentice."

He sat down again and rubbed his face in his hands, "Look you, Nicodemus. I will take you with me and I will seek to let out whatever music you might have inside but I cannot put in what isn't there. I cannot take as apprentice one without the gift. I'll give you half a year. But," he raised a cautionary finger, "An I decide you've not the gift, then we find you something else."

All you can ask of the god is a chance. "How do we get you out? I've no hope of getting a key."

He went to the window. "Is that the shed with the horses and the postern gate?" I craned my neck, then nodded. "I thought so. A rope from this window puts me outside the walls." He smiled, "The lady plans well. I was held in my room last night and only moved here this morning. There's a rope in my saddle bags. An I know her, she knows about it. All you have to do is get me the rope."

We laid our plans for the following night, giving us a day at least before Cromart's return. "The less men out on our track, the better I'll like it," was Bellarus final comment.

Chapter 8

I stole into the shed before first light. Gentling both mounts to keep them quiet, I found the rope in one of Bellarus' saddle bags. Smug with cleverness I clambered up to the tiny loft where I could try the rope unseen but my smile soon came unstuck. No matter how cunningly I coiled there was too much of it to conceal beneath my clothes. By the time Baldric arrived I had it back in the bag and was currying Megan, worrying more at my problem than such snarls as were in her coat. All I had worked out was Bellarus' window was too high for me to dare to cut it.

I gnawed at it off and on all day but Baldric brooked too little inattention for me to make very much progress. Such plans as I did concoct were improbable at best. Despite the old man seemed not to want to work the mare too hard, so that I was sure he was privy to what was in the wind, he had no end of horselore. It was late in the afternoon before I could get away. Finding my sour mood sharpened by hunger—I'd been too intent that morning upon the shed to break my fast—I went to the kitchens. Kat would let me cadge and I could consider anew at my table.

"Well, Edgar's taken a dislike to you and no mistake!" Kat slipped me an apple and some cheese.

As this was not new to me, I only grunted, concerned to find the answer to my problem. She turned away. The guard was sure to search any bag I carried, nor could I see any way to distract him from his post. I sighed and at last heard what she'd said, or rather, how she'd said it.

"Kat!" I had to call her, "What makes you say that about Edgar?"

She came back slowly and, sitting opposite, leaned well across the table until our heads had all but touched. "'E called you Jarn's bastard spawn," I felt my face twist at that, "And 'e gave orders you were to take no more meals to t'arper." Blood roared in my ears and her face in front of me quivered through a veil of red while the room behind surged back and forth in waves. Had it been Edgar there in front of me and I the means, I think I would have tried to stain him red for good. *Which is what he wants,* I thought as I fought to bring myself to control. *Does he know?* The waves receded and the veil dissolved and I heard Kat's voice as if from a distance.

"Nikki, be you all right?" and then normal and close at hand and sharp, "Nikki, what 'ave you got yourself into?"

I shook my head to clear the last of the fit. "Just faint. I rode all day with Baldric and forgot to break my fast." I wondered an I could trust her, then knew in a heartbeat I could. That was not the issue.

"Best for yourself that you not know, Kat. Leave me and let me think."

She stared at me with worried eyes but she was serf enough to know I said true. Breaking off the stare with a funny little shrug, she backed away and left me to my thoughts. They were bleak enough. We had a day in hand to Cromart's return. Before Kat spoke, it had been in my mind to see at supper an Bellarus could sniff a way where I could not. Now Edgar had sealed me off. Despairingly, I wondered who I was to think the god had signs for me, else how should I be brought to this pass? I should have known that the god speaks seldom and tips less the dice of humankind, lest all our work be rendered mere illusion; but I was young and much afraid. At last, knowing such thoughts would get me nowhere, I fought to think.

An she would, the lady could overset her son, but she was playing know-not as well as the least of her serfs. Besides, the cost would be to alert Edgar. The problem was mine to solve. Unhappily, I wrestled with it but always dark Edgar rose in my mind to bar the way. Weary with it, I sat back, defeated, and bit unthinking into my apple. As the juices of my mouth flowed out to meet the tartness, reminding me of my hunger, the key fell into my hand with a slap—put there, as it were, by Edgar. I almost laughed aloud.

Finishing hastily my rough meal, I slipped out in high excitement, to find the things that were needful. They weren't so hard to find but I feared to ask for them, less Edgar hear and work out my intent. So I waited until all had left their work for supper, to steal what would have gladly been given. It took some time, and longer yet to put it all together, but at last I could back to the kitchens for a meal myself, very late, but happy at last to see my way.

§

"You're late!"

Kat slapped supper down before me and I looked at her closely then, an for the first time, aware suddenly how much she had been my friend. I remembered her laughter at my bath when first I came to the castle. Since then, she'd been part of my daily life and had become one with her surroundings, seen but never looked at. She was young, with laughing eyes and great round arms, strong from slinging pots in the kitchen. Yet I could see by the wing of gray in her hair she tried to hide and her roughened hands that age would take her soon, coming quick as it always did to serfs. I ate my supper slowly, thinking of her and Edgar. It had been in my mind to ask her for food for the journey but I put the thought away, knowing I could not beg help from a friend then leave her for him. As it was it must come to his attention that she had been my friend. When it did, I knew he'd put the laughter out of her eyes.

"Kat!"

I'd finished my meal and called softly to her as she passed and she stopped and I stood. How much could I say? "I'll always be proud you were my friend, Kat," I hissed, low as I could, "But Edgar must not think so."

The slap rang round the kitchen and heads turned towards us all about the room. The print of my hand warred with rage and baffled hurt across her features as she recoiled while I stepped to the side that my face might be better seen. Watching her coldly, I searched her eyes and saw at last a flicker of understanding.

"Leave me be, wench, I need take no insolence from a common kitchen drudge!" My voice was raised and few could have missed the words. They spoke a language Edgar could understand.

"Proud talk for a draggled little field rat!" she spat and walked off like a queen, rage in every step.

It was all I could think of. Leaving my table for the last time, I pondered an our little scene would deflect or simply intensify Edgar's interest. 'Twas a sore heart I took upstairs.

In my room I made up a little bundle using the cloak I'd got from Annie, putting in my mother's fork and father's tools, a few other little things I'd come by at the castle, and my spare clothes. These were old castoffs of Edgar's and such was my distaste of him that I briefly thought to leave them behind. Then I grimaced at my foolishness. Would I go naked? The clothes I wore were his as well, the ones I'd come in having long since disappeared. Sliding my father's knife into a sheath I'd made of leather scraps, I clasped it to my belt beneath my jerkin and found myself ready. With hours to go before I could move.

Restlessly, I paced to the window, the bundle still bulky in my hand. I forced myself along my way in my mind, picking down the stairs and courts and passages in the dark, choosing which would be the fastest and which the most unseen. *The bundle.* I thumped it against my knee, considering how I might pass it off in a chance encounter. My position reminded me that harpers were not all could fly from windows. Scraping up what string I had, I tested its length. Short. Yet close enough, I judged, to let the bundle land softly, drawing no attention. Tying it up I settled down to wait, watching the guards upon the walls, remembering ruefully their emptiness when I arrived. My coming had changed that. Still, I could only find two, one to a side. For as long as I watched, they kept their stations, their care all for the approaches across Tansley Plain, not a sally from the Castle. In all the weary hours, they glanced at the foot of the castle but a time or two, and then only directly underneath.

At last, it was time to go, the castle all asleep but for the guards. Softly the bundle went out the window on the string. 'Twas not quite long enough so I had to let it drop the last few feet into the courtyard below. The *whump* it made as it landed rose to my room and I fell back to the shadows. The near guard turned, his head cocked like a terrier, and methodically began to scan the inner wall. I prayed the bundle was against the wall and not in the open where he would surely see it in the moonlight but I dared not check to see. In the end he turned back to the plain, but his head was stiff with listening, so I stayed frozen, deep in the shadows. For minutes he stayed like that, with the stillness of the dead, so I daren't move, not even in my room. Finally, he stretched his shoulders and stamped a foot and leaned forward over the battlement.

Wearily, I slumped down the wall. Watching him all that time I'd been struck by the obvious—I'd never considered the weather. The night was too quiet to cover our sounds, the moonlight too bright. For a hand of heartbeats the though kept me pinned against the stone, before I struggled angrily to my feet. The god sent what the god sent. It had to be tonight—Cromart's return tomorrow with his hunting party would more than double the garrison. I pushed away the thought that mayhap the god was not with us and stepped out in the passage, squaring my shoulders. 'Twould not do look furtive. The dark and the shadows soon built fear atop the worry and I began to sweat, despite the cold, making my shirt wet and my hair lank.

"Going somewhere, bastard?"

"My Lord Edgar!" He looked smug and satisfied. The smell clung round him suggested a recent assignation and I wondered briefly an the wench had been willing. With a chill, that made me think again of Kat.

"I…I couldn't sleep. I have dreams, still, of the raiders." The fear, which was real enough, showed in my speech, and he smiled, fingering his knife.

"So, even in your dreams, you're a coward!" He toyed with the hilt a while, then withdrew his hand, "'Tis well for you my mood is good. Get you back to your place and face your bogies yourself instead of dragging them all about the castle!" He dropped his hand back to the knife, this time with purpose, and the smile fell away from his face. "Mark you, bastard, our time will come." He leered, "You can add me to the bogies in your dreams!"

Back in the room I was as bare of resources as it was of my belongings, a boy, terrified, with none of the training that came later and could so easily have sustained me. My fear rose up to eat me and I felt myself swallowed in its maw and wallowing in its belly. I lay on my pallet, crying silently, hopelessly, bitter at the Lady Beatrice to ever have thought that I could rescue Bellarus.

§

A shutter banged. The wind elbowed through my window and rippled its fingers along my spine. In an instant my body went from sobs to laughter. That gave me pause for I'd still sense enough to know that meant I was stretched far beyond myself. Sitting up slowly, I thought of my father and all he'd done in his life and what he'd had to overcome to get there; and so I brought myself in hand. I laughed softly to myself, with something like real amusement. Thank the god or thank Edgar, the wind was up in the delay. The night was full of sounds to give us cover.

Somehow the dark and shadows had lost their power. I went easier, slipping through the night noise down to the kitchens for food. I took good care to spill some apples on the floor and leave covers off and doors ajar. 'Twouldn't do for anyone to think that I'd had help. Outside, I went soft across the cobbles, keeping back in the shadows, collecting my bundle and reaching the shed without incident. The guards never so much as turned.

Reaching Megan, I ran my hand upon her neck. A shadow moved and I went for my knife, trailing my bundles on the floor. The horses shied but kept silent, though I cared no more for that. My only thought was to hurt Edgar before he took me, to leave him, an I could, something to curse me by the rest of his life.

"Faith, 'ere's a cockerel!"

"Baldric!" I eased from my crouch but kept my knife before me, relieved it was not Edgar, uncertain where he stood. "I thought you were Edgar."

He snorted, "I'm thinking that's no compliment. Put up your knife, lad, I'm 'ere to 'elp you."

"You've orders from the Lady Beatrice?"

"Ssst, lad! No names!" He relented, "We'm not exactly chatty, mind, but I can count ta fingers on my 'and. I've been keepin' watch these last two nights. Do ye pack the bags while I muff t'orse's 'ooves."

My part was quick so I joined him and he showed me how to lace on the leather booties. "Don't be trying to ride with them on. Just get ta beasts a safe ways apart from ta castle before you removes them."

"Baldric, you put yourself in much danger."

"Lord Edgar?" his contempt was plain again. "'Oo do ye think taught my lady to ride when she was small?" he demanded, then his face twisted into a smile, "And grand she was, pluck for anything. She's worth two of 'er son!"

"Do you think Edgar cares who taught his mother to ride?"

"No fear. She'll keep me from 'arm. I'm for Cooling in a day or two, to 'elp resettle."

I considered that. "Can you take Kat?"

He sighed, "I've no overmuch control of 'er Lady's dispositions." He considered, "She knows Edgar's temper so 'appen I can manage." He looked up. "Now, be off with ye, lad, its over late. The bar and the 'inge are greased so now 'tis up to you."

From the shed to the gate was a matter of yards, all out of sight of the guards a courtyard away and the wind swallowed the little noise I made. Quicker than thought, to a whispered, *The god go wi' you,* I was safe outside, the weakest link in the plan behind me. I'd a bad moment with the door as I could not bar it from without and feared lest the wind catch it and bang it about. It couldn't fail to bring the guards. Baldric could do it an I went back to fetch him but that was to shout of help inside. In the end, blessing my father's good steel, I cut some woody stems. Wedging them between the door and frame, I managed to pull it firmly to. Breathing hard, I made my way to a tree I'd marked behind the castle where I tethered the horses. They were too close there under the walls for the guards to see even should they look back.

Beneath Bellarus' window, my fears began anew. We'd agreed on no signal and he could not even know that I was coming; mayhap he was asleep or, worse, had been moved. Who knew but a guard, or even Edgar waited above. My mind whirled like a rolling dice, the headman etched on five sides out of six, and I had to sit against the stone and force myself to think. An he'd been moved there was naught I could do, but I did not think the Lady would sit still for that. As for a signal, any call I made loud enough to wake him might reach the guards instead. Surely, an my aim were true, it should be signal enough. Sending first a brief prayer to the god, I stepped away from the wall and made a cast.

The old stirrup I'd found for weight clattered against the stone, full ten feet below the window. Wincing at the sound, I ducked back. A gust rattled the chimneys far above then I heard no more though my nerves seemed to stretch out my ears with the trying. At length, timid as a mouse and feeling just as naked against the barren earth, I crept away from the wall. Should the guard be coming to investigate he could not fail to see me but I could not hug the wall forever, nor risk a second cast until I saw where he was and whether he listened. I must go a long way out to find him. To my relief, the man on my side was still at his station. The far one would hardly have moved for a sound that was opposite to him. Sweating again, I moved back to the wall, bracing myself for a second throw, when sudden I saw a head at the window. Bellarus looked out and grinned, then held his hand out.

Neatly, he reached down and caught the stirrup at the top of its arc, pulled up the string and then the whole of the rope. To my dismay, as he lowered his bundle and then his harp, he must use the string to get them to me. The rope was not long enough and 'twas hardly a trick he could employ upon himself. Indeed, by the time he'd secured the end he was short by almost fifteen feet. I tried to wave him back but he only shook his head. Tugging at the rope a time or two, he squeezed himself through the window and started slowly down. He walked himself along the wall, for all the land like a large, ungainly spider. That illusion soon gave way, for he'd not a spider's legs. His all too human ones slipped out beneath him and he was left swinging in the wind, kicking them wildly. I held my breath but he managed to wrap his feet about the rope. For a moment he hung there, then came down yet more slowly, his progress measured in inches.

Aching from holding myself in I wondered how much worse it must be for him. So locked were my eyes upon him that I almost missed the guard until too late. A flicker caught the corner and I saw him coming down the battlements towards us and flung myself against the stone waving urgently at the figure above. Bellarus must have seen me, for he froze. I prayed furiously, hearing the footsteps now, above the wind. While the guard might miss me beneath the walls, he could hardly fail to spot the harper on the rope. The steps stopped abruptly and there was silence. Even the wind fell in a lull an everything had somehow gone and hung itself from Bellarus' rope, just to see how it looked, time and space, frozen in the moonlight.

'Twas that same moonlight broke the spell, twinkling to my right from something that arched golden from the wall and fell to the ground with a splatter. Time froze again, so only the arc was added to the landscape, suspended once more, an all were turned to stone. Still the man went on and on and I felt a mad desire to laugh, an only I had the breath. He finished at last with a grunt and I slumped as his footsteps receded, then slipped out and looked him back to his position before waving to Bellarus. This time he came down with a rush to the bottom of the rope, then somehow slid so only his hands grasped the very end. Stretching out, his feet were little more than the height of a man from the ground. He let himself go with a sigh and a thump.

He lay, not from hurt but to catch his breath, and between his pants breathed, "Well done, Nicodemus. I hoped, when you didn't come, that the fault lay elsewhere and you'd contrive."

"Edgar," I said shortly. "We'd best be gone."

He picked himself slowly up, "An he'd gone on any longer then I must drop!" and rubbed his shoulders, "Ah but he was close enough that I could see why he had such capacity!" That did it. Sudden, we were both helplessly laughing.

§

When he'd stowed his gear to his satisfaction, the harp carefully in a cunning bag made just for it, we led the horses away from the castle and along the stream behind. The trees that grew along its banks provided cover and for a mile or so we were safe from the watchers' eyes, as we worked our way upstream. Of a sudden it ended in a cleft from which bubbled the spring that fed the stream.

"Ah," said Bellarus, regarding with ill-favor the moonlit plain ahead, "I wondered that the Lord Cromart would let such cover grow so close to his castle!"

" 'Tis pleasant in summer and the guards can see the approach from any one of the towers."

"I have eyes!" he growled, and saw my face. "I'm sorry Nicodemus, that was unworthy. You've risked much to get me here and, an we're caught, you'll share my fate. How go we from here?"

"I'd thought to pick our way to Farleigh's Snitch and so join the road through the Southing Wood to the border beyond. The guards, an they're awake at all, will be looking for a troop, so two, mayhap, can pass unnoticed."

"'Tis chancy. We're safe for a bit. Let's uncover the horses hooves and take counsel while we can."

In truth, we'd but a single choice, and that was to wait for an end to the moonlight or to go at once, and the risks were great in either case. Waiting gave us but three hours of darkness before the dawn after which the alarm might go at any time. Going gave us half the night but only an we could escape detection. When we'd done with the horses Bellarus wriggled up the little hill behind the spring and motioned me to follow. There we lay and watched the guards in the distance for minutes on end.

"They're none too active." He turned and looked away to the south, "Is Farleigh's Snitch that hamlet yonder?" I nodded and he studied the land awhile then motioned us both down. "There's hedgerows halfway in look tall enough to provide some cover and there's boulders and shadows enough between. I think we're better to go." He shook his head, "'Twould be easy without horses, but we'll need them. We'll have to go roundabout, to give them less profile. Keep an eye to the guards, as far as we can. An they move we freeze. The eye at night needs movement." I nodded and motioned him to lead but he said, "I'll take both horses. Do you think you can lie backwards on the saddle and have an eye to the guards?"

We went that way awhile, and it worked after a fashion. Twice I saw a guard move in the distance, though whether to turn or ease his stance was more than I could tell. I hissed and we stopped, to my great relief, for my arms grew weary with gripping and the saddle slammed my stomach 'till I thought I would be sick. At length we reached a copse and I called a third halt and slid off gasping. "An I hold a bridle, I could walk backwards at the pace we're going and still keep watch."

He looked at my face, "Mayhap, 'twould be better, " he said, "At least an I'm to keep your dinner off my shoes!" I managed a smile at that and we set off again and, indeed it was better, though the going was slow and I often stumbled and stubbed my heels. 'Twas a laggard's pace we made, stopping a fist of times for my alarms, so the castle got smaller behindhand; but at length I could no longer tell the guards from the towers. Bellarus grunted at that and led us behind one of the great stones that broke that part of the plain.

"'Tis well for us the god was none too tidy when he made this part of the land," he grunted, patting the stone, then looking up. "'Twill soon be low enough to be behind us and we must turn. 'Tis only half a mile to the rows but we'll be seen an they look. This creeping will no longer serve. We gallop and hope or wait it out." We were now three miles from the castle and but two from the road, so that waiting seemed the safest course. But the dark in the fields would slow us down, while the light, could we make the rows, might get us to the road before it fully failed. Distance was our need so boldness must be our course. Even so, as we swung to our saddles, I couldn't help pulling my hood low over my head, though I knew it could make no difference. The ground was too broken for a full gallop and I felt, as I watched the windbreak, that it would never come up, that we were somehow going slower than before, pinned perhaps to a pair of rocking horses, riding to nowhere on the flat floor of the plain, like naughty children waiting to be found out.

The feeling dissolved abruptly as we dashed behind the first of the rows, finding not hedges but trees well above our heads, and dismounted to discover the effect of our ride. The wind, by now, was down and between the trunks, the castle lay silent, one with its lengthening shadow. We banged each other's fists as soldiers will, knowing ourselves to be fairly away. Remounting, we found our risk rewarded as there was still light enough to make good speed and we closed rapidly on Farleigh's Snitch and the road beyond. Remembering the geese at Pudding Hill, I hissed to Bellarus to give wide passage to the hamlet.

"No fear!" he said, " I…what's that?" He'd stopped his horse and was on the ground in an instant, holding his hand to his mouth for silence.

"I… hear nothing," but he shook his head sharply and, throwing me his reins, ducked between the trunks. Hitching the horses, I joined him, just in time to hear the faint note of a horn, winding in the night from the castle.

"They saw us after all!"

He shook his head. "Too long. Mayhap the guard, the god rot his ungainly tool, needed to water again and saw the rope."

"What difference!" I despaired, "We are undone."

"An they know where we are. An 'twas the rope they saw, then they don't. Watch."

Terror yawed in my face again and I closed my eyes and found it inside and not in the night. "Edgar was right. I am a terrible coward."

Bellarus kept his eye on the castle but quoted softly,

When the trumpets blow and the hosts draw near
'Tis only the fool who feels no fear
Sore afraid at the battle's dawn
Courage grasps for its sword and presses on.

"'Tis from *The Song of Cuthbert*," he said. "I must teach it you."

I felt better after that and began to take some interest in what he watched so keenly. An on cue, a mounted party issued forth from the castle and began to gallop down the road. For long minutes we watched them, hardly daring to breath, willing them to pass us, please pass us. In the last strands of moonlight we saw them obey, hewing to the road past Farleigh's Snitch, and fading off to the south, putting Bellarus in the right of it. As one, we rolled over and sat against a pair of trunks and expelled a pair of gusty sighs.

"They're to close the road against us."

He nodded somberly, "Any other routes?"

I considered and we talked through our choices. There were tracks through the Southing Wood, I knew, but you needed to know them not to get lost, as I did not. Finding a guide was perilous, for him an he were honest, for us an he were not. Besides, though his argument with his father had held him back, Edgar was a hunter and would know the woods, *putting us on his ground* as Bellarus phrased it. In the end, we decided on the hill country. Though I had never been this far south, I knew the woods ran out in the hills and that the hills themselves were seldom visited, being barren and lacking game enough to draw the hunt.

We mounted in full dark and picked our way straight to the road, seeing as we went torches out behind the castle. As we crossed the ditch and settled down to ride I heard a sound behind that pulled me up abruptly.

"Dear the god! Hounds!" My voice cracked, the fear washing back.

Bellarus considered for a moment. "Did you ever hear of Cromart hunting a man with dogs?" I never had and told him so. "And did Lord Cromart take his deer hounds with him to the hunt?" I thought back, seeing again the train going out the gate, two handlers and both braces of the great beasts. He laughed at my reply, "Then all that Edgar has is rabbit dogs. He'll get tired enough of them when they've run him down a dozen trails!" Again he was right, for we rode then and the sound of the hounds died back in the night. We never heard them more.

§

Pudding Hill loomed in the predawn and we swung west from the road, lest the party had stayed or left a guard behind. Dawn itself was slow, the clouds that came in the night dropping to meet the rising downs as we tended west and south, seeking the edge of the wood. It began to rain, soaking my aching buttocks and turning them numb, and time turned gray and got wet at the edges and then dissolved. When at last the trees arrived, I didn't know whether it was noon or night and Bellarus had to pull me from the saddle.

"We rest here."

He found a glade a short way in the wood and we pulled the horses in and made a wet and weary meal. Halfway through I fell sound asleep. My dreams were full of baying hounds and cold and dripping dungeons and I awoke, wet and shivering beneath my cloak, feeling more tired than when I'd begun. Bellarus was up before me, an he'd ever, indeed, been asleep. I forced myself to my feet and bolted the remains of my meal at his insistence. Much thereafter is broken into pieces, dozing in the saddle, making camp again at the edge of the hills, being shaken from my sleep to take the second watch. The next clear memory I have is of being shaken again and waking to chagrin and sunlight. It was the end of my watch, but Bellarus said nothing, only bidding me change my clothes spreading, as I shed them, my wet ones on the rocks aside his own. We were in a rocky bowl with grass enough to graze the horses, a suntrap, out of the wind, that, despite the lateness of the year, would be hot by the end of the day. Not yet, though it was a blessing to be dry, and I felt almost cheerful as I slipped shivering up the rim at his beckon and lay beside him.

"'Tis well you slept," was as close as he came to scolding, "We'll need your hillcraft now," and he pointed down.

I forgot the cold and stared at the figures on the plain below, "They've tracked us!"

He shook his head, "They seek the spoor," and he pointed again and yet again, "There are several parties but," he managed a grin, "no dogs. When they missed us on the road it was natural to turn this way. I'll warrant there are more search the forest tracks. We've time, but let's away, before they find our trail."

'Twas weary work and slow, now riding, now leading, with me to pick the trend of the hills to move us south and he the local ground, the better to cover our trail. Twice we had to double back from tracks that proved dead ends, the second coming near to be our undoing. Only Edgar's rage and the broken ground that forced us off our mounts kept us from running into him, or at least across him, which would have had the same effect. We came not strictly back, but were casting south, seeking the valley I was sure, from childhood stories as well as the twisted ranges behind, must turn and lead us through. Of a sudden his voice rang round the hills. We thought we were discovered but it went on and on until at last we pinned its source from amongst the echoes, and, hitching the horses, scaled the little ridge between.

Edgar was below with five of his men, and he was screaming at one whose eyes showed white in fear.

"My lord, must be they comes this way," the man protested, "'Tis ta only valley goes through!"

"Then why are there no tracks?" demanded Edgar, trembling in his anger. "That bastard grew up in these hills and must have found another way. You've missed his trail!"

"My lord, ta ground be stony, and you gave me little time to cast."

Edgar crowded his horse at him, then vaulted off, "So now 'tis my fault," he screamed, "Get you down, fellow, and I will teach you manners!" He motioned to the men on either side of the luckless guide, and they pulled him from his horse, the fear in his eyes now catching theirs as well. "Hold him!" Edgar commanded, pulling out his knife. He moved in front, grabbing the man by his helmet, and there was a terrible scream that rose on the mountain air, going up and up until it met its own echo. When Edgar stepped back, the man's face was covered with blood.

"Dear the god, he's slit his nose!" whispered Bellarus in horror. "An he'll do that to a free man, the god help the serfs when he becomes Baron!"

The party rode out behind Edgar, white-faced and stiff, leading the horse of the guide, who they left behind, his screams having sunk to a queer, bubbling sob. Seeing them go, he gave a cry, and stumbled after, his hands clutched across his face. We lay a long time, sick at what we'd seen, watching them disappear down the valley, first the mounted group and then the wretched figure after.

As we rode away, set unwittingly on the right path at last by Edgar himself, my thoughts were all on my friends, Brychan and Annie and Kat, and what life would be under Edgar. It did not seem meet to me to pray for death but I could ask for life. So I prayed long and hard to the god that Cromart would outlive his twisted son.

Part II
Apprentice

Chapter 9

An hour before dawn we crossed the border. That, in itself was not important, though I remember it because it is a time of day I have always loved. As we turned east, down and out of the hills, Umber crept up before us in the sky thrown glow of the not yet risen sun. Goff's country, no different from my own really, yet, looking back, I seem to see that sun rising on a whole different world.

We were safe enough. Goff was no friend of Edgar's then; even so Bellarus kept us going across his lands. 'Twas no hardship. By then, I was into the rhythm of the thing, but even was that not the case, I would have ridden without complaint. I'd no wish to stay beneath the roof of my parents' murderer and Bellarus must have known it, though he never said. He simply kept on. For all his bluff ways he knew what ran in people's hearts.

By nightfall, we were deep into Umber, and put up at some other lord's—I've long since forgotten who—and sudden, I was his body servant. He'd only time to sketch my duties before we went down to supper. I was shockingly green and it must have showed at the table, yet they were simple enough. I'd little more to do than stand at his elbow, look to his glass and bring him his harp when he was ready. Light duty, particularly since no harper will dip deeply who has to play. I cannot recall that I made any very great blunder. In fact I recall little, except the music. I'm sure I would not think so very much of it now, a casual performance for a country baron, given after long days in the saddle, yet to me it seemed just as wonderful as what I had heard at Halting. More than anything, I was struck that, for all I was just a body servant, this was now part of my life—the hall, the high table with its flashing talk, and most of all, that glorious baritone served up on its bed of notes—all mine. *For six months,* he had said, *Six months to try me to see an I could be apprentice.* I listened, hardly believing that I could ever have been so bold as to think I could do what it was that he did now. Even as the music lifted me and took me with it

I heard a wail down inside, *To love it is not the same as doing it. Six months, Nicodemus!*

I didn't tell him of my fears. How could I? He had said he would give me my chance and I believed him. More I could not ask so I rose with the fear each morning and hugged it to me when I went to bed at night. In a funny way it became a litany. An I could not believe in myself, still I could hold to the amount of time I had left, *Twenty-three weeks to go, twenty-three!* What I would do when it got down to two or three didn't bear thinking about.

It didn't help that all his care was to teach me service. The harper's life is a self reliant one and he made it plain he asked nothing of me he hadn't done a thousand times himself—making camp, brewing tea, taking care of the horses and his kit, and mine, for he bought me one; cleaning the dishes, learning to cook and carry out the myriad of little tasks that made sure life on the road remained a pleasure. He was a patient teacher, a quality he didn't always find reflected in his pupil, though in the main I bit my tongue and buckled down as best I might, hoping, the sooner through this, the sooner to the music. Still I had to admit to myself that those lessons would stand me in good stead. *Aye, skills to fall back on, Nicodemus.* It helped that I liked the life, then hurt as well as I realized it was one more thing to lose. It added to the litany.

My duties were fewer when we guested, which was mostly. I must keep our quarters, run his errands and continue to stand at his elbow and his wine at dinner. I minded none of the actual work itself, for he was a fair, an exacting, master; but the best was to stand at table. It meant jostling afterwards for my own food with the pages and squires. Eating last, we ate not so well as I had at Halting and my companions were sometimes loud in their complaints and inclined to be haughty with a harper's boy; yet I always found it worth the wait. Even after I came to know all Bellarus' songs, I would have waited far longer just for the music. I was astounded to find not all my fellows felt the same. They took care not to say too much in my presence, lest it come to my master and so rebound upon their shoulders, but 'twas plain that not all regarded a harper as a treat. Sa. I have said I was green. I am sure they must have laughed at me behind my back; but, beyond the natural chagrin of a shy boy, I am not so sure I would have cared. A whole world was opening up before me. And not just the music. There was the talk as well.

At home the concern of the kitchen folk had been all for Tansley and little had I heard there of affairs without, and that little always of Anglesea. Now my ears feasted, an my belly did not. At first much flew past my understanding. Bellarus would fill it for me as we rode so the words came to make more and more sense. The names were hardest. They flickered through the talk like conies in a thicket, so you were never sure an the one you glimpsed was one you'd met before. In the end I sorted out even them, and held them while I needed them, though most are dust in the wind by now. 'Twas the first I'd heard of large affairs and I was dazzled. More than ever, I yearned to be harper, to stay in the midst of all this whirl and not be pawned off and dealt out as apprentice to some trader of dusty bales of wool.

Still, an Bellarus was satisfied with my work, he made no push to try me as apprentice beyond having me sing scales with him when he would warm up his voice.

"A harper must take care of his voice as well as his harp, boy!" he would say, "$Da\text{-}da\text{-}^{da\text{-}}da\text{-}da\text{-}da\text{-}^{dah!}$" He cleared his throat carefully, "Better. One can always get a new harp!" He thrust, "No, not you. There! Da…to there…$^{dah!}$" then he would go back to his own, paying no attention to my efforts. Yet, I dared not protest. I had found, for all his patience, he had a chancy temper when he was taken where he did not want to go.

§

I had considered it only fair he tell me why he was barred from Anglesea. I'd asked him almost as soon as we had cleared the border, but he had only bade me gruffly mind my business. Another attempt a day or two later was met with an even sterner rejoinder. It nagged at me as we worked our way down through Umber into Dankar proper and I resolved to try him again. Between fiefs, we'd camped in a pleasant coll and caught a coney and found herbs I recognized from my mother's garden. The stew was as savory as you'd get in a good inn and I'd got his tea steeped just as he liked it. With the dishes done and the horses looked to my tasks were done for the night. It seemed a propitious time.

"I told you to mind your business," he growled.

Resentment flared like fire in dry grass, "It *is* my business! Do you think the Lord Edgar is like to forget who it was got you out the castle? I am banned from Anglesea as much as you and on account of you. The difference is, Anglesea is home for me!"

And flickered out. He had warned me not to pry. He stared at me so fiercely 'twas like being caught in the veer of a mountain squall. I dropped my eyes before its fury and at once it broke over me. I felt my ear seized and was dragged up to my feet.

"An you would be harper, boy, *never* drop your eyes!" My ear burned painfully. "*Look* at me!" He tugged again and my eyes came up to his hawk ones through a veil of water. I had to fight to hold them there, for his gaze was a physical thing. It overset even the throb where his fingers gripped.

"Better." He let me go and returned to his place opposite while I rubbed the afflicted ear. "As much as a priest is a harper a creature of the god." He was staring into the fire now, but the eyes looked inward and the words came slow, like a chant. "More. A priest is always subject to the discipline of the Temple which can rob him of his mind. A harper has only music and the god." The eyes came back to me, gentler now, "An a harper will not bear true witness, Nicodemus, who will?" He held me a long minute, before saying, "Better. When you're right, boy, don't ever drop your eyes."

I felt some of my anger return, "I am no serf!"

"Don't you think I know that?" His grin was a lopsided thing, an old ghost tugging up one corner of his mouth, "I knew your grandfather."

He said it an that explained everything, but I saw only nothing. My ear throbbed, more with resentment I think than pain. I could not follow his twists and felt as if the ground were shifting at my feet, and so hurled back, "Is that why you agreed to take me?"

"Go to, boy." His grin was full now and genuine, "As you have so carefully pointed out, 'twas you took me. I owe you far more than I ever did your granfer, a debt I mean to pay. But debts cannot make you harper. Only you can do that." He sighed, resigned or bitter with old memories, I could not tell. "Still, you're right. The debt demands the tale, at least."

Despite that admission, I didn't get it all that night. It came in bits and pieces, over time, for he couldn't bear to talk of it for long. Though he never flared at me again for asking, I learned when I could tease from him a little and also the signs that he'd had enough. There was old pain there, buried deep and festering enough that he'd no desire to dig it up.

Here then is the tapestry, as I have pieced it together, though the threads are much as he gave them me, oft in the high, old, formal language of the harper.

"A young man I was, then, when I came to Estonval, of high hopes, the robe that marked my elevation to master harper splendid in my pack. Elinor was Queen in Dankar, as newly minted as I, and I thought I could smell a fresh wind in the land. 'Twas not before time. The old covenant, that the lords would protect and serve the people, was breaking down. The dogs set over the sheep had become a ravening pack with a taste for lamb. For two generations, no king in the land has stood between the barons and the people."

The day he said that, I objected, "I never heard it said that Queen Elinor stood for the people."

"A maid, to take on the barons? She was lucky to keep her crown. The old lords were not pleased to have a queen at all, much less one with new ideas. But there was no other legitimate heir to Dankar and an empty throne would have plunged the kingdom into chaos. There's precious little profit in a civil war. Better to sit snug in your castle and raid the neighbours back and forth. No tumbling of keeps or breaking of noble heads, there, just cattle and pigs and sometimes even a little gold—faster than taxing and much more thorough—and an excuse to stay in arms!"

"Were your parents serfs?" I remember asking, surprised by the depth of his passion. Somehow, that had never struck me as a possibility.

"Nay! I was the fourth son of a Suthy knight, with but a single manor. No way to inherit there, nor revenues enough to equip us all for martial valor. And I didn't care for orders. They were pleased enough to see me go a harpering..." he didn't say it, but I got the sense they had not been so pleased since,"...I simply have eyes, Nicodemus, and a harper's training. I know the Tales from end to end. I know what we were at the Coming, and what we've lost."

"The Tales are sung everywhere," I said, astonished, "You sang two yourself last night!"

"Aye, so I did. And *Very nice, harper,* with just the right degree of appreciation, then, *How about something with a little more thump a da tiddley dump?*"

I was silenced by that. It had been news to me that people could listen to songs over and over without once hearing the words, but so it was. For many words were but a pleasing noise. As well, I discovered barons were better than most at the trick of hearing only what they wanted. I suppose Elinor found that, too. As Bellarus told it, they had hedged her about with advisors, then, discounting her as a maid, had gone on with their ways.

"The Queen had a longer vision. She set about to make her court the most admired in the land. She sent out for masons and jewelsmiths and cooks, for weavers, for carpenters, for workers of stained glass...and for harpers."

I smiled. No doubt which he thought were the most important. Seeing it, he smiled back, "She built a whole new street for tailors."

I was startled, "For tailors?"

"Aye. She decreed she'd none about her that were not splendid and she gave them the means to accomplish that. It seemed a small thing, a woman's thing, so though her advisors grumbled, they gave way. 'Twas a meet concern for a maid and they'd rather have her at that than affairs of state. Live and let live was a bargain they understood, so they peacocked around the court for her, all the while trying to quietly abrogate the crown's prerogatives away to the barons. Yet, while they tried to push the power outward, she was slowly gathering it in."

"I don't understand."

He chuckled deeply, "No more did they, until it was too late. Over time, to be at court came to be a cachet. The most powerful barons lurked in their castles at first but you can't expect a man to spend the worth of a good charger on three sets of court clothes for he and his lady and not lord it over his country cousins. It took her twenty years, but now there's a season at Estonval, two months, an you please, after the spring plantings, when not a baron in Dankar proper but will be in the city, vying to be seen at court. Naturally, almost any business of note, is transacted there."

"Under the Queen's eye. Didn't the advisors try to put a stop to it?"

"'Twas too late. By the time they'd realized what was going on she'd already changed the worst of them. Ambrey was first. He got caught with a page, which was a great shock to his friends, but it ruined him, despite their protests. He had to retire in disgrace and the Queen appointed Ralven in his place before the barons rightly knew what was happening."

"She set him up?" The shock showed on my face, "She seems an ill ruler."

"Don't be so quick to judge, Nicodemus." His tone was soft, though his eyes were bleak, "What would you? They wouldn't let her play the man, so she chose other weapons." He stood up, kicking the last log into the fire, signaling there would be no more talk that night. "I'll tell you this. She's a woman stands by those who stand by her. And she loves Dankar and the land. Which is more than you can say for most of our rulers."

'Twas the last time he talked of the Queen direct. He would talk of the court, of the jousts and banquets, of the harping. He would talk of himself, *young*, he would say, *fresh minted, shiny as new coin*... sounding an he spoke of someone else, just an his younger self had been a different person. But, in all these tales, the Queen was missing, like the dark heart of a rainbow, marked only by where the colors didn't run. In my naiveté, thinking of what he had said before, I saw her as a spider in the center of her web, and so thought he had come to hate her; but now I think the truth was just the opposite. I think he had loved Elinor as a man does a maid. And though I have no scrap of proof, beyond the man himself, who never said, I think she must have felt something for him. He was not the man to be so wounded where love was not, at least in some measure, returned. But, of course, he was just a harper; she was the Queen.

How else to explain, 'twas he was picked for the mission? A perfect mission for a harper, you will say, but one so young? When she had so many older and more experienced at her court from whom to choose? But such a mission. Surely, you will say, her lover, an was he so, would be the very last she'd send? Nay, the first. Bellarus was a rock, a man who'd never swerve from his sworn word. So how, in that great swirling court with its hands and hands of harpers, did she come to know that?

I debate with ghosts. There is no one left to tell the tale, now, but only me. 'Twill have to be told as I see it. He went, a young man, full of purpose and resolve, from the court at Estonval to the one at Carvigal, as an emissary, to propose a marriage between the Queen of Dankar and the King of Anglesea. An my suspicions were correct, it must have been a torment to him, but he was a proud man. 'Tis in my mind he did it proudly. Besides, I think he knew that love was not in her mind, but only politics. She wanted to wield the two Kingdoms into one, a first step in putting the land back together. 'Twas an idea to fire a young harper, but, strangely, my grandfather as well, who Bellarus had met at the Carvigal court.

"He was a profoundly conservative man. Nowadays that means he would stand for baron's rights and prerogatives, against crown, against people, with no more said, but then it meant he stood for the old ways. I was out at his manor a time or two. He husbanded his folk as well as his land."

"Like my lord Cromart?"

"Aye," he said heavily, "Tansley has been luckier than most." He said no more but we both knew they would be making up for it sooner or later.

Sa. I spin it out. Suffice it to say, the mission was a tricky business, that few of even Elinor's people knew about. As the smaller nation, Anglesea had a long and deep seated suspicion of

Dankar. Bellarus and my grandfather had made common cause and Cantor, at first, was willing. Elinor had been wise enough not ask for the joint crown to sit upon her head but what she did propose Bellarus was charged not to reveal until he had gauged Cantor' interest. The King of Anglesea assumed all the power would be his until Bellarus finally made it plain that each would hew to their own jointure and the united crown would only fall to their eldest born upon both their deaths. A reasonable plan, but Cantor's hopes were dashed. He took offense. My grandfather was so rash as urge the marriage past the point where the King had set his face against it, with what unhappy outcome I have already told. As an envoy, Bellarus was allowed to leave, but told he was not welcome back in Anglesea.

"So why did you go back?"

"Partly to see old friends. But mostly because it is not meet a harper should be denied any part of the land." He threw the lees in the fire—we always had these talks in camp, away from prying ears—and stretched, "Should have been safe enough. I've bulked and bearded and grayed over all these years. I'd thought I was discreet in Carvigal, but someone must have known me and told the King. So the writ was issued, but only after I'd left. 'Twas my bad luck that Edgar heard of it."

"Well, I wonder…"

"Enough, youngster! No more of this. I've paid that debt off fair and full, 'tis time to be looking forward. Stand up." I did so. "You've worked hard, Nicodemus. You'd do anyone proud, now, as a body servant." I held my breath, by no means sure this was what I wanted to hear. He seemed to contemplate a moment, then sighed and stood back.

"Warm up your voice. Just as I showed you." He listened without comment, then waved me to a halt. "That first song I did last night, do you mind it?"

"Lord Dagnard's Bane?"

"Aye, that's it. Sing it for me—nay, not that way! Take a few breaths, first, while you think about it. Then let it come. The first verse will do."

So I did as I was bid and sure enough, I saw him singing it in my head and then the words came, and the tune. When I had done, he shook his head sorrowfully.

"Sounds like a cat with a mouthful of marbles!" I closed my eyes, feeling my hopes fall through the sudden emptiness of my chest, so I hardly heard his next words. "…start you on the Tales, tomorrow." I felt a hand come out and tousle my hair. "Eh, lad, happen you'll do. It seems I have me an apprentice!"

Chapter 10

It was April month. All day we had been riding across the Dreydich Hills through high meadows awash with wildflowers. The rising scent had mingled in our nostrils with the dust and the smell of sweating horseflesh, familiar marks of the warmer summer season just beginning. Late in the afternoon, the track widened and started down so that we were able to ride into Tamus town with the evening sun still warming our backs, a welcome friend after a long and bitter winter.

I had been with Bellarus for more than six years now, as his servant and then as his apprentice. Truth to tell, the latter was no easier since the duties were simply added to the former. I didn't mind. Apprentice to a man like Bellarus was higher than I'd looked to reach, six years before, and time would make me my own master. Already, I'd a defter touch with the harp than he and my ear was better, though he grumbled to hear it said. I did no boasting, but listeners will remark after a song and drink will sometimes make it loud enough for harpers to hear. A teacher born, Bellarus had no envy. I think he was secretly pleased though he'd make a show of putting me in my place by correcting my phrasing or fingering a variation for me. In most things he was still my master. In some he always would be. He'd a way with a tale that would hold an audience, commoner and noble alike, almost without breath, where I could only speak to them through song. And his memory was a gift from the god. Let him hear a ballad of tens of verses one time through and it was his. Demand of him the song a twelvemonth later and, though he has not played it in between, yet not a note would be missed or a false word sung.

Since not all of our coin came from the exercise of our art, which often was exchanged for bed and board, but some from the scribing of missives and contracts for the unlettered, this gift was put to good use. We could set up for custom on market day and Bellarus would listen to a dozen clients, either word for word or setting their thoughts into fair language as was needed, firing it all back at me between. My hand, mayhap because I had more patience, was the neater. His performance did no little to attract custom and invariably we could take in enough coin in half a day to retire to the taverns where we could *Wash out the taste of all that ink*. Despite I was the one who wielded the quill, Bellarus would do most of the washing.

Though our backsides were sore from a day in the saddle, we were both pleased to be about our travels again. The winter snows had come early that year, and heavier than usual, and we'd been held since just before mid-winter's day in a village in the high passes on the edge of the Fastness. It had been too small, even, for a proper name, though the people themselves had called it *the town*. 'Twas the best joke we were to enjoy throughout all the long, dark months as we moved from attic to steepled attic, each colder than the last. Though no one would turn away a minstrel, they were too poor to keep us for long so we were passed from hearth to hearth like a jug of ale going round the table. Always, we were given the best room, the master's and mistress's, tucked up in the lofts, away from the fire. They were a hardy folk, used to the cold, and so thought little of it; but they were also a proud folk. Much as we would have preferred the common room below with the dying embers of the fire and the warmth of the family around, and the animals too, they would have taken it unkind. No harper will willingly give offense, at least to that kind of folk. So we put up with it and tried to make our fingers dance a gladness we didn't always feel. We wore out a good many strings. Though the food was scarce and got more so as the long months wore on, there was gut and to spare for the making of new ones, better than ever we'd seen. Bellarus swore he'd never use lowland gut again. It was the only real satisfaction he got in all that time.

Truth to tell, he was tried more sorely than I. An they were a poor people, they were also free, with no overlord to exact tribute from them, nor none close enough to find it worth worrying them from their mountain aerie. In principle, the Fastness was a vassal duchy of Dankar, but the highland clans would have none of that. Dukes sent by Dankar somehow always managed to fall off a mountain, while the Fastness chiefs were unwilling to accept what was held to be a foreign post. Queen Elinor, for all that some called her the unready, was yet wiser than her kingly forebears. She declined to push the point. The ducal seat was currently empty.

Such places are few enough and it held the feeling of home for me. Foothills Croft had been far enough from Holding Castle that, child as I was, I had never really felt the heat of the baron's breath upon my neck.

Anglesea aside, we had been all over the land, following the fairs in the summer season and wintering in some great lord's palace or castle. Bellarus was a restless man and it was his boast that there was no fair in all the land, great or small, that he had not been to; and it was his charm that he worked the small as hard as the great, shunning the disdain of his fellows, holding harping to be the god's work and not to be held back. Although his skill and reputation gained us entry to any noble hall, he was never happier than playing in a tavern or at a country fair, with a steaming crowd and plenty of ale. *People are like horses,* he would say. *An you would know them you must get the stink into your nostrils.* Not for him was the life of a minstrel kept, for, however honored, he felt like a servant in the noble halls. He was touchy, with a fine nose for condescension. More than once, in winter, we moved halls and, however gracious our hosts, he was always pleased when the spring came and he could take to the road, his own man again.

A single season sufficed for but a fraction of the fairs, so we crossed the land again and again, from kingdom to kingdom, taking always a different route, a wandering life that suited me as well as it did him. It chafed him that Anglesea was barred, not from any particular affection for it but that he saw the land as a whole and his to wander. He swore bitterly at politics, which harpers held themselves outside. Not even for love would he ever undertake another mission.

§

The sun slanted pink of the old stone walls as we reached Tamas Town, striping the Western Gate about with battlemented shadows. To our surprise we could not just pass in but we must wait and be questioned by the town guard, on orders from the sheriff.

"Something's afoot," muttered Bellarus but they were civil enough and after a few questions, as to our business, from where we came and whence we journeyed, they were quick to pass us in, saying respectfully,

"There's always a welcome for a harper at the sheriff's hall."

Not being one to close a door against himself, Bellarus thanked the man without committing, his intentions all for the taverns, the more so as there was news in the air. As we rode across the little square, bright with the sun dying in the mountains behind us, he leaned forward in his saddle, every line of his body shouting his anticipation. He turned off into a narrow street to the right and I followed him, amused, knowing it would fall to me to drag him to his bed that night.

After the brightness of the plaza the street was dark as a cave. For a moment it blinded me so even Bellarus and his horse disappeared while my eyes fought to readjust. Slowly sight came back, but still, I saw ahead of me no rider. Instead, up out of the dark loomed a knife, quivering in its pool of black. A plain blade, I noted absurdly, much used but sharp. A blade, it seemed to me, that searched, hunting with a glittering, baleful, mindless malevolence. As from a distance, or in a dream, I heard a voice. For a wonder, it was my own, though it did not seem to me that I talked. I watched the knife. Side to side it moved, an alive or driven by a hand unseen. At last it stilled, then struck, moving swiftly forward while the blade snuffed out and left only the hilt, outlined in the dark. Of a sudden Bellarus was beside me and I could see the street, dim on either side. The hilt dissolved into the crossed shape of a hoist away in the dark at the end, unsecured and stirring in the evening breeze. I stared at it, uncertain, while my master laid siege to me with questions, buzzing them at me like angry quarrels spent futile against the stonework of a tower.

"Back!" I gasped.

At once I forced my horse around, grabbing his bridle. Willy-nilly, he must follow to the square. Twice before the god had spoken to me true. Was this a third time? I was unsure but it seemed a small enough thing to find a different route to the tavern. When we reached the square I told him only that he should take us by another way, one roundabout, coming at the inn from another side altogether. I sought for a way to explain myself, unsure of my own belief in the knife, strangely desperate to gain his. My only certainty was, an it was a blade, it had been aimed at Bellarus' back and not at mine.

To my surprise he consented at once, dismounting and leading the horses to another street, at the far end of the square from the gate. Entering, he looked at me inquiringly. I nodded, seeing only what you would expect—houses, elbow to elbow away in a line, hunkered down and spilling the sounds of the supper hour out over the empty cobbled street. By ways and ways he led us, staying to the wide ones where he could, with an eye for trouble. Strangely weary, I began to question the worth of so devious an approach, thinking I must have dozed, then doing it. Looming in the dark, the sign of the Boar startled me awake.

A slack jawed ostler ambled out to receive us.

"Move it, fellow!" Bellarus snapped, thrusting the reins at him. Before the man could answer he helped me slide down from my horse and was hustling me inside.

"Steady, Nikki," he whispered at the entrance.

"Sorry," I murmured.

Straightening up my shoulders with an effort, I shook him off and motioned him ahead. We were barely through the door when the landlord spotted us. With a roar he rushed over and Bellarus was greeted by a clout on the back would have felled a smaller man.

"And Nicodemus," he bruited, when they had done roaring at each other. I braced my back, surprised he should remember me, but he only wrung my hand between the two of his.

"You were but a boy, last time I saw you. You come back to us a man!"

His name came back in a rush. "Well met, Tandor." He grinned hugely and would have gone on but for Bellarus' ruthless interruption.

"Find us a table, Nikki!" he waved me away and at once reclaimed Tandor's attention.

I wandered to a table and bespoke two pots of ale from a passing maid. While I waited I had to fight hard not to put my head down on my folded arms and go to sleep. Bellarus broke free and joined me just as the beer arrived. Downing half in a gulp he waved her two more and leaned forward.

"What was all that about?" I told him plainly, as best as I could remember, doubts included.

He grunted, "An 'twas a dream, 'twas no ordinary one! You spoke aloud." His eyes drifted left, remembering. "The voice was yours, and yet not yours, somehow. The sound alone was the scrape of nails upon my soul."

Of a sudden, I was wide awake, "What did I say?"

He looked at me sharply, "You don't know?"

"I remember nothing but the knife, until it dissolved into the end of the street, and you were shaking me."

"You said *All paths lead to the grave in the end but the end is closest down this one. The knife! Turn back! The knife waits for thy back.*"

"Not very good poetry," I essayed a laugh but it fell lame. Even as I did so, I knew it must have been the god. The vision came back with a rush, "I remember a voice, and that I thought it might be mine; but not the words." I added wonderingly, "I don't believe I could make out the words at the time."

He sucked his teeth, "Why don't you order us some supper while I have a think?" After a long pull at his mug, he added with a grin, "Make sure there's some meat in it!" Then he settled to his ale, deep in thought.

The supper came, a steaming pie of beef and kidneys, savory with onions, watering mouths long dry with mountain fare. No sooner was it put down than there was the sound of boots at the door. Before we could so much as cut the pie the sergeant from the gate was striding over.

"Harper." He stood against the table so his mailed form loomed above us.

"Sergeant." Bellarus nodded, sitting back. The two regarded each other for moments, taking each other's measure but five beefless months and the rising steam got the better of Bellarus. He waved at the table.

"Join us... or state your business and let us get on. This pie is a noble one and will not wait for commoners!"

The joke was an old one but it served, possibly because of the feeling with which it was said.

The Sergeant smiled, "Thank you, harper, but duty calls tonight. Did you see anything untoward between the gate and here?"

As he said it, he watched my master closely, but he picked the wrong man. Bellarus was a teller born, who could switch from role to role just by shifting his voice. What was harder, he could hold to a role as long as he chose, with never so much as a tone or syllable false.

"Nothing," he replied evenly, "What should we have seen?" Too late the sergeant shifted his gaze to me. I leaned forward to hear his answer with an interest I need not feign.

"A man was killed, knifed in the back, just down the street you rode to come to the tavern, at about sunset. Indeed, when I heard, I thought at first it might be one of you, but it was a local man."

"Which street was that, Sergeant?"

His gaze shifted back to my master, "Battlement Lane, which runs out of the square on the right. The one you took."

"You are misinformed. We went by High Street."

The sergeant's gaze grew cold, "I saw you go to the right myself."

"True enough. But you must have turned at once, else you would have seen us come back and take the other way. Ask your men, or inquire of the houses in High Street. Someone must have seen us."

"I'll do that, harper. But why did you change your mind and take such a roundabout route?"

Bellarus looked amused and a trifle embarrassed. "I remembered an old friend, and thought to look her up but she wasn't home."

"Her name?" the sergeant demanded.

My master switched his look to pained, painted over with just a touch of hauteur, "Please, sergeant. I'd keep her out of this, an I could. Should the mystery not be cleared up and the sheriff insist, time enough to name her. Meantime you may confirm our route."

With this, the sergeant must be content. Bidding us hold ourselves in Tamus Town until further notice, which Bellarus answered with a wave, he marched out. His mail clinking his dissatisfaction. On the way, he had a word with Tandor so Bellarus was unsurprised when the landlord arrived and told us our horses were under interdict.

Observing sadly the fallen pie he announced in a mournful voice, "I'm too hungry to wait for another one. This will have to do, though 'tis sadly past its prime. Nicodemus, do you serve while I discuss old friends with Tandor here." Turning to him, he said lightly, "The good sergeant thinks that we've been doing murder."

"He'll catch cold at that. Sheriff Sandold is a hard man but I'm thinking he won't be too quick to condemn a harper."

"Why, so I think, but it does me good to hear you say it. Tandor," he continued with a wink, laying a finger alongside his nose in caution, "Where exactly was it that Marilenya lived?" The landlord told him and they discussed the ways of the town until Bellarus nodded, "I have it now. We must have a gossip when I'm done my supper."

Tandor took the hint and returned to the bar. Bellarus let out a great breath, as if he'd been holding it since the sergeant arrived.

"It seems I owe you thanks, young Nicodemus. I'd rather the good sergeant kept me from my dinner than 'twas done by that knife of yours. My back itches at the very thought."

"I am but the god's vessel in this."

He answered slowly, "Those other times you spoke of—the sunset and the chapel—they might have been but a boy's fancy. But this…" he shook his head and I could see awe start in his eyes, "You have the sight!"

Such wonder tinged his voice that I pleaded, "I am still Nicodemus, apprentice to Bellarus the Harper."

He smiled at that, "Aye, lad, so you are. But 'tis a rare gift and chancy. You'll not find it easy. It changes things and no mistake, how I still am thinking on." He turned to the pie, "This poor beef has died two deaths, I fear!"

There'd be no more out of him until he'd taken thought. He bit off an enormous piece, while I busied my mother's fork, letting him, as he no doubt would have put it himself, commune with the dear departed.

When half the pie had disappeared I found the silence weighing heavy and asked, "Was Marilenya the lady whose name you'd keep from the sergeant?"

He nodded, grinning, "Her name had no need of protection but I must needs halt the sergeant's inquiry until I had her street."

"And what an they insist and find that she was in?"

"Difficult, dear Nikki. Though they'll have trouble proving that I knew it, she's died two years agone!" He grinned like a little boy, and helped himself to another great slab of pie, "Never tell a lie an you don't have to, especially to the law."

I fell into the trap, insisting, "We knocked at no doors. Whoever lives there now might well be home!"

"Indeed. But Marilenya, bless her heart, was quite," he paused, "*Professional*. When she was in to visitors she'd hang from the balcony a certain scarf she wore. Not even I was privileged to knock at Marilenya's door without the scarf was out. I doubt not but 'twas buried with her." He roared at my discomfiture, "Ah Nicodemus. 'Tis past time we did something about your precious innocence!"

After supper, he called for more ale and sat Tandor down, telling him of our winter exile, and begging him for the news, "For I'll swear something's afoot, when Tamas soldiers question travelers at the gate."

Tandor was blithe enough to answer and names flew thick and fast between them. Much was lost on me, but the gist could be gained and the news was sobering. A dispute that for long had smoked between Queen Elinor and Granly, Duke of Umber, was dangerously near to flame. Elinor had called the Duke to her court for neglect of his duties as a vassal but Granly was skulking in his castle, refusing to come. Elinor's kinsman, next in line for the throne, he was the most powerful lord in the north. He'd a string of castles and a great number of vassal barons, so that, direct or indirect, upwards of a thousand knights owed him fealty. Elinor had assembled her army but not all the barons had answered her call, with those in the north favoring Granly, while many in the west were waiting to see who should prevail before declaring.

"And the Queen bites her nails in Estonval, while her army stands around."

Bellarus lifted his eyebrows at that, "How many days?"

"Six weeks for most, some more, some less."

"While Granly's knights polish their armor at home?" Bellarus whistled softly as Tandor nodded, his beard bare back from his teeth in an unhallowed grin, and I had to ask for explanation.

"Vassals owe but forty days a year to their suzerain in the field and thirty more as castle guard. After that they stay at their lord's expense." Bellarus gave it, slowly, as if thinking it out as he talked. "Elinor's used her days of castle guard and twelve days in the field without ever moving, while Granly has yet to spend a day. How stands Queen Elinor's treasury?"

Tandor spread his hands, "Am I the lord of the exchequer? But I'll tell you this—for two years no taxes have come from the north and much of this year's collection is slow from the rest of Dankar. Money paid now to the Queen might have to be paid again to Granly should he win."

Of other names there were plenty. Some stood in hopes of picking up the pieces should both combatants fall or be weakened enough, while, free of the royal eyes for a time, a dozen private wars flared about Dankar as ancient scores were settled. Some loyal to Elinor yet left their posts in Estonval to succor castles threatened while other held to their oaths and hoped the Queen would prevail and make good their losses.

The names they spoke were knightly, and it was noble fortunes stood to be won or lost in the great game then unfolding. As I listened I saw in my mind the common folk, rooted to the land in nameless rows like so much corn, able only to hope that the scythe of war would pass them by.

"'Tis mostly quiet in these parts," Tandor concluded, "but trade's down with fewer on the roads than ever I remember. The fairs will be small this year." He heaved himself up, a worried man, reflecting my thoughts, "Eh 'tis the common man as bears the brunt. But come, harper, 'tis time we both were to work!"

§

Earlier he'd passed the word there was a harper in so by now the room was full with a crowd more military than usual. Whatever Tandor's worries, war was not at Tamus' door and they were cheerful enough, quaffing their ale and thumping the tables good naturedly as they called for the harper. It was Bellarus' way to leave them some minutes at this before stepping out sudden and giving them a song. As apprentice, I filled in between his sets, so I settled in to watch the crowd and enjoy our first real performance in many months.

Just as Bellarus seemed about to rise, the sergeant appeared at the door again. A pall of silence spread out from him until it had engulfed the crowd entire.

"Easy, lads," he raised his hands. "But let me through and I promise not to take away your harper."

They relaxed at that and even bantered with him as he passed, making straight for our table once again. "You're off the hook, harper. We just caught our man."

"Who was he?"

He looked at me somewhat quizzically, but then said easily enough, "One of the masterless men running from the troubles in the east. He was half starved and desperate and never should have gotten by the gate." Curiously sympathetic, he added heavily, "At least he'll eat in the little time he's left," an he realized how little separated the fugitives on the road from his mates around him in the tavern. On the point of turning to find a seat, he threw in, "I'd say the god likes you, harper. From what we know now of the time of the murder, it could easily have been you got knifed!"

Seeing us left behind, the crowd gave a little cheer, and made space for him, and took up their thumping an nothing had happened. Bellarus said nothing, ignoring them, deep in thought.

Then, to my surprise, he thrust my harp at me from beneath the table.

"You do it."

I tried to protest I had ready too few songs but he would none of it.

"You know them all. Don't fight them, but let the music take you." He held up a single finger, "On the table at my sign." For a few moments he listened to the crowd then banged down his hand.

I was up in the hush that followed, not knowing even how I should start. Of their own accord my fingers stroked the harp, a plaintive sound, and I was minded sudden of his own lament. Walking the chord down to the key, I watched the faces turned up in the dark. It was a strong beginning, the farm wife's cry reminding them of just what was loose in the land, and they gave me good applause, even the soldiers. I listened to it die while I pondered what piece next, thinking, as an apprentice does, of chords or phrasing or what best fit my range. As usual, I'd a hand of pieces ready for the interval though none seemed quite to fit.

On the edge of giving them the one I thought the best, their mood reached out with lazy pipe-blue fingers and took a grip on me. Quick as thought, I gave them a ballad, unpracticed in a year, old and brave and romantic, a counterpoint to the serf's lament. I let the harp run in behind it, and carry it simply, without elaboration. They knew it, it suited them and the way they felt. From that point they were mine. After that I chose simply what would fit, first responding to their mood, then playing on it, taking them high and low as I would, the crowd become my instrument. At the last we drove each other, joined into one, like some great lute with I the strings and they the body, resonating, magnifying and giving depth, throwing back the sound and out until it seemed we shook the night.

I took no break, understanding Bellarus would not want to play the apprentice, but went straight through, then had to give them a pair of encores. They wanted more, but I spread my hands, exhausted. They subsided with good grace, leaving me to the ale which Bellarus thrust into my hands as I sat down a final time.

§

Even as I quaffed it, I regarded him over the tankard, trying to read in his eyes what he thought of my first performance. He stared back at me gravely and my heart sank. Deliberately, gently, I put the tankard down, afraid that I might bang it else.

"Well?"

"I'm sorry, lad," he smiled, but ruefully and I realized with a start that he'd drunk but little ale that night. "You're a harper born. That concert was a trial should please the sternest master. By rights I should set you free and name you harper now." He stared intently at me, and I could see he was deeply troubled, "The sight's a rarer gift by far than music but, as I apprehend the matter, as much in need of training."

Training? "A monastery?" He nodded.

I thought it over. The sight? That should surprise me, scare me, but somehow, it did not. 'Twas not a gift I'd asked for—who would?—but the god has been good to me in other things. Seemed it to me 'twas not my part to pick and choose. Besides, harpers often trained at monasteries. Bellarus, I knew, had done so. I felt excitement quicken.

"That doesn't sound so bad," I offered cautiously, afraid to hurt his feelings more than anything. "What do a couple of more years matter? Monastery training can only help a harper."

He looked at me sadly, "And do you truly think, an you really have the sight, they'll let you be harper?"

Chapter 11

For two days we'd ridden single file, Bellarus guiding, winding steadily higher into that great upthrust of mountains on the coast of Westernesse called The Welling. The monastery at The Welling is the least of the ten founded in the first years of the people's coming as retreats and places of training. 'Tis but a tenth part of the size of the great Weirston Abbey, near to Estonval, seat of the Abbot's council. Folk in Dankar are wont to speak of the Archabbot of Weirston, since he presides at council, though that is not a title he dare use himself, however much his monks promote it. Yet, an Weirston is the seat of the Temple's power, there is a saying among the brethren that while Weirston has an Archabbot, 'tis at The Welling you'll most likely find the god.

Bellarus had told me most of this when he proposed to take me there. At the time it seemed to me disrespectful, an not of the Abbot of Weirston, then at least of the god. The god is of the land and in it, everywhere at once, and therefore not of one place alone. 'Tis true that the presence is local on those occasions it makes itself manifest. Even so, I thought the god would make it without favor, at need throughout the land. Yet rounding the crest of the trail, it was not difficult to see how such a saying might come to be.

There's no warning. The flinty track twists up between the peaks, rounding ridge after wall after ridge, in interminable succession, each promising then giving way to yet another of its dreary brethren. The mind becomes as weary as the bottom, *dunched* as they used to say in Cooling. The eyes dull with endless miles of dun-heather-furred dun rock. Naught marks the final corner. The path turns right, hard in by the mountain wall, just one more twist in an incessant parade of blind curves. Bellarus disappeared then hove into view again as Megan rounded the corner. He was stopped, twisted in the saddle grinning back at me.

He was gratified by my gasp. 'Tis cloud roiled country, the weather boiling about the peaks and spilling into the valleys in helter-skelter fashion, but that day was sunny. Welling Fjord sparkled below us, held blue in offering, cupped between the Fingers of The God thrusting, as sheer above us as the water was below. Four to a side, the fingers were green at the bottom with great trees growing impossibly out from the cliffs that rose straight from the sea. Impossibly, the tops were tipped white with snow. The track dropped down in zigzags, a ribbon uncoiling as it fell into the void at our feet. I felt I could shy a stone to the water, or even dive. Yet it was noon as we looked and almost sunset by the time we reached the bottom.

The monastery itself was a jewel matched to its setting. 'Twas on an island in the middle, buttressed by rock on the west rising fifty feet above the land before plunging three hundred down to the fjord below. Behind the ground sloped eastward to the sea so that the whole island, a tilted mile in length and half across, appeared to be leaping from the waters like some gigantic sea beast. A natural gap in the western wall had been filled by the monks forming the whole into an unbroken shield against the prevailing wind. Hard in behind the buildings were tucked, made of the self same stone: a great central temple, ancient, surrounded by cells and workshops, barns and hospice and library. Eastwards lay a miracle of gardens and ponds and fields. One island, fertile, in a land of jagged stone, green with clover grass and darker bands of trees, dotted with sheep and fringed on the east with sand.

§

Incoming parties are seen hours before they reach the bottom. A boat arrived at the little mainland jetty even as we did. That careful coinciding sums nicely the Welling brethren's approach to life: the courtesy not to keep us waiting combined with a concern to be doing all the time. The boat was run by a single brother, his robe, brown and clean except for the new dirt of the day at its hem. He wore it rolled up to the elbows and open at the neck, showing him to be a man of thews, ruddy with sun. Greeting us jovially he had us and the horses aboard, the ropes slipped and the sail bellying for the island with an ease that bespoke the waterman born. Yet what speech we had with him on the passage belied that, for he came from far inland in Westernesse. He had never seen the water until he entered the monastery at seventeen; nor was he regularly the boatman but simply the closest brother to hand when we arrived.

We were to see the abbot the following morning, an interview that worried Bellarus, though he had known him of old as a good man and a fair one.

"And not such a stickler, either, which is most important. At least he wasn't when we were novices together." He paced about our modest quarters, tugging at his beard, and muttered, "Trouble is, thirty years changes a man!"

It had surprised me when he'd told me he'd done his training at Welling, coming at the age of sixteen.

"'Twas the music that brought me," he'd replied. "They played fair with me and made me a harper in five years. I was not so good at the other things that they were too sorry to see me go. Since harpers are sacred to the god, the Temple is glad to have a hand in their making." I knew all this, of course, but he was not a man spoke much of his past. I'd assumed he'd been at Weirston Abbey with its special school for minstrels. An he would sponsor me I'd even thoughts of trying to spend a year or two there myself, *Before all this*. He was not the only one was nervous, but at least I felt no guilt. Bellarus was plagued by a growing doubt he should have brought me there at all.

He had no need to fear of changes in Abbott Herrick. In the presence of the brother who admitted us, we went through the business of kissing his ring, as was proper, only to have him throw his arms about Bellarus, the moment the brother had bowed himself out.

"How are you, you old rascal, 'tis marvelous to see you!" he exclaimed. They reminisced for a while, then Bellarus introduced me and we sat down and talked as man to man, an he'd hung his office on the wall.

Bellarus told him why we'd come, of the dagger in the dark and of my warning. Then he had me relate my side of it as well, the sunset and Halting chapel. When I had done, the abbot asked me with grave courtesy to step outside.

Bellarus must have been interrogated as to my character, for when I returned he said, "I've had a good report," and fell to probing me more about my experiences. At length he was satisfied and sat back with a sigh.

"I think you're right, Bellarus."

Steepling his fingers, he explained carefully how meditation could be used to sharpen my appreciation of the god and tune me closer to the presence. While it seemed to me the god had found me without I had their training, yet I felt 'twas the god set my feet on the path that had lead to The Welling. 'Twas not for me to turn aside. I didn't argue, but simply listened.

"Bellarus has told you of his fears?" he inquired.

"He has told me something of your inquiries, and that in training me you might decide I was candidate to be a conduit of the god."

He nodded somberly, "His fear is not misguided." He seemed to wince a little at the word, then continued, "Let me explain our procedures in exact detail, so you know what you're up against."

Whether layman or priest, he explained, students who follow deeply into the paths of meditation were subjected to examination, *strictly an internal affair*, he assured me. The verdict returned was always either *inspired by the god* or *not inspired by the god*.

"'Tis honorary, in large degree, the holder being entitled to no benefice from the Temple on that account."

An inquiry, on the other hand, was used for cases where a claim was made of special contact with the god. There were two kinds, a simple inquiry, again a local affair, being empowered to return one of three verdicts. *Fraudulent,* for cases in which outright deceit was involved, generally for purposes of profiting off the peasantry, in which case the claimant was turned over to the secular authorities for punishment. *Misguided,* applied to simple souls who genuinely believed they had a special channel to the god, which signified the temple's disagreement. Action was seldom taken, the label usually being sufficient to discourage any followers. Or, they could be declared *inspired of the god,* in which case they were offered training in meditation.

"So how does *the conduit of the god* fit in?" I asked.

"The fourth verdict," he replied. "An there is even a suspicion that it might be appropriate, a full inquiry must be held, as it may never be returned by a simple inquiry. This requires the presence of a second abbot or an official from the holy office. An the verdict is returned, *conduit of the god,* it must be confirmed by the council of abbots, for it means the Temple considers that the god actually speaks through the man. The conduit of the god, for there is seldom more than one, holds a very elevated position in the Temple, yet few would construe it as a happy one. There is much demand on the part of kings and other high nobles for prophecies. *The conduit of the god* is very much a..." he groped for words, "...servant of the temple."

"The case does not arise. Train me how you will, I am very sure that I could not call the god even at the command of a king."

The abbot looked unhappy. "Though it was not always so, for about a hundred years the conduit's keepers have been using drugs."

I was horrified, "This has nothing to do with the god!"

I heard Bellarus gasp, that I should speak so to an abbot, but good man that he was, he only nodded, "I'm afraid you're right. I've tried to have this stopped, but the practice is well entrenched and I've not enough support on the council. The temple is run by men, my son. It is not always as we would like."

I thought hard about what he had told me. "An I take the training, then it sounds a simple matter of internal examination, with inspired or not inspired the only verdicts."

He shook his head, "As matters stand, that's so. Only Bellarus and yourself have direct knowledge of the matter of the dagger, so I can safely ignore it. But," he raised a finger, "An such a thing were to occur here, I must perforce take notice. An it be compelling enough, I would have no choice but to call for a full inquiry."

I felt as if the walls were closing in on me, not only those of the Abbey but the great fingers about the fjord as well. Could this be the god's intent? Why all the years at harping an I were to be no more than a drugged puppet on a string?

The abbot's gentle voice cut through, "There's no need of any decision today, Nicodemus. Take all the time you want. I'll direct the hospice to put no limits on your visit."

I nodded blankly. 'Twas a dismissal and Bellarus and I both got up to leave. Some of my disquiet began to subside.

"Tell me, lord abbot, what you think men should do with gifts given them by the god."

He looked over to the door where I had paused. "In the normal way," he said carefully, "Make the most of them, as Bellarus tells me you have done with your music." He regarded me a long moment, "But normal is a word I would hesitate to apply to this case. "

"Wheew!" Outside, Bellarus slumped against the wall. "I'm sorry Nicodemus," he said miserably.

"You didn't know?"

"Not like that, I didn't. I knew the temple would be interested, but not to make you conduit of the god!"

"It doesn't matter."

Indeed, I'd more than half made up my mind already but I wanted to confirm it, an I could. I spent the afternoon alone, wandering through the meadows surrounding by the towering mountain walls. By the end of the day I knew. There was no message. It simply felt right and I was content with that. After all, the god had not misled me up to now. I told Bellarus at once and spent the rest of the evening reconciling him to it. Next day I confirmed it with Abbott Herrick. I would stay.

§

Though I'd been happy on the road I found a peace at Welling, in the learning and the slow cycle of the seasons, that I could respond to as poor Bellarus could not. He stopped the winter, to see me right for he was worried about the position he'd put me in; but he could see I was happy. In the spring I convinced him that I was fine. Indeed, I was convinced myself, for the great fingered walls of the fjord thrummed at me like the chapel at Halting. Though I got no sign direct I was sure at least that the god was not unhappy with my presence there.

So Bellarus rode out in April, seeming sudden old though he was gay enough. He promised me faithfully that he would find a boy to serve him as soon as he cleared the Welling. Throughout the day I watched him dwindle up the ribbon until at last he blinked out of sight at the high corner and I turned back to my work. My heart was heavy at his going, though I knew he must.

The monkly life is strictly regulated, with bells pealing throughout the day the hours of prayer and work, of meals and sleep, each of those activities fenced with rules abounding. Strangely, I found a freedom there I had never known. Before I had always been at someone's beck and call, even at Halting where I had danced to the Lady Beatrice' tune. The monastery expected its novices to learn basic skills in all areas of interest to it and I must take instruction in ritual and meditation along with all the rest. Beyond that, as a harper in all but name I was accorded a special status. Once Brother Gingold, master of the novices, found that as well as letters and music, I'd enough of farming and husbandry from my father and herbal lore from my mother to satisfy their requirements, he gave me my head. His only demand was that I use my time well. My music I kept up by assisting Brother Jerome, the music master, in the teaching of the novices, and found, to my early dismay, that I was learning more than they. He only chuckled, a deep rolling rumble.

"Truly, 'tis said, an you would really know something, then you must teach it."

Buried deep in The Welling, the monastery got little news of the outside world and that only infrequently. By and by we heard that Queen Elinor had patched up her differences with Duke Granly which pleased me. Less misery for the commons, less masterless men upon the roads. Unhappily, the brother that brought the news was of the opinion it couldn't last.

The isolation meant The Welling also had to be self-sustaining. With news so infrequent, I began to put the outside world aside. I found myself fascinated by the making of things, wine and beer and cheese. With meat on the table only twice a week, the monks ate great quantities of cheese. I spent hours at the vats learning the process and how to control it. Brother Rufinus harbored hopes, I think, that one day I would take over from him as cheesemaster. I'd never the heart to tell him that it was the whole idea of process that fascinated me and not the cheese itself.

In the first of the autumn storms some months after Bellarus left an old storehouse collapsed and I, with some knowledge of stonemasonry from helping my father, was sent to assist in its rebuilding. I went willingly enough, but with no feeling of pleasure. Stonework, as I knew it, was brutal work. To my surprise, it went quite easy, for an I'd not my father's inches, I had vastly more than I had at twelve, and Brother Canus knew how to gentle a stone where my father, no mason, had not. He worked at an easy pace, liking to talk as he went, yet the walls went up like butter castles on a cake. Much of his talk was monastery gossip, but he would work in snippets of his craft. Later he'd tease them back to see an I'd been minding. The more I learned, the more I wanted, and the more I took the more he gave.

He could wall in stone, and arch and fenester, as high or wide as you wanted; he could even roof or dome. For him, the heights and widths and thicknesses were matters for calculation, and he took me, who could barely count a hundred, through the magic and mystery of numbers with a rush I could almost hear. He taught me all the mason's formulae and turned my interest back at Brother Tantran, the transcendentalist, saying that calculation was general. It could be used in music or even the making of cheese. Indeed, before I left, I had succeeded in computing the volume of one of the oval Welling Monastery cheeses merely by measuring its major dimensions.

Brother Rufinus was unimpressed, "I could get the answer faster by dipping the cheese in water," he grumbled, "Always supposing I wanted it in the first place."

I didn't mind. For me, calculation was a wondrous thing. Much was I to owe the little mason for starting me down that path, as well as brother Tantran, who was patient with my pestering, even though calculation was but the smallest part of his purview.

Poor Brother Canus. Sometimes when he talked, you could hear he dreamed of temples, but the Monastery had one, and ancient and splendid at that. All he could do was maintain it, which he did with care and pride, and build the odd wall or storehouse. I never did find out why he took orders. Such things were not discussed unless a brother wanted it, but his reasons must have been strong to so bury himself when he could have built greatly in the world. He never complained. In the end, the abbot, deciding that the god's gifts should never be ignored, set him to building a little chapel for smaller ceremonies. Nowadays, travelers returned from Welling Monastery speak of it in the same tones as the temple or the island itself, so it is in my heart the little man died content.

Where Canus gave of his craft to any who cared, Brother Manfred, the herbalist, as masterful in his way, was jealous of his. I spent many hours with him, working to his direction, taking my knowledge far past that of my mother; but what he did, he would never tell. I must learn by watching, a slow, painstaking process that eked the knowledge out in grains, where it should have been a flowing stream. There were times he would accuse me of trying to steal from him and I would learn nothing for days until he'd been placated. This went on for years, I being the only novice willing to stay with him so long, until at length we had it out. By then I was sure of my place. One day, my craw full of his vituperative remarks, I hurled at him that in not giving freely of his knowledge he was neglecting his duties. He loomed above me like a battlement as he raged he would take me to the proctor but I was too gone to care. Angrily, I challenged him to do it. The sweat that started on my back as I thought what the proctor would do cooled me quick enough. Strangely, the old man collapsed like a wall of sand. Thereafter, I had less trouble. He became careful of giving offense, and made more effort to teach. Yet it was not in his nature to give freely, and I never learned more than a part of what he knew. He died just before I left. True miser that he was, he went happy, I think as if by not leaving all his craft behind he was taking something with him to the grave. Well, I have more of herbal lore than the common run and he taught me the value of standing up for myself. I have little complaint.

§

When I had learned the basic skills of meditation, I started special sessions with Brother Tantran. He alone, besides the abbot, knew of the incident of the dagger in the dark, and why I was really there. A gentle man, and learned beyond any other I've ever encountered, I quickly grew fond of him. Yet my feeling of freedom fled at these sessions, as the shadow of the Temple official seemed to loom behind him in his cell. My fear distressed him, both because it encumbered what we sought and because he knew it to be real and reasonable and felt it for me too. He, however, could put it aside and go deep inside himself, where I could not. Endlessly patient he tried a number of artifices, chanting and herbs and incense, which I disliked as he had no need of them himself. This pleased him. In the end I succeeded simply because my intrigue with what he could do overcame my fear of what might happen to me an I did it. The tipping point occurred when he tried to put me in a trance himself, and couldn't do it.

Putting away his spinning disk he commented, "Your will is strong. There are few, untrained, who can resist as you do."

"Does that mean that I can control when I go to trance?"

"Of course. No one can force trance onto a trained master. It comes only at his call."

I let go after that, and he taught me to go down inside myself, merely by composing my muscles and breathing, and then by willing it. I learned to ride my heart beat and swim with the strange creatures that make up my blood, shutting out the world without. Then I learned to rise again to that world, without ever leaving the trance, and to fuse with it and tune it, sifting it for nuances. He called it *making a channel for the god* and taught me that. Though I could never call the god, I could listen for the presence as I never had before.

"The presence is closer than people know, and comes and goes more often than they think. The inspired of the god are those who learn to listen."

When I told him of the chapel walls at Halting, he took me to the meadows on a quiet day, when the brothers were at their noonday meal. Then he bade me go down then rise up again and listen. I heard the Fingers of the God, strong now as in the chapel, not the first time, but those after. The message was the same as it had been those years before. When I told him, he smiled.

"Patience is not such a bad message," he said and left it at that; but I think he was satisfied.

Chapter 12

I stayed six years at Welling Abbey and came to love the place with a deepness that scoured my bones. Years later, when asked to name what there was in all the land I might want, it came to my mind to be Abbot of Welling and so end my days there serving the god; but that's a thing not even a king can grant and I kept silent. Now, I would go as a simple brother, but my bones are too old to cross the passes and I must keep my place.

Six years was the limit of my staying, without I took my vows and became a brother. Save the few who had gone, all those who had been novice when I came were brothers now and I must touch my lock to them. By my fifth year, I knew in my heart I would go but hung on as long as I could for love and because I felt no great call to move. Events, as they always had, overtook me. My leaving was precipitated by a pair of deaths.

Though second in time, the first we knew of was Abbott Herrick, who passed away sudden in his sleep. He was greatly mourned. As his loss was unexpected, he being hale to the day of his death, the Monastery, twenty years under his calm and benevolent rule, was thrown into disarray. It was clear that, in the absence of the abbot, the prior presided, but just how a new abbot was elected was not straightened out until days after the old was interred. In the end, a message had to be sent to the Office of the Council of Abbots calling for an external convenor to preside over an election.

As it turned out the Office could nominate its own candidate so this necessity was not overpleasing to Brother Grenson, the prior, who coveted the abbacy. Time, depending how you saw it, was on his side or not; it was early spring and the pass outside was not yet open.

While we waited on the god, Grenson set about consolidating his position. He was too careful to move into the abbot's quarters, but used his study, hailing in brother after brother to sound out their positions, and making, I suspected, a few judicious promises. Thereafter, his cronies started a campaign, praising his virtues and subtly denigrating the rule of Abbot Herrick. There being no other obvious candidate, too many brothers nodded their heads, not wanting to stand against him. He was a narrow and uncompromising man and many, seeing his rule as inevitable, secretly feared him. Still, time was in a fair way to undoing Grenson. He played his hand so hard that when the convenor arrived many of the brethren were quietly ready to vote against him. All they needed was a creditable alternative but no internal candidates were quite ready to take on the prior.

Grenson's worst fears were realized when the convenor brought that alternative in the person of Brother Fernand, sub-prior of Weirston Abbey and nominee of the Council Office. He was a quiet little man, but with a sparkle in his eye and a determination that the brothers liked. I think they would have elected him. Unhappily, Brother Andrea, the convenor, and he were adversaries of old nor had the lengthy trip from Estonval improved their understanding. In Grenson Andrea recognized a fellow traveler. Since the Abbott of Welling sits on the council, he must have decided that Grenson would do him far more good there than Fernand. Shamelessly, he turned convention into intervention.

After the candidates addressed the brethren, he called the role with them still in the hall. Moreover, he called it by name, going first to the known supporters of Grenson and then to the waverers, leaving his opponents to the end. Voting under Grenson's eye, with an apparently rapidly rising toll in his favor, most of the waverers stood for him, so that Andrea never even got to his opponents. He simply declared Grenson Abbot the moment he had collected enough votes. I could see from the back of the hall, where the novices were allowed to observe, that Fernand knew something was wrong, but he didn't know the brothers well enough to spot the pattern of Andrea's calling until it was too late to protest. He said nothing, but his lips thinned out. I wondered an Brother Andrea knew just how determined an enemy he had created.

It disgusted me that a high official of the Temple could stoop to such manipulation and saddened me that the Abbey and all its brethren should become simply a tool for such ambition. Under Abbott Grenson, it would not be the happy place it had been under Herrick. I determined it was time to leave. I'd only a matter of months in any case, and spring was a better time for a harper to take to the road than autumn. That decided, I went to see Brother Tantran for the old transcendentalist had become my mentor and I wanted to tell him first.

§

The god did not betray my trust. In the years since I had overcome my fear and let myself go, I had become adept at meditation. There were those for whom it became a drug and they must perform it daily so it became a ritual and not the thing itself. Tantran accepted that and advised them when they would, but taught me to use it at need, refining it as I went.

"The skill itself is simple," he said, "And once acquired, is never lost. But 'tis a sword gets dulled by constant sharpening. It should only be stropped as 'tis used."

So I used it when I felt the need of peace, or sometimes in exaltation, with the wind through my hair on the high wall, the waves thundering below and the fingers reaching for the sun. At times I could feel the presence pulsing strongly with the blood in my veins, leaving me content that my feet were on the right path. Yet not once, in all those years, did the god speak through me. There was no question of an inquiry, either simple or full.

Tantran was unsurprised at my visit and simply said, "'Twas in the wind. I'll arrange for your examination and have a quiet word with brother Gingold to get you released from your duties. There's no need to tell the abbot for a day or two yet."

I was moved, for it would give me time to say my good-byes. Under Herrick, I could have expected a week's grace but we both knew that Grenson was unlikely to be so generous. As for the examination, the label *inspired of the god* would mean little to me as a harper, outside the bounds of the temple; but it meant much to him. I held my peace.

Grenson fulfilled expectations, by steepling his fingers two days later, and saying in his abrupt way, "Your examination will be on the morrow and the Abbey will be pleased to guest you one day farther."

I blessed Tantran's forethought and managed to bow myself out with tolerable grace. Tantran frowned at the day, but said nothing, restricting himself to instructing me what to expect at the examination.

"'Tis a simple enough affair. The abbot will ask one other to join him, probably brother Gingold, and I will advance your case. They will put a few questions, which you should answer truthfully and modestly, and then they make their decision. If I know Abbott Grenson, he would be more pleased to grant it an you were staying, as it would reflect credit on the abbey, but he hardly can refuse you an you play your part."

The night was clear. I elected to do my vigil in Canus' little chapel, half finished though it was. The walls would shelter me from any wind and I could see the promise of its beauty, as well as the god's in its roof of stars. I waited a long while, letting the peace seep through me, and then, abruptly, went down deep. I seemed to expand through the almost finished walls, and loomed above, outside, looking down at myself in the dark. The presence was all around me now and I felt my heart slow and take up its beat, 'till all, flesh and blood and stars, and walls, man made and god made, thrummed steady through the night as one. I felt exalted, at peace, as much a part of that holy place as the fingers themselves.

Then, for the first time in all those years, the rhythm began to alter. I saw a shift emerge in the message, not like a sea change, but more as a step built atop another or a chord that begins to shimmer over a note. Strength had been added to patience and a small part of me wondered what was coming while another little part thanked brother Tantran for his desire that I be declared inspired. Left to myself, I would have missed the vigil. And its message.

§

The stars stayed long past dawn. It was brother Tantran's hand upon my shoulder that brought me back to the light.

"You've seen something!" he said, looking at my face.

I shook my head and explained that I had simply felt the presence with a shifted rhythm. He looked relieved, but I could see he was deeply worried.

"What's amiss?"

"I…I…I'm sorry, Nicodemus," he stammered, "I could not refuse to answer the abbot when questioned direct. He was asking for your history, for the examination, and I had to give him all of it." His eyes looked anguished, "It seems the *conduit of the god* died a few months ago and the Temple is searching for a new one. 'Tis not to be an examination but an inquiry!"

"A full one?"

"Yes," he nodded miserably, "Brothers Andrea and Fernand to be external examiners."

I started to protest but broke it off aborning. There was nothing he could do. Wonderingly, I remembered the changed message and felt strangely at peace.

"Will you be my advocate?"

"Willingly," he replied, "But they have given us no time to prepare a case. By rights, it should be put off a week, but brother Andrea is in a hurry to leave, and has insisted it go forward as scheduled."

I reassured him as we walked to the hall, thinking that the message had not been for nothing and that I would rather have the god on my side than brother Andrea.

Echoing my thought, I said to him, "It is in the hands of the god."

He stopped abruptly. "It is in the hands of brother Andrea. How much do you think the god had to do with the election of our new abbot?"

"Mayhap it is the god's intention that I become the new conduit."

He shook his head impatiently, "I have seen the conduit of the god at work. 'Twas not a pretty sight. He drooled incessantly from the drug, and babbled a lot of nonsense that his brother keepers *interpreted* for the supplicant." He drew a deep breath, "How the temple came to this pass, I don't know, but I am sure the god is far from these proceedings." This was plain speaking from him, but there was more.

He grasped my arms firmly, facing me, "Nikki, this saintliness just won't do." I blushed at that, for indeed I think I had been too full of myself. "We must *fight.* There is naught here but brother Andrea's overreaching ambition. He means to be the one to provide the conduit and it doesn't much matter to him who it is."

That put a different slant on the message, "Be strong for the fight, and not for what the god intends?"

He nodded. "So I think."

I mulled it over as we resumed our walk, but it felt right to me. I almost missed his final muttered comment as we came to the great hall, "Our best hope is that the verdict must be unanimous."

§

To my surprise, the hall was filled with the assembled brethren. Unlike an examination, an inquiry was public. An there was excitement there—for such a thing had not happened at Welling in living memory and the brothers were only human—it was subdued and somber. Familiar faces swam up from the crowd, each meeting my eye, each muting support and concern. More than brother Tantran's warning did that bring home how dangerous a proceedings this could be. I trailed my advocate to the front of the hall feeling sudden downcast. Forcing my thoughts back to the message and it's invocation, *be strong,* I tried to regain my feeling of being ready, though that was somewhat spoiled by the rueful realization I hadn't had a chance to break my fast.

Brother Andrea presided. The concern for my stomach receded quickly before the growing appreciation of just how dangerous an adversary he was. Though the verdict must be unanimous, procedure was in his hands alone. Ferociously, unremittingly, he wielded it like a weapon.

He had me sit to one side, seated on a narrow stool set high upon a desk, an on display. Did I as much as shift position, he coldly bade me still. Twice the glass on his desk was turned and still I was given no voice. I was treated by him as an object, less than a worm found beneath a stone examined by a farmer, less, an that were possible, than the stone itself. My name he would not speak, except once for the record, but referred always to me as *the novice*. I went from anger, to contempt, to a kind of icy respect.

He started by questioning brother Gingold on the circumstances of my arrival and quickly passed to Tantran who was the only brother, after good abbot Herrick, to speak to Bellarus about why I had come. They questioned him closely as to what Bellarus had said and then to what his version of my version had been. Brother Fernand intervened to have me tell it but was over-ruled by Andrea. Tantran told the story true, but minimized it as he could, stressing the dagger shape of the hoist in the dark and the fact that it was uncertain there was any actual danger to Bellarus.

Switching back to Gingold they had him read my progress as a novice. He did me proud, stressing what I had accomplished, and pointing out I made no claims to be in touch with the god, but *proceeded in quite the ordinary way*. The questions seemed routine, but I noticed that Grenson, newly abbot, followed Andrea's lead while Fernand was most careful to refer to me by name. There seemed little doubt which wind was blowing from which quarter. Nevertheless I started to study them more carefully. In the end, all must vote.

Tantran was questioned again, this time about my progress in meditation. The old man had courage. Despite Grenson's deepening frown, which boded ill for him when this was over and he must face him as brother to abbot, he stood on his right as advocate, asserting unequivocally that the verdict should be *inspired of the god*.

"Nicodemus has great skill at meditation, and is able to feel the presence when it is there, but not once, in six years at Welling, has there been the slightest sign of anything else!"

He sat down, and I saw Grenson nod his head, but Andrea seemed unperturbed, reaching even beneath the table to restrain the abbot from retort, a movement only I could see from my aerie. I mistrusted his calm. He gave me no chance to dwell on it.

"The novice will now tell the inquiry what he saw in the lane in Tamus Town."

I took my cue from Tantran saying what I saw, but stressing the doubt. The tack seemed reasonable, yet Andrea worried me by not attacking it, as I expected, but by playing to it. Again, he asked me of Halting chapel, and again of the Foothills sunset, working with me to stress just how indeterminate each incident really was. By the end, Tantran was smiling openly, so I think he believed that Andrea had changed his mind but I was still uneasy. It didn't square with what I knew of the man.

"Thank you, novice."

His smile and his refusal to give me back my name confirmed my fears. Turning to his right, he asked the abbot what was known about Bellarus. I listened as the oily voice of a man who'd never known him described Bellarus as a harper known throughout the land and a true son of Welling Abbey. His time as novice was described in such terms that the puzzlement bloomed in Tantran's eyes, who'd known him then. The smile slipped away from his mouth.

When Grenson finished his recitation on the virtues of a man he'd never met, Andrea thanked him and sat back.

"If there is no one else to add to the testimony?" he cocked his head and waited the barest fraction of a heartbeat, "I think then, 'tis time to get a sense of how the examiners feel. An we are unanimous we can draw this matter to a close." He smiled graciously at Grenson, "Abbot?"

"I'm afraid there is some doubt."

He had not the look of a man who was torn, but said it precisely, an it were a set piece between them. Already Andrea was inclining his head to his left, instead of waiting to find out about the doubt.

"Brother Fernand?"

"Six years at Welling Abbey and not a shred of direct evidence. I say *inspired of the god,* and no more."

Brother Andrea smiled and spread his hands in a gesture like a newly apprenticed player. "I find myself in agreement with both my brothers," he began. "On the one hand," and he fluttered at Fernand, "There is no evidence direct. Yet, on the other," and now at Grenson, "We have this *doubt*." He looked down, letting the word hang in the air, before taking up the thread again. "*Doubt* permeates this case. Brother Tantran," and his hands were at work again, "*Doubts* whether the candidate actually saw a dagger and *doubts* that the harper would actually have been killed. It is reported that the harper *doubted* these events, and the candidate himself," and here he waved at me, "Has cast some *doubt* upon them."

By now the one doubt that didn't exist in all the hall, not even in me, was that the man was good. Advocate and spectator and victim, we leaned forward for his every word, even the abbot who, I was sure, knew, as I did not, exactly where he was going.

Andrea spun the silence out for moments, before going on, "Just what is it that we *doubt*? Surely not that the candidate is inspired of the god?" He looked to his right and the abbot shook his head in agreement, "Then we *doubt* that he is conduit of the god."

I saw the trap and felt sudden an claws were tearing at my stomach. How he would spring it was beyond me but he was a man knew the ways of the Temple through and through. I was sure it was clear to him. His hands came to rest at last in front of him.

"What an we are wrong?" he asked very softly, "What an the harper Bellarus, who thought enough of the candidate's powers to bring him to Welling, were here before us? Would we not then have evidence direct? The conduit of the god is too important to the Temple for us to be ruled by doubt." He sat back like a man who has made the decisive throw at dice, "Let us put him to the test."

Tantran was on his feet, "What test? There is no test can be made of this issue!" he protested.

Brother Andrea smiled, something he was doing altogether too much of for my liking, "Oh but there is. We can give him the conduit's drug."

The protest spread to the audience and Grenson was on his feet, all outraged abbot, "Silence!" he roared. "You forget yourselves!"

Fernand took over from the brethren, "You can't," he said flatly, "In the first place there is no precedent and in the second, I'll not agree to it."

Andrea was ready for that as well, "No precedent, agreed. But an inquiry has wide discretion. I think it will encompass this procedure. As for your agreement," he raised his voice, "Scribe, you may enter brother Fernand's dissension into the record." He said it pleasantly enough then turned to Fernand. "Consensus is needed only for the verdict. Majority suffices on issues of procedure. Abbot Grenson?"

The abbot's assent, ready and untroubled, confirmed my fears that this had been worked out beforehand. Tantran made a desperate last cast, "We have not the drug!" but I knew Andrea would not miss so obvious a trick and, indeed, his smile lost none of its satisfaction.

"I've been a keeper. I know the formula. Abbot Grenson, an you would be good enough to send for your herbalist, mayhap we could reconvene after the noonday meal?" As the hall cleared out, he issued one last command, "The candidate will keep his vigil and his fast within his cell." He didn't even bother to look at me.

§

Alone, I paced the scant and barren feet of my cell, unable to settle, unable to contain my fear or even my hunger. After minutes of this, the door opened, and brother Tantran entered, concern writ in every wrinkle of his good old face.

"Nicodemus, this will not do. You must get a grip upon yourself."

"I'll refuse the drug!" I exploded.

He looked at me, like a child, "Then he'll have it forced down your throat," he said calmly. "This is not the way to fight him."

"It would help an I were allowed to eat!" I shot back petulantly.

He snorted, "Which is why he won't allow it! Come, Nicodemus. Where is your teaching? Hunger is the easiest of your appetites to control. Sit down, and take a few deep breaths."

Automatically, despondently, I did so. I felt quickly better as my training reasserted itself. He watched me a while, then nodding his satisfaction, carefully closed the door and pulled a fresh loaf and some cheese from beneath his gown.

"Brother Barry in the kitchens has little use for our new abbot, either," he commented cheerfully.

I couldn't keep from smiling, "That's outright disobedience."

"Aye, " he agreed. "It seemed the least we could do. The food will help a little in your fight with the drug."

Tucking into my meal, there was one thing I still could not puzzle out, "What does he hope to gain by this?"

"Enough of a show to convince brother Fernand to vote you conduit. An the drug is given to one untrained, it simply knocks him out or even kills him. 'Tis a sore trial even for the most adept, and few enough of them would bring forth anything of use. I've always feared you might be one of the few and brother Andrea smelled that out when first he questioned me."

He talked of the ordeal to come, telling me I must use all my training and call on all my resources. As no one could fight off the drug completely he advised me to go with it, like a swimmer on the tide who seeks only to keep his head above the water, except it was my tongue that I must govern.

"Let it take you where it may, but hold onto your core and know yourself as Nicodemus and so strive to say nothing at all. An you come silent from the drug, you will be of no use to them as conduit."

I nodded and finished my meal in silence, whereupon he carefully swept away the crumbs, and stood to leave. "Compose yourself, until they come. When they give it you, take it, seating, tranquilly but fast, then go inside yourself before the drug can take you. I will be there but they may not let me speak." He opened the door softly, then smiled at me anxiously, "The god be with you, my son. An any one can fight it, you can."

I took his advice and composed myself upon my pallet, then started the breathing, working through the exercises, as a novice would and I had not for years. The rhythm, the second, strong one, thrummed up slow and I had no doubt as to its meaning now. Idly, I wondered an there were others. Then it took me and washed away the cell and suspended me somewhere in space, oblivious to all but its heartening pulse.

§

It receded as the door opened, but I heard its echo even as I was walked to the ordeal, escorted by a silent brother Gingold. He left me at the hall, empty now of all save the three inquisitors, the scribe, a creature of the abbot who I knew but slightly and whose name has long departed me, and brother Tantran as my advocate.

I advanced, and nodded at the scribe, feeling strangely in control, as I had not that morning.

"For the record, I refuse to partake in this ordeal."

Brother Andrea regarded me, tight lipped, "I can have you forced."

Watching the scribe complete his scribble as pointedly as I could, I replied, "Then let my compliance not be recorded as willing but under duress." The scribe looked up at the abbot at that, who nodded reluctantly. My protest was duly entered.

Brother Andrea pushed forward the cup before him, "Let's get on with it!" he exclaimed testily, but I shook my head.

"I require a seat."

He seemed on the point of protest but Fernand quickly intervened, "The request is reasonable. The drug is strong and the conduit is always seated before he's given it."

He nodded to brother Tantran who hastened for a chair before Andrea could object. Ignoring the convenor's drumming impatience, I composed myself again, closing my eyes and taking far more time than I really needed, simply to gall him. At length, I held out my hand and Tantran passed me the cup. 'Twas but a quarter full of fluid, innocent of color, even of odor. For all the land it might have been water but I knew that it was not. Brother Grenson was too implacable. Remembering Tantran's words, I took a breath and drank it off, then breathed again and went down quickly.

'Twas well I did, for the drug took me even as I reached the thrum and I must swim hard to have it swell to anything approaching its full resonance. Thereafter, I focused on the rhythm, weaving into it my name, then reached for the muscles of my jaw and locked them tight. Instead of going into stillness remote from where I was, as usually happened, I swooped into a maelstrom. The hall swirled all around me, my chair seemed to dip and go with it, and then I shredded to my fibers and went spinning piece by piece off into the void. Desperately, I held to my rhythm and my purpose, shrieking my name to myself, alternating it with the great pulse of strength, while letting no sound out from between my lips.

Abruptly, the whirlpool stopped, an it had a bottom and I'd fallen through, and I could see clear again the room. Now time changed, slowing down, and my vision magnified. I could see each grain of sand tumbling from the abbot's glass, slipping between them an I wanted, dancing with them an I cared to, until almost I lost my rhythm in their slow dance to oblivion. Then it speeded up, so I could see the pulse in brother Andrea's neck throb and begin to race, to blur and buzz like the wings of a bee, and then like the string on a harp. The abbot's neck joined in and the beat jumped out between them so the musician in me yearned to reach out and tune them. Somehow I caught myself and found again *strength* and *Nicodemus,* now faint and far behind.

No sooner had I got them than time began to veer, back and forth between fast and slow, so that I could hear it shriek as it shifted. I lost my name in the wail and could hear only the echo of *strength.* I no longer knew what it meant and wished it away, but it buzzed at me, always the same. At last I knew it for my drummer, and cued to it and time shuddered and, quite suddenly, marched beneath its beat. *Strength* and *Nicodemus* once again were woven to the rhythm, so that I knew myself, but something somehow important slid beyond my grasp. *Nicodemus* had shifted to the downbeat, so it led *strength* instead of trailing, was that it?

Then I heard a voice and fear went through me, for what was important came back. Talk. I should not talk; but the drug was gone and I could hear the voice and it was not mine. Was I being called? I could not puzzle it but silently thanked the god for keeping me quiet then fell into a faint.

§

I awoke on my own pallet. The sunlight streamed through the high window of my cell, and Tantran eyed me anxiously, "How are you feeling?"

I felt an urgency I could not define, so proffered my other need, "Hungry!"

He laughed, "I'm not surprised. You've been asleep for a day and a half and you had precious little the day before that."

He stepped into the corridor and I heard a murmur of voices before he returned to announce, "Food will be along shortly."

I was still trying to grapple with the length of my sleep when the import of that hit me, "Food is being served to me in my cell? Not even the abbot gets that! Tantran, what has happened?"

He eyed me warily, "What do you remember?"

"Not much. Drug dreams. Relief that I didn't talk. And at the very end, when I thought the drug had passed, a voice that was trying to reach me, then I passed out and missed the message."

He sat down and faced me, his expression strange so that it seemed to me that pride and awe chased one another across his face.

"You did talk, just as Bellarus said, *in a voice not yours.* Nor was it the drug, for I'll swear you had thrown it off."

Then he told me how I had wrestled it for hours, saying nothing, the muscles standing out upon my jaw from the effort, "Much to Brother Andrea's chagrin. Finally you opened your eyes, and I could see the drug was gone, and suddenly you seized the cup and stood and strode to Brother Andrea. He quailed like a frightened rabbit at the look on your face. You held out the cup in your hand and said, in a voice that made me shiver, *unclean!* Then you crushed the cup and let it drop before him. And you said, *You cannot call the god with drugs. Let the temple mend its ways.*

After that you turned and came back to your stool and I heard you say, *South comes the sky fire,* before you fainted."

Something in me stirred, "*South comes the sky fire.* Did anyone else hear me say that?"

He shook his head, "I don't think so. You said it quietly. I was the only one who was close."

Focused still on the urgency inside of me and fearing that I'd missed a message, I felt only relief, knowing this to be it, though I did not yet understand it.

"Thank you, Tantran."

He looked at me strangely, but my food arrived and we did not talk while the tray was disposed. The brother who brought it fairly fled. We had been on passable terms so I began to feel uneasy, but the waft from the bowls before me reached my nose and my stomach lurched to tell me its presence. I reached for the spoon.

"Out with it, Tantran! What is the matter?"

He stared at me as I ate and said slowly, "You have become more ... *commanding.*"

Instantly, I felt contrite, then realized that I did feel different. For six years now, he had been my master in all but name and now I felt as if I had passed him. 'Twas not in command I had spoken, but in banter, as one would with an old friend.

"I'm sorry," I apologized, "I had not the right."

He shook his head, "You have all the right. They'll never admit it above, but you *are* the conduit of the god, one of the old sort, from before the drug." He was whispering now, his eyes staring, "'Tis said you only come in times of need."

More than his words, the look in his face shook me so that I put down the spoon and reached across and took his hand, noticing suddenly how frail it was in mine.

"Whatever else I am I am still Nicodemus, who was your pupil and feels your friend. For the rest," I shrugged, feeling nothing, knowing I was still myself, "Time and the god will tell, but however I am touched I can tell you this. It confers no special merit. I am still Nicodemus," I repeated. 'Twas like a mantra, one I needed. He essayed a smile at that and seemed a trifle easier, so I thought of what he had said, "What did the inquiry find?"

"They could have only declared you *inspired* but I don't know for I was here with you. I did hear they debated long into the night."

"What makes you think they decided on *inspired?*"

He snorted, "They could hardly declare you conduit else they'd have to take you at your word and dismantle the whole office. Besides, Brother Andrea left yesterday. An they declared you conduit you can be sure he would have waited to escort you himself. Brother Fernand stayed and wants to see you when you've eaten, I believe to convey the verdict." He chuckled, "As far as I can tell, our good abbot wants nothing more to do with you!"

To my surprise, Fernand came himself to my cell as soon as my tray was cleared, an he had been waiting outside. Ill at ease, he waffled about to a degree that seemed very much at odds with the incisive man I'd seen earlier. At last he blurted out that the inquiry had found me *misguided.* Tantran was beside himself at that, and I had a job to calm them both down before I could ask Fernand for the story entire.

"I'm sorry, Nicodemus. And for you, too, Tantran, since it is quite a slap to your face, he having been your student."

He seemed sincere and more at ease since he had got the verdict off his chest. As the story unfolded, Tantran sputtered to life a few more times, but I felt strangely unmoved. It was simple enough, an one read between Fernand's blandly reported lines. Andrea had been horrified and wanted to bury the inquiry as deeply as he could. He had held out to have me branded *fraudulent.*

"He could have turned you over to the secular court in Westernesse, then. With a little conniving he might have convinced them to turn it into a death sentence."

Apparently the abbot for long had said little. In the end, though, even he did not agree with Andrea's solution.

"An only to protect the good name of Welling Abbey," Fernand allowed himself to comment.

On his own score he was more eloquent. The gist of it was that he agreed with Tantran, but knew that the inquiry would never find me conduit. He claimed to be afraid that, an it did, the Temple would try to subject me with the drug. It was quite an admission for a man who represented the Temple official and I looked at him narrowly.

He returned my gaze calmly enough, "Consider, Nicodemus. When I return to Estonval, I am but the sub-prior of Weirston Abbey. Abbot Grenson will sit on the council, and brother Andrea is Secretary of the Council Office. I would not be able to help you and a conduit of the god has no power in his own right, but is *kept,*" and here his face distorted into a slight grimace, "For what he can provide. An you are truly conduit of the god, of the old sort, then it is in my mind that you will come to us in the god's good time, without the need of inquiry."

"And officially discredited by the temple!" snapped Tantran.

Fernand's smile was wry now, "Just so. It was your new abbot's idea and he brought Andrea round to it. Somehow, in view of events, I could not think it mattered much to the god and as it was the best could be got from good brother Andrea, I agreed."

"And did you think that it might matter to Nicodemus?" Tantran persisted. Fernand said nothing, but raised his brows at me in inquiry.

As gently as I could I said, "He's right, Tantran. It matters little. I've no urge to go off preaching and there is a matter must be attended." I turned to the envoy. "Why are you here to tell me all this? Why was the verdict simply not pushed at me?"

"It would have been more in keeping," he acknowledged. "Put baldly, the *committee,*" and here he was ironic, "Wants no trouble and would be happy an you just disappeared. Since I consider that the best course for you, I engaged to talk you into keeping quiet."

This I could turn to my advantage, "There are conditions." He smiled, but said nothing, while I considered. "First, Bellarus would have declared me harper, but forbore as it would have been unseemly in one to become a novice. He expected the Abbey would do so when I finished here and so they must."

He inclined his head, "The abbot will be embarrassed, to declare you *misguided* and then *harper,* almost in a breath, but I think it safe to say he will agree. What else?"

"Simply supplies and a boat to get me away to the south, as quickly as possible."

"That, he will be happy to do. Why to the south?"

"Let's just say that I would start my harpering without I run into Brother Andrea again."

He looked askance, but said nothing, and shortly left. Seeing him to the door, I managed a word in private. He engaged to find a way to warn the abbot out of venting his displeasure on Brother Tantran.

Chapter 13

"We'll be landing you there, harper."

Brother Linfred's tone was respectful but his mouth was a tight line as he pointed. I couldn't blame him. This was far farther than they were wont to go, the coast rocky and without harbor to shelter them an it came to a storm. Only the fact that it was spring, when the storms were few, together with his strong desire to be rid of me, had prevailed upon the abbot to order this trip. That I was risking the lives of the brothers sent as crew, I knew, but the urgency to get south was tight in my gut. I reasoned an the god wanted me there, there would be no storms.

Yet the brothers' constraint was more than resentment, for they were cheerful enough in their work, and only quieted in my presence. They'd all been at my inquiry, and though the ordeal and verdict had not been public, every brother in the monastery knew more or less what had transpired. From the moment I stepped from my cell, I found myself surrounded, not by contempt at being branded *misguided,* but a kind of awe. 'Twas a poor substitute for the companionship I'd known. I quickly tired of it and was glad to be away. On the boat they settled in to calling me *harper* and though I was proud of the title, it was used to distance me so I yearned for the simple *Nicodemus* of old. A week before I'd been one of them. Now I was not, nor ever could be again. I sighed, trying to shake off my melancholy, and directed my attention along his line.

There was little there to reassure me. The shore was rocky, seeded with reefs and studded with sea stacks, so the swells boomed and broke in countless ragged edges. Behind, the hills marched down in ranks, sere and brown, spreading their barren little valleys to the sea. How, in all the miles of coast we'd passed and stretched ahead, he knew this for the spot seemed a mystery beyond any poor powers that I might have. He'd told me he'd never been there; instead he worked from old pilot notes made years before by a brother swept down by a storm while fishing outside the fjord. Somehow he'd found a haven and then managed to sail back when the storm had cleared. His notes were kept as a matter of course, but they seemed desperately scant to me. I was amazed to see a gap grow sudden in the reefs as we drew in with a beach of sand behind it.

My misgivings rose up as I watched the little lugger rowed out past the gap. It raised its sail and swiftly started its long reach home, stranding me on the sand, one hand high in farewell, the other to Megan's bridle. As she tucked her shoulder into the swell, I saw a hand come up, whose I couldn't tell, and wave in return. Inexplicably, that last little touch of humanity made me feel sudden better. I turned and explored the place, which I'm sure had seen no person since the long dead brother had sailed his boat back home.

Though the beach was pretty enough, it quickly gave way to a barren, boulder strewn heath, stretching back for miles to a crescent of hills that bounded it all around. Hauling my supplies behind the beach I made my camp and settled to consider. Though the shore trended south and east for some miles still, so that I would have landed farther down had brother Linfred been willing, yet I could not see that I could pick my way by land. I was close to the southern tip of Westernesse and that would have to suffice. While the thought that I could go a deal farther south in Suthy niggled in my mind like a ragged nail, the urgency that still throbbed inside would not admit the time to get there. The muscles in my jaw locked down hard. This was not the place to second guess myself. I must put my doubts aside and settle down to wait, trusting that time and the god would reveal whether I was right. The urgency at least warranted that I should know soon.

Two days later, I began to wonder. Had I been the untrained boy who came to Welling, the doubt would have eaten me whole. As it was, I contained it, longing for the presence to confirm to me my choice, but knowing I must accept that the god had spoken and would come to me in time. Yet 'twas hard. As a boy, frightened, alone in a great warren of a castle, the presence held out hope of something better an only I had patience. Now, I was a harper, trained by a master and an abbey both, ready for the road. What was I doing, waiting on a barren beach? I needed nothing. *But the god does!*

I spent my time reacquainting myself with the saddle and my songs, riding back and forth along the strip of sand, sitting over my harp. And always I watched, looking for a sign. Remembering where this journey had begun, I regarded particularly the setting of the sun, enjoying for the first time the sight of its slide directly into the sea, almost an it were snuffed out each night. 'Twas easy to see the hand of the god in that and such a wonder should never be called ordinary, but I went unsatisfied to bed both nights. I could not help but think, on the third night, after two full days on the beach, that, an I had taken the ordinary way, I would be clear of The Welling and able to turn south by now. My only consolation was that the weather meant the lugger must have got back safely.

§

The third sunset, with a sky completely clear, was more meager than its brethren. Once the sun had gone I sat down to meditate, waiting for one of the moons to rise. The wind had died so it was completely calm, with only the swell making surf a gentle threnody with just the bass line present. I felt myself expand and match the canopy, looking down at the darkening land below, then inverting effortlessly, like a swimmer turning on to his back, to see the stars.

One by one they came up as the light faded, old friends making their bow and taking their appointed place. The trio, first, twining their perpetual way about their pole, marking the north. Then Ryan, the hunter, chasing Artos, the horse, condemned to run the night until he should get his leg astride just before the dawn, only to start again tomorrow. Feeling a kinship for his fate, I waved him on his way. I felt the start of words I could mold into a song.

Next the Drift, stars like snowflakes piled beneath the eaves. I felt the tug of the child who had wanted to dive into the middle and toss them laughing. One by one they came, the constellations, each touching me in its own way, telling me that all was in its place, myself included. *South comes the sky fire!* I had been blind, looking vaguely at the sunsets. The sign must be here, a comet perhaps, or the fabled aurora that my father told me he had once seen. Even now, I could hear the whispered awe of his voice, *'Twas like sky fire, Nicodemus, flickering in the north.*

Now, I began to scan the heavens in earnest, looking for the flicker, not sure whether it would be north, as it was for my father, or south, as I had been told. *Dear the god! Did south mean south in the sky? Had I come to this wilderness in vain?* Pushing down the thought, I kept to the search, and blinked to see a star fall. Common enough and not to the purpose.

And then I saw it. A new star, brighter than the trio, glowed almost directly overhead. How I'd come to miss it, I could not think, for bright as it was it should have shown up early. *Unless it wasn't there!* Could this be the birth of a new star? Brother Tantran had told me such things happened and pointed me to Pedantrus, born a century and a half before and recorded by the monks at Welling. I watched in awe. Even as I looked it bloomed and seemed to snuff its neighbor. Still it grew until I saw its neighbor come again, this time above it, and realized sudden that it moved. East it went, and somewhat north, not fast like a falling star, but slow as breath. I could track it just by the steady winking on and off of its brethren as it passed. And always it grew, getting larger, elongating, white, with tips of blue at the bottom.

Abruptly, I stood on the heath, looking with my own eyes. Beneath the sound of the surf I could hear a deeper roar. I had to turn and gentle Megan, who, catching it too, grew restive. Even as I calmed her, the sound rose so the surf disappeared, like thunder heard distant in the hills, except this went on and on, without break or let. Then it struck me the sky fire was coming down, moving faster now, dropping northeast. In my awe, I let go of Megan, and she broke and bolted in the dark all in an instant. I heard one wild neigh and the drumming of hooves, quickly gone in the swelling roar that rebounded from the hills so that, was there nothing to see, I would never tell from where it came. Yet the fire was now so bright, I think even the blind would have sensed it through their lids, and I had to shield my eyes.

At that, it snuffed behind the hills, like a candle going out with only a wickling glow behind. Quickly that went out as well.

The thunder died. Then distantly, there came a great metallic clash, like two armies that surged together in the night and then at once were still. In the sudden silence, the land seemed almost dead. Then, softly, the sound of the surf asserted itself. I whistled for Megan and heard her whinny in the distance, distressed still but not, I thought, unduly. Content she was all right, I left her for the morning, seeing little profit in trying to recover her in the dark. She could not go far, no more could I. Whatever the god had sent, it must wait until there was light. I composed myself for sleep as best I could. For all of Tantran's training, it came hard that night. 'Twas difficult not to think on what it was I had seen and heard. At one point I got up and drew a line in the dirt, marking the direction of the sky fire's fall, then tried to settle in again.

'Twas well I made the mark. By dawn, the sky was overcast. Without the arrow I would have been hard pressed to say exactly where to seek. As it was, breaking my fast and my camp, I stared at the featureless hills, memorizing each contour until I was sure I had the line. Megan came to my whistle, a little wild eyed, but settled to my hand and let me saddle her easy enough. Checking a final time my distant point against the dirt, I rode out into the lowering morning.

§

The arid plain grew only tussock in scattered tufts, but it was peppered with flint so, though we made good enough time, it was a fussy passage, demanding of my attention. At the hills, I must dismount and lead the mare up through a thousand feet of gorse and knife grass, a trying business with not so much as a coney trail as guide. By noon, we made the top at last, and, tired already, I stared at the plain below. 'Twas the twin of the one behind me.

It dawned on me then that I little knew what it was I was seeking. Consumed with the problem of getting there, I had put no thought into what it was I might find. Nothing stood out on the plain below and I was minded of the pot of gold my mother always laughed was at the end of a rainbow. The trick, I found as a child, was to find the end, for it always moved as I did and I never could quite see where it came down. Sa. I was adult now and it seemed to me so large a fire, unless truly like a rainbow, should leave a mark. I could see no blackening. *Where was the end of the rainbow?* I only had its line. For all I knew it could be behind the next hill. *Or the one after that,* I thought gloomily, remembering the approach to Welling Fjord, through the passes. I thought of the sound, that I had judged it close, an indeed I could judge such a thing. The plains were miles across and I refused to believe that the fire had come down too many ranges away. I would make for the next line of hills and see beyond them, watching on the way for anything that might mark the rainbow. *And if nothing then?* I shrugged it off, knowing I would have to see before I could decide, and tried to find my line.

Since I was at my final point I had to turn and look back. To my dismay, the ocean rolled for miles and I could not find my little beach with any certainty. Cursing myself that I had not thought to keep its mark as I rode away, I searched for Brother Linfred's gap. From my angle, 'twas as hard to find from the hills as it had been at sea. At last I marked where I thought it was and drew another line. Before I left, I raised a cairn that I could see against the skyline. All across the weary plain below I kept casting back at it. I could see it well enough but worried still that I had already put myself off my course and might well pass whatever it was I sought.

It was twilight by the time I reached the opposite hills and, look as I might, I had seen nothing. Making my evening meal over a fire of twigs, I considered whether there was anything at all. Could it be that the fire itself was the sign and that I must somehow read it? It would take a better hand than I at reading portents and I thought wryly of the brother keepers of the conduit of the god before I fell asleep. Perhaps one of them could interpret what I'd seen. I'd no intention to ask.

In the middle of the night I woke to find the sky largely cleared again, Aurelia riding through the heavens, dodging through what wisps of cloud were left, with little Aries rising in chase behind. Suddenly sleepless, I looked at the hill looming before me, and decided there was light enough to get up and at least have a look. Leaving the mare behind, I slipped up the hillside glad, in the chill, the climb was stiff enough to warm me. Just below the top, I hesitated, afraid to see a repetition of what I'd seen already, just another plain stretching off to another wall of hill. In the end, I inched up and stuck only my head above the ridge. There was another plain all right, a small one, ending in cliffs above the sea where the coast turned north; but what else there was stilled all the breath in my body.

Now, these many years later, I can see it in my mind as clear an still I lay atop that hill. Yet I know that what I see now is not what I saw then, that time and understanding have shifted my perceptions. The picture is the same, that is etched for always, but the realities are different. At the far edge, by the sea cliffs, was a vast black circle of blasted ground, resting my fears of rainbows. From dead in the center of the circle lay what seemed like a great arrow of purest silver, for all the land like a pointer. My heart turned over. Was this a second sign, made by the sky fire, tacking me east, straight at the sea? An to underscore 'twas the sea was meant, the very end hung out over the cliff, as much of it as there is head on a man. I glanced up at Orion, in the midst of his endless chase, wondering bitterly just how long this might go on and how I was supposed to take to the sea again. Then I looked back and saw that the pointer was crumpled and torn, an a great tower had toppled on its side. There was no rubble of shattered stone to speak of masonry. Instead its walls were smooth or jagged where torn. Pondering that, it struck me it must be made completely of metal, silver or mayhap sword bright steel, not just stained its color by Aurelia. Was it forged then? Had the sky fire somehow come down and kindled the heath and drawn iron from the land and so raised the tower? It seemed doubtful. I'd seen no red in the rock around that speaks of iron, nor did it seem to me the god would raise a tower to fall. No other thought would come so I settled down to watch, warding the chill with my mind and seeking for the presence.

I was no wiser by morning, except to know that, whatever it was the god had brought, the presence was not there. I must make of it what I could upon my own. Waves of heat shimmering off the plain reminded me I'd little water left. Whatever I would

do I must do quickly. I slithered back over the crown of the hill
and went for Megan.

§

Riding to the tower, as I'd come to think of it, it seemed
both larger and smaller than I'd first thought. It was shorter by
far than it seemed from the hill, more like five hundred feet than
a mile; but as I closed, it loomed above me, a sweep of steel so
vast it crushed me to insignificance. The damage grew as well, so
I could see it burned and buckled and torn, making it at once
more ordinary, a thing made and used and broken, and all the
more extraordinary. What smith had so wrought?

I rode around as much of it as I could, not daring to go too
close to the edges of the cliff. I could see a ragged edge where a
great piece had broken off in the tower's fall and I had no wish to
discover an more was ready to go. The tower itself was not a
tower at all but was made in pieces like a ship, ribbed and
skinned, every part of steel instead of wood. At the end in the
center of the circle was a dome of black, like the inside of a great
bell fifty or more feet across. The metal around it was blackened
as well and soot came off on my hand so I had little doubt that
here was the source of the fire.

Making a second circuit, I found my eye caught sudden by a
gleam, an steel had winked across the sun. Looking, I found
instead of a wink, a glow, that, move my head as I would, stayed
steady on. A light, from inside the tower, shining from a rent
above my head.

Keeping Megan still I found that I could stand in the saddle
by leaning against the side and just reach a hand to the tear. There
was room to pass inside. Taking a deep breath, I levered myself
up and in with no worse than a knuckle skinned against the tear
in the metal.

Inside was a passageway, all of metal, standing on what once
had been a wall. Brighter than any candle, the light came from the
end, shining from a wall that I judged had been the ceiling. Even
so, it was darker by far than the plain outside. I approached it
carefully, trying to tune my eyes to its light. Where it shone, the

passage seemed to turn, but as I reached it, it went out. Grabbing a bar in front of me, I steeled myself against turning back for the day and peered instead around the turn.

Even as I did, a second light came on ahead, an beckoning. It showed a staircase passage, like a ladder in a ship, except that up now meant simply north. Treading on what must have been wall I edged along the rail trying to hold the way in my mind lest the light go out for good. Again, the light went out as I reached it and again another came on, leading me deeper into the tower. Much I saw that was strange, but only in flashes, for the light was insistent. An I stopped to examine a thing, it went out regardless, so I must hurry to catch it. At least I saw I needed it only to lead me and not to see, for enough light came through the rents and even a window or two, that I was confident I could get back out so long as it was day.

At last I passed through a room that looked something like a room, with a table and two long couches bolted down, though even here there was more I didn't recognize than I did, and that little strange in its design. Like all the rest, the light there went out as soon as I came in, so I had little time to look. Another came on, in a room now above, so I must climb some twenty feet, using the furniture as my ladder.

Hauling my way up through the door, I saw this room was smaller than the rest, with no second way out. The glow held steady, but threw its light across the chamber instead of shining all about as it had before. It fell on a single object, an that were the one thing I was meant to see. What it was was no more obvious to me than all the rest. But as I studied it, I saw there was a quality about it was different.

It was simple enough. Hanging from the wall that once was a floor, fastened to it, was an oblong box raised on a table so that, could I stand by it, 'twould come to my hip. Built of light blue bricks, it had an unfinished look, as if the whole tower and everything that was in it had been built by master craftsmen and this one piece made by the rawest apprentice.

Yet this, which should be the least important, was all that was lit by the unblinking eye of light. I touched the object and found it rough, where all else had been smooth or carefully textured. To my surprise, I felt the brick move fractionally beneath my hand, and before I could think, had pulled it from its place. Beneath lay another object, in the style of the masters, so that I could see it had been but shelled by the apprentice, an in afterthought. *Or packed up against the fall?* I beat the other bricks aside, my heart like a hammer as I saw what lay beneath. 'Twas a box, like a coffin with a dome of glass. Inside, half slumped against the straps that held him, lay a man.

All this time 'twas an I'd been in a dream or still in the grip of brother Andrea's foul drug; from the watch at the beach to the plains to following the lights, I had done what seemed to me must be done, without ever thinking too much what I might find. Whatever I had expected, a sign or a revelation or a symbol, it had not been this.

I felt strangely diminished, and realized sudden that part of me had yearned to be *conduit of the god,* an I could but forgo the drugs. It had a ring to it, like *right knee to the king,* and I knew then it was the title I wanted and not the office. To be hailed as chosen of the god seemed a very fine thing and I had ridden through the barrens like a hero in a ballad, expecting somehow to be covered in glory when the verses were sung. 'Twas the trappings I had wanted, threads of finest gold and brightest scarlet to make for me a place of pride within the tapestry, without ever seeing it would pin me there.

Well, here was my place. An it was a man I'd been sent to find, then that man was who the god sought. I was but a page sent to seek. So it was that the journey did bring me revelation. In that one moment, it freed me of my dagger in the dark I'd lived with for years. An I was not *conduit,* why then I was *harper* and that was place enough for me. I smiled. Halfway to hating the unknown man, I realized sudden he was my freedom. Leaning forward, I looked at him more closely.

Part III
Damonryan

Chapter 14

Slowly, at the very edges of my ears, I became aware of a sound like the distant summer thrum of insects. Touching the casket, I could feel it through my fingers. Look as I might I could see no sign of breathing, yet he had not the look of death. Unbidden, the tales of my childhood rose in my mind. *Enchanted? Am I to break the spell?* As I considered that, the light waned like a moon slipping into the clouds. Then it went out altogether.

The dark surged over me. For a moment I thought I was lost, but slowly, lit by the glow of far-off daylight from the door beneath my feet, the room came ghostly back. The cask emerged above my head, a darkness against a darker gloom, its occupant swallowed in its shadows. For heartbeat after heartbeat, I regarded it, wondering what to do. My instincts were all to leave, but surely I had been summoned to do more than just bear witness. Sudden, there flickered on its side a small square of red like a precious stone that catches at the light. It went out again then winked back, and off and on, a ragged rhythm, something small on the edge of death.

Each time it glowed I could see letters, strange, etched upright in black, straight backed as soldiers, too regular for mortal scribe—a single word, easily read: **OVERRIDE**.

An incantation? I scarcely knew but traced the letters with a fingertip and said the word aloud. Nothing. I worried at the meaning but could make no sense of it. *Ride over what?* Staring about me I shook my head in disbelief. Even right way up I would never be able to get Megan inside this topsy-turvy place; there was no room for a horse. The jewel died as I puzzled, forlornly sputtering into a final fade. I reached out, touching it again, assuring myself it still was there. My fingers felt its edges where it was raised from out the casket and excitement quickened. Could it be that the jewel itself was the key?

Gripping its edges, I tried to move it, side to side at first, then twisting, and finally plucking. Each time nothing; 'twas fixed immovable. More in frustration than out of any rational thought I thumped it with my fist, an to say *let go your secret!* I felt it yield. There was a click, loud as a drum in the little space, and the dome on the casket sprung out. A fraction only, a line at the bottom, nothing more, but I pressed against it. 'Twas hinged above so I found could swing it part way open. Were the tower erect, I might have opened it full, but a foot was all I could reach. Turning, I swept the gloom to see an there were something I could stand upon.

From behind my back came a sudden hissing sound. There was a smell, slight but foul, unknown to my nose though it echoed of wine gone bad. Even as I twisted back the sleeper, visible now with the cover up, stirred and opened his eyes. In the dark, I saw mostly hair. He was human, that much I could tell, but the rest was hidden behind a wild tangle of mane and beard. Weakly, he began to struggle with his bonds. I tried to help, but they were strange and barely in reach. Then, before I could resume my search for something to stand on, they gave with a rush. As best I could I broke his fall, putting us both in a heap and knocking the breath from out my body.

As I lay gasping, he rose, staring at me, and said, "Yer hewmn!"

For the life of me, I could not answer, but retched for breath. Understanding, he seized my legs and pumped them until I got my wind then broke into excited speech. His words were fast, the patter of rain on a pond, except they rose and fell, both in pitch and volume, like gusts that raced patches across the water.

I shook my head and said, as slowly and clearly as I might, "I…don't…understand. Slow…down."

That set him off again and I got little for a spell besides *hewmn,* by which I was tolerably sure he meant *human,* and *Anglisch* which meant nothing to me at all. Seeing my bewilderment, he stopped and spoke slowly.

"Yew…spayke…Anglisch."

His accent was strange beyond my poor art as a scribe, but I could grasp the words, if not what they meant.

"I *speak,*" I said, "Now…that…I…have…breath."

He seemed delighted, almost to dancing, "Yew…do…spayke…Anglisch!"

"What…is…Anglisch?"

"The…langwidge…yew…are…spayking."

I considered that. "All men have language. 'Tis what separates us from the beasts." Remembering Brychan's comments about *lordtalk* I wanted to ask him an he had meant that, but already I had gone too fast and he shook his head to show he had not understood. In frustration I asked, "Did…you…think…a…man…would…whinny…like…a…horse?"

He laughed, a sound so gay and gusty I couldn't help but join in, though I didn't see 'twas all that funny. "Yew…have…horses…tew?"

I nodded, finding it strange he was so surprised about horses or that I was human and could speak. There was much more here than I could understand though he appeared ordinary enough in the dark of the tower and I had been relieved to hear such unaffected laughter. Suspicion welled but I started too fast and must simplify and start again.

"Do…you…come…from…the…Great…Land?"

"No…I…", he hesitated, "I…will…explain…later. Must…check my ship," he finished in a rush, peering about the room, muttering something too low and fast to catch. Then he called into the dark, "Josh? Josh-u-a?" There was only silence.

"I…saw…no one…else," I told him, but added, in the halting way we had developed, that it was dark and I had been led straight there. "I…help…you…look." By now, I was dropping words just to get the message out.

He looked at me sharply, "Led? How?" I explained about the lights and he questioned me a little. "No…lights…now," he observed. "Poor Josh. Must be out of power." This last was said fast, an to himself, but I was getting the trick of his speech.

"Out…of…power?" I asked.

He looked at me carefully, then spoke simply, but closer to normal speed, "It was Josh who led you here and showed you the release. No need to look for him. He's here." He hesitated, his eyes wary, even in the dark. "Josh is a *machine.*" An he was expecting something, he was disappointed.

"I do not know the word."

He sighed, and rubbed his hands across his eyes. "There's a lot to explain." To my surprise, he extended his hand, "I'm Damonryan."

A knight or noble then. Well, I had seen Bellarus shake the hand of a knight once or twice, and I was harper now, an hardly of his esteem. Hiding my doubt, I took his hand and completed the ceremony.

"Nicodemus, harper, late of Welling." I must think on that. After the inquiry I might not want my name tied back there quite so readily, "I'm honored to meet you Damonryan."

He smiled, "Damon Ryan. Two names, not one. Can we go outside? I want to see what it's like!"

As we stumbled out in the half dark, I heard him curse a time or two, but I wasn't really listening. There was much to ponder and I tried to make some sense of what I'd seen and heard already. At last he reached the rent and I heard him give a whistle of dismay as he looked out.

"How does anybody live here?"

"No one does," I answered, sure by now he came from the Great Land. "We call this the barrens. 'Tis not like the rest of the land at all."

He looked at me over his shoulder, "So how come you're here?"

"The god sent me."

He turned then, so that I saw his face in the light for the first time. In the dark, it had been dominated by his hair, long as a woman's but tousled about his head, unclasped and uncombed, running altogether with a great beard below. Now it was his eyes that held me, blue, quite still, though I had the sense that he looked me up and down, and unreadable. He stared at me two fists of beats and more. Behind them I saw the hair's uncommon color, straw touched by the evening sun, curling to a deeper red in the beard. Neither illness nor age had marred his skin and his teeth, when he broke off his stare at last and flashed a rueful smile, were white and straight, all present. My age, then, or mayhap younger. The smile, I noted, touched into his eyes.

"We do have a lot to talk about," he said finally and vaulted lightly through the rent.

A man who journeyed through the sky on a tower of steel? Following him more gingerly, I could only agree.

§

Outside, the first thing to take my eye was his garment. He wore just the one, from neck to ankle, as strange as what he called his ship; it fit so close that, except where he kept his manhood, I could see each muscle and its flow beneath, more a second skin than clothing, without seam or buckle or tie. As he moved the garment shimmered, shifting colors in the sun an a hundred rainbows had been caught and twisted into threads and so wove together. It held my gaze as brother Tantran's spinning disk could not. 'Twas all I could do to force them back to the man.

He seemed ordinary enough, except for that glory of hair. About my stature, though heavier built, with wider shoulders, and straight as a soldier. A young man in the full prime of his strength, though oddly, his blue eyes, cooler now than the Drift, seemed somehow older than the rest of him. They watched me take him in then, when I had done, just swept along his ship, reckoning the damage. Sudden they sparkled and he strode forward.

"You really do have horses!" He stroked Megan's nose and scratched her ear, clicking at her like a delighted child.

Moving beside him, I flipped open the saddle bag and took out a fresh round of cheese and the last of my waterskins, thinking he might like to break his fast after his time in the casket, and also that he might talk easier over food. Watching me warily as I cut two wedges he took the offered piece gingerly and looked at it carefully. To show him it was good, I bit a large chunk from mine and chewed it ostentatiously.

He grinned at that, "Sorry, Nicodemus. I didn't think you were trying to poison me. Food from a different …*place* can be trouble." Looking at the cheese again he shrugged, "I suppose if you can eat it, I can. And sooner or later I'm going to have to." He took a bite and chewed absently, staring at his ship, then broke off in quick surprise, "This is *good!*"

"The cheese of Welling is renowned through all the land."

He looked a little more cheerful, "Do you brew beer here as well?"

"I've none with me but you can get it at any tavern."

"Taverns!" he breathed, then quickly, "Dark or light?"

It seemed a strange question. "Their custom is mostly done at night…"

"Not the taverns!" he interrupted, "The beer!"

I laughed at that and told him that lager was light and the darkness of the ale depended upon the publican.

"Brew pubs!" he said, half to himself, "Damon, old son, you may just have landed on your feet!" Then, quickly to me, "Sorry Nicodemus. Spacers get in the habit of talking to themselves."

Was spacer a common term for a drunkard where he came from? Given his ecstasy at the mention of taverns, it seemed likely, but I could see no way to ask.

My face must have done it for me. "Oh lord!" he exclaimed, "I'm just glad to find some amenities!" He blew out his cheeks, "If I could have some more of your excellent cheese, perhaps we could sit down and I'll do my best to explain." While I cut him another piece, he looked at me shrewdly, "I suspect this will be harder for you than for me."

At that, he was right. By then we could understand fairly well the words each other made, so long as we spoke with care, but what he had to say made for hard believing. In the end I did because I must, because there was too much about him and his clothes and his ship that were different. The clothes I could see, flashing before me, but the hardest was the *ship*. I must imagine the awesome bulk of that shattered tower of steel riding a tail of fire lightly between the stars. Yet I had seen the fire come down, seen its power etched black across the plain, seen the great fire saddle of the bell at the bottom of the ship. In the end I managed it.

Damonryan seemed surprised, "I must say, you take all this more calmly than I expected," he commented.

"That a man can fly at all, much less something so big, is a great wonder and hard to grasp."

Shaking his head, he said, "I didn't mean that. For a man who didn't know what a machine was and uses a horse to get around, you seem remarkably calm about the idea I would come from the stars."

"Why should our sun be the only star to have world with people?" I asked, puzzled as to why that had anything to do with horses and machines.

"So you know your sun is just another star?" When I nodded, he continued, "Where is this Great Land you talked of?"

"Many months sail across the sea. The Tales seem to indicate it was to the northeast somewhere."

For a moment he considered, saying nothing, then, "I want to check something and I need to have a look through the ship anyway. Want to come?"

Inside, he moved deftly through the dark, bringing us quickly back to the large room that had looked most like a room. "Main cabin," he explained as we clambered through the doorway, "Spent most of my time here. Hang on and I'll get a light."

Working his way across the cabin, he extracted a tube from a cupboard on the floor and flared it to light in his hand. Alone in that mystery of a ship, when I had followed the lights, I had been striving for the message and missing the messengers, never considering what a marvel they were. Now, as I watched him search the cabin, I considered his lamp with growing delight. He could make it bright as the sun, so it would burn the eyes but never a hand put to the glass that held it, which felt only cold when I tried it. At need, as I followed him, I saw him spread the light like a lamp, or narrow it to a cone or even a needle to probe into the vitals of one of his machines. Once, he changed its colors, playing a rainbow across a crystal surface, first steady, an the colors one by one were dropped into a pool; then fast, in a flickering dance, that drew a gasp from me, but only a grunt from him.

There were other wonders, in plenty. I remember a thing he called the *console,* a plate of glass like a window with a wall behind and rows of *keys* below, small squares for touching with letters marked upon them, one or two per square. Nothing happened when he touched a few of the keys and he quickly gave it up with a muttered, "No power!"

Thence we clambered along to what he called his *engine room,* engines being machines, as he explained, for driving the ship through space. To my bewilderment, the room was smaller than the cabin, with walls that were almost smooth. He laughed at my dismay, "The engines are beneath us, Nicodemus, or would be if we were upright. And they *are* big, about three quarters of the ship. Most of these," he waved at the walls, "Are simply access panels." He sighed, "And the one I want is now on the roof! Give us a boost up, will you?"

By standing on my shoulders, he managed to reach the panel he wanted, though it was no mean feat to swing it down out of the way. That done, he pulled himself up and disappeared inside, like a coney going into a hole in a cliff. 'Twasn't long before he popped back out of his burrow. "Just as I thought," he said when he had dropped to the floor again, "There's no power left at all. It looks as though Josh didn't really have enough to get her down properly, which is why she crashed. He must have had to bring her in too fast, buckling that landing strut outside and pitching her on her side. Beats me how he kept enough to signal you with the lights."

When at last we were outside again he said, "Since you like the light so much, you may take it as a gift."

I shook my head, "I have nothing of this worth I can give to you."

"Just my life, Nicodemus," he laughed. "Without you, I would have died in my tomb. The remotes were damaged in the crash and Josh wasn't able to release me."

Then he showed me how to use it. 'Twere flimsy, you would say, to look at it and heft it in your hand, but even now, after all these years, it has taken no mark that I can find, though its fire has gone at last. It could be played like an instrument, changing its light to the pressure in my fingers. Turning it over I found it cunningly made, seamless like his clothes, so the black that fit into the hand and the glassine globe all seemed one.

"Where do you put the oil?"

"You don't. When the light goes out, it is finished. It's cheaper to make a new one than to replenish an old," he added, half apologetically. He checked, looking at my face, "Does that shock you?"

"This is beautifully wrought and would have taken months of the craftsman's time. You must be a very high baron indeed, to discard so valuable a piece."

He laughed uproariously at the thought of being a baron, and tried to explain. It took a time, trying this and that, before we hit upon the way that cheese was made at Welling. It seems his people made lamps that way, and most other things as well, using molds, making them by the thousands, and thousands of thousands, using machines instead of people. Machines were constructions for doing work, like water wheels or windmills, except they had machines would fly them through the air, or carry them like wagons without horses. They had machines to wash their clothes and cook their food, machines which entertained them or mined their ore or farmed their fields. They even had machines that built their machines for them.

"What do people do?" I asked.

The answer, it seemed, was both much and nothing. They had many what he called *professions* which we should label *crafts,* far more than I could well imagine. No simple harpers, there. My brethren and I had a thousand counterparts, people who would spend a lifetime playing one instrument in a vast assemblage of different instruments, pipes and horns and flutes, lutes of many sizes played with a bow, instruments keyed like the lamp. Music was divided, cut like a pie into countless *styles,* with different singers for each. Every craft was the same, so an you had a pain in your foot, you saw a different physician than an it were in your head. Many, it seemed, did little real work, other than to guide the machines that did it for them.

"I was right to call you baron," I said slowly, "All your folk are lords. Your machines are serfs."

He smiled assent, then, "Serfs?" he queried. "Don't tell me you've got knights and dragons and stuff!"

"Dragons?"

And so it went. For two days we talked, each questioning and telling in turn, finding out all we could about each other and our peoples. Many were the turns in the track and sometimes we went wrong for though our words were the same, our ideas were not. In that way, new ideas like machines were easier for me to grasp than the difference in existing ideas. In the land, *language* is what people speak, but for him people spoke one *language* or another.

Imagine two people talking, both able speakers, but both using completely different words for the same things so that neither could understand each other. Thus his people came to label the languages they spoke with names and it appears *the* language is actually *a* language his people call *English!* Much more was there of that ilk.

Time was needed to build our understanding so it was not complete at our leaving, but must be steady filled as we went. Some of what I say mayhap I didn't know or grasp, until days or even years afterwards though most I got in those days beside his ship. Enough! I will spin my story without worrying overmuch about what was learned when.

He was born, Damon Patrick Ryan, the first names being his own and the last carried by his forefathers, on a planet called Unity, fair by his reckoning, and rich. There were no barons or knights or serfs on unity, only *citizens,* each equal before the law. Instead of a king, they were ruled by a *government,* a group of citizens elected by the people, a little like the abbot of Welling except the election was revocable. An the people didn't like their government they elected a new one. At first, he made it sound like paradise, but I came to understand, in conversations over the years, that his equality was a slippery thing. As he put it once, long after, *some citizens were more equal than others.* He was full of such tortuous concepts.

Unity was only one of thirty-eight worlds settled by humankind, spread among the stars, but thin, very thin. They had machines could move them from one end of the land to the other in merely minutes and circle a world in an hour or two. Messages could be woven in a web of light and spun between the worlds in minutes, but to cross between the farthest of the worlds took more than a score of years. Since, even with hard riding, it took months to cross the land, this seemed to me of little moment but not to Damonryan. He said it had been the dream of his people to stretch out and spread through all the stars; but the distances slowed them down and splintered their efforts. At the frontier, twelve years travel from the center, with the space outside it barren, *Unity just lost interest* he had said with a look on his face that said to me *here is one who has not given up the dream.*

"Do others search?" I asked.

"Yes, from Desolation. I couldn't join them so I decided to do a bit of digging on my own. "

"Were they hostile to one from Unity?"

"No, we don't have that kind of trouble. Desolation is twenty years from Unity. Nicodemus, that's a tenth of a *lifetime!*"

That's how I learned both of his age and that his people knew no war. As he talked I had revised my estimate of his age to somewhat older than myself, thirty mayhap, thinking his people's span to be the same as ours. Instead, he said he was fifty and five, a graybeard were he one of us. I could see no signs of it in all that hair.

"It isn't dyed either," he said, laughing at my inspection in his unaffected way. "We have simply learned to slow the aging process a little." He ran his hand through his hair and cursed at its length, "Keeps growing in the Medicom!" he grunted, "I need a shower and a haircut." Then he looked suddenly woeful, "I'll bet you don't have showers here, do you?"

Again I was puzzled, "Not all the land is as dry as this. It rains quite frequently elsewhere."

He groaned at my reply. "A *shower* is a device that sprays water all over you. We use it for washing…", he hesitated, looking at me challengingly, "…every day!"

Puzzled by his manner I said, mildly enough, "We have baths. Will they do?"

"With hot, running water?"

"Running?" I tried to imagine water with legs, then thought I saw what he meant, "You mean flowing all the time, like a stream?" I shook my head, "Even well kept houses and inns couldn't afford that. There's a pipe from the kitchen stove to the bath-house, with a stopper for letting heated water in."

He relaxed a bit at that, but still, not completely. I thought of his *every day* and a suspicion crossed my mind as to his manner. I was five days out from Welling, with only a cold swim in the sea for the wastes had little water. I was almost as travel worn as he. "A bath would feel good right now," I assayed.

He relaxed all the way. Somehow, he'd been afraid we didn't wash.

My feelings must have shown in my face, for he muttered, "Sorry Nicodemus, no offense. Many centuries ago they used to have knights and castles and such on old Earth and it sticks in my mind that they never bathed."

It seemed so bizarre. It was so long ago I suspected that was one he had gotten wrong.

§

He questioned me like an abbot about the land, making it plain he was stranded, "The *Loribel* will never fly again, Nicodemus, and there's no one going to come and look for me. When I don't return, they'll write me off, and one or two will even think *good riddance!*" Of a sudden I felt abashed, thinking, after his stories of the reaches of space, that there was little I could tell him that was wonderful. Seeing the land as I thought he would see it, it seemed a little place, and poor. In that I was wrong, for he was strangely joyful.

"I think I am," he answered thoughtfully, at my comment. "When I went to sleep in the Medicom, I didn't even expect to survive, so I've much to be grateful for. But it's more than that. Life in the Settled Worlds was *bland;* I was looking for some spice. I think maybe I've found it."

Unable to go exploring, he had become what he had hoped was the next best thing, a trader moving goods between the stars.

"I was a kid, what did I know? I wanted the *stars,* Nikki!" he said with such a hunger that I saw Unity for him was what Halting Castle had been to me. A strange equivalence but I think flame riding steeds of steel must do that. They fling themselves so far and so fast that worlds are shrunk to castles; and the land to what?—a room?

"I was *bored,* Nicodemus. Two years to Jansen's World, and six months more to either Paradisio or Twistensen. Twenty years I plied that run, enough to get me all the way to Desolation, if only I had gone. The boredom ate my soul!"

It seems he'd determined to give it up when he happened on some cases of rare wine that had come all the way from a place called Franz on old Earth. Apparently they had the right to a certain amount of cargo of their own so, back on his home world, he made what he called a *killing.* I thought he had done murder for the wine and my face showed it but he only laughed.

"A *profit,* Nikki, a huge profit. The guy found it in his old man's cellar when he died and didn't like wine. I swapped him for the same number of bottles of Baktra whiskey and he was sure he had swindled me!"

The profit must have been huge. He used it to buy the *Loribel* then made a voyage or two on her to get what he called a *stake.* "Then I struck out for the stars!"

I thought of that, my eyes shining, "'Tis a lucky man who gets to follow his dream!"

He laughed. "To be honest, until I got here, it was even more boring than the run to Jansen's World!" He was like that. He would never let me make him out to be more than he thought he should be.

§

Inevitably, we came back to my presence on the plain. When he asked me I took a breath and told him the story, more by far than I was wont to tell to strangers. But 'twas he I'd been sent for. He had the right. I started with the monastery, but he questioned again, now in a way that minded me of Cromart. So I told him all, back to my childhood in Anglesea. When I had done, he thanked me, saying that he had learned more about the land in my history than in all my other tellings. Then he seemed to falter.

"What is it, Damonryan?"

He smiled, "I think that will have to be my name here," then grew serious, "Nicodemus, you've been straight with me, but ...well...I don't want to offend you."

"How should you offend?"

He considered then said carefully, "My beliefs are not the same as yours."

I frowned, "A man believes what a man believes. An my grandfather believed that children should be taught their letters and Lord Cromart did not, where is there cause for offense?"

He hesitated a moment, then, like a man who runs at cold water, "Where I come from, few people believe in a god of any kind!"

Bemused, I answered, "What does *believe* have to do with the god? Believe is next to hope, for things that might or might not be, as that your friend afar is well, or that none will come to seek you." He smiled at that. "Do they believe in stones and the sky? They are or are not and so it is with the god."

"They can see stones and the sky."

"And they can commune the god," I returned, puzzled.

He reflected my puzzlement. "Commune *with* the god?" he ventured at last.

My bewilderment grew, "Do we see *with* the stones and sky? No, we see *with* eyes. When talking of what we see, we say, simply, *see*. How can you commune *with* the god? You commune the god."

"With?"

"The spirit."

"The spirit is a sense?"

I felt an I conducted a temple school. "An organ, like the ear, that contains the sense." Then I stopped and looked at him wonderingly, "You *have* no spirit?"

He answered slowly, "I have heard of the spirit, but not as a sense of the god. Where I come from only five senses are recognized."

"And without that sense, you do not believe in the god." He nodded. *Aiee! To span the stars and yet be so savage!* I saw that he watched with eyes of strange compassion. *He thinks me savage!* I asked angrily, "Did you think you've loosed a stone would make the wall come tumbling down?"

Again he nodded, still watching me with those eyes, "Something like that."

"'Tis not a wall but a castle, with a town around it of walls. Nay, more than that, it is the very fabric of the land itself, with its mountains and its hills. One stone will make no difference." *Would it?* I wondered, or was I just talking, the savage to the star man? No. The god had sent me here so it couldn't matter to the god and the simile was apt. It was hard to see how belief in men of Brother Andrea's ilk was more than a cloak lightly worn. It must be missing entirely in Edgar.

I had never thought of belief in just that way before, but there were stones enough pulled out and lying about that one more would make no difference. The god would care no more than the sky for mortal's belief. Whatever anger I felt was gone replaced now by a sadness for him. We have the words *deafness* and *blindness* but none for the absence of any of the other four. I am very sure I would rather walk the land without my sense of sight or sound than without my sense of the god.

Then I bethought me of how he had talked of *believing in a god* and I asked him about that. He told me that different groups of people believed in different gods, each with a separate name.

"Though some argue that all are the same god, just going by a different name. Your god, what do you call him?"

I felt bewildered. "The god is not my god. The god is just the god like the sky is the sky. And the god is not," and I had trouble saying it, "…a *him!*"

"A woman?" he seemed surprised.

"No, no. I had never really thought about it before, but we only talk of the god or the presence. We never refer to the god with words like *him* or *her* or *it.*" I found it easier to get out the words a second time and we talked a while more, of the god and of my coming, but I could see that he had trouble accepting it.

"I'm sorry, Nicodemus. I know it's real to you and I've no wish to tamper with that. A man's beliefs are his own. I'm afraid how you got here beats me, but I'm grateful you came. I'm satisfied to leave it at that."

I was not so sure that I was. When the first spate of revelation ran down I had time to think at last. I recall asking him some question—I've long since forgotten what—and not listening to the answer but watching him instead. He seemed so ordinary, 'twas hard to credit he'd been sent by the god. *And from the great land!* The tales did not equivocate. 'Twas the god had commanded the people leave the evil of that place, an evil so great they had shed the very memory of what it was lest that be enough to break it out all over again. So why had the god sent a man from the great land now? Was the evil purged? How would I know?

I went troubled to bed that night and woke, sweating, from a dream, convinced he loomed above me, his hands reaching to throttle around my throat. Yet the embers of the fire showed him safely rolled into his blanket, blissfully asleep. Drifting down again, I felt the roles reverse, my hands now reaching out and grasping and that forced me wide awake. Damonryan didn't think he'd been sent by the god. Could it be that he was right, that only I was there by design? *Death dream.* I slid from my sleeping roll. *God sent?* Trying to ignore the pooling cold of the sweat in the pit behind my shoulders, I flexed my fingers. An memory could contaminate, what of a man? Mayhap 'twas the god's intent that this Greatlander never made it from the wastes? I flexed my hands a second time, looking at them. Long fingers, flickering red by the embers. I shivered, seeing them bloody. *Harper's fingers, Nicodemus, not soldiers.* All my life the god had been with me. I had been carefully led from the killing road.

I slipped back to the warmth of my bag and my foolishness washed over me like a wave. I'd so clearly been sent *for* him. He'd told me himself, had I, against all expectations, not arrived, he would have been dead within the month. Yet it begged the questions. Why was he there? What was I to do with him? The god works in strange ways. One thing my dream had made clear was I could not introduce him as a Greatlander. He'd be dead, or worse, a guest of the Temple, within a week. Whatever we did, we must go carefully. Somehow I'd have to pass him off as of the land.

§

Revelations seemed endless. Our talks conjured up the image of old Baldric teaching me to ride on Megan, except it was my mind grew sore and not my seat. Eventually, the talk ran down and we began to take thought for what he should do. Since I had come for him, it seemed to me that we should travel together, an he would, and, indeed, he was grateful for the suggestion. We agreed 'twere best he not seem to be too different. Since we were of a size, he fitted well enough into my spare set of clothes. Shoes were another problem. I'd only the boots I'd brought to Welling, kept carefully by the monks through all my years against my going, and when he looked at them he said bluntly that he wouldn't wear them anyway.

"Boots like that would kill my feet!" and from that he would not budge. Indeed, he had a point, for we tumbled out his clothes finding at last a pair of plain brown boots with the look of leather, though no one would mistake them for a pair made anywhere in the land. I gazed at the wealth of clothes strewn out so carelessly, so he said, "Would you like a pair?" Would I? The colors of the rainbow, with the lack of seams that I was coming to know, so that I was sure they would leak no water. Light, half the weight of my own, yet so sturdy that he said they would last for years, showing me no knife could cut them. Even the soles, patterned for grip with that peculiar precision that marked all the works his people wrought, would not wear out. Sorely was I tempted, for even our feet were of a size, but they would lead to more questions than I was ready to answer. I shook my head.

We agreed he would start by playing my servant.

§

I cut his hair and trimmed his beard for him, short, like a knight, for though he would play the merchant, he said that on a world without showers he must go closely cropped or go mad. What goods he might trade seemed to me a problem, the more so as he had need of a horse, "Which I'll bet won't come cheap?" he asked. I nodded, thinking of Megan who was worth half a manor, so that how I should ever replace her when she grew too old was more than I knew. "Well," he said with a grin, "Let's see what I can come up with."

Back in the cabin, he went straight to a cupboard and drew out a little box. "Will this do?" he asked, opening it like a conjurer and shining his light off a stack of tiny bars of the purest gold. "Currency's a little volatile when you voyage two years between worlds," he said, "So I always carry a little for emergencies. There's a couple of *kilograms* here, which would buy me a reasonably fine horse at home." Then his smile faded, and he looked at me anxiously, "Is gold valuable here?"

Chalices or candlesticks were all that I'd ever seen with that much gold and I tried to see the size of cup that it might make. Not so big as the great one upon the high altar at Welling Temple, but none so mean as even a duke would despise it. "There's far more than enough for a horse here," I reassured him, "Though 'twould take a goldsmith to tell you what 'tis really worth."

"Good. Let's see if there's anything else I need." As he searched I tried to imagine what it had been like when the ship, as he put it, had been alive. Already it had a ghostly air, cavern dark except where pierced by our lamps, filmed with the dry brown dust of the plain outside which blurred the wonderful surfaces and hid their subtle colors. Saddened by that, for it was those perfect surfaces, as well as the sheer size and shape of the ship, that, more than anything else, set it apart, I drifted to the console. 'Twas a machine for scribes, a letter to a key, with other keys with numbers and symbols, often in pairs, some of which I knew and others not. By pushing keys I could form any word I wanted and just to see how it might feel I picked out NICODEMUS. Nothing happened, and I tried to imagine the window above glowing white and the letters appearing in black, as Damonryan had said they would an only there were power.

Even had it worked, it seemed a tedious business, slower by far than writing, slower even than the copyists who painstakingly copied out the books in Welling's library, before the old ones should fade. About to turn away, my eyes caught sight of something above the console that I had not noticed before. Black, like the lamp that he had given me, it lay enshrined in a glassine globe, rather like Damonryan, when first I found him. Even so, I probably would have said nothing an he had not come up behind me just then, "What's this?"

"Just an info unit. It's strapped to your wrist on the ground, when you're away from the main computer. Don't need it on the ship but it's great for finding bars on Jansen's World. I keep it in that programming unit so Josh can download the latest information just before I go…" he stared at it, "…ashore." Sudden he was reaching forward and popping open the cover, "Bloody hell! I wonder."

Quickly, he strapped it to his wrist, then pushed something on the side, "Hello there!" he intoned, "Testing, one, two, three…"

A tiny, tinny voice replied, "Hello, mannikin. This is a recording."

Chapter 15

"Glory hallelujah!" He pounded me on the back, "Well done, Nicodemus. I should have thought of that." Then, in a voice of flat command, he said, "Continue message."

The little voice started up again. "Sorry about not waking you earlier, boss. I calculated you would be safer in the medicom than anywhere else and I haven't energy enough to argue with you. This planet is at the extreme limit of our range and I'm almost out of fuel. Even taking the *Loribel* straight in our landing speed will be 3.3 times normal. I don't like the range of probabilities on the deceleration forces. I'm not sure we'll make it. What I am sure of is that there won't be power enough for me when I'm done so I made this recording now. I'll be certain I save just enough to release the medicom." Damonryan gave a little snort at that. "…way, the fact that you are listening to this means you made it. Your proverbial human luck is with you.

"I hope it *is* with you, boss. There are only three planets in all the Settled Worlds with conditions closer to Terran than this one. G3 sun with 1.07 standard solar radiation, .96 standard grav. breathable air. The complete statistics are in a file marked New World. All that suggests your luck is staggering, but there is, as you would say, a wild card. Indications are this world is inhabited by intelligent life. There are no electromagnetic emissions, but roads and evidence of cultivation are visible from space. Infrared and visible emissions at night are consistent with small towns. I judge a post-bronze, pre-machine age culture, but what sorts of beings they might be I cannot tell, beyond that life seems to be carbon based. I hope you don't end up as someone's pet, or worse, their lunch. That I must leave in your hands.

"I've done my best. Sixty percent of the planet is ocean with the rest being almost all low lying swamp and reef with a few tiny, rocky islands. There is only one habitable area on the entire planet, a large mountainous island 120,000 square km. Have a look at the map. I've dropped you in a barren plain in the southwestern corner, where you should be undisturbed for a while.

"I've also downloaded to the infocom anything I thought might be useful. It won't hold all my library but its capacity might surprise you. Based on the known distribution of habitable planets I've computed it could list the inventory of every bar in the galaxy!

"So long, boss. I'll miss you. If you ever figure how to pipe enough power aboard, I'll be here."

"In a pig's eye!" Damonryan looked haunted, "Don't see any way to rig power here," he muttered, then whispered, "So long, Josh," like a man who stands, then turns from a grave.

The voice was tiny, male somehow, but high, without the rumble, so that you would never account it human when first you heard it. Yet, as he talked, you forgot that, so that the humanity came through. It would not have been hard to think some evil spirit had caught up a man and shrunk him and his voice and locked them in the box on Damonryan's wrist. The silence stretched, so I said something of the voice and the humanity I'd heard.

Idly, he strapped the little unit to his left wrist, then started to rub the great knuckles on his other hand, staring at them and rubbing, until he saw what he was doing. His mouth tightened and he abruptly stopped, "He wouldn't thank you for saying so," he said softly, "He didn't have a very high opinion of humans." The lips twisted into a wry grin, "If you'd heard him on the ship, you'd say he *was* human. He was designed that way of course—by humans, something I would twit him with when he got too unbearable." He shrugged his shoulders, "This little squeak is simply due to the smallness of the speaker in the info unit. It's not much more than a toy, really."

He turned his gray eyes on me, "He was just a *machine,* Nicodemus, an artifact, fashioned for human use. Yet I miss him." He hesitated, then asked "Does that seem strange to you?"

I thought of the voice, tiny though it was, and shook my head, "It is right for a man to mourn the death of a friend."

"Mourning." He looked back at his hands, quiet now, "I suppose that is what I'm doing. I haven't had much experience at it."

He was quiet for a time then stood up and, almost, he seemed to shake himself, like a dog coming out of water. "This settles something that's been on my mind for a while." He looked at the infocom strapped to his wrist, "Watch, Nicodemus." He turned to face me, then slowly, spinning it out, held out his wrist so the infocom faced up. His eyes found mine, and I realized he was gauging how I'd react to what it was he was about to show me. Somewhere, deep within, a smile lurked, but he made no comment, just paused a moment longer before snapping quietly, "Map!"

Despite all my resolve, I sprang back striking my head against the wall behind. It was hard enough that I think there was pain. An so, 'twas a sixteenth note, high and sharp mayhap, but swallowed whole by the chord of awe that swelled behind. I stared at what it was he'd wrought—a ball of purest light that glowed between us, hanging in the air and yet, somehow, writhing with life. For a moment I felt an the presence hovered there, not as a voice heard distant in my brain but revealed full in awful majesty. Without thinking, I began to sink to my knees when he stopped me.

"It's all right." The voice was gentle, an to a child, "It's just a picture of your world."

A picture! Another of his artifacts, but dear the god, what artist ever drew in such colors, or used the living air as his canvas? I stared at it, trying to force myself to see past the wonder, to see what it was he saw. A ball, a ball in the air two spans and a bit across, of the purest colors, glowing blues and greens and blacks, almost hurtful in its beauty; a ball that turned stately there before us so that we could see all its aspects.

"My ...*world?*"

"That's right." He nodded his head up and down and his wrist trembled with the motion so the ball, the *world,* quivered with it. Somehow, the image was coming from the infocom.

"More or less as I would have seen it from space," he continued. Moving his finger, he stroked a patch of green,

"Label: the land," he said, in what I was coming to recognize as his speaking-to-the-infocom-voice. "Expand, to the land."

At once the ball disappeared, to be replaced by what I slowly recognized as a map of the land. But what a map! The sea in blue and blues, shading darker outward in stripes as it moved away. The land itself in greens and browns, with mountains standing up and out from it, so real I could find the fingers of the god and see each one. I tried to touch them, but my hand passed through, the map rippling an it were smoke, then closing faultlessly behind as I withdrew in haste.

"This red X is where we are," his voice broke in upon my reverie, "And these ones mark what Josh thought were probably towns." I studied them with a frown, walking the land in my mind, not used to maps though I had seen enough at Welling to recognize this for what it was.

"Carvigal," I said at last, pointing, "And Estonval..." He repeated the names to the units, and letters like the ones on the jewel on the side of the casket sprung up on the map, tiny but readable, marking the towns.

'Twas purest magic, and yet he'd called it a toy. Then I laughed, "It spelled them wrong!"

"Ah well. Can't hold it responsible for foreign spellings. Correct it. Just say the letters," he prompted.

And so I did, and so it did, reforming the words in an instant. Delighted, catching suddenly the spirit of the toy, I named all the towns it had found, then pointed at the fingers of the god and had it label Welling Abbey.

Damonryan smiled at that and said softly, "Magnify!"

Again the image changed and it seemed I flew with the clouds, and below me lay Welling Fjord, cupped in the fingers, the islands clear and even the serpentine track with a box at the bottom.

"The jetty!" I breathed, pointing at it.

"And this must be the monastery," he agreed, "Did Josh get the buildings right?"

I stared, trying to see the marks as buildings, recognizing them at last as outlines, "Yes. This is the temple and here the barns..." Once I got the trick of it the rest became clear, though I laughed, "Brother Canus would not be pleased to see his new chapel abuilding called a ruin!"

He joined into the laughter, though not with his usual gusto, "Well, you can fix it later, and label all the buildings as well if you've a mind." He took a breath, "So you understand my map, Nicodemus, and that it is accurate?" I nodded, wondering where he was driving. "Stand behind me so we get the same point of view."

As soon as I had moved he snapped a string of commands and again the ball of the world floated before me, turning now, dark on the left and bright on the right. "This is the dawn line," he said, pointing, "And here, the land rotates into it."

Even as I watched, the sun caught the tops of the mountains of the Fastness, then burst upon the plains of Dankar, Angleterre and Suthy, before catching again the Welling and then finally lighting up Westernesse. "See how green the land appears in the light. That is caused by the vegetation. Now, let's look at the rest of your world, let's look for the Great Land."

"Here," I pointed to a great blue green band wound round the center of the world like a sash.

"Can't be. Josh said it was all swamp and reef. It must be ungodly hot, up there on the equator." He watched it turn for a moment, then said reflectively, "It girdles your whole world. That's what keeps your atmosphere going —there's probably as much *chlorophyll* there as in all the forests of Unity." He brought his gaze back to me, "It's no place for humans, Nicodemus."

I watched as the world turned before me, "It must be. There's nowhere else."

"Mmm." The sound was non-committal, "Expand." He traced the lines on the image that flew before us, "Josh had no time to do a proper survey so there's not the same detail here as for the land. Still, you can see there's no real *land* here. No one could live here."

Long I watched where his fingers traced, thinking over what it was he was telling me. The land came up again and then departed, but his fingers never wavered.

"You are saying there is no Great Land."

Flicking his wrist, the image disappeared and he turned to me, "Not quite. I'm saying it was not on this planet."

I gazed hard at him, struggling to grasp where it was he drove, part of me reaching out for it and part of me thrusting it away.

He sighed, "I've known since I first saw you, Nicodemus. In twelve hundred and fifty years of space travel we have never encountered another intelligent race. That doesn't mean they're not out there, just that space is so damn *big*. But we did find plenty of life and though it was often similar to ours—most plants have some form of leaf, for example—it was also wildly different. But you are *human* and…," he paused, "We speak the same language. That was the clincher. There have been some crazy theories that humans did not evolve on earth but were seeded there by space spores borne on meteorites, or some other such silly nonsense. I suppose it might just be possible, that it could explain human beings evolving on two separate worlds. But there's no way they could speak the same language. Face it, Nicodemus. Your own history says you came from elsewhere, from the great land. True enough except that the ship must have been a space ship and the great land another planet."

"We have no *machines,* none of this, this *technology* you speak of. We could never build such a ship!" I protested.

"Not now, perhaps. What year did you say this was?"

"Seven hundred and ninety-one."

"And you date that from your Coming?" I nodded. "Mmm. Your year's shorter than ours on Unity but it's only a little longer than a standard year. Time enough for your ancestors to lose their skills, particularly since they didn't have to build the ship anyway, only buy it. From what you've told me of your Tales, it sounds as if they were pretty agrarian in their outlook in the first place."

I was about to protest when the floor dropped with a massive shuddering jerk that sprawled us sliding down the floor to fetch up sharply against a wall. "What was that?"

"The ship." I tried to struggle up but he grabbed me, "Freeze! Something's given way. Anything could set it off again." We lay in a tangle for long seconds, listening. At length, he let go

my arm, and said just three clipped words, "Out. Now. Quietly."
Gently, he pushed me. What had been more or less level floor
before, now tilted wildly, making passage difficult. 'Twas as well it
had been wall before for there were fittings enough to give us
handholds. It seemed an eon but at last I made the rent we used
for a door. Peering out, I found to my dismay, the ground had
receded.

"What's the matter?"

"'Tis almost twenty feet."

He wriggled up beside me, "Space! We'd better jump."

'Twas a long drop. As dry as the barrens are the ground is
like stone. Even hanging first by my fingertips I'd the breath
knocked out of me. Sa. At that we were lucky we did nothing
worse.

When at last I got to my feet I found Damonryan inspecting
his ship. He said nothing as I joined him. He didn't have to. The
problem was clear. A great section of the cliff top had sheared
away under the weight of his steel steed and now it balanced very
precariously on the edge. The starman got down and crawled
carefully up to the precipice. When at length he got back he stood
up and dusted off his pants, "Gone," he said in an awed voice.
"Fifty *meters* of cliff top and it has disappeared into the sea as if it
had never been. Only the scar is left."

The ship shimmered in the sunshine, balanced like a plank
left by children who'd been playing at see-and-saw. For the first
time, with its nose thrust out into open space I could see how it
must have looked in flight. But it couldn't last. All its weight was
on its fulcrum, now the new edge of the cliff. 'Tis not for nothing
the Westernesse fisherfolk call that kind of stone *rottenrock*. With a
grinding roar, the pivot point sheared away and Damonryan's
ship overbalanced and toppled down the cliff face and into the
sea.

§

There must have been strong currents there for by next day
the plume of dirt had cleared from the water. Lying gingerly on
the cliff edge we thought we could see a long way but the water

went down a long way. 'Twas hot and windless, so it sparkled deep green at us and we could see the flashing schools of fish but no sign of the Loribel.

Easing back from the edge, Damonryan stood up and brushed his clothes, "That's it," he said, "She's gone." His face was a mask. Whatever he was thinking, I couldn't tell.

I squinted at the sun and thought of my water. We'd gotten some from the ship, but not much. "Best we go too."

§

We kept to our own thoughts as we worked our way north. I think he mourned his ship but he wouldn't talk of it. I had much to think on myself. What he had told me was a hard thing and a great idea to accept; but I meditated upon it as we walked and found it had the taste of truth. Hearing him talk of languages, I had still thought in my old way, that people speak language, so that it did not seem to me strange that a starman and I should understand one another. Even when I had grasped his surprise and its roots, I had seen no farther. Now I rehearsed the Tales from end to end, carding them in my mind to look for errant strands. Not a line was there to say we had come for the stars; but an for ship you saw a tower of steel like Damonryan's, and for Great Land you read Great World and for seas you put in the reaches of space, neither was there a line to say it nay. Most telling was that the tales used only words for these three things, like the labels on Damonryan's map that could be changed in an instant. Not even the sea is described, though the stars are, by which they steered, or *through which they came.* In the end I thought, *the truth of it we'll never know, and mayhap it doesn't matter* but I also thought that Damonryan was in the right of it. What else had we lost in coming to the land?

I thought of the man himself. At his ship, times he'd been like a child, voluble, excited, laughing at newness; times he was a baron, commanding, used to being obeyed; but always, he was familiar, not talking up or down but always to, always *with*—a man I hardly knew, treating me as his oldest friend. I found it disconcerting. True, I'd rescued him, but, short of being a baron,

I would have expected that would make him talk *up*, at least at first. And a baron would never talk aught but *down*, no matter how beholden. Not knowing what to make of this, I found I'd fallen into the habit of thinking him a little simple. Glancing over, I found him watching me, an he knew what was going on in my mind. There was more than mourning here. Startled, I realized he was deliberately holding his peace. Before his ship had slipped over the edge he had made his point. Now he was showing a tact and subtlety I'd not known he had.

I found myself studying him as we walked. He had a softness about the edges that you didn't see often, like a priest whose fiefly sinecure comes with more good living than duties. He walked like one too, not easily, but an he'd to master it at first, then painfully as the miles came on. Not a man used to riding shank's mare for any great way. *And is that surprising, given what he's told you?* Why should a people who can fly on steel walk? Yet he simply set his lips and kept on, and I realized he would come to it, faster than any priest. For all his softness, he had moved round our little camp like a tumbler, supple of body and quick of foot.

When we switched, it became plain he was not used to any kind of mare. "Don't your steel steeds have saddles, then?"

"Contoured seats," he grimaced, "Well padded ones that accommodate themselves to your body. Christ! I don't know that I wouldn't rather walk!"

"We can both walk," I offered, "And lead Megan."

"Don't tempt me." His lips narrowed to a line, "I've got to learn sometime."

Chapter 16

Though I did not know the country, we had as guide his map which had more detail the closer you came to his ship, so in the country we crossed even the streams and tracks were marked. By the first night we had reached water and by the second had gained the first of the tracks. We rode by turns, but Damonryan those first two days grew weary either way and dropped to sleep before even he had finished his evening meal. Yet he was a good companion, always uncomplaining, gay or serious as the turn required, a man who could talk or listen and always knew when I had need of thought and so held his peace. By the third day he'd bounced back, and took great interest in how to catch a coney and find the herbs and cook it on the fire. After the meal was finished he rolled up his sleeve and declared his intention *to see what Josh had packed.* He laughed as he said it but that died quickly to a low whistle, "Josh wasn't kidding!"

Moving behind him I saw, above his wrist, a glowing page of white that floated in the air, covered in colored letters and symbols. Some of the words were clear enough but I could make little sense of the whole.

"It's a catalogue," he explained, "A list of the books he put into the infocom. I'd no idea it would hold so much." *Books!* They were not books as I knew them. Oh they had writing all right, or printing, in the perfect letters I'd already come to expect; but they could create things in the space before us, exactly like the map. An you would read about horses, then it would show the beast to you, or have it run, so you would swear 'twas the creature itself before you. I saw there the insides of a man, the bones, the nerves, the muscles, you could dress him layer by layer, or turn him about or expand the *image,* as he called these wondrous pictures, to look at any part, to see how the heart or lungs were built, or even the eyes or the mind. There were a thousand thousand other things and more, numbers then I had no names for.

" 'Tis the fount of all knowledge!" I exclaimed at last.

"Not quite," he replied. "Josh has all of it. He's a copy of the entire Congress Library aboard, which includes every book known on the Settled Worlds. This is just a small sample, but since it includes the *Encyclopedia Galactica* you're not far wrong. It comes as close to being a fount as a thousand volume compendium can."

"A thousand volumes. That's almost as many as in Welling Library."

"Nicodemus, old son," he said, grinning, "There's over twenty-three thousand volumes in here!"

How can a library that exceeds even that of Weirston Abbey, that holds rooms and rooms of books, packed so high the monks must get the top ones with a ladder, how can all that be strapped to a man's wrist? I had seen his tower and its great black bell, seen the sky fire and the gigantic ring it left upon the plain; even his name rang of Ryan, the nightrider, so I saw him ride his steed of steel across the stars. But this, this infocom, this tiny little thing of mundane name that held such awesome power and beauty, this passed belief.

Surely it was magic! An I, who should have known better, could think so, how then to blame the simpler souls that after were to see only mystery, an object of awe, a talisman of great potency held up to them, the Oracle; but he was able to show me, there, that night, that it was not magic. He showed me the simple bricks, called *atoms,* of which all matter is composed. There are scarce two hundred in all so that some things, like iron and gold, are bricked up of atoms of a single kind, atoms of iron and gold, while bricks of two kinds must be used for water.

There are youngsters now can tell this tale better than I, but what matters is how small these atoms are. Small beyond imagining, so the number of them that dances upon the head of the pin needs almost a score of zeroes to write, more atoms of iron than a beach has grains of sand, or a plain blades of grass. Inside the Oracle is a simple crystal wafer, half an inch on a side and a tenth in thickness. And though it takes a hundred atoms to hold a single letter, yet I have done the calculations and there are atoms and greatly to spare to hold all those volumes.

Ah well, I worked with it for long and mayhap I take for granted what I should not. I know I sometimes joined with Damonryan in cursing it when it was slow to find a thing we wanted. Wonder is no bad thing when it is not misused. It is only its misuse I rail against.

Even late to our sleeping rolls and late abroad, we crested the last of the barren ridges by mid afternoon the following day and gazed down on the southernmost of the Westernesse baronies, the strangely named Stanley's Pipe. Children the land over would mock one of their number as the Baron of Stanley's Pipe, most never knowing there really was such a man. The fields and vineyards of the barony stretched out across the plain, spring green still but shimmering in a sun would make them sere by summer. Eastwards lay the Bay of Rundel, close enough that we could hear the distant crash of breakers, then racing away north and east in a great sweeping curve of blue that disappeared into the rising purple of the Fastness, lost in the heat haze behind.

"An honest-to-god working castle!" breathed Damonryan behind me, pointing away to the north.

"Why do you shake your head like that?"

"Was I?" he seemed bemused, "It looks just like pictures I've seen of castles back on old Earth. I feel as if I've come through some kind of time warp. You must have had some pretty romantic folk to bring those along with you."

I shrugged, "That one is the seat of Baron Brunil. 'Tis a pleasant enough place—I was there with Bellarus, years ago, when we worked their harvest fair—but *romantic* is not the word I would have chosen. Anyway, castles were not brought by the people."

He turned from his awed regard of the distant keep and stared at me, "What do you mean?"

"The Temple keeps records. The first castle was built at Anendor, here in the Westernesse, only about three hundred years ago." 'Twas my turn to point, "But there is our destination." In all the sweep of shore there was but a single inlet, somewhat to the north of us, in which nestled a tiny fishing village. No ships of any size could shelter there but I hoped to find a fisherman would take us across to Suthy. After six years spent in Welling, I'd an itch to see the eastern plains again and it was a long and wet and weary ride through Westernesse, with its endless rains north of Stanley's Pipe and its dripping, tangled woods that marched all the way up the western walls of the Fastness.

As we moved off, down the path, he took one last long look at the castle. "Someone brought a book," he muttered.

§

The village held but a single tavern, small and mean from without but snug enough inside, an you didn't mind the smell of fish that soaked it through and through. With no coin between us we had decided he should play my servant and the landlord was happy enough to feed us both and let us have one of his two tiny rooms. Inspecting it, I found it clean and nodded my agreement, though in truth we had but little choice.

Damonryan sputtered, as soon as he had left, "But there's only one bed."

I smiled at his discomfiture, "Aye. 'Tis usual for the servant to sleep on a rug upon the floor, but never mind. The bed will hold us both." In the event, I had misread him. Unless they were lovers or children, his people never slept more than one to a bed. "I'm sorry, Damonryan. He must needs keep his other room for paying customers. Besides," I could not resist adding, "An another party were to come in, you might have to share that bed with three or four!" It was the first of many such shocks for him and, though I was often amused, he rode them like a seaman on rough waves, lurching a little from time to time but always recovering to take the next one easily. I wondered an I would do as well were our roles reversed.

Supper came early. An it was plain, it was also good, so even Damonryan exclaimed. "Excellent! What is it?"

"Sounderfish, probably caught fresh today, and grilled very lightly over the fire."

He pushed his fork in again and took another bite, rolling it around on his tongue, "Hmmmm! I could sell it for a fortune back at the Settled Worlds."

"It's expensive enough in Dankar, as it is only caught in the Bay of Rundel." I stopped then, "You don't exclaim at potatoes or carrots or horses. How is it you don't have sounderfish?"

"Because it's native to the land. Anything we have in common, horses and carrots and potatoes and lots of other things I've noticed, like rabbits and grass and elm trees, must have been brought by the people. Anything we don't have in common, is native."

He went back to his eating, watching me over his fork while I thought that through, "The Tales do say that the people brought seed and livestock and planted grain when they arrived…" I thought about his comment and grinned, "…but no books. They wanted as little contamination from the Great Land as possible."

He ignored the last, "They planted more than grain. Nicodemus, I'm no biologist, but even out in the barrens I saw more plants that looked familiar than not. My guess is that the local species don't compete well with the imports, but even so, that must have been a hell of a big ship the people came on!" He said no more, though for a time it became a game between us to mark what had been of the land and what had been brought, with the infocom our referee. His guess was good, as so many of them were, for the brought prevailed above the native. I viewed that with no little pride until he showed me how the native were still in full retreat. Older plants filled many parts of the herbalist's chest. From that point on I viewed the land through somewhat different eyes.

As fisher folk must be at their nets and traps before the dawn, I started as soon we were done, nervous to be playing again after all these years, knowing I must give them my best, and concerned how Damonryan would make out on his own. I need not have worried. They kept me at it until the small hours. I was pleased enough to oblige, happy to have an audience again, not realizing how I had missed a crowd. As for the starman, he had the knack for getting on with people, I was to find out who it didn't matter. He soon was elbows deep in fishermen, talking and laughing an he'd known them all his life. An they found his way of talking strange, why they knew enough to know that theirs was not the only accent in the land, yet not enough to know that his was nowhere of the land.

At last, as I was about to help him stagger off to bed, the landlord said, "I'm sorry about the hour, Harper, but fishermen do like to have a time, and there's precious little chance they gets, 'ereabouts." He bent to wipe a table and I waited. The Rundel fisher folk won't look at you when they make a request, nor make it direct either. "They'd be pleased an you were staying a little."

That was the opening I'd been waiting for, "Enough to take us and my horse across to Suthy?"

He pulled a face at that, "There only be one boat big enough for the 'orse, sir. But I'll see what I can do."

By next day it had been arranged. For three nights more play, the fisherman who owned the biggest boat would take us across. How he was to be paid or by whom I never found out. 'Tis best not to inquire too closely into such arrangements, but the landlord took good care to let the word out about the countryside. By the third night there were soldiers down from the castle.

Knowing I would be playing again, the crowd was not too loath to let us earlier to our beds on the intervening evenings. Any fears that Damonryan renewed in me that he might be overfond of his drink he put to rest, for never again did he need to be helped off to the bed. Indeed, an he had, 'twould not have been me who helped him. Both nights he went with a serving wench, but I saw he went under his own sail and was content. Even then I need not have worried. I was to find that even on the very rare occasions he drank to staggering, still he could hold his tongue. The real wonder though was that he took a different wench each night, with never a penny for either; yet had both in charity with him and even each other.

Never one to simply hold to what he had when he could go forward, he decided on the final eve, once I was safely playing, to see an he could get the soldiers to accept him. Halfway through the night he was sitting at their table and to look, but for the lack of mail you would say he were one of them. Though I tightened my lips at the risk, we would be soon in more knowledgeable company, so who could say but that the bolder course were best.

At any rate, he was getting on, except mayhap with the sergeant, who seemed put out at his popularity with the serving girls.

Though we'd arranged to go at dawn, the company was not content to let us early to our beds, wanting the fullest measure from this their final night. 'Twas a hard life they lived and *times* as they called them, like this were scarce enough, so I could not find it in my heart to blame them; and in truth, they were a good audience, as simple folk often are, so there was much for me to enjoy. Three hours before the dawn the landlord flared his torches and called out for the final round. Fingering the harp, wondering what I might give them for a final song, I saw Damonryan signaling a serving wench, his empty tankard on his head, a look of comic misery painted on his face. Behind him, the sergeant was staring and I saw to my horror that his sleeve had slipped back and exposed the infocom strapped to his wrist. Looking at the server, he didn't see what he'd exposed, or the sergeant's stare.

"What's that then?" As he spoke the sergeant reached up and struck Damonryan's wrist. Whirling back and pulling his hand down, he was yet too late to stop the infocom which sprang to life and hurled the map into the air before the goggling eyes of those around him. The howl of surprise and the map itself, bright as a flame in the tavern's dark, drew the eyes of all in the room. There was pandemonium before he could switch it off, and no few cries of *Demon!*

Before things could get out of hand I stood tall and cried out, "Hold! 'Tis no such thing. Strange, it may be, but I have looked at it closely and there is no harm in it." I used the most powerful of my voices, and they quieted, uneasy still, but respectful of a harper.

"What is it, then?" a voice called out.

Before I could answer, Damonryan answered smoothly, almost disdainfully, "A toy, to amuse the ladies, I hope to sell in Dankar. 'Tis a crystal that catches the sun and holds its light until it is rubbed."

I held my breath, hoping that would suffice. "Let us see the trick again," another called.

"Nay, I cannot," he answered easily, "One flash and it is gone until next I charge it with the sun."

There was a long silence and they looked at each other, then one man said, "Well, an the harper says 'tis all right" and I took that as a cue and announced the final song, trailing the opening chords as I did so. That settled them, and I gave them another pair to get them through their drink, then bowed to uneasy applause.

"And so, goodnight!" I bowed again, catching the landlord's eye, and he started to gentle them out.

When most had gone, Damonryan began to rise, but the sergeant grabbed his wrist again, so that I prayed he would not start the infocom and give him the lie. "Tales for fishermen!" he muttered, "That's no toy. What's a draggletail like you doing with a thing like that? I'm thinking that's something the Baron would like to know."

I started forward but Damonryan caught my eye and shook his head, with a commanding look I'd not seen before. "I believe that's my wrist you're holding," he said to the sergeant, pleasantly enough.

"So I am," the sergeant growled, "What of it?"

He shrugged, and with little effort that I could see, stood up twisting his way from the sergeant's grip with a flick that had the massive soldier rubbing his thumb. "Good night to you, sergeant," he said pleasantly.

That was too much for the man. With a bellow, he flung the table aside into splinters and charged. Moving faster than any man I'd ever seen, Damonryan shifted slightly to one side like summer lightning that dances from cloud to cloud. Instead of sweeping his opponent before him, as I, and no doubt he, expected, the sergeant left only his arm behind while he flew past so there was a pop and a squeal of pain even before he hit the floor. Leaving him gasping, the starman turned and disposed as quickly of two soldiers who tried to circle him, flowing like water, a foot whirling high in an arc that somehow came in from the wrong side to kick a knife from one man's hand. Faster than thought, it was done, three men on the floor. The rest of the soldiery hung back before his smile, awe and fear in their eyes, some no doubt thinking that the demon was the man and not what he bore on his wrist.

Urgent in me was the thought that now we must leave, must put this behind us before folk inquired too close, and I feared lest the sergeant had slammed the door. He was sitting now, groaning and holding his shoulder, all fight gone out of him. All around me were eyes, white with concern, the landlord and the fisher folk that were left, thinking what this should mean. Striding over, I examined his shoulder to give me time to think, though I'd little doubt it was dislocated.

"I have played at Stanley castle and know your lord of old for an honorable man," I began. This was to stretch the truth a bit, for it had been Bellarus who played and I'd not the slightest idea how honorable Lord Brunil was; but it seemed to me I had thought him a hard master and my shaft was rewarded. I saw alarm start in the sergeant's eyes. Whatever I knew of his lord, I was almost certain he had wanted the infocom for his own, and his eyes confirmed my suspicion. Rather than accuse him outright, I said, "This man," nodding with some disdain at Damonryan, whose eyes twinkled in appreciation, "Is my servant. To steal from him is to steal from a harper." The point was contentious in law, but I doubted the sergeant was in any shape to appreciate such fine distinctions and, indeed, he began to look thoroughly uneasy. "An I come before the Baron, be sure that I shall press charges; but I have urgent business in Suthy and am willing to let this matter drop, an you give your word to a harper you will do likewise."

Hoarsely, he replied, "I didn't know he was your servant, harper. There was no 'arm intended. I was only trying to do my duty." Steadily I regarded him, and he dropped his eyes, "Aye, harper. T'affair's over as far as I'm concerned."

"Witness?" I called.

There was a chorus of gleeful replies, "Aye. Witness!"

That put paid to it as far as the sergeant was concerned. He would get no credit out of this affair by bringing it to the Baron. He would keep his mouth shut and I rather thought I could depend on him to see that his men toed the line as well.

With Damonryan's help, an irony that made the starman grin even as the sweat started out on his victim's forehead, I popped his shoulder back in place and bound it for him, bidding him give it a chance to heal. Then extracting from him the price of the table, I sent him on his way. Since a man with a useless shoulder would not long be a sergeant in Baron Brunil's pay, he went not only cowed but grateful.

§

"I'm sorry, Nicodemus."

"Hmmm. Not your fault." I pulled off my boots, "Still, 'tis a dangerous toy," that was putting it mildly. For all its marvels, I was tempted to bury it deep in some hole, but that the god had so clearly meant for him to have it. "Best you pack it out of sight. Get some sleep." I rolled determinedly into the bed. 'Twas late, and we were away at first light.

"I can't keep it packed away all the time. Away from the ship it needs sunlight to run."

I rolled back on my elbow, "I thought that a merry tale!"

"No tale. It *is* a crystal, I told you that already. The only stretch I made was the single flash. It'll run a week on a few hours of good sunshine."

I whistled low. An he would use it, meant he must carry it in plain sight at least some of the time.

"But, Nikki, it was my fault. I never thought of it, but I could have secured it. Here I'll show you. Activate."

Obediently, the infocom switched on.

"Password, Activation, Damonryan," he thought a moment, then grinned, "Jaysus, Mary and Joseff!" He turned to me, "Now you think of one."

"Me?"

"Sure, something could happen to me. You might as well be able to use it. It keys to each voice that's authorized to use it, so you need your own password. Something not too obvious."

I hesitated, "Password?" and looked at him. He nodded, "Activation," I said slowly, "Nicodemus," then thought a moment longer, before giving it my key.

"Good. Shutdown!" he said, then, with satisfaction, "It won't make a peep until it hears the right password in the right voice. Let's get some sleep."

Chapter 17

The fisher folk hewed to their bargain. In fact, the village complete turned out in the dawning mists to see us off with a gusto that told me our besting of the soldiers had been popular. The boatman chortled most of the day across, and would see again the crystal flash that was the sergeant's undoing. Happily, it was cloudy all the way, so Damonryan could tell him straightfaced, there was too little sun to capture.

I smiled at that but little else. The fisherman would prattle happily to Damonryan but was in awe of a harper, so I was left to my own thoughts. Our first encounter had gone both better and worse than I'd imagined, but we'd rubbed tolerably through. Suthy, with its quicksilver folk and their well honed delight in mischief would prove a sterner test. I'd no doubt but we'd troubles to come. Yet, watching him with the old fisherman, I could not see their shape and it seemed bootless to worry about what I could not see. The god would send what the god would send.

'Twas the god's sending that worried me. While made sense for Damonryan to continue to play my attendant, it didn't take the conduit of the god to see a greater pattern than that was in the weaving. Idly, I picked a thread from a hole in the hose they'd given me so grudgingly at Welling, and twirled it between my fingers. Harper green. One color of one strand I knew and mayhap that it was a leader for a second, to shepherd it along, tucked under, until it should find its proper place in the pattern. I could not even tell what Damonryan's color might be. Wryly, an to discard the first would reveal the second, I flipped the thread into the sea; but the wind snatched at it before it hit the waves and threw it back in my lap. Not yet then. I sighed, hearing the sounds of the waves against a cliff. We were there. I looked at the thread again, only sure that Damonryan's would not be the lighter green of my servant. An 'twas me that was sent to the barrens, it seemed more like I would end as his servant.

§

Tanrith looked a sleepy place, washed in a sun that had emerged at last, and ringed with hills that hem it in so much you'd say there was scarce room left for a cat. The houses wink whitely up the hillside so steeply that, from out to sea, they seem to be stacked, each on top of each. From the headland juts a mole, as the locals like to call it, though 'tis only boulders they have tumbled into the sea, without bole or fender or hoist upon all its length. Still, it makes a harbor, which otherwise would just have been a dint in the coast, and ships are safe when tied behind it. 'Twas proper port enough for our purposes. Not wishing to voice aloud our need, we tramped its winding lanes a while, and found Damonryan a goldsmith.

"What poor assistance may I render to a harper?"

After the heat and the glare of whitewashed walls outside, it was like stepping into a cave. Our eyes must fight to regain the dark, but as they did so, I found my image fading. Cool it was, certainly, how not? With walls of sunbaked mud full two feet thick. But not dank like a cave, dry instead, with only the smell of long dead dust.

My inquisitor stared calmly at me, used to waiting for his visitor's eyes, taking the time to sum us up. He was a little man, old and bald and fat, in a robe of some faded red stuff, who might have been ridiculous were it not for the coldness in his eyes. *Not much profit in penurious harpers.* Somehow, he didn't strike me as a man cared much for music.

"My friend, here," I indicated. Damonryan had insisted, before we went in, on doing the talking. I was not so sure it was wise but I had at last agreed when he pointed out it *was* his gold.

The old man's eyes shifted and I saw there a look of uncertainty that he could not quite hold back, but he said nothing, trying to keep his gaze now on Damonryan, while all the time watching me from out the corner.

The starman started, like a guilty child. He'd been peering all around the shop, though I saw nothing there to wonder at, one goldsmith being much of a muchness with any other. Then I remembered 'twas all new to him and looked again to see it as he might: small and dingy, with darkwashed walls that hid from what little light slipped in through the slits of windows; a gold bracelet or two upon display, well out of reach, just good enough to pique the buyer's interest, the rest locked away, out back, some of it, some of it at home, never too much in one place; a set of scales, well oiled I saw, the cleanest thing in the place; the inevitable display of used goods, small and shabby, traded for a few coppers, and now displayed for sale for a few more. I clucked to myself, knowing I should have warned him that looks meant nothing, that no goldsmith will willingly show how much wealth he truly has.

The cold little man came to his inevitable conclusion. Waving at the display, he said smoothly, "There is something the young sir fancies?"

"Just," he replied, ignoring the dusty case, "Fair value for…this," with great delicacy he extracted a package from his pocket, unwrapped it and placed five of his bars upon the scales. "Can you change us this and as much again," he asked, looking scornfully around the shop, "Or do we go elsewhere?"

'Twas clear the bars were strange to him, rectangular but rounded everywhere, perfect pieces of some jeweler's art though 'twere but bars, smooth and gleaming with a whiteness I'd never seen before in gold. Damonryan had told me 'twas the purest possible gold, down to the last of his atoms. To judge by the look in the goldsmith's face, he'd never seen that color either. He stared at it as if he thought it was a rabbit would bolt back down its hole at any moment. Convinced at last it would not disappear, he shifted his gaze back to Damonryan, seeing him, I think, for the first time.

"Elsewhere?" He wet his lips thinly, "No, good master, you've come to the right place. No better price will you get than Sharf's!" From beneath the counter the goldsmith extracted a box of weights and at once set about with his balancing.

"A strange size," he muttered, "Two pounds, and a bit more." He kept up his muttering, adding weights until shortly he had balanced out the bar. "There," he beamed.

My companion looked at him and then at the pan and then back at the goldsmith. From where I stood, he got stare for level stare, but he must have seen something I didn't. All at once, his eyes never leaving the man, he reached out and, almost delicately, brushed the weights from the pan.

"Oh, sir, have a care!" the little man screeched angrily, scuttling to catch them before they hit the table, "These are most precise and not to be battered about!"

Ignoring him, Damonryan extracted from his pocket the second packet, unwrapped it and placed the other five bars on the pan where the weights had been. The scales quivered in equivalence. Swiftly, like a magician at a fair, he switched bars between the pans and found the same again.

"Scales are all right," he grunted, "And the bars undamaged." He looked the smith, "Which leaves your …ah, precision, weights."

Picking up one of the two larger weights, the starman asked, "How much?"

"A pound!" snapped the smith, all indignation, "Scaled to the standard pound kept in the Prince's own vaults. The same, good sir, as a pound in Dankar or Westernesse or even," he sniffed his suspicions, "The wilds of the Fastness!"

Damonryan ignored his sarcasm and picked up a smaller weight, "And this?"

"One ounce,…"

"Verified by the Prince himself, I know. This?"

"A grain."

"Which is?"

"One two hundred and fortieth part of a pound." The smith seemed emboldened by this ignorance, "These are yearly checked, there is naught wrong …"

"So, the fifteenth part of an ounce." Seeing the look on the little man's face, he laughed, "Surprised a barbarian from the Fastness can calculate?" Damonryan picked up the two large weights, and clicked them against the counter one by one, "Two pounds, and fifteen, and thirty," here he clicked down the two one ounce weights, "And five more grains. Thirteen grains short."

"Sir, my weights are true!"

"You mean they would be by the time we got back with the Prince's measurer." He regarded him for a long moment, before saying quietly, "Why don't you get out your other set?"

"Sir, I…"

"Never mind. Come, Nicodemus, let us go in search of an honest man!" He reached for the gold.

The smith fairly screeched, "Sir, let us not be hasty. 'Tis possible my old set has been knocked about a whit. I do keep another set, for my better customers you understand…"

Damonryan smiled at him sweetly, "Including the Prince and his men, no doubt."

The gold seemed to fascinate the smith. His eye never left it as he reached slowly down and back, coming up with a second box of weights. The box was cleaner, the weights more carefully packed than the first.

"It seems you have few better customers," I observed, amused.

He shot me a dirty look for my troubles, but said nothing further, concentrating instead on weighing up the gold.

"Two pounds, three and two, sir," he was almost apologetic, "That's forty-seven grains above two pounds."

Damonryan nodded curt acceptance and they began to dicker over the price and the assay, but 'twas clear the heart had gone from the little smith. In the end they settled for full face value, forty-four nobles, and the wristbands thrown in for good measure. The starman rang a coin for me and when I nodded, he quickly did the rest but the smith had abandoned the lists. All chimed true.

Outside, I asked him how it was he'd known the weights were heavy.

"I didn't. But after thirty years of trading, I know a cheat when I see one. It was simply a matter of working out how he was doing it."

"But it was in pounds." I was still bemused, "You said you didn't use them. And how could you know of the Prince's measurer? I didn't even know he had one."

"Neither did I. But nobody keeps standard weights in a vault unless they use them for reference, and it was a fair bet whatever official they use works for the Prince. As for the pounds, I looked up the conversion in the infocom. My only gamble was that they hadn't changed in eight hundred years." He cracked a laugh, then grew pensive, "You know, Nikki, pounds were out of date long before your people left Earth. Someone had to work fairly hard to reinstate them. I wonder why they bothered."

We inquired where we might buy a horse and, in gay good spirits, he bought me lunch in a tavern.

"Why so glum?" The server had left us with our food and the beer that he so loved.

"Am I?" I toyed with the pie, pushing pastry flakes around in the steaming gravy.

"What?"

I realized I was bothered, and sudden, I knew why. "You're usually an easy man, Damonryan, and that's just fine. Getting on with folks is a good way to put talk to rest." I chased a pea around with my mother's fork, trying to find how to explain to him what I was having trouble explaining to myself. "When you talked—no, *dealt*—with that smith, I felt I was in the presence of a noble, a baron, or at least a powerful knight." I snorted, "I doubt an the smith would be surprised an you were the Prince himself, dressed up in motley."

He laughed at that, disposed more to be pleased with the image than worried.

"'Tis all very well with a little mouse of a goldsmith, but try that with a knight or a baron and it will lead to serious trouble."

Seeing me offended, he was at once contrite, "I'm sorry, Nikki. It *is* your planet." He chewed for a while, deep in thought, then said finally, "My worlds are just as hierarchical as yours. Call it human nature, call it efficient management, all societies seem to need a pyramid. The only difference is you're born to your places, while we earn ours, but you yourself are proof that even that can be changed. Sure I've a rough tongue when I need it, but I never sassed my captain. I know how to deal up the hierarchy as well as down."

I saw the flaw. "You respected your captain. He earned his position..." he grinned at that but said nothing and I plowed on, "...how an you don't respect a man yet he holds position over you because he was born to it?"

"Just because I think our system is better doesn't mean it's perfect," he growled. "The incompetents have to do something and some positions seem to positively attract them. Anyone who's had to stroke a Dalmity customs agent or a jumped-up Unitarian senator can talk to one of your knights or barons!"

With that, I had to be satisfied. For all his talk, I knew the differences ran deep, and felt the seeds of trouble; but where or how I knew not. I consoled myself that, in the end, he must make his own way. Yet 'twas into my hands the god had dropped him, and I must do all I could in the meantime to ease his course.

Since only donkeys could negotiate the steep ways of Tanrith with anything like a load, we must go to a manor on the terraces above. As this meant dealing direct with the knight who held it, I wanted to make the buy myself, but he would none of it. Yet he was as good as his word, being as respectful as you please, while somehow managing to buy a pretty little mare at not much more than half the asking price. Further, he got the man to throw a usable saddle into the bargain. I had thought to use my harper green to get him a good price but he far outstripped my expectations.

"I've had years at that game," he said when I commented. "Besides, these knights may have plenty of land but it's obvious they see precious little cash." He looked at me sideways, "Admit it, Nicodemus, I *do* know how to stroke!"

"For all his pride, he was as courteous as a good knight should be," I sniffed, "They won't all be like that."

"Makes no never mind to me. He could have been rude as he liked, I still would have got my Jenny!"

Leaning forward he rubbed her ear and I smiled despite my fears. He was pleased as a child with her and with himself, and why not? Though he'd made sure I approved his choice, he'd picked out the mare unaided from the little herd. Then, when her old name was not to his liking, he named her too, saying to the startled knight.

"They always called the mares Jenny in the stories when I was a kid."

Sa, the man was a trader. Whatever harpers get, room or meat or drink or coin, is not traded but freely given, as is the song, both being a sort of gift to the god. True, there are customary tithes, but they may be varied from, and not a word said on either side. One does not haggle with the god.

Yet real skill is not to be despised. A man can not do a thing and still admire it in others. I resolved to swallow my misgivings and leave him to do the dealings.

Chapter 18

He leaned back from scratching his horse.

"I don't suppose the word *bank* means anything to you?"

"The side of a river?"

"A place to keep your money. It's just struck me that between the bars and the coins that are left, I'm carrying around a lot more than most of these fellows see in a lifetime. I'd be happier if I had somewhere safe to keep it."

"'Tis a problem harpers little reck with!" I snorted, then, seeing his point, added slowly, "Or many else. I doubt Lord Cromart himself had that much ready gold. I suppose most people bury their coins, or mortar them into their houses."

"Marvelous!" he said, morosely. "There's only one place I can think of to bury it in a horse and I suspect Jenny here would object." He rubbed her ear again. "Where to?"

I thought of our trip from the wastes. By rights, we should take it slow, until he were used to riding, but he'd set the seeds now. There were two in Tanrith knew of his wealth.

"Best we move on," I grunted.

A league along the road we turned off on the track that wound directly up the back of the mountain. That way, I hoped, pursuit would pass us, then cursed to myself as the first of the tangled forest branches slapped me in the face. One old goldsmith and a knight! 'Twas hardly likely we'd be followed, but I resisted the urge to turn and take the easy way. Safe was seldom sorry. Megan leapt in surprise at a savage dig from my heels.

We rode through all that afternoon in silence, forced on us by the mountain path. 'Twas not that it was treacherous, or even so very steep, but narrow and twisting through riotous woods, where a myriad kinds of trees and vines and creepers fought twig and spine for light and space. Two could not go abreast and Damonryan must ride well behind to avoid the backwards sweep of the ever encroaching branches. There was no place one could stop and 'twas not the easiest sort of riding. Even I found it taxing and how he must be feeling I could only imagine; but I heard no cry for quarter. At weary last, just at evening, we came out on a road that rolled its way across the mountain heights to a small town in the distance.

"Thank the lord Harry!"

He pulled abreast of me and I could see how tenderly he rode.

"We could walk the rest of the way."

He shook his head sharply, "I'll get used to it," then grinned painfully, "I'd gallop for a cold one!"

"Too far for that." I gauged the distance, "An hour at a trot."

He tried not to groan. To take his mind off his seat I asked him what had been on my mind a while but we'd had no chance to talk about.

"How is it, an your people no longer make war, that you are such a good fighter?"

He winced and shifted about, "Sport. Trips take a couple of years at low gees, so you have to exercise constantly. I've seen people carried off a ship because they didn't. And unless you're on a big liner, there's not all that much room. Karate fits the bill." He managed a lopsided grin, "The spaceports can be rough enough to give us all the practice at regular gravity we need. Most spacers learn the basics."

"Basics!" I whistled, thinking of three men down in two hands of beats.

"Mmm. A fourth degree black belt is a little higher than that, I guess."

A little! Later on, I looked it up in the infocom. They had more grades than there are eggs in a henhouse, but 'twas clear he was no mere journeyman.

Seeing my look he added with a twinkle, "There were plenty higher. My old skipper was sixth degree. Not much bigger than a minute, but she could whup me five times out of six."

I mistrusted that twinkle. *She?* I was sure he was joking as he'd done a time or two already, telling me something outrageous about his people only to say after that he had been pulling my leg. I refused the bait, simply sniffing and urging Megan to a little faster trot. I was weary enough myself not to be the butt of one of his jokes. He could suffer in silence.

§

Liguria was a pretty town, tucked into the mountain's shoulder just where it began to drop down the other side, with granite houses softened at the edges with tangled vines of moonbloom. The great white blossoms were out already, even before the sun had gone, twisting east to track little Aries, puffing their perfume to the air. We found the only inn and the landlord was pleased enough to see a new harper and willing enough to trade a decent room and board for a night's play. I made sure we took the saddlebags before the ostler led away the horses.

"I could have paid for it, Nikki," he said, as he dumped the saddlebags on the bed.

I looked at him, wondering whether that were some sort of apology, but he just seemed sore and tired. "'Twould not be like a harper, to pay when he could play," I said mildly, eyeing the shutters at the window. "Besides, it *is* my trade. Best I were at it." I pulled the shutters to and barred them, eyeing them with misgivings. "Will have to do. I can hardly complain to mine host."

He whistled in exasperation, "I'm sorry I mentioned the bank. You weren't worried back in Westernesse."

"The fisher folk wouldn't rob any guest, much less a harper. Life is easier here and fingers lighter." I crossed restlessly back to the bed, "No, that's unfair. Even a Suthy thief would not toss us knowingly, not for a harper's normal purse. But minstrels are thick on the ground here so we're not much of an event. A thief could rob us never knowing I was a harper." I stared at the bags, "We should find some paint, tomorrow, and slash those across with green."

"Whatever. But that's tomorrow." He stretched painfully, "I'm for a pint!"

I smiled tightly and locked the door, finding myself conscious of how much more gold weighed than the mere metal.

'Twas a weight I didn't like. *'Tis his gold. Why should I worry?* But that didn't wash and I knew it. The god had sent him to me.

§

Downstairs, he pushed straight to the bar, and from there, would not be moved, not even for supper. He was willing to have me laugh at him and even grinned back in my face, but his supper he took standing up. Though they'd cleared us a table, and I feign would sit, I stayed. I owed him that. A man who can laugh at himself deserves better than to be snubbed for his little jokes.

The landlord played his part, for the supper was fine, more spiced than savory, as you'd expect in the south, but done with skill and not just the heavy hand that sometimes passes there for good cooking. Afterwards, I went upstairs, for I'd left behind my harp on purpose. To my relief, everything was as it should be, but I resolved on the morrow to do better than paint. We'd get a moneybelt and strap the stuff straight to Damonryan. I'd not stand the worry else.

When I returned, I found the room packed and the landlord called me straight to the stage. The crowd went still as a morning pond and my words to Damonryan echoed in my head. The Suthy folk are no simple Westernesse fishermen; they've more harpers there than in all the rest of the land put together. I fussed with the strings on my harp for a few moments then straightened my shoulders. An there was one thing I knew how to do, it was to play. I went at it as they do at Welling, sweetly, seemly, not putting myself before the god. The harp rippled and the notes dropped out into the quiet and I lost myself in the music. I felt like brother Canus, building chapels in the air, with notes for blocks and chords for beams and flying buttresses stepping up out of arpeggios.

So I was startled, after the third song, to hear a little shuffle of applause. The song was much of a muchness, no more special than the others, so that I wondered what it was they liked about it to thus applaud before I was done. Nor did it die back, as I would expect so soft and mannered a clapping to do, but just went flatly on.

Before I rightly knew what was happening, a local harper ambled up, his eyes sly in a reddened face, his greens faded and stained. Winking at the crowd, he thanked me gravely for a pretty performance, and began to unsling his harp. Understanding came at last. For a moment I stood stock still with shock, but he'd left me with naught to do but retreat. 'Twas in me to flee the room completely, but my pride would not let me. In the end I settled for the darkest corner. For two hands of songs I stared, too much put out to really see him or to hear his music. At last, my brain began to function. I saw what he was doing, and began, willy-nilly, to listen. Hard use had burred his voice, *Not just from song!* I though sourly, and his playing would not have stood for the apprentice' prize at even the smallest fair. Yet he had more tricks than a performing dog and he kept them pleased. I had to admit he did it well, the whole rose well above its parts. I knew my mistake.

In an abbey, one sings in choir, raising pieces to the god like stained glass windows, each voice a dappled fragment that fits tightly in a whole. The song is all, the rush and color paramount. A harper sings for the god as well, but he must *perform,* the road to the god is through his audience; he must take them with him and not just throw the song above their heads. I'd ignored my audience and they do not take kindly to that in Suthy. Mayhap they'd not catcall a harper as they might a mountebank but, as I'd just found out, they'll shame him with small applause. In that land of minstrels, there's always another to take his place.

"You all right?" he quizzed me softly. 'Twas borne on me that he'd been watching all along, biding his time and I was reminded that, when he wanted, he had a rare tact.

"Just my pride." He'd only seen me play for fishermen and it was sudden important to me what he thought. "I know my mistake," I added, "Too many years at Welling. I played like a monk and not like a harper. 'Tis not one I'll make again."

No fear they'd let me back on that night, however. The landlord was good about it, he didn't charge me for our room; neither did he extend his invitation for another night. I thought of explaining but it would have sounded lame so I left it; there were other towns and other inns.

Unlocking our door, it was a relief, in the stuffy upper regions of that house, to find a cooling sift of night air.

"We've had a visitor."

"What!" I stared at the crack between the shutters I had so carefully closed, while he strode to the bed and went swiftly through the bags.

"Gone," he said tersely, "Gold and infocom both."

Chapter 19

"There's a footprint on the windowsill." He threw the shutters open and I saw it gleam wetly in the moonlight, a partial print. Bending down I picked up the crushed vial of one of my medicines.

"Tincture of *chial*. 'Twill dry quickly. He can't have been gone long." Even as I spoke, the night breeze whispered across the sill and the print began to disappear.

"If he can do it so can I."

So saying he levered himself through the window and was gone. Rushing to the casement, I found him edging along the demi-roof below, his hands gripping the eave above. 'Twent down steeply and the two converged fast enough he was soon forced to stop. By then though he was much closer to the ground and I saw him slip over the edge and, with a last whitening of his knuckles, drop silently to the street.

By the time I'd swung my leg out over the still, he was out of sight. Trying to ease my weight through the window, I felt the night wind shiver fingers along my stretched out groin. The house seemed to lurch like a fishing smack hit by a wave and I was left gasping and clutching the frame an it were flotsam in the flood. Call it cowardice an you will but I crawled back shaking. They talk of fear of heights but that is nonsense. I'm happy enough in the mountains so long as I stay away from steep edges. 'Tis not the height, but the drop. Almost, I stayed. They were both long gone, 'twould only be playing tag in the dark, but I could not convince myself. In the end, I took the stairs.

Slipping out the back gate from the courtyard, I found myself in the street below our window. A glance up and back was enough to confirm for me the narrow alley Damonryan had taken but, despite the moonlight, I could see little down its gloom.

"Nikki. Over here."

I traced down the wall, a matter of a hundred feet or so, and there found Damonryan. Alone.

"You lost him." I felt dismay stretch at my ribs.

"Not yet. He's gone to ground. I don't think he's moved since."

I saw what he meant. There were only three buildings at this end of the alley, which, at its far remove, turned into a country lane. 'Twas not much of a town after all. Where I'd expected a maze there was only this one lane, and not so very long at that.

"Take that one," he pointed to the largest of the buildings, "I think I can search the other two without letting him slip away."

§

'Twas a stone barn, still warm from the day, long and high, full of shadows, black voids that hung between grayer patches spattered through the gaps by the moonlight. I froze in the dark, waiting for my eyes to adapt, listening, listening. At length, I thought I filtered the edge of a loft, floating up out of the blackness, and then a second one above it. Ahead, what seemed to be a long row of stalls and a ladder, rising up to the first of the lofts; but no sounds. The place was musty with disuse and vast, a perfect hiding place. I crept forward, then spoiled my stealth as my toe come up sharp against an uneven flag and pitched me to the floor. My cry was followed by an answering rustle, somewhere up above, and then silence. An it was our quarry, 'twas sure by now he knew that I was there.

"Nikki?"

"In here."

"No luck," he said softly, groping towards me, "Brother, this is a cave!"

"I heard a sound just before you came in."

"Our boy?"

"Mayhap. Or a rat." Still, we whispered.

"Mmm. There's some houses down the road. For all we know he's tucked up snug in bed." He stared around, trying to pierce through the blackness that surrounded us. "We'll need help to search this place Nikki. And torches."

"No! There will be more questions from the sheriff than we can answer."

"The landlord."

"Who will go to the sheriff. I've a better idea."

Unthinking, I stepped forward, to clear a space around me, as if I were on stage.

"Who steals from a harper?" I called, pitching my voice to carry to the rafters, but not outside. "To rob a harper is to rob the god!" I paused to let that sink in. Another rustle, far up again, but no more than a rat might make, disgusted with human idiocy. Sa, in for a penny. "'Tis Nicodemus. Be revealed then, by *the fingers of the god!*" Brother Tantran would have had a fit. 'Tis one thing to call a ring of mountains around an abbey by that name, and quite another to suggest that the god really had a human anatomy or that anatomy could act as an agent.

There was nothing. Even the rats had given up.

"The fingers of the god," I called, trying all at once to raise my voice as loud as I could without changing its normal tones or cadences.

Sudden, there was a yelp, and a figure hurtled from the straw in the lower loft, an stuck by a pitchfork.

"Brilliant, Nikki!" With that, he swarmed up the ladder to collar our thief.

Sa. I thought it was. *The fingers of the god* was my password for the infocom and though I'd not heard it respond, the thief must have. Coming in the wake of my little invocation, it had clearly scared him silly. I heard a scuffle up above.

"By Aries, Nikki, he's just a boy."

That might make things easier, though I'd have to see him first to be sure.

"The Sheriff will hang him just as high."

There was a meatier oath and my partner's scandalized head appeared at the top of the ladder, "You can't be serious! He's not even eleven."

I shrugged, "So he gets a smaller rope. Bring him down."

"Sa, a rat indeed," I proclaimed disdainfully, hoping he could see my face in the dark. The little figure cowered back against Damonryan, whether because he conceived of him as his protector or simply because he feared the power of a harper who could call the god I couldn't tell. Reaching out, I seized him by the ear and dragged him forward, into a little patch of light.

"Fie on you, Damonryan, you're losing your touch. 'Tis not a boy but a girl." The child whimpered and tried to draw back until I pinched down hard.

"Jesus, Nikki, that only makes it worse! We're going to have to let her go…"

"…with a gold piece for her trouble," I continued silkily. "Did you get back the gold?"

"All of it."

"Why did you steal from a harper?"

"Ah…ah…ah didn't *know!*" she stammered out in a squeaky voice, "Nuthin' marked the bags as yours and who'd think a harper'd have so much money?"

"No one. 'Tis why I carry it. 'Tis Temple gold…" she shrank back at that; an they love the god, the poor have no reason to love the Temple, "… which I take to the great abbey in Dankar." I let her go, and she collapsed back against Damonryan, "And now you have broached the secret."

"Not if we let her go, Nikki. That way the sheriff would never know." He looked down at her and said roughly, "You can keep your mouth shut, can't you kid?"

The little head went up and down violently, but 'twas not a promise I'd trust, even to morning.

"All right," I agreed, "To keep the sheriff out of it. But look you," I drew myself to my full height and pointed the hand that held the infocom at her, "An we have the stain of trouble on our journey, I'm going to assume 'tis because you prattled, and I'll come back for you." I paused, to let that sink in, then shook the infocom at her, "Be sure, I'll find you."

The starman turned her loose and she fled.

"Jesus, Nikki! I thought for a moment you were serious."

"*Aries,* remember," I said absently, then shook my head, "I'd never hurt a child. I doubt her thieving is even her fault. I just wanted to hold her tongue long enough to get us gone."

He clapped me on the shoulder, "Well, I think you did the trick!"

I felt no elation. Doubly I'd failed the god: my carelessness had led to the theft of the gold and infocom that, somehow, were a part of Damonryan's being here; and harpers were meant to elevate and not demean the god by seeming to play with power like a third-rate magician at a country fair. But the worst of it, I knew, as we made our slow way back to the inn, was that we'd not saved her from the hangman. 'Twas the knife in the dark, all over again; not the voice, I didn't speak, and it only lasted a heartbeat. Behind her, even as we let her go, I saw the noose, not dark and shadowed, but clear as the day. I was glad 'twas too dark for him to have seen my face. That we'd only stayed her time I was sure.

I said naught. What point? Even an Damonryan believed me, which was doubtful, 'twould only ruin his sleep to little purpose. So I left it and he slept in on the morrow.

§

"Get up!" I kicked the bottom of his bed, "They've cleared the tables already. An the maid finds you here, our host will want payment for today."

He grumbled without much heat, but came soon enough and got us saddled. As we mounted up, the old landlord came out and piped, "No offense, harper, but seems you were abbey trained. Not so saintly the next time." He lowered his voice, "Voice is better than Cobham's, you should be all right, just keep it in mind."

I felt the blood rush to my face and bit back a sharp retort. *Dear the god, my pride is as raw as Damonryan's backside!* 'Twas no way for a harper to go on, so I thanked him for his advice, as gravely as I could. Then I asked after a leather worker.

"Third street down an' all the way right. You'll have no trouble."

I nodded my thanks and heeled Megan. My companion held his shout of laughter until we got outside the gate.

Sa. He was right about the leather worker, too. We found him easily enough, but we were there a time, getting not one, but two money belts as well as a broad strap for the infocom. Damonryan had insisted upon the two belts as we rode over there.

"It's only sense, Nikki. We're just splitting our eggs between two baskets."

"Your eggs," I reminded him.

"Don't be so stiff-necked," he retorted, then sighed, "All right, have it your way. *My* eggs. Do you mind carrying half of them?"

Put that way, it did make sense, and I agreed, but we had to wait. The leatherworker had but a single belt and must needs make up the other. As well, he made a simple, broad wrist band up to Damonryan's orders, with a square hole cut carefully in the center. Afterwards, he wore it always, strapped over the infocom, covering up its strap, with only the crystal poking through the hole. 'Twas marvelous to see how ordinary it looked, just a polished black stone set in a leather band. Not just in the common style mayhap, with something of a knightly feel, but no more unusual than that. 'Twas the strap gave it its unlandly look.

Stepping out into the sunshine at last, while Damonryan paid the reckoning, I heard a commotion in the street and stopped a child pelting along for all he was worth.

"What is it?"

"Nothing, sir," he wriggled, then caught sight of me, "Er, Harper." He gulped, his eyes wide in his grimy face, "They do say they caught a thief. A *girl thief!*" he added impressively. "Hang her at sunset they will and, please sur …," he swallowed, and corrected again, "Harper… I wants to be early, for to get a good seat."

Waving him on his way, I stood up, stunned. *Already.* I felt responsible, an my seeing the noose the night before had somehow put it there today.

"Are you all right? You look like you've seen a ghost?"

I shook my head but said nothing. At the end of the street, I turned Megan away from where the child had run and managed to get him out of town without him noting anything was wrong beyond my face. I never did tell him.

Chapter 20

Suthy is a blessed land, with five great lazy valleys, swimming in the sun, each one fertile, river ribboned and fielded, with vineyards marching up the mountain slopes. They spread like fingers, from the palm of the central plain, where lies Caitlon, central jewel in the Suthy crown, her five-rivered waters glittering in the endless sun. Even the mountains are benign, low and round, forested where there are not fields, cool against the summer's heat and deep with soil. There were fairs aplenty, and taverns and noble halls, all happy to welcome a minstrel.

We harpered about, following the fairs, stopping a day or two at tavern or castle. It gave Damonryan a chance to gain his feet. In public, he played my servant, lest there be too many questions. As it was, I had to deal with no few upon his speech or his manners, and once upon *that wrist band he affects*. Always we moved on before the queries became too searching.

Having been chased from Welling with a kit too small for one, never mind the pair of us, we bought bits and pieces here and there, never too much at once. As the days and the little market towns passed by we took on more of the look of man and master, at least as to our clothes. Nothing could make him walk like a servant, nor, having learned at last the art, to ride like one either. His shoulders he carried too straight and his gaze too high and clear, so that he reminded me more of a Fastness warrior than anything else. Indeed, there were times that I hinted at something of the sort but that were a dangerous game. As insular as they are in Suthy and smug behind their mountain wall, sooner or later I'd run into someone who knew better.

To give him his due, he did his best, studying his role at every turn. In the taverns he achieved just that blend of deference and chaffering you'd expect of an old retainer and we spent some comfortable hours over a pot or a pie, when I was not playing or he chasing after the bar maids. In the markets, 'twas he that held our little purse and he that bargained, while I drifted along behind. All the while he showed by his manner 'twas beneath his master but not a common fellow like him. At a high table, he would stand behind me, vying with his fellows as to who could be the most attentive. More than one baron commented to me that I had a good man there; only by the gleam in his eye would he show that he had heard.

Yet, withal, 'twas just a game to him. He was not long discovering that rank in the serving hall can be just as strict as at the high table, each according to the standing of his master. Thereafter, he took no little glee in puffing off my consequence. 'Tis part of a servant's job to do so, of course—how else to deal with a landlord?—but it never struck me 'til then that it was done to puff the servant. He cared no button for that, but the real servants did and so it amused him. He did it for that and because he thought I took too little care of my own importance.

Nor was there any sign of that lordliness that had worried me in Tanrith; week by week we rubbed through it a little more tolerably than before, until I found my fears slowly slipping away.

Oh there were gaffes. I mind the time in a tavern he was drinking with some soldiers, not so plentiful in Suthy, lounging and laughing with them in his easy way. Of a sudden I heard some kind of oath from their table and saw him holding his elbow, his companions drawing back with slitted eyes and tautened mouths. *Now what!* I thought, expecting trouble, but the soldiers shortly left, stalking stiff legged out like outraged dogs.

"What happened?" I asked as he joined me at my table.

"I hit my funny bone and swore."

"Dear the god! Whatever did you say?"

He looked at the door where his companions had departed, "Better not," he said ruefully, "I don't want you walking out on me too."

Now I was curious, "I deal in words, Damonryan," I cajoled.

So he told me and was right—better he had not. I felt the gorge rise in my throat. 'Twas hard to believe a man could even think thoughts like that, much less put them into words.

"Sorry Nikki. I'll find another way to swear."

Sa! I had asked for it. I wanted to drop it but, beneath his apology I heard puzzlement. Best we both understand. "Do…ah, your people say that commonly?" I groped, unable to use his words.

He scratched his head, "My mother wouldn't have liked it," he admitted, "But, it's common enough in the back streets and bars, even something of an art." My opinion of his people dropped a little then, but he added, "I don't think words have quite the same force for us."

Indeed, he was to show me after that words are strange things; what can be said in jest in Suthy would cost your life in the Fastness and vice-versa. His folk hold you cannot kill a man simply for what he says. 'Tis hard to fault them for that but it makes them much freer with their words.

Yet he never repeated the mistake. Instead he became fluent in the soldiers' curses, even, to their admiration, inventive, though he sighed to me from time to time that he found it pretty tame. Likewise, he was able to change both the manner of his speech, and even his accent. Day by day, the questions they aroused grew fewer.

For myself, I felt a whole new sense of freedom. Dearly as I had loved Welling, I had not thought of the rules as bonds; but now I felt their loosening. No one, save mayhap the tinker who mends where he may and moves on, is as free as a harper. I was on the road and my own man, could choose to go or stay, seek out fair or castle, decide when to sing and what. I've heard of narrow souls who returned to the cloister, overwhelmed with choice, but I was not one of their number. Instead, I felt like a cat who, waking, stretches, then bounds outside into the sun.

I might lack a master's cloak, but I wore the harper green; journeyman or master, 'tis all one along the way or in the taverns. A cloak comes out on only the most formal of occasions.

The deference I found strange. Oh, there was a tug of pride at first: the fussing of a landlord, the seat of honor at a high table, the pulling of a forelock or a little curtsey as folk went past. Heady stuff, for a young fellow off a farm in Anglesea, but it quickly palled. 'Twas much as on the boat from Welling, in the end it only served to set me apart from my fellows. I might be welcome at the high table, but noble I was not and now I found myself cut off from the kitchens as well. Remembering Bellarus at Halting, I tried it a time or two, but 'twas all very distrained. Mayhap 'twas Damonryan's presence, which made me wonder an that was why Bellarus had had no servant when I met him; more like I'd not the old man's knack. At any rate, I soon gave it up.

The taverns were better, so crowded one got to push together with all sorts of folk, but even there I was harper, and apart. At least Damonryan and I could share table, and not cause comment. I began to feel as I had at Halting Castle, neither fish nor fowl. In placing me between two worlds, I wondered an the god had not always intended me to be harper.

Only in the music itself could I reach truly out. The night after the infocom was stolen, we rode in to another of the little mountain towns and found another of the taverns. 'Twas coming on for sunset, and between the image of the little thief who was likely even now kicking out her life at the end of a sheriff's rope, and my memory of last night's failure, I was in no mood for chaffering. I barely saw the landlord, just asked for a room and promised him something special.

Giving way to the look on my face, he simply bowed us in. We must have been fed, I don't recall. All I remember was a taproom packed to bulging, so he must have passed some kind of word, and a crowd looking to be pleased, by me an I could, or else at my expense. I felt fey, an my weird was on me, an that one night would decide whether I would truly be harper or no. Sa, not all sendings are true ones, sometimes what swells within is simply the ardor of youth. At any event, I had thought hard about how I would begin. I wanted no repeat of yesterday, so I eschewed my harp at first and got a stool from the bar and sat it upon the little stage.

"I'm going to tell you a story," I began.

Then I gave them my own, while all the time talking an he were another boy, which, of course, in a way he was. My sadness that I could not save the girl reached back to my sorrow of early years. I made them see the snow blowing across the frozen ground, which they never see in Suthy, not even in what they call their mountains. I made hunger pinch at southern bellies that had never felt it and scattered the bodies before them in tattered bundles upon the earth. I took harper's license and made the lad a hero.

"...At last he won to the castle and, dying, brought warning to his lord." 'Twas not a time for verity; the harper's task is to move an audience. And death was on my mind. I picked up the harp, "As it happened, there was a harper there."

Now I gave them Bellarus' Serf's Lament. I played no games with the tapers, that was my master's trick and besides I didn't need to. I'd brought my own dark into the place and I could see I had them. So I chased the shadows away with a couple of old Earth drinking songs taught to me by Damonryan, that I had phrased down a bit. They were too raw else, even in ribald Suthy, but reworked, they were a big hit, and no one could accuse me of building chapels in the air. From there I could do what I want, an I did it passing well. Mine host was pleased. I felt I was harper at last. At the same time, a little shadow passed away.

For a time, thereafter, performing was pure joy. I would reach out and play the crowd again, drawing them into my harp, each a string, with their own note and sound—a widow, withered, swaying with a dying babe; a maid, bright cheeked at a love song, looking shy under lashes beside her; a peasant lad, wide eyed, side by side with a soldier who just thumped his tankard along to a marching song.

Coming down from one such performance, Damonryan said, "It's like watching someone make love!"

"You should know," I grinned back at him. Yet he was right. An the common folk would never let me set aside the dignity of a harper, still, on stage, I could reach through it and sometimes 'twould feel uncommon like an embrace.

§

The castles, in Suthy, were something of another matter.

This one was very grand, newly built, the seat of Lord Cozumel, Baron of Monza, and no fortress. Safe behind the mountain wall that separated it from Dankar, Suthy had seen no foreign army in eight generations. The newer castles reflected that, keeping the look, but not the substance. The only moat was my lady's rose gardens, planted hard beneath the walls, and the windows were wide, sited for light and air and not defense. Great areas of the base could not be covered by crossbow fire from the walls.

Our quarters were sumptuous. Outwardly, all the old courtesies were kept. I was to have the seat of honor at the high table, and though the lord was too busy to see me, the chamberlain himself led us in, informing me of the arrangements. Loftily, he also told me that Baron Cozumel kept not one, but two, harpers of his own.

Which puts me in my place! I didn't like these new developments in Suthy. Unless he be old, a harper should have no sinecure. Song comes from the god and should be at no man's beck and call; nor was art ever meant to be padded at the edges. We belong on the road, but kept bards were all the rage in that country. An that became the general style, all the land would be the poorer.

It also meant tonight would be a competition. Contests happen often enough at the great fairs and, even as an apprentice, I had entered them. There was always an honest attempt at judging, and one felt the god looked over, and that a good performance could sweep all before it. This would be different. Nothing would be announced, no formal judgments made. I might even be the only one that played, though I doubted that, with two kept harpers. Yet I would be measured against them, the whole hall alert to see an they were worth their keep or whether their lord could do better. I had learned to hold back a little on such occasions, but it rankled. Knowing my dislike, Damonryan made himself scarce, doubtless bound for the kitchens in search of ale or cozy company for later on that night.

'Twas worse than I imagined. The hall was large and full, all that a harper could want, but Lord Cozumel had one of his men play through supper, and that put my teeth on edge. He could make no song, just a pretty tinkling to curve about the edges of the talk. 'Twas not a style I could admire. Coming from the god, music should be listened to, not hung on the wall like a tapestry.

The *place of honor* was not up by the baron and his lady but down at the end, by a knight, young, newly spurred, and far too full of himself. I made what talk I could and was thankful to find him more interested in his wine than a visiting harper. He'd brought only his groom, not good enough for Cozumel's table, so, Damonryan behind me as always, served us both. Until then he'd found it useful for it gave him a chance to listen in without having to speak himself. The nobles, being better traveled than the common folk, were more apt to wonder at his speech. That night, there was no talk worth hearing, and no other servant nearby to outperform, so I could hear him, bored, shifting from foot to foot.

My companion did not help. He was too young to be sure of himself, new to command and peremptory in a way that, grating on me, must have sounded like bone on bone to the starman. 'Twas done thoughtlessly, not with Edgar's purpose, more to raise his consequence than out of malice, but I could see that Damonryan was on the burn. Not for nothing had he spent time in the kitchens, and he began to play the serf, slow and dumb and deaf. He did it well. Had I been in a better mood I might have found it funny.

At last, they called for harpers, first the other two and then myself. I quickly saw the game. They played almost wholly their own compositions, long languid pieces that reminded me of southern gardens: decoration everywhere, with phrases running riotous as Suthy passion blossoms, virtuosity splashed freely, entirely for its own sake. I found them strangely passionless, even, never loud enough to offend an aristocratic ear, I suppose, or soft enough to make it strain. But Cozumel liked it. That, of course, was all that mattered.

Out of sheer bravado, I opened with a fragment from the last cadenza, rippling it back at them, trying for some of the passion I found so wanting. There's little that any man can do with a harp that I cannot and I saw its author pale. *Unworthy, Nicodemus. He at least wrote it!* I'd done little writing at Welling and less on the road with Damonryan. That of course was the challenge, and I could not meet it. *I don't spend my time in perfumed gardens!* but I knew that was not all the reason.

I bowed to the man, thirty summers mayhap, small and neat, but old already in unease, "A worthy piece. I fear you are my better in composition." Sa. At least the second part was true.

He relaxed at that and I gave them my best at the old time ballads. It went well enough. The harpers, no longer feeling threatened, were inclined to be gracious and Cozumel, an it was not what he really liked, at least was ready to give it the courtesy it deserved. There was no reaching out that night, except perhaps, to a few of the servants on the edges of the light. I played only as long as was strictly necessary.

As I finished, and started back to my seat, I heard my dinner companion.

"Boy!" to a man three times his age, though he looked much less than twice it, "Are you deaf? I said more wine!"

"I be coomin', zur!" I heard the north country brogue, a bit of which he must have picked up from me around the campfire, with misgiving. Damonryan seized the pitcher from its stand with a look I didn't like and then made awkward haste. I thought to stop him, but I was too far and would only make what was to come look less like an accident. Holding the pitcher high, my erstwhile servant stumbled as he approached, and with nearly perfect aim, dumped it entire upon his tormentor's head.

"You did that deliberately!" he screeched, his voice breaking in his rage, "I'll have you flogged!"

Damonryan said nothing but just glowered at him, willing him to try it then and there. In fury, the young knight thrust back his bench and stumbled to his feet. He was stopped by the silky strands of Baron.

"Dantine," Cozumel's lazy voice drawled down the table, "Most inconvenient I know, but I do believe the fellow is *not* your servant."

There was iron beneath the silk, and it stopped the knight where he stood. "My lord," he said, bowing to hide his chagrin.

"Harper?"

I knew my cue, "My lord," I bowed to him and then the soaking, outraged knight, "I shall deal straightway with it, just as the matter deserves."

Happily, the fool was too drunk and thought too much of himself to suspect that he and I might differ in our opinion of what was a just desert. I saw a glimmer of amusement in Cozumel's eyes but he just inclined his head. Motioning to

Damonryan with an anger I had no need to counterfeit, I left the hall.

"Well," he said, when we reached our room, "Shall you pound on the bed while I give a few judicious screams?"

"You reck too finely!" I hissed at him. "This is no game. Was Cozumel annoyed and not amused, I would have been hard put to stop a public flogging."

"It might still have been worth it!" he said defiantly.

I stared in dismay. When he'd told me his people would not even smack a child, so great was their horror of physical punishment, I'd assumed 'twould make him cautious. Instead it meant he had no more notion of what was at stake than a child who'd never been smacked. I felt my fears for his ways rekindle, and went to bed in no little turmoil.

'Twas only prudence to make an early start so we were away before most of the high folk were up. Damonryan bustled about, packing, calling for the horses, and loading them, for all the land a model servant. Mounting up, I viewed him with disfavor, but he just smiled me blandly back. He was too blithe with too much spring in his step for my taste, an he thought last night a victory. I determined to talk to him once we cleared the gates, but the sun struck us, the day was warm and fine, and, resolutely, I shut my mouth. Talking would pay no toll. Must needs I show him.

Though we'd mostly kept to the hills, I turned us downwards, dropping into the heat of the valley below, Monza, source of Cozumel's wealth, even if he didn't choose to live there. 'Twas named after the river that winds through it, the greatest of Suthy's five. Where the valley opened into the central plain lay Monzantus, largest of the Suthy valley towns, a brawling broth of a city, tucked into a great meander in the river. By royal decree, commerce is forbidden the capital, so Monzantus, serving in Caitlon's place, is heart of the river trade. 'Tis as graceless as Caitlon is fair, a dark and stooping brother to what the Southron's are wont to call the queen of cities, dirty, squat, swart, full of warehouses and workshops, and swarming with river serfs. Coming in across the northern bridgegate, I checked with the sergeant on duty and was grimly satisfied.

§

"Phaaw! No wonder you kept to the hills!"

I smiled thinly, "Most of the market towns aren't as bad as this. Monzantus is … special."

We'd left our horses at a stable and made our way on foot. It put us closer to the smell that coiled from the cobbles in the late afternoon heat and we must pick our way about things better not looked at.

"Why are we here? And where are we going?"

"To further your education." He looked at me suspiciously. "Ahh," I said as bland as he had been that morning, "I believe we are here."

An alley ran out from our street, narrow and short, walled in by the blank sides of the adjacent houses. A few strides brought us into a cobbled square, ringed three sides around with houses, fine once, long ago, but now ill kempt, hard used, a warren swarming with the most miserable serfs in all the land. The fourth side had been a palace once but whatever grace it might have possessed had long since fled, shorn brutally away in its making over to a barracks and a jail. The smell in the square was worse than in the streets outside, a presence so physical I felt my arms come up, though whether to ward it off or cut it through was more than I could tell.

"Jesus, Nikki!" He had stopped and turned away, hunched over, his hand across his face, "Whatever you want to show me, it can't be worth this!"

Grabbing his wrist, I pulled him forward, "'Twon't kill you, outlander," I retorted. "*They* have to live with it all their lives."

The crowd parted as I dragged him through, staring as we went. My harper green assured the passage, though there were many there, I was sure, had never seen one of my calling before. I'd not dare the square without it.

In the center stood a scaffold, mercifully unused, and a pair of sturdy posts set deep into the cobblestones. I'd timed it well. As we emerged from the crowd the first pair of what looked like a half dozen malefactors were having their manacles hooked over a bolt set high in the post. The sergeant in charge of the punishment party checked them both, hooking up another link so the hapless serf was forced up on his toes.

" Ya got to stretch 'em, Guido!" he clucked at his man and stepped back.

Both men were bare to the waist, their arms stretched up and around the posts, their backs tensed against what was to come. One was crisscrossed whitely back and forth with scars, mute witness to an earlier embrace with a pillory. Other than a few half-hearted jibes and one or two shouts of encouragement, the crowd was largely indifferent; most had not turned out for this, they'd seen it all a thousand times before, they were here solely because this was the only place they could come. We were of more interest.

One old dame, short and stout and very labored of breath, wheezed up beside us, dressed in a gown so patched there was more yarn than cloth.

"Brought thy boy so ye could show him why he ought to behave?" she gasped shrewdly, completely ignoring Damonryan's age.

"Just so, madam," I bowed my respect. Here, at least, she was a queen of sorts.

"Thought so," her bosom heaved comfortably, "The swells does it from time to time." Then, lest I mistake her, "Not that ye be a swell, harper," she added, "'Tis just ye be doing what the swells does."

"I quite understand," I assured her gravely.

"Aye. 'Tis best place in Suthy for thy lesson, young feller," she said brightly. She seemed obscurely proud of that fact, "Make sure he pays it some mind."

Not sure what to say, Damonryan was saved by the sergeant.

"Room!" he yelled and at once lashed back with the whip.

Watching for it, the crowd parted, just enough for his backwards cast. 'Twas an old ritual, and they were used to it and the sergeant both. To my fascination, I saw them leave him little more than a foot all around, yet his aim was true and the whip danced in and out of the throng behind without ever touching a soul. He was a professional, stepping forward into the stroke and flicking his wrist just so, working for his best speed in the scope of a steady rhythm. With five men to go, 'twould be his pride to give the last as good as the first.

My detachment could not survive the first horrible *thup* the whip made slicing into human meat. Though there's hardly a village in the land without a pillory they are seldom used and I was never one to take a flogging as a holiday. I'd not been since my father had dragged me in Cooling for the same reasons I now took Damonryan. Sa, I knew to what it was we'd been coming and I schooled my face. Beside me, the old woman wheezed companionably on, comparing the sergeant's technique with some of the others, but it was more than I could do to answer her.

On the second stroke, the man at the post screamed, and by the fifth, he was crying continuously, trying vainly to writhe away from the lash and begging the sergeant to stop. That worthy went stolidly on. The only effect was that his companion, the man already striped tied to the other post, twisted awkwardly against his stretch and spat noisily on the cobbles.

"Shut yer gob!" he yelled disgustedly, "Fella can't get no peace around here!"

Some of the crowd laughed at that but it was quickly drowned by the high pitched scream as a sixth line of red sprung from the victim's back.

By a dozen lashes, Damonryan was white to the roots of his hair. Deeming it enough, I pulled him from the square, the beldame's parting crack rising to follow us out.

"Ye'll have no more trouble with him, harper, I'll be bound!" she cackled.

Doubtless she was wrong, but as I stopped and let him be sick in the alley, I thought that, for this at least, mayhap he had taken my point.

§

"Are you all right?"

We had camped that night away from all towns, no trial in a Suthy spring and safer for talk. He'd not said a word the whole of the ride or while we were setting up. Remembering how often he'd respected my silences I had left him to his, but 'twas getting late.

"Mmm." He nodded, "Guess I just realized how far I really am from home."

I wondered what that must be like, to be so unimaginably far and know you could never go back, to be surrounded by an alien people who thought differently, spoke differently, ate differently. I thought of the smug kept harpers and the indifferent chamberlain, the heads that bobbed down as I passed and the voices that fell silent an I'd walk into a kitchen. *Like me.* Foolish. It had to be a thousand times worse for him.

I started. I'd wanted him to talk. "Wishing you could return?" I blurted and bit my lip. *Of course he does. What would you?*

"This afternoon, maybe, but not now." He lapsed into a long silence, so I thought he was done, then started to speak, "That's the nub, though, isn't it? Not going home." He tossed another stick on the fire, "You know what a *tourist* is?"

I shook my head.

"Used to carry them, sometimes," he mused. "Hated the bastards."

"So what are they?"

"Sorry. People who travel to another planet just to…," he snorted, "…e*xperience* what it's like. Then they get upset when the hotels and the food are not just like home. They claim to want adventure but its really only the *illusion* of adventure they're after." He looked at me ruefully, "That's me, Nikki. I've been acting like a tourist."

"You seem to like the food well enough."

"Jee…Aries, I'd kill for a cup of *coffee!* But you know the real hallmark of a tourist? They always think they can play by their own rules." He shivered, "When that little bastard jumped up last night I was ready for a fight. In my mind it was him against me, all nice and tight and fair and square." He closed his eyes and I knew he was seeing the flogging again. "That could have been *me* in that square and there would have been no diplomat from Unity to pull me out." He flexed his hands, then said quietly, "Past time I learned your rules."

Then he gave me a wry smile, "Don't look so down, Nikki, I'm lucky to be here. By rights I should be entombed in the reaches of space."

"Escaping the halter does not reconcile a man to the dungeon."

"Ahh," he looked around him where the grove of thousandleafs shimmered in the dark, "This is no dungeon. Thinking this all through has made me realize that I *like* it here. There's more *life*, somehow," the muscle jumped in his cheek, "Except when you're trying to beat it out of some poor bastard."

I grinned at that and sudden, we were both laughing. When we had done he reached out and bumped me lightly on the shoulder, "Thanks, Nikki. You're a good friend."

Friend. I stared at him, wondering, realizing sudden it might have been one of his strange out-of-the-land words like *machine* or *language* for all it meant to me. All those years, at the croft, with Bellarus, at Welling, and I'd never had a friend. Not even at the monastery. I'd been too old and too apart from the other apprentices for that.

"What's the matter?" He cocked his head sideways, "Another of your ghosts?"

I shook my head, not trusting myself to speak. Not a ghost. A revelation.

I had one now.

§

He changed after that. Not a great lot, as they'd say at home: certainly not his carriage, nothing could take away that. He was still easy, enjoying his mug and joke, with a knee ready and a buss for any maid who was willing; but, what I now realized had been mockery was gone, replaced by a kind of dignity in the pursuit of his official duties that armored him against worse abuse than Cozumel's knight could have handed out. He let his bearing speak for him. *I am the harper's man*, it seemed to say, *and nothing you can do can take that from me.*

The rub, of course, was that he was not. At best he was marking time. Servants of harpers don't loom large in the pattern so 'twas plainly my part to help him to whatever destiny made it important enough to send me to the barrens. But what was that? I mulled the question for weeks, even trying him as a minstrel. After all, 'twas by the harper's road the god had sent me. He'd a fine, deep voice and a fund of scandalous songs, but that was as far as it went. An errant note never worried him. As for the harp, he could as well have played it with his elbows. I was unsurprised. He liked a song as well as any man but, when all was said and done, 'twas just a song, no more than the draught of ale that went with it. He'd no fire for music.

Toss the sticks as I may, they always came down in the same direction. The man was a trader born. Why the god should want another merchant was beyond me but I could read the riddle no other way. Afraid of seeming to want to be rid of him, I'd kept my thoughts to myself. Still 'twas evident that Damonryan's mind ran on similar paths for he had taken to poking into every dark and dusty workshop he could find, seeing what it was they did and how they did it. In the taprooms he would seek out what tradesman or merchants were there and ply them with gentle questions. Indeed, I worried lest I find him knifed in a ditch as a spy but I need not. He'd a knack for getting on with people that he coupled with a sure instinct for when to shear off.

To combat my fears, and mayhap to find an answer there, I took more to the infocom. Damonryan has taught me how to use it and was content to leave it with me while he rambled off on his expeditions. 'Twas time I should have used to practice but I found myself restless. Whenever I was sure I was safe from prying eyes and clinging ears it was so easy to whisper to my wrist, and have unfold a world I never knew existed. A lifetime and more one could spend on even a tiny part of what it held.

For a time I delved back into Mathematics, learning far more and more simply than ever Brother Tantran taught. 'Twas pure joy so I wondered what the old man would think of it, but I found the lore it held grew quickly past what I could grasp. Physics, the study of things, I assayed, but, even with Damonryan's help, all but the simplest of its ideas were beyond me. How a people can embrace a study so strange, so far outside the realm of our experience, then reject the god before them for lack of what they called proofs quite passes my understanding. When I commented Damonryan only smiled and said nothing and we left it at that.

Chemistry, however, the study of how atoms combine, was the sheerest poetry, and I reveled in its mysteries, its symmetry, its marvelous, interlocking nature, where piece fit into piece, building, from the simplest blocks, the entirety of the world around us. I was caught by that and stayed with it some weeks; but it too passed beyond me.

Alas, I was not helping Damonryan. Those studies were the sheerest indulgence, yet I could not resist. Most of what I learned, of course, he already knew and he would explain sometimes a point I simply could not make out from the machine. Often, he would smile as he did so, as aware as I that whatever answer he sought lay down none of the paths I searched. He was like a parent, indulging a child with some new toy bought at the autumn fair. Then the smile began to fade.

He'd been used to his Joshua. Yet the more he helped me, the more his scorn at this tiny toy version of what he'd known went missing. Gradually, he began to delve himself, a little at first, then deep and even deeper. I no longer had the luxury of the device to myself.

He started with things, in the beginning, noting some need as we traveled about and then exploring it. Waterwheels, mayhap, or a better way of making pipes for water or paper; or sometimes things I had never heard of, some kind of gum for making better wheels, he called *rubber,* and many others. He would list them out, considering *where I might make a start.* More and more, however, he became interested in the history of his own people, and would mutter things to me like *Did you know that most knights hadn't the slightest idea of how to win a battle?* or, again, *Ready money undercuts the landed classes!* His paths seemed to lead as far away as mine.

§

"What is it you seek?" The last embers of our fire licked lazily between us.

"Hmm…sorry." He looked up, then ordered the little machine to shut itself down. "Sifting, mostly."

"For what?"

"I hardly know. Something to give me an edge." He hesitated, looking strangely shy, "Well…maybe, more than that. Maybe…" he finished in a rush, "…something that could make a difference."

"How do you mean?"

"Something like the printing press."

His latest efforts had got me reading a little of the history of his Earth myself. Not an elevating story on the whole—no wonder the people left an 'twas the great land as Damonryan claimed—but I seemed to remember the press was a device for making hundreds of copies of a book at once. The writer claimed it had changed the world.

I felt the first rising of excitement. "Could you do that?"

"Probably. The technology is pretty simple." He didn't seem very enthusiastic.

I pondered that, "Are you afraid of the Temple?"

He grinned, "They've got the book market all to themselves, huh?" then turned serious. "It's not that, Nicodemus, although from what you've told me, they'd be an enemy to fear. But who'd read the books?"

"I would. The brothers at Welling would be delighted, the…"I stammered to a stop.

"You see. It can be argued that Gutenberg invented the press precisely *because* the demand for books in his time was overwhelming the copyists. Whatever. He couldn't have succeeded without a lot of readers. If I tried that here, sure as black holes, I'd go broke!" He yawned and stretched, "Don't look so down. There's bound to be something else!" He reached for his bed roll then stopped, "By the way. I did find out one thing. You know how the similarities between here and old earth bothered me?" I nodded and he reached for the roll again and stretched himself into it. "Turns out that castles were developed independently in medieval Europe and in feudal Japan. *And* both societies had serfs." He yawned again, "Maybe your people could have developed it all over again, though I still suspect someone must have brought along a few hints!"

§

Long after he'd gone asleep I lay awake, staring at where the coals roiled red. So simple, yet I'd missed it! A parade of those impossibly, militarily straight letters, lined up into countless regiments of books, marched endlessly through my mind. 'Twas not just Damonryan I'd been sent for, 'twas the infocom as well. The parade died slowly out. I could see just enough of the force of his argument to trust that his judgment was sound. It didn't matter. The books stood for the power of the infocom and Damonryan was the key. It was only a matter of time until he found something else. At last it made sense he be a trader.

Made sense, but that didn't tell me how. Wool or silk, tobacco or tea, all the great trades were governed by license and the licenses by the guilds. Thinking of the books, I had at once thought of the Temple. No matter what he tried, he'd attract attention and it would be none of it friendly. He'd no chance without a guild. But what guild? And how to get him in once we knew? I knew little of the guilds, only that Cromart had thought he could get me into one, a dozen years before. Was Cromart still alive? An he were, would he do for Damonryan what he'd half promised to do for me? I didn't know. I was an obscure harper, suspect by the Temple and I didn't know enough about anything.

I needed help and not just for Damonryan's sake. Until I'd seen his feet set firmly on their way, I'd not be free to follow my own road. 'Twas time and past to find Bellarus. I only hoped he was still alive.

Part IV
Dankar

Chapter 21

So we took the Masser Pass and crossed northwards into Dankar. My fear for Bellarus was well founded. Despite he wouldn't approve the southern twist had been given to harping, 'twas a point of pride with him that the land entire was his stage; yet, in all our wanderings in Suthy, I had not caught so much as a murmur of his passing. The last anyone had seen of him had been four years agone, too long for him. An he was anywhere, 'twould be here.

Dankar is mostly one vast fertile plain, quilted with fields and woods, cut across with rivers that keep it watered and broken here and there by softly rolling hills and little market towns. An it has not in summer the sweetness of Anglesea, it is yet a gentle land, kind to an old man's bones, with little of the northern bite, nor yet the southern sear. 'Tis the land of fruit and flowers. In the east the lemon bears year round and the seasons are marked not by what falls from the sky but only by what blossoms or grows in the ground. 'Twas my intent to harper across it, from fair to hall to tavern, casting for my old master as we went. Yet, as we broke down from the pass, I became aware of how much I was looking forward to simply showing off the country.

'Twas not the land of my remembering. Oh, the hills were the same, as green as ever, and the wind as soft; but every wall winked weapons and in every tavern the talk died stone dead at a new shadow in the doorway.

In Suthy I'd heard from time to time talk of trouble in the north, a new Duke in Umber, restless, and by all accounts, a bloody man. I'd questioned carefully but found it hard to know. They do love sensation there but seldom consider northern affairs worth more than a few mouthfuls of conversation. The accounts of Duke Granly's darker doings I halved and then halved again. Such tales grow as they spread, the more so in the south. 'Twas one more case of a young man succeeding to his father's honors, and stretching out, to try his reach. An he wanted the Dankar throne, why he was not the first. In the end, his neighbors would restrain him, or the Queen would see him caged, with no one the worse except the poor serfs who had the bad judgment to get in the way. I'd seen it before and I'd the grim certitude I'd see it again. A sorry tale but no reason not to go north.

Yet the stories swelled as we went north, instead of shrinking as I had expected. So far as I could tell, Granly's deeds were all in his own Umber and he'd made no move against Dankar proper. But he was up to Seton's old tricks, no taxes had come south to Carvigal since he had stepped into his father's boots. No one doubted but war was coming. Not a castle or manor but whose court echoed daylong with the clash of swords an every man in Dankar of the warrior class, knight and squire and soldier, sought to forge his steel anew in the practice yards. We were welcome enough, but at night, in the halls, the call was always for songs of valor and the men would drink and bellow the chorus and clash their goblets as hard as their swords.

In the taverns, the fear of the common folk dripped thicker than year old syrup. *The old Queen was for it this time,* they whispered. The tales out of Umber made them shiver at the thought of Granly as overlord. Nor was it only the northern bogie they had to fear. They found their own lords resty and moody and hard to please.

§

Tappingsworth is an old town, unwalled, but gray stone everywhere, wrested from the hills around, so every house can be its own fortress an need be. Beforetimes all had been softened with ivy, but every stone was stripped bare now, giving the place a raw and sullen look. Even the tavern, hunkered hard below the towering sweep of the castle wall, took on a mean and unwelcoming air. *The Mason's Arms,* I knew it of old, its sign, tongue-in cheek, an one can say that of a sign, a pair of brawny arms each holding up a great stone. I had always liked the place when I had gone with Bellarus, and was sad to see it so come down. Yet the fire inside was bright, the beams and polished bar warm as only old wood can be, and there were encouraging smells from the kitchen. The place was thin of company. The talk died, as usual, until I stepped into the light and let them see the harper green.

"Harper." The landlord, a tiny little man, gleaming bald save for an absurd fringe of white above each ear, nodded and managed a smile. He didn't look as if he'd been smiling much lately, but I remembered him anyway. I managed to dredge for the name.

"Balzan."

His head cocked like a bird so I saw that, indeed, the two little fringes did not even meet at the back, and the eyes narrowed as he looked at me askew. Then the hand came up from the depths of his towel and one small finger jabbed.

"Nicodemus?" This time the smile was genuine, "By all that's wonderful! Bellarus' boy." In a trice, he'd slapped two mugs on the bar and had them filled to overflowing, "'Ee, thee's grown lad!" he exclaimed, leaning back to get a better look at me, while still holding on to the bar. I remembered now. There was a platform built, all along, just behind the bar, put there just for him to stand on.

"Whew! Look, Nicodemus."

The remnants of a substantial meal lay all about us. Mine host had done us proud, bustling about, fetching the best of everything. He'd high hopes for a good night out of me, but it was still early yet, and people had only started to drift in. I looked where Damonryan nodded.

I smiled wryly, sure of where he would spend the evening. "Not my type."

He was already half way to his feet, but he stopped at that, "What *is* your type?"

"Not bar maids, that's sure." Seeing his anxious look, I added, "Don't worry." I knew his fears. In his view any man not attracted to women must be interested in men, "I simply haven't found the right woman yet."

I didn't tell him Bellarus had tried to rid me of what he called my precious innocence before he took me to Welling. 'Twas not a success. She was comely enough, at once lithe and buxom, with crow black hair, and not much older than I; but she'd seen much usage and had a hard edge to her that she took care to hide from my master, for fear of her fee. Sometimes, I am told, such women are pleased to school a young man but she was simply impatient. Pulling me into her airless little attic room, she kicked the door shut, and at once flopped back on the pallet that was all the furniture the wretched little closet could hold. Even so, for all I was nervous, I thought myself still willing. Without more ado, she pulled up her dress, clear above her head as if she didn't even want to watch. At once, all I could think of was *soldier's meat!* All I could see was my mother's torn and bleeding body. The room closed in on me like the grave and the gorge rose up in my throat. I turned and fled. The look in her eyes as I wrested open the door never made me anxious to repeat the experience. Sa. I had grown up with love and knew its resonance, deep and steady. In my mind, that can't be bought or taken, or even bartered, one to one, for the night, as both Damonryan and Bellarus did so readily. Seemed it of more moment to my friends than me. An nothing else, the god had taught me patience.

I waved him away and he went, that easy grin of his back firm where it belonged. With some interest I watched and it didn't take him long—a few words back and forth, a laugh, a head tossed and a hand held out and he was pulling out a chair to sit at her table. She smiled as he sat and I saw he was right about her looks, which were well beyond the common. She was smaller than the robust types he usually liked, but beautiful, dark-haired and lithe, with fine gray eyes, soft against a skin like fine china. Yet, believe it an you choose, I felt no envy; one can admire the deft strokes of a smith without ever wanting to take his place.

I went to work on couplets. There was a piece I'd been shaping but I needed yet a few rhymes to round it out. How long I worked them I don't know, only that I was not unhappy with my efforts when I became aware again and found the big room filling up. Balzan's satisfaction was evident. Seeing me scan the place he flipped up a tiny thumb from his perch behind the bar, then made a filling motion. I just shook my head. More ale would not improve my performance. I saw approval light his eyes, touching off amusement in mine. He'd had his share of drunken harpers, then.

There was a great thump at the door. Even as I swung my head, I caught the blaze of the little landlord's eyes, before he dropped them to the floor. Anger. And something, of fear as well I thought, though I couldn't be sure. I wouldn't have seen it at all had I not been looking right at him when it happened.

The door was flung back and one of the biggest men I had ever seen was in the act of straightening from where he'd had to duck through. 'Twas hard to see as he was still half in the dark. It looked an he were dressed in servant's livery, though he scowled about the room like a sergeant-at-arms. I caught the flash of a dagger at his belt. An he were a retainer, he was a privileged one. 'Tis seldom that such a one will not nod at least to a harper, but his eyes slid past me an I wasn't there. At length, he was satisfied, and stepped into the light where I saw plain the servant brown with the yellow tabs at the shoulders, that marked him for a noble's. Behind him, stepped his master.

Like a nightbird an image of Edgar flickered across my mind, surging a sudden, bitter wash of fear in my throat. I knew it for foolishness. Edgar was older than I, a solid man by now, an he lived, still. What would he care for the wanderings of an itinerant harper? Then the man moved forward in the light and I saw the difference. His face lacked the glittering malevolence of Edgar, carrying only its bored and sulky shadow. And where Edgar went light, always on the front of his feet, this one went flat with a heavy tread, letting the weight of his footfall proclaim his consequence. The image flitted off into the dark and with it the fear; but all around me, I saw eyes hooded down and shoulders hunched. The youth, it seemed, was known.

I studied him. How not? I faced the door and Damonryan was away across the room, busy at his favorite pursuit. I'd no one to bend in talk to. A noble sprig, or rather, a sprig of the nobility, young, sixteen mayhap, and too sure of his consequence for my taste. *Which is why he reminded you of Edgar.* He wore a shirt whose cost would have kept a harper for a year, but carelessly, open at the collar and recently stained. *With wine. Half in his cups already.* The white and rounded skin beneath bespoke too much time in taverns and not enough in the practice yard. Despite that, he wore a sword.

Becoming aware at last that one pair of eyes at least was on him he turned my way. I schooled my face and met his stare easily across my cup, then nodded briefly.

His answering nod was stiff, "Harper," he grudged, then flushed and swung his gaze to the bar. "Balzan, you little toad! Port! A bottle of your best." Too loud. Volume to sweep awkwardness.

"My lord!" the publican squeaked and backed away, bowing, then fled for his cellar.

So, a lord. Early then to his father's honors which would explain a lot. *No.* Memory picked at me. Hakford Castle, at whose very foot we were, was the only one in the vicinity, but Baron Runholt had a string of them and the titles to go with them. Titles to spare. *And no time for the schooling of his son.* I remembered now, the last time I'd been through, with Bellarus. An old man, even then, with a son for his dotage, he'd be much older now, but he was still alive, I was sure. I'd heard his name not long ago, in Suthy, somewhere. Looking at the son I was glad I'd decided on the tavern first, and for no better reason than I'd been bored of castles. 'Twould have been a trial, I decided, to spend a meal trying to talk to this one.

The port was back and he gestured impatiently to his servant who, for all his size, had the trick of silence so complete you lost him in all his master's noise. *Unpleasant cub.* I tried to catch Damonryan's eye across the room, but he'd returned to the girl. Who could blame him? Shrugging to myself I dismissed them all, fixing my gaze deliberately on the table, seeking in the scars yet one more rhyme. 'Twas on an odd meter I'd settled, so the lines were trickier than usual, but I was close now and flattering myself the result would be worth the effort.

"Move, peasant, this one's mine!"

The words were loud. He didn't care who heard him or, more like, took care that all did. When I looked up the big servant had reached over and was putting down the bottle, a little bang on the table to punctuate his master. As he stepped back, I saw the girl framed between them and the hairs on the back of my neck rose in sudden apprehension. Since Cozumel, Damonryan had shown me a time or two he could stand up to provocation, but it had always been aimed at himself. Fear lay naked, slashed ugly across that beautiful china face.

She's only a doxie, Damonryan. She goes with anyone who pays. For all that was sense I started to rise. *My skipper was a woman!* I'd been affronted when he told me that, sure he was pulling my leg, but he'd convinced me later he was deadly serious. In some strange way, that belied his eyes and common experience, he saw women as just the same as himself. I was only halfway to my feet when I saw his head come between the two who stood before him. Quite deliberately, he caught my eye, and the head gave a sharp little shake, then watched me back down to the chair, before leisurely pulling back.

"I'm afraid the lady wants to stay with me." His voice floated easily across the room, not loud, but quite audible in the silence that hung thicker than smoke.

"It doesn't matter what the *tart* wants," the youth said thickly, "It only matters what I want!"

"No good, my lord," I could still hear no sign of strain in his respectful tones. "Neither of us are serfs. You have no office over us."

The stripling laughed high and nasty, "Lars, throw this dung outside." He giggled again, "In the midden, where he belongs."

Stolidly, the big man moved in, seizing Damonryan by the scruff and one arm. He'd done it all before and he expected no resistance. He knew his master too powerful for that and for once Damonryan seemed inclined to be sensible. He made no demur but let the man drag him to his feet. I doubted big Lars would even use the midden, just getting Damonryan out of sight would do, but I still thought it time to call a halt. Only the shattered look on the girl's face held my call. I could follow the man outside after all and make sure he did no real harm. Preferable, mayhap, to making even more trouble for her. Whatever the outcome, she'd be behind when we left.

I should have known better. Lars was just propelling him past his master when Damonryan struck. A elbow back and up, into the pit and point of the retainer's stomach. A quick twist around as Lars began to double and a lightning strike upwards to the chin with the heel of his hand. His neck flung back, the servant straightened, willy-nilly, and Damonryan finished him with a strange, sideways, kick of his heel, deep between the big man's legs. Three blows, faster than it takes to say them, and somehow he was back and face to face with the youth before his follower had even reached the floor.

The cheeks of the scion of castle Hakford stained slowly red with fury. Not for the massive Lars bubbling deep in agony on the floor beside him, whom he simply ignored, but for his own affronted dignity. In front of him, Damonryan seemed to stand easy, but I could tell that the rage ran clear through him, though the god knows where it had come from. Red anger against the black. Call me coward an you will, but I knew no purpose could be served by now trying to come between them. In their present mood, I doubt they knew there was any other in the room. The die was cast and though you would say to look at them, 'twas no contest, that the starman could toss aside three or four of the lordling and never know they were there, yet 'twas all the other way. Damonryan's fists and feet would avail him little against the lethal whisper of Suthy steel. For a long moment the youth stared at Damonryan, and it seemed to me that as he did so generations of his ancestors ranged up and took their place behind him. Sure of his right, he slowly reached for his sword. 'Twas in his face he'd no intent to put it back unblooded.

Any other man, unarmed, would have fallen back before that threat. Certes, 'twas what the cub expected, but Damonryan moved in a step, his eyes glittering. Then he spoke him soft, too soft for aught but the two of them. The hand stopped. The nostrils flared and the cheek I could see went from red to white, but the hand still stayed though the fingers flexed as if they yearned for the hilt. Damonryan spoke again, as quiet as before, and even the fingers stopped. 'Twas an the sprig were turned to stone and indeed, you could have picked him up and placed him in any castle garden, called him *Uncertainty* and folk would exclaim at the sculptor's art. Then he trembled and the hand fell back. One by one, as it seemed to me, all the old lords he'd ranged behind him started slipping off.

He fell back half a step, but Damonryan held up his hand and he stopped. They had more words. Then, quick as a cat, the starman stooped and, without ever taking his eyes from the other's face, relieved the still groaning Lars of his knife. Holding the hilt in his right hand, he started slowly tapping the blade against the palm of his left, then nodded curtly at the youth. This worthy's lips worked, then he spat deliberately on the floor at Damonryan's boot, spun on his heel and stalked straight from the inn. Not once, in all the confrontation, had he looked to his servant, nor did he spare as much as a glance for him now.

With a curse, Damonryan stabbed the knife deep into the wood of the table, then moved around and dropped back into his seat. He had no eyes for the girl who still sat frozen, more white faced than ever, but watched instead the servant Lars get slowly to his feet. To my surprise, where I'd expected a rage more profound than his master's, I saw only respect.

"Thee knows how to fight," the big man wheezed painfully.

A mort of the anger drained from Damonryan's face, "I've been around a bit." He looked at Lars with some sympathy, and pushed the bottle across the table, "Drink?"

"I'd be proud to but…" he looked at the door where his master had gone, his expression unreadable. "Best not."

"Take the knife, then."

Lars raised his hand to where his blade still quivered in the table, then let it fall. "Best not," he repeated, then gave a ghost of a grin. "My lord would never understand 'ow I come to get it back." With a nod of his great head he started for the door, his gait slightly lurching now, distinctly tender.

§

"What did you say to him?"

"I asked him how he thought he was going to get his sword clear of his scabbard before I broke his arm? That's why I waited. Not only to put poor Lars off his guard but to finish up close enough to his high and mightiness that I could catch hold of his sword arm if I needed."

"The god, starman…" the girl had long fled, afraid of any violence, either from Vlastus, as I'd found the lordling called, or from Damonryan. I could safely use what terms I wanted, "…he might have turned once you let him go, and spit you with a will!"

"You forget the knife. I told him I could put it between his eyes at twenty feet." He grinned, some of the tension easing, "Never thrown one in my life. I'd have been lucky to hit him with the hilt!" He was scornful now, "I was safe enough. His type live by the bluff, and believe it. It makes them afraid to call someone else's."

"His power is no bluff!"

"Jesus, Nikki!" the grin waxed into red-hot anger, "What do you want me to do? Stand aside? Analla was terrified." The anger was in his eyes, now. "He beats his women bloody before he takes them!"

I felt sick at that. You hear of such things, but I'd not run into them before. Nevertheless, he needed to understand there was naught we could do. "Look around," I flung back at him, coldly. The girl had not been alone in her flight. Except for Balzan, who eyed us resentfully from behind the bar, the big public room was empty. "They were all afraid to be found here when Vlastus comes back. When he finds us gone, who do you suppose he'll take it out on? Lars?' I shook my head, "'Twill be the wench takes the brunt, and I'll warrant it worse by far than what he'd have done to her an you let him alone."

"Goddamn it, Nikki! Is there no justice in this bloody place? You mean that jumped-up little bastard thinks he can get away with it just because his father is lord high something or other?"

"Something or other! Lord Runholt?" I felt my brows go up, then started to intone, making the titles roll like a herald does, so they come at you in waves, "Baron of Lansing, of Hakford, and of Harting, Master of the Royal Hunt, Privy to the Queen's Council, and the god and the baron himself only know what else. And *thinks* is not in it, my friend. He answers only to his father and the Queen. He'd have to do a good deal more than knock about a bar girl to attract their attention."

We stood, locked eye to eye for a dozen heartbeats, then I nodded at the door, "Come on. Best we were going. Balzan wants us out of here."

I'd already had words with Balzan, or rather he'd had them with me. Vlastus was well known to him and the little landlord was one with his customers in fearing the lordling would return and find Damonryan there.

"After what you said?" He shook his head, "No way do I leave Analla to his tender mercies!"

"An he comes back with half his garrison?" He stood his ground, with a look in his eyes said I would never move him. I considered. "I'll talk to Balzan."

§

We rode low, hooves ringing off a western road etched clear by both the flying moons. No way for a harper to be leaving town but haste mattered more than dignity. The landlord had agreed to move Analla to Estonval but not until he had promised to do it that night and at once had Damonryan at last consented to leave. 'Twas not until the long reaches of the outlying fields began finally to stutter into woods that I felt safe enough to drop the horses back to a walk. We went in silence a while, catching our breaths.

"You did her no favors, you know." I was still bitter against him, determined he should see, once and for all, this was not his world. An I didn't, he would kill us both.

"What do you mean?"

"Whatever evils there are in the land are always magnified in a town as big as Estonval. She had a place in Tappingsworth, friends, a family. She'll have no one in the city, and rats in plenty to prey on her."

He said nothing. We rode on, his silence more bitter than reproach, and sudden, again I saw my mother's body, faceless behind its thrown up dress, the blood pooled pathetically beneath. For the first time since I'd become his guide, I felt ashamed of the land. My way might be sensible, would certainly keep us alive the longer, but, even to me, it had little of the savor of what was right.

Chapter 22

I had a bad night. Murder and rapine stalked my dreams, while I played my pretty, useless harp. There is never any sound in dreams, or at least in mine. Wherefore, to what end a harp? Would my tinklings seem as silent amidst the roar and clash of war? That thought thrashed back and forth between broken bouts of sleeping, all jumbled with the notion that Vlastus was just a symptom of the ill that infected Dankar, and that could I but physic the growth that curled blackly out of Umber, mayhap I yet could find the cure. Beneath all, lay thickly the worry that I'd driven a deep and irreparable rift in the only real friendship I'd ever known.

I woke in the morning to the sweet smell of burning gumwood, laid over with the waft of tea. Before I could even break from my roll he'd brought me a mug and had squatted down before me. This was a reversal. In camp we generally abandoned our roles as servant and master. Since I was invariably first one up, 'twas usually I who made the tea.

"I'm sorry, Nicodemus."

I regarded him ruefully, "You were right."

"Mmm. I know." He scratched briefly at the ground with a stick, then looked up, "Trouble is, so were you."

I took refuge in the tea, glad my worst fears of the night were not to be realized, and he stood up, tossing the stick away.

"Is there any reason I shouldn't carry a sword?"

I almost choked. "Other than the fact it will get you killed?"

"You mean it's forbidden?"

"Only to serfs," I admitted. "But you can't bluff everybody. An you carry a sword, sooner or later you might have to use it."

"I'm not worried about that."

I stared at him, "You should be. Knights and even men-at-arms train with weapons for *years*. You'd never catch up."

He didn't answer, but removed the covering strap from the infocom and began to search. After a time, he grunted, "Thought so. See here?"

He twisted round the unit and swords beyond imagining marched slowly through the steam of my tea, a vast array of types and sizes, some so strange you'd never think them swords at all, except for the companies in which they marched.

"These are of the kind used in the land." He ran his thumb through the quivering image, "See the thickness of the blade and the width of the point."

Then he showed me others with blades that, did ours bespeak the stolid knight in armor, these conjured instead the waist of a Suthy dancer, some even lithely curved, but wicked edged—

"These were used to slice..."

And yet a third set, like daggers drawn to impossible lengths or even great needles—

"...and these to pierce. Your pattern sword is designed to chop, and that doesn't take a great deal of skill." He caught my look and gave a tiny half laugh, "I know. Easy for me to say. Watch..." he whispered a single word, *"Samurai."*

There sprang up the image of a man with long hair and a strange flowing costume that made me think at first he was a woman. That thought fled as he wielded a pair of curved, slicing swords in a flashing display that would have silenced the most rabid knights.

I whistled, "And I thought he was a woman!"

"And so wrote him off," he snorted. "Well, originally the Samurai *were* all men, but what would you say if I told you I've seen a cast of a woman who could dice one of your knights into stewing cubes before he could ever get his clumsy sword clear of its scabbard?"

I looked closely at his face, but he seemed too serious just now for this to be one of his jokes. He sighed in exasperation, "I'm sorry I ever pulled your leg about anything in the Settled Worlds!"

I poured out the leas of my tea and sighed in my turn, "It seems not natural."

"Well. Point is, these skills are still practiced on the Settled Worlds and they really do take years to master. I could never survive against..." he raised his eyebrows, "That *woman,* but..."

he'd picked up his stick again and now slashed down at the ground, "With my training, I believe I could learn to use one of your kind of sword well enough."

§

At the next town he bought a sword, old but serviceable enough. From time to time thereafter, he would find a companionable soldier who would tutor him for a coin or two. He practiced daily, by himself for the most part, which seemed of little use to me, but he laughed.

"I know how to fight already. What I seek now is to learn the weapon and how to wield it."

Indeed, within a month he managed to surprise one of his teachers, winning, with wooden practice swords, three flights out of three. It cost him a deal of ale to satisfy the fellow's discontent and after that he was more circumspect, chaffering his companions for practice rather than lessons. Though I suspected the capability of the man he beat, still it seemed he began to win as often as not. I began to have fears that he was seeking to become a man-at-arms and at last I broached the issue.

"A hired bully-boy, like poor Lars!" he scoffed. "Don't fret, Nicodemus, I've no taste for another's dirty work. It's just that I refuse to walk blind in the land of the one eyed."

The analogy seemed a little rough to me, but I didn't quibble. There were other signs 'twas not his intent. In Dankar we were camping more and harpering less than we had in Suthy, in part because distances are a little greater and in part because I grew weary of the endless requests for battle songs and the ballads of great deeds. The whole kingdom was preoccupied with war, though so far, it seemed all posturing, with no movement of troops.

It gave us more time with the infocom and Damonryan seemed bent on putting it to good use. Several new schemes were hit upon and then dropped, better glass for one, and something to do with pipes. He was fascinated by a thing called electricity—lightning in a bottle was as close as I could get to it— coming back to it over and over but always leaving it again.

"Too complex," he would mutter.

Trying to grasp the physics of the thing one day, I could only agree but when I said so, he only snorted, "Not that way. Same old story. Too much infrastructure for one man."

§

I had another worry to occupy me. Try as I might I could get no word of Bellarus. Castle or tavern, 'twas always the same. He was remembered well enough, but no one had seen him for at least four years. The only good news was that no one had heard of his death. I began to search in earnest, seeking out such old friends of his as I could recall and inquiring close into what they knew. At last, I ran to earth one old fellow, at Burangary Castle, who had competed hands of times against my old master and who had made some attempt to keep up with his former rivals.

"Retired, I heard," he piped, "Somewhere up near Tamus." He said a great deal more, in fact, but that was all was to the point.

I took my leave of the old fellow feeling all betwixt and between. At least there was some solid hope my master were still alive but I could not make myself believe that he would find the life of a kept harper at all pleasing. His ancient colleague, as emptily garrulous as only the lonely can be, had made the evils of such a position plain. Though 'twould be beneath his lord to starve or otherwise abuse him, he felt like an old dog, unable to hunt, kept on sufferance, for charity and consequence, rather than because he was really wanted. 'Twas seldom now he was allowed to raise his reedy old pipes in song which fretted him worse than all the rest. The light was gone from his eyes. 'Twould not be long, I judged, before he simply turned his face against the wall.

§

"To Tamus then?"

"Do you mind?" It meant doubling back, for lately we had been working our way east. Burangary was not so very far from

Estonval and I think he had been looking forward to seeing that city.

"You're leading the parade," he laughed. "After the trouble I've caused you, it's a wonder you still let me march along!"

So we rode to Tamus, coming in, of course, by the Eastern Gate. It and the square inside were pattern enough of the Western that, for a heartbeat, I shivered and wondered, had we arrived by its fellow, just which street I would have taken to get to the Boar. Yet nothing untoward happened this time. The inn was the same. Not even the ostler had changed. Inside I found Tandor, large as ever, still behind his great bar, polishing his tankards, only the thinning of his hair giving any sign of the years that had intervened. He looked up as we entered.

"Ha! Nicodemus!"

"Well met, Tandor." I suffered his great embrace then introduced my companion while he swept us all an ale. "You're one of the few to recognize me," I told him after we'd all taken a companionable pull and Damonryan had commented suitably on his brew.

"Been watching for you anytime these two years gone, is why," he smiled. "Happen t'auld man will be pleased to see you."

"So he *is* here. I'd heard he retired."

"Aye. He's with Lord Tanfred and 'is lady, at Bannering."

I shook my head, "I don't mind them, well, Tandor, beyond the name of course. Is he much fretted?"

"Fretted?" Tandor pulled a long face, "Ah, well…" then he burst into a great roar of laughter at my look, "*Fretted,* Nicodemus? Well, I suppose you might call it so, with the snuggest little sergeantry you ever saw. *Peacocking* is more what it minds *me* of, though!"

"Sergeantry? Tandor you're joking!"

"Never a word!" he swore, "Tanfred and 'is lady are what gentles is *supposed* to be. They took a shine to the old man, see, and they could see 'e was beginning to 'ave a 'ard time of it. They 'it upon that as a way of gettin' 'im to stay."

Sudden, I was anxious again, "Has he grown so very old?"

"Naow, naow, master Nicodemus, don't be takin' on so. 'E's too old to be travelin' in all weathers, but 'e's spry enough for all that." He drained his drink, then heaved his bulk to his feet, "Going to play tonight?" he asked hopefully.

I shook my head, "Next time. Can you give me his direction?"

"As I feared." He told me the way, then seized me in another of his crushing hugs before setting me down, "But next time you plays, mind."

"What was that all about?" asked Damonryan as we left the tavern.

"A sergeantry? It means he's a place of his own. They are seldom granted, and then only for exceptional service to an old and valued retainer. I've never heard of a harper getting one before." I thought a little as we rode, "Should give him dignity and mayhap a little independence. I only hope it doesn't mean he's just got a little bigger kennel."

§

We found the place, late in the afternoon, an ample house with a pretty garden and a couple of fields about. My old master had done well. I knew knights who would not despise it. Before it an old man leaned upon a gate, watching the pigs in the yard, then turning to us as we cantered up.

"Well met, uncle," I nodded, giving him the kind of back handed title the west riding folk use for their elders, "Can you tell us, is the harper Bellarus to be found within?"

To my horror, the old eyes twinkled, then the old lips parted in a fearsome grin, "Uncle, is it?" The lips twisted even harder, "Rogue, do you not recognize me?"

"T…too late!" I stammered, "Y…you've shaved off your beard!"

"You always were a bad liar, Nicodemus!" he slapped his thigh in glee, "Eh, but come down from Megan, there, and let me see you!"

I slid from the saddle, shocked by how much he had aged since last I saw him. His hair had thinned, lying lank and white upon his scalp, and he leaned upon a stick, his great frame shrunk in upon itself. For all of that, there was strength yet in the arms that wrapped around me and a lively quickness to his movements. Then, to show me he still could, he near flattened me with a blow between the shoulders, "'Tis *good* to see you!"

I made him known to Damonryan and we walked, all three, to a small barn, out behind the house. There the starman clucked at Megan, "I'll take care of the horses," and drew her and his own mount into the building.

"Let me show you my roses," offered Bellarus, taking me by the elbow, "They're fine old roses, much neglected, but I think mayhap I have succeeded in bringing them back." As we left the barn, he jerked his head behind, "There's a tale, there, I take it?"

"Now, how did you know that?"

He chuckled, "Servants don't generally dismiss their masters to spend time alone with old friends!"

As he showed off the place, he affected diffidence but his casual words could not mask the deep delight. "Just fieldstone," he waved at the house, and so it was, rough shaped and fitted, with an amount of mortar that would have had Brother Canus pursing his lips, but beautiful for all that, with its weathered, rounded surfaces. "Crude," he deprecated, "But these rural masons exhibited a skill that is not often appreciated. I am oft amazed at how well the stones are fit!"

I looked closer and found he was right; at least I was sure I would not have wanted to try. Easier to first cut the stone into blocks, but already he'd passed on. Catching him up and just looking at him as he talked, I saw the years fall away. The aging was all on the surface. Inside the man was as solid as the wall behind us, his mind as good as ever, his faultless memory unimpaired. We passed on to something else, but more of the same from him, and I found myself amused. Most important of all, his hands were strong and straight and his voice was clear, *so I can still sing for my supper* he laughed. "I've only to sing for it once a week, and on feastdays," he added, "And ..." giving me a jab with his sharp old elbow, "I've a snug little widow to care for me!"

He passed on to discourse of his timbering, how 'twas cut and pegged, what tenons worked best in thousand leaf and what in oak; then 'twas the apples in his orchard, what he used for scaffold and what to graft. The deeper rooted something was, I was amused to see, the deeper his interest. 'Twas plain the life suited him, at least in his old age; the road held no more allure.

Sa. He had much to hold him. His sergeantry was almost a third of a manor in extent, with an ample farmhouse that would have been called a manor house when first it was built, and several crofts, each with a family of serfs to run it. I could see his people were fond of the old man, who knew each of their names down to the smallest child, and that he was an easy master. Even so, the place had a well tended look.

"Nlandeth," he said when I commented. "She was the headman's wife before he took sick and died, and she will stand for little slackness. We make for a good team."

Though she wore the widow's bun, *snug* was not the word that I would have applied to Nlandeth. She was of that nameless age that female serfs seem to come to so quickly, and then live in until they die, a coiled and dried up leaf of a woman, fierce as hunger. She said barely a word when we were introduced, but ducked her head to hide her eyes, then went and sat apart, alone. Still, for all she didn't move, it felt an we circled, a pair of crouching, wary dogs sidling endlessly about a single, elderly bone. At length she got up and left for the kitchen. Bellarus looked troubled but said naught and we talked of old times until she served the supper.

To give her credit, there was nothing mean about the meal. Still, 'twas not a success. Against her wishes, Bellarus insisted that she should sit with us, so she did but she would say no word. A harper learns to talk with anyone at dinner, but I might as well have addressed my remarks to the farthest of the moons, for all the response I got. What, beyond her undoubted skill as a goodwife, Bellarus could see in her was more than I could understand; then, as we stood up, I saw him smile at her. 'Twas all he did. He was discomfited by her behavior, I knew it, and she must have too, but still he made the smile. She gave him one, back, not even a whole one, but a little, twisted up half smile, and, sudden, I saw a bit of Annie, and realized she must have been fierce to outsiders as well. It made her a little more human, his attachment for her a little more understandable. Still, I resolved we wouldn't linger. Tomorrow, I'd get Bellarus on his own, and pick his brains on the subject of Damonryan, and then we'd depart. No harper should stay where he isn't welcome—'twas he himself had taught me that.

§

"'Arper?"

'Twas a double rise that night and I'd been watching the moons swim up out of the field together, Aries, now that they were gate high, already ahead of Aurelia. Somewhere I had heard the *thwick-thwick-thwick* of a thresher, and had thought *ours*. A glider, not a true flier like the birds the people had brought with them to the land, a difference I had never noticed before I met Damonryan.

"No feathers, either," I murmured, and turned to the voice.

She looked startled. "Nlandeth?" I realized I hadn't even heard her enough to recognize her voice.

The *thwicking* sounded again, "Ohh!" she gave a nervous little laugh, "T'resher bird. Folks do say t'at means a good 'arvest."

"They used to say that at home, too," I offered, then turned half back to the gate, "I always liked a double rise." Whatever she had been sent out to say, she might find easier were we not quite face to face.

She gave me no answer, but confirmed my instinct by moving to the other end of the gate. Yet her face was darkly sharp against the moons and her silence coiled about her. We stood like that a while.

"I won't be staying long, Nlandeth," I said, gently as I could muster, against the bitter taste of bile inside.

"No, 'arper, no! You must stay!"

"He won't beat you, you know," I said somewhat sharply.

"I knows t'at!" she said scornfully, then, even in the dark, I could see the sharp little face soften, "But 'e *will* be un'appy."

"Does that matter to you so much?"

"Aye," she lifted her head, "It does so."

"Then why…?" I let the question hang, unwilling to reproach her. She knew well enough what it was I was talking about. For the longest time there was silence.

"'E talks of the road, sometimes," she said at last, picking at a sleeve, then abruptly looking at me full in the eyes for the first time, "'Tis like 'e's talkin' about anutter woman!"

"You're afraid I'll take him away?"

Wordlessly, she nodded, a jerky movement, like a bird that dips its beak then tries to watch.

I thought of the old roses tumbling down the stones of the garden wall, "Never," I said flatly, "I'd no intention of trying but I couldn't even an I would. He's completely happy here, Nlandeth. Those times are done for him. He'll talk about the road until the end of his days, but that's all 'twill be—just talk. He'll not go back."

She watched me as I talked, never moving, then said wonderingly, "You cares for 'im!"

"Of course."

"Young men often don't," she shrugged, then added quickly, "I'm sorry, Nicodemus. I 'ave been a fool. Trut' is, 'e 'as talked tat much of you, it made me right nervous." She looked back at the house, an seeking Bellarus through the thick old walls, "'Twould do 'im a deal of good an you could stay awhile. 'Tis the talk 'e chiefly misses."

'Twas not the most gracious invitation I'd ever had but I believe she meant it. She had a fierce loyalty for the old man which was hard to hold against her and I think she felt the same way about me. In the end, 'twas almost all we had in common but 'twas enough for an uneasy peace. I agreed to stay for a while.

Not that it was so very hard to importune us, once I was sure she did not actively want us gone. Damonryan got a room of his own and I was glad of the chance to talk to my old master, whose mind had not shrunk with his frame. With the starman's consent, I told him all that had passed, and the three of us talked late into many nights about what it all might mean and what could be done. Where I still tended to treat the infocom as a wonder or something that Damonryan could use in his search, Bellarus almost at once regarded it as a resource, to be pressed somehow into service for all of the land.

"'Tis a veritable oracle!" he said, not the least overawed by Damonryan's demonstration.

Remembering my own first reaction I was a little chagrined by his. Oh, he exclaimed suitably over its colors and its impossible letters and whooped over the glowing globe of our world, but he was not the slightest taken aback. I suppose the fact that I saw it all unprepared while he came to it only after a deal of talk about it made some difference. I was childishly pleased when Nlandeth treated it as the sheerest black magic.

§

As courtesy demanded I accompanied Bellarus on his weekly visit to his Baron. Damonryan was thought to come in his old role, but already that felt wrong to me and I put him off. Now that we were staying in one place a spell, better he not be seen. What the future held for him I was not sure, only that it was not to be as my servant.

The steward took us straight through to the solar, as soon as we arrived, an unlooked for privilege that told me much about my old master's standing. The Lord Tanfred, Baron of Bannering, stood beside a chair, a spear of a man, tall and straight and thin and silent, with steel gray locks that only needed to be drawn to a point to make complete the illusion. Indeed, I found out later, he was still known as *the lance,* though not only for his aspect; despite he was whisper thin his prowess with that weapon had won him no little renown in his youth.

A lady as different from him as she could be exploded from the chair like a pigeon from a thicket. She was small and plump, soft edged where he was angled, brown haired and eyed and gowned, brown on brown on brown, not dull and sere, but rather sparkling, the flash of feathers in the sun.

"Well met, Bellarus!" She kissed him on the cheek, for all the land an he were an old friend who'd chanced by instead of a retainer upon a mandatory call. "And this is…?" her head canted sideways, "Nicodemus!" she hazarded, then clapped her hands when Bellarus nodded that it was so.

I made my bow and found her as effulgent at seeing me as she had been at my master. Though she was engaging as a child, I sensed behind it a graciousness that went far past childhood's years and beneath and behind that again, a hint of steel of the oldest and longest tempered sort.

Through all of this, her lord had never moved; now at last he came forward. An he was as spare of speech as his lady was not, still he was her perfect counterpoint and made us feel as welcome. As a young man he'd traveled the land and he asked me now about Suthy and Welling, using as few words as he could to keep me talking. And so, in easy stages, they moved us down to supper. Only once did I hear him hold forth in the slightest, and that was on the subject of the Duke of Umber. I had just commented that people seemed not so upset in the west as they were in the east.

"Make no mistake," he said grimly, "Granly is a man to fear. He wants to be King and he's already shown in Umber he don't much care how he gets his way. Folk here think it don't concern them for well they know the battles will be fought over other's fields. An he wins, they will sing a different tune. They'll have a different overlord, one very much in debt to Granly, and expected to pay that debt."

"Carstead!" added the Lady Masra, with evident loathing.

"Very likely," agreed the Baron mildly, "The Duke, Nicodemus, sees the land in simple terms. You are either for him or against him."

"And you, my lord, stand for the Queen."

"Just so." He gave one of his rare smiles, "It does stiffen the resolve something wonderful." I smiled back, finding it hard to believe he was a man in need of such stiffening, though doubtless there were others that did. He said little else on the subject except to say in his mild way that there would be war come spring. He made it sound as common as apple blight but, for all his blitheness, trouble lurked in those steady eyes.

Afterwards, both of us played, a bittersweet joy at first, for it was evident I had surpassed my old master. Yet it was not a competition so neither of us essayed to do too much and even played together, me underpinning his lead, as was fitting. An his fingers were a little stiff, he knew well his limits, and never pushed into what he could do no more. Nothing could ever take his basic sense of music, though, and I went from being afraid of offending him, to marveling how well he used the tools he had remaining.

At the end, before we left, the Lady Masra discreetly pulled me to the side and murmured quietly, "I saw you watch how we treated the old man. Do we pass muster?"

There was no point in denying it. I bowed and simply said, "He was a good master to me."

"I'm not offended, harper." She smiled, "'Tis my lord's intent to grant him tenure at Warely for life." A shadow crossed her face, "I'll see he does before he rides to this war."

On the way back, I asked Bellarus how it was they were so sure who Umber would give Bannering to, an he took the crown.

"Carstead? He is due to inherit in any case, and he is Umber's creature." He looked at me sideways, "You must have seen how they dealt together, Nicodemus. She is barren—'tis known he had his byblows as a younger man, though none since they were married—yet Tanfred would never countenance that she be set aside."

So, good and ill, then. An his voice or hands gave out, Bellarus would not be back begging on the road. Once given, such grants were not lightly set aside. Still, I couldn't help wonder, should the Queen go down to defeat, how he would prosper beneath the despised Carstead.

§

Despite that shadow, 'twas easy to fall into the way of the local peasantry. Peace, there, seemed to rise from the very ground, like deep, still water, and for once we had time on our hands, without the need to be moving on every day or two. It gave the starman time to think, and more and more, he began to talk of glass and better papers and ink as a place to start. There was something else, I knew, but though he seemed on the verge of discussing it a time or two, always he pulled back. I didn't press him, feeling he would bring it up when he was ready.

More and more, as the days passed, plans to make things would lead him to thoughts of places he might do it. He talked of workshops laid in a town somewhere, or of warehouses converted, and we even rode to Tamus, where I'd to make good my promise to Tandor. The trip was a sore disappointment to Damonryan, for he found the streets largely organized by craft, and not a premise did business but held a license from the sheriff. A particular license, the coopers to coop, and the goldsmiths and silversmiths to make jewelry, but always of their own kind and never the others.

He blew out his cheeks, "No scope for me here," he muttered.

When we got back to Bellarus', he stared out over the fields, watching the men and beasts returning in the gathering dark.

"You know," he said thoughtfully, "I could do worse things with my money than buy a spread like this."

"Difficult," I replied, "An you are not noble. Except for the odd little sergeantry like Bellarus', the manors are all held by knights or barons."

"Damn!" he swore, adding a few expressions of his own safely under his breath, "Space, Nicodemus! Is there anything they don't control?"

I smiled, understanding his frustration, but thinking it something he must deal with himself, "The trouble with you is that you *act* like a baron."

He stared at me a moment, then grinned, "Nikki, you're a genius!"

Chapter 23

As he had been sharing a pot with Bellarus when I went to bed, I thought little of Damonryan's absence next morning when I came to break my fast but by midday I taxed my old master an he knew where he was.

"Not here," he said with something of a gleam in his eye, "At dawn he rode to Tamas Town. I wouldn't look for him for a day or two yet."

Regarding him with some suspicion, I demanded to know what the two of them were up to.

"'Tis a surprise," he retorted. "He thought you wouldn't quite approve and looking at your face I can see why. Cut rein, Nicodemus! The lad's got to be able to stand on his own sometime."

"Lad? He's almost as old as you."

"Is he now?" Bellarus stroked his beard in some chagrin. "Well, well. Whoever would have thought it?" Then he shot at me, "All the more reason to let him go."

Though I knew he was right, I had misgivings remembering all the scrapes he had got himself into, and there wasn't an hour went by in the next two days that I didn't consider saddling my horse and riding after him. The track I watched continuously so that Bellarus grumbled I was a mother hen. Even so, I missed him, for he slipped round behind and quietly stabled his horse, strolling in upon us just as we sat to supper.

Bellarus swept him a magnificent bow, "Good, my lord," he said, "Would'st deign to join us in our simple supper?"

I could only stare. From his gaudy velvet hat to his lemon yellow boots he was the picture of a town lord, a very gentleman of fashion, straight from the court of the Queen. Making us an elegant leg, he then pirouetted so we could admire him at all points.

"Will I do?" 'Twas directed at Bellarus.

"Indeed you will. Nicodemus was in the right of it. You *do* act very like a lord."

"It will *not* do!" I spluttered, "Looks make not a lord and a commoner caught acting above his station will get the shortest sort of shrift!"

"You're looking at it backwards," said Damonryan, "Who is it to say I'm not a lord where I come from?"

"You'll never say you're from the stars!" I protested. "You'd not like to be believed and 'twould cause an almighty uproar. Of a surety, the temple would come sniffing about, and your only witness they have most thoroughly discredited."

"I could probably sell it to them eventually, but you're right, it's likely to cause more trouble than it's worth. Bellarus and I have a simpler plan."

Never one to miss a cue, Bellarus spoke up, "Damonryan is to enter the Great Autumn Tourney at the Estonval Fair. There are always a few places left in the lists."

"Dear the god, Bellarus, are you in your dotage?" Sudden, I found myself in a rage, "The man has only just learned to ride a horse! He has never held a lance, never worn armor! An he gets on the field, he's like to find the sheer weight of the stuff dragging him from his horse." That last thought stuck, cooling some of my choler, "But they *won't* let him on the field. The heralds would never permit it."

Although he'd fluffed up at the mention of his dotage Bellarus now brought the weight of all his considerable dignity to bear, "So long as the heralds believe him noble he may enter the lists anonymously. I believe they will accept *my* surety on that point."

"Wonderful!" my anger rekindled in an instant, "And when he fights like a commoner and *dies* like a commoner, what are you going to tell them over his body?"

"It's just a tourney," the old man protested, a shade less sure.

"Aye. And you know well that knights get killed at tourneys. Particularly inexperienced ones."

Through all of this the starman had let us brangle. Now he said quietly, "I won't get killed."

"The god, Damonryan! These people have been training all their *lives!*"

He shrugged, "I have three months," just as if that were sufficient.

Exasperated, I turned back to the old man, "All right. Just suppose you manage to get him on the field; and just suppose he somehow manages to survive. What, in the name of all the kingdoms, is the point?"

"We tell them he's a knight. He will be dressed as a knight. As *you* said, he already *acts* like a knight. An he can learn to fight like one, their very pride would be loathe to make them believe otherwise."

"That won't wash, Bellarus and you know it," I retorted, "The heralds know the patrimony and style of every knight in the land, down to the lowest cadet of the least important house in Westernesse."

"Ah, but once we've shown them a knight, and they want to believe, we've got a little story for the Queen!"

They told me their tale and I told them just what I thought of it; throughout all that supper we contended and then well into the night. At length Damonryan stood up, "I'm for bed," he yawned then looked hard at me, "I'm going to do this, Nicodemus," he said flatly, "With, or without, your support."

After he had gone, I turned on Bellarus. "Look you, old man," something I should never have said, would never have said but that I was cold angry, "This is a game to you. Something to fill your empty hours here. But 'tis not you will pay the price of failure."

"Nikki," he said quietly, not putting on his dignity and so putting me far more effectively in my place than if he had, "'Tis not the least use insulting me. 'Tis the lad's plan, by far more than mine, and he'll not be swayed from it now." His old eyes twinkled, "Ye put me in mind of a mother hen trying to squat on a cockerel!"

I gave it up for the nonce. "He's not a lad," I said crossly.

§

Certes the bit was full and fair between his teeth. In the morning both were up before me, Nlandeth reporting that

Bellarus was gone to the village and Damonryan was somewhere out by the barn. I found him behind it, surrounded by gear he'd already bought, from the sheriff's own armorer, no less, an the markings were anything to go by. He'd on an iron codpiece and a shirt of close-linked mail and was now examining the straps on a gorget.

"Should I have put this on first, I wonder?"

I shrugged my lack of knowledge and leaned against the barn, watching the struggle.

"You need a squire."

He stopped and looked at me quizzically, "Now, why do I have the feeling that that is not intended to be helpful?"

"No, no," I protested, "An I knew of one, I would be happy to furnish you with the name of a young fellow, at once knowledgeable about armor and blithe that his new master was not!"

I ducked away as a mailed glove sailed past my ear, "Not all squires are apprentices," he called after me.

His words were prophetic, but of course he knew. I looked up to find Bellarus, returning from the village, with a burly graybeard stumping along on a gimpy leg beside him. For all his peasant's smock, he had the close hacked hair and even, through the limp, the carriage of a soldier. Bellarus introduced us, telling me something of the fellow's history. Sure enough, he was an old man-at-arms, brother to a woman who lived in one of Bellarus' crofts, though he did not. I glared at my old master, for it meant this Barth had been sent for, a matter of at least a day or two before. He was come to stand both as trainer and squire, a request he seemed perfectly ready to fall in with, though he said nothing.

In fact, he let Bellarus do all the talking, limiting his conversation to a laconic, "'Arper,' when first we were introduced. Though he'd seldom fought on horse himself, Barth had garrisoned a castle in his younger days and Bellarus claimed for him a professional interest in how the knights were trained. At the sound of our voices, Damonryan came round the corner and I found myself quickly ignored as Barth took the starman straight off to start his training. I noted with dismay that the planning had been sufficiently detailed that Damonryan had equipment for Barth who, despite his injury, was still well able to wield a sword.

'Twas not until evening that I had a chance to get the man alone. I steered him out of doors, where we could talk unheard.

"Barth. …" I paused, realizing this was going to be more difficult than I thought. I'd no idea what he'd been told, certainly not that Damonryan came from the stars, but how had they explained that a noble had no knightly training? Whatever they had said, I didn't want to contradict them. I tried again.

"This is not going to work. The…ah…*other* knights have been training all their lives. You must know already he has no chance to beat them. I don't mind him getting knocked into the dust a bit but I don't want to see him killed. He won't listen to any arguments of mine, though. 'Tis up to you to show him that he can't compete."

I went on in this vein while Barth listened attentively, nodding at what he considered particularly telling points, chewing on some kind of leaf. When I had done he spat thoughtfully out on the grass.

"Master said you'd be talkin' to me," he said with a conspiratory nod, "Meanin' no disrepeck, 'arper, but 'appen 'tis 'im as is payin' me!"

Then he stood, perfectly pleased to hear what else I might have to say, though 'twas plain 'twould make not the slightest difference. Apparently he regarded my pleading as more in the nature of a performance than anything to be taken seriously.

They went back at it the next morning, then day after day, Damonryan always in his armor. 'Twas plain enough, a suit of mail, with breastplate, gauntlets and grieves of steel and an old fashioned tourney helm, not much more than a padded bucket, with slits for seeing and breathing. He fought in it, walked in it, ran in it, striving to get used to the unaccustomed weight. He even rode Jenny in it. She was not really up to all the extra load, though she carried him bravely, even managing to sweep into a gallop. I had to admit that he did pretty well though not even the dullest serf, watching his antics as he tried to mount, would ever mistake him for a knight.

The mail he didn't mind, but the gauntlets and helm he despised, finding them clumsy and disputing constantly with Barth their drawbacks. Once, to prove his point, he threw them off and challenged the old soldier to lay sword upon him. Barth was tentative at first, but Damonryan rang a clout flatly off his helmet that nearly felled him, and he set to with a will thereafter. Barth's breath soon gave out, so they didn't fight for long, but not one of the two or three dozen blows he aimed came even close to the starman, who fought in a blur.

Awed, Barth gasped to a halt, "I've never seen a man so fast!"

That had been in my mind before, but to hear it said by a seasoned fighter aroused my curiosity and I asked him about it over our evening meal.

"It's no special talent," he answered, "In an emergency, the brain releases a chemical that speeds it up, something most people might experience only three or four times in their lives. But it can be trained. Because the mind moves faster, the world around appears to slow down, so Barth's sword floats towards me and I have plenty of time to avoid it. The same process also allows me to move my muscles quicker, though not so much for it can only affect how quickly I start them, and not their speed of contraction."

"Why don't we simply do it all the time?"

He shrugged, "Double the speed and you double the energy, double the energy and you double the heat. Do it all the time and you quite literally bake your brains."

I chewed on that a while, "How do you train for it?"

"Meditation. Not so very different from what you've told me of your Tantran's training at Welling Abbey." He looked at me quizzically for a moment, then added, "The technique's been known for two or three thousand years so I've been surprised your people didn't bring it with them. They couldn't have been very militarily inclined when they arrived which confirms my suspicion that all this stuff about knights and serfs was grafted on later." He looked thoughtful for a moment, then said, "What I must guard against is not to count on it too much."

When I asked him why, he told me that some people learned to do it naturally. "I'm willing to bet that the best of your knights can do it, even if they don't realize it. If I get used to everyone being slow, I'm liable to be in for a big surprise."

I narrowed my eyes at that, "It sounds as if you plan to fight a lot more than a tourney."

"There's a war coming, Nicodemus. If I'm to be a knight, I can hardly avoid it. And," he added hastily, seeing my face, "Before you start on one of your diatribes…"

I made to protest.

"Diatribes!" he said firmly, "Just consider. Seems to me there are far worse things to be in one of your wars than a fully armored knight!"

"Harpers remain neutral."

He pushed back from the table and grinned, "I can't sing, remember." With that, he was gone, bawling for Barth, leaving me biting my lip. The better argument was that however fine a thing he might think it to be a knight, that didn't make him one; but even as I groused at myself for debating on his ground, I knew inside no ground would have made a difference. 'Twas plain he would go his way and no fears of mine, however apt or well founded, were going to make the slightest mark.

My best hope now was the lack of a horse. Destriers are no ordinary beasts, being well above the common in size and with years of training to boot. Jenny, despite her great heart, was by far too small to do. Trained chargers were rare and very valuable, worth more than Bellarus beloved manor house put together with all his grounds and his little village. With war in the air, finding one would be hard and purchasing it more ticklish yet, for who but a belted knight would want such a beast? Yet, after a pair of weeks, anxious for me lest he succeed and for Damonryan lest he did not, Bellarus heard of a newly widowed dame, with a suitable beast on offer. When I heard that the animal lay but two days ride away, almost I could believe that the god was taking a hand. I shook my head at that and sniffed the wind but I could feel no breath of the presence. Though I knew that chance casts the dice

with men far more often than the god, it made me jumpy. With
sour eyes I watched Damonryan take his leave of a gleeful
Bellarus, every inch the traveling trader on the lookout for
breeding stock. In all of this I was become like the sailor's Jonah,
worse than superfluous.

§

"No wonder knights are so poor!"

As always, he had traded well, yet between steed and gear
and his new courtier's clothes, his gold was by now sundered in
two. The beast was a mettlesome stallion, Darksome, well named,
an animal who demanded to be mastered before ever he would
show his training. It took him a week just to learn to ride him.
Under Barth's watchful eye, he managed it at last, so that he
could urge the horse into a full gallop, or veer it left or right, or
even rear and stamp, all simply by using his knees. And while all
of this went on, Barth at last found me something to do.

"I 'ears you'm good with yer 'ands?"

I shrugged non-commitally, "What is it you want?"

"A quintain."

I felt a gleam inside and wondered an he had known it and
whether there was more to Barth than there seemed, but all I said
was, "Describe it."

'Twas fairly simple, a crude figure on a stick, with a helm and
shield to represent a knight, and a pair of outstretched sticks for
arms. An 'twas not struck fair by the lance, 'twould rotate and an
arm would catch the rider. Even as he talked, I could see
possibilities for an improvement, and so I agreed and set to work.

"Never saw one like that!" Barth whistled, though he had the
wit to see at once what it was I had done. In his usual laconic
way, he said no more but simply pulled the dummy back hard
against the springy plank I had it mounted on. Should
Damonryan ever manage to hit it square, the mannikin would
give instead of breaking, and mayhap turn still when it bobbed
back up. Barth grinned his approval and bawled around the barn
for his pupil.

Bellarus turned up for the show as well. Damonryan managed to canter Darksome down to the end of the makeshift list and get him wheeled and to drop his lance across the saddle rest. The great horse must have seen the little figure waiting at the far end for he broke into a gallop without any urging from his would be master. The lance bounced violently in the crupper, and he fought it, so that the point swung wildly in the air. It passed the mannikin a good two feet to the left but the jutting stick arm caught a badly off-balance Damonryan square across the chest, and swept him with a crash into a stunned and winded heap.

Bellarus hobbled over and leaned his stick upon his helm. "I claim this horse and his arms by right of combat!" he cackled, playing, for the moment, the oldster with glee. Gasped out though they were, the string of oaths that followed drew another of Barth's admiring whistles.

Twice more he rode at the wooden knight with the very same result except that Bellarus kept wisely quiet while he thrashed around on the ground. In dismay, I saw him stumble to the horse a fourth time and, in a rage now, ride at the target without ever trying to point the lance at it, taking it instead full on his chest and bulling his way through. When he rode up in triumph, flipping up his visor, Barth looked dourly at the spinning quintain, "Try that in combat, you'll be spit like a chicken."

"Maybe so," glared the would-be knight, then grinned like a boy, "Makes me feel better, though!" and he kneed Darksome around for one more charge.

This time, more by chance than any control he exerted over his wildly errant point, he struck the target a swiping, sideways blow. His yell of triumph wailed into despair as the quintain spun and caught him behind the kidneys, boosting him from his saddle and past his charger's ears. Had the beast been not well trained, he might have been trampled, but it veered and braced, then whickered where it stood.

"I think the damn animal's laughing at me," glared Damonryan, sitting painfully up. "No apple for you, tonight!" Darksome, every inch the haughty destrier, just whickered again. The starman heaved himself to his feet, "Enough for one day!"

and gingerly set off towards the house, leaving Barth to bed the animal. I was not fooled. He'd be back tomorrow, and I felt despair. More than a month of his three gone by and he couldn't even hold his seat against a wooden dummy. What chance had he against a real knight? Yet I knew his stubbornness and sudden I'd no wish to stand and watch him through the weeks with little else to do but bray from the sidelines. The time had come to leave but even as I turned to Bellarus to tell him, it came to me like a cold wind that I had no heart for harping. I hung there, stunned, like my wooden man upon his stick, wondering just what it was the god had done to me. For better or for worse, my star appeared to be tied to Damonryan's. Bellarus eyed me askance. Then there drifted across my mind something I'd toyed with for a while to do and I made a sudden decision.

"Lend me your donkey."

Chapter 24

The road wound left into the rise then abruptly fell away, leaving me looking down again at Halting Castle. With its hard old northern stone stained rose by the westering sun and a rich quilt of fields tucked almost to its walls it looked peaceful enough. Serfs streamed home to catch their evening meal, black dots in the distance with an intermittent firefly flash that, an the scent of new mown grass was anything to go by, must have come from shouldered scythes.

Wearily, I heeled forward my reluctant mount. No mendicant friar ever had such a horse as Megan so I'd had to take Bellarus' donkey instead. Shank's mare would have been faster but the beast carried the load of phials and implements and essences I needed for my role as itinerant herbalist. I'd also had to stop more. Despite all he had done to prevent it, I'd learned much from Brother Manfred and I found my skills in great demand by the country folk amongst whom I chiefly went. So I stopped and held my court, took their pennies, mixed their medicines and salves, and came to know the trade.

'Twas not always an honest one. There was a steady demand for philters or potions to raise flagging husbands or other charms of that sort. Yet every time I was reviled for refusing them I noticed that my ordinary business picked up. I soon discovered there was no disease but had to have a medicine. Instructions to bathe a fever cool, or take plenty of water or work a wasted leg were so much air without a potion or ointment to go with them, the nastier the better. At Welling we'd taken great pride in our ability to smooth out the taste of even the bitterest of herbs but the peasants would none of it. They wanted every copper's worth and could not be brought to believe that sweet smelling salves or elixirs that tasted good had any healing power at all. The cherry water and lemon balm I'd taken so much trouble to bring might just as well have been left behind. An I used no pounded spiders, I did not tell them that but simply took to adding bitter herbs to potions they found too sweet. My medicines were popular enough after that I had to spend no little time in the gathering of new ingredients.

Sa. There were rewards. Folk eased or sometimes even outright healed were gifts in themselves, though the ones I couldn't help oppressed me more than usual. Having seen the infocom I knew how much better Damonryan's people could have done and resolved to spend more time looking into his medicine. On top of that, they shared their homes and food with me in a way they never would a harper. I gave out I was a simple man, come from the north, abbey trained, to be sure, but still of the people. While they cosseted me as they would a harper, with the best seat and pride of cooking, they did it an I were one of them and not apart. 'Twas a comfy feeling.

§

The gates of Halting loomed above. Unlike the last time I'd arrived, the battlements were fully manned and a guard sang down to the courtyard below at my approach. The sergeant at the portal was as surly as old Rufus but he let me in readily enough.

"Doss ta mule in ta stables," he jerked a dirty thumb, "And, be you fast enough, 'ee might get a bite in ta kitchens."

No groom came for my beast, nor steward to greet me. I was not important enough for that. Not wanting to seem too familiar with the place I asked my way once I'd seen to the mule. Dropping down the stairs brought back so many memories that I stopped and rubbed at my beard, sudden nervous, afraid 'twould never be enough. Twelve years is a long time but I'd known everyone in the kitchens; surely there'd be someone who, looking at the man, would still see the boy. *Foolish, Nicodemus. You did not even know yourself in the glass!*

It was the same and yet, somehow, completely different. My eyes sought the groom's table and found it, still in its corner, more battered than ever. *And greasy!* I sat, startled, and looked about, knowing sudden what the change was. Always the kitchens had been a warm and happy place, and spotless. It was warm all right. 'Twas midsummer and the place was ferocious with the heat from the great central oven. No Kat, though. In fact, no one that I knew and no laughter either, just surliness and silence broken here and there by the staccato clatter of dirty platters come back from the hall above.

"'Ere!"

A bowl and mug were slapped in front of me. Cold porridge, a single carrot tossed on top, withered, last year's stock when fresh must even now be juicy in the ground, and small ale which I was to find watered past a point would have been tolerated by even the meanest goodwife.

I cocked an eyebrow, "'Alting's not too fond of strangers."

"'Tis what we eat," she said dully, then with more snap, "An you be too fine for it, could try your luck upstairs!"

Dirty hair wisped across a face that had flickered just for that moment but fell back hollow now against bones too high. Thinness poked here and there through a dress too torn for decency but the eyes didn't care. They gazed flatly to the side, not meeting mine, out of habit though and not shame. With nothing more to say she twisted slowly back and in that instant, recognition shook me like a dog. 'Twas well she wasn't looking at me. As it was her name was at my tongue unbidden so 'twas only with difficulty I could bite it back. *Janna!* To hide my shock I bent and stuffed in a spoonful of the porridge. Mayhap it had been all right in the morn when I suspect it had been made, but now, cold and greasy from standing, it served to legitimize whatever dismay still registered on my face.

Janna. I remembered her now, a vixen, irrepressible, always skirting the edge of trouble and wild to be like Kat. Three years my senior but you'd never credit it to look at her now. Between bites of the disgusting stuff, I scanned the kitchen much more carefully. Two more I found, an undercook who I thought had been a spitboy, and another drudge, all aged, all thin and ragged as beggars, all beaten. Still no Kat, for which I was beginning to be grateful. I saw other things. Though it was dying now, only the central fire had been banked; the rest had the cold, dead look of pits not used for days. The leavings from upstairs, which included one complete capon, untouched so far as I could see, were carefully scraped onto a wooden tray, and handed to a boy with a vacant look who was even dirtier than the kitchen staff. *The kennel boy*. Edgar's dogs were better fed than his people. 'Twas telling not a morsel was taken, though even as he left I saw the dog boy eyeing which portion he would have for his own.

§

I paced the tiny margins of my room. Room! Was a cell, windowless, airless and none too clean, with only a curtain for a door. My sojourn in the kitchen had turned up little except that the Lord Edgar was out hunting, Kat was not there and the Lady Beatrice was. Confined to her quarters, it sounded like, though I'd had small conversation and even less opportunity to probe. The little biplay with the capon and the dog boy had said it all. He would eat alone what none dared touch in the open room. An Edgar had somehow turned his people, each against their own, what chance had I an someone tumbled who I really was? Best I be away on the morrow to Pudding Hill. I'd only stopped at Halting because it was the nearer and there was some chance Kat might be there. It had been in my mind to see Beatrice an I could but 'the state of the castle proved she no longer ruled as chatelaine. Stopping my pacing, I sudden made up my mind and thrust the packet I had made up back in my pack. Too dangerous, with nothing to be gained. I'd hold my promised clinic in the morning and be on my way.

'Twas not a pleasant night, the cell stuffy and the pallet too dirty and full of pests for me to even contemplate. Stiff and tired, I was nevertheless grateful for morning, not minding even the lukewarm porridge. At least it was fresh and the apple with it firm and sweet and not too bruised. Stretching I rose and told Janna I'd be holding a clinic out behind the stables before I left. I'd no desire to hang about but 'twould have been out of character not to have done so. Behind the stables had the virtue that it was out of the public eye, which is to say Edgar's and in the normal way, the telling of a single servant would be enough to spread the word. An it did not, I could be gone the faster.

Business was slow at first but not even Edgar could wholly stamp out the castle gossip, so it picked up through the morning, mostly men at arms or their women, with a handful of upper servants. A few I recognized but I saw no answering spark which began to make me feel more comfortable in my chosen role. My observations from the kitchens fresh in my mind, I refused to let them crowd about my little table, but waved them back so I could see them one at a time. 'Tis hard for a body who has acquired the habit to shake the sense of always being watched but furtive answers make for bad medicine; they loosened up a little, knowing their fellows could not hear them.

"Next."

I looked up and was startled to see the self same maid that Beatrice had sent for me to tell me of my riding lessons. She was old now and a little bent, her face pulled permanently into the hard lines that seemed a feature of every visage in Halting, but there was still vigor in her walk.

"What can I do for you, mother?"

She snorted and began a rambling dissertation which came down to very little but the normal aches of age and that she was bored and had heard my medicines were cheap. At length I began to mix her up a salve.

"Are you maid to the lady?"

She looked at me sharply, "How did you know that?"

"Your clothes," I shrugged, "'Tis my business to observe such things." Almost without thinking I reached into my pack. "Give her this, with my compliments." Along with the salve I held out the little packet I had made up. Inclining my head, I said, as unctuously as I could, "There is no charge, of course."

She stayed her hand, "She will not see you!"

"Nevertheless." I continued to hold them out, "The fortunes of business, madam."

I could not have been the first peddler to have tried this ploy for she took them and went without another word. Watching her stride away, I felt the sweat begin. While the contents of the packet would mean nothing to Edgar he would see at once 'twas not the normal offering of a peddler of herbs to a chatelaine. I remembered that Beatrice had refused to speak to me plainly in front of her maids but surely it had not been this one, who she'd sent in secrecy, that she mistrusted. For the rest of the morning I kept watch, angry with myself for being so foolish, half hoping—

Nessa, that's her name—would come back, half afraid that Edgar's men at arms would be down for me.

In the event, neither happened, and at midday I declared the clinic closed and put away my wares. Eschewing the kitchens— I'd quite enough of Halting's porridge—I went straight to the stables and began to pack up my mule. It took me a time. One of the straps had frayed but the saddler had gone to his midday meal, along with all the grooms and stable boys, so I had to jury rig it with a piece of rope. A hand brushed my shoulder and I started so the mule reared back.

"Nessa!"

She looked as frightened as I but even so, her eyes narrowed, "How is it you know my name?"

"I…I asked," I replied, fighting to recover.

"Well," she thought about it, seemed satisfied, "I'm glad I found you. I waited by the kitchen stairs and when you didn't come I thought you'd left."

"I almost did," I replied, pointing to the offending strap. "I've had enough of Halting hospitality."

Her mouth tightened even more at that, "My Lady will see you. But have a care. She's not supposed to have visitors." Without another word she beckoned me to follow and slipped quietly from the stable. Even as I trailed after her the thought crossed my mind, *Dear the god, it might still be to Edgar!*

§

"Nikki!"

Twelve years dropped away, the same room, newly swept, the same scents, the old chair, the regal way she had of sitting in it; the only difference from the last time, she was in the shadow now, where the sun had gone round from her morning window.

"My lady!"

I stepped close and saw her properly and all the years flooded back and more, piling up on her like waves as they grow where they beat upon the shore. Her face was gaunt with lines and the light had gone from her shining hair leaving it flat and dead. The sparkling colors of her clothes, white slashed through with blue, had been changed for black vented on dullest black. And her hands, those pale and slender hands that had flashed from her sleeves like birds, now held the arms of the chair in a static grip, all ribbed veins and twisted knuckles. Yet the voice was clear, and the eyes, for all they spoke a sadness I could not begin to touch, still held something of their old command. I felt my heart go out to her as it never had before.

She smiled grimly, "Here's a sight. I'd thought we'd sent you out a harper!"

"And so I am. Circumstances required I come in disguise."

"Edgar." She said it flatly, no inflection, the one word explaining everything. For a moment she was gone, as old people go, making me think, mayhap, she were half senile.

"I sometimes wonder an I haven't fostered a changeling," she said softly; then the eyes came back to me and they were anything but foolish. The grief in her was a solid thing, enough to crush her, yet her back was straight as any queen's and her head erect. She looked me over long moments then smiled.

"Come, buss me boy. 'Tis plain my sweet Constance had no such problem." I kissed the proffered cheek and she laughed, "Never did care for beards! Eh, but 'tis good to see you, Nikki. Do you give me a jar or two of your ointments, that I'll have something to show for your visit, then sit you down and tell me all about yourself."

I did as I was bid, leaving open my case of medicines. Nessa kept watch outside but we might get little warning. Just before I seated myself she said sudden, "Here. Before I forget," and she handed me back my mother's fork, that I had sent to her packed in a bag of herbs, as a sign.

So I told her what had passed since I had seen her last, leaving out only the sendings of the god and Damonryan. We talked of my life for an hour and I found best the little happenings that made her laugh, like my first concert in Suthy. In the end she clapped her hands like a young girl.

"Has done me more good than any of your medicines just to hear you talk!" she exclaimed. She was silent a while, turning over in her mind all that I had told her. I left her to it.

"Well! You haven't come all this way just to talk to an old woman."

"In part," I smiled, "I came to see old friends."

"Seems to me, I was not one of them," she challenged.

"I think you were. Mayhap more than I knew."

"You see far, child. Like your mother." Her eyes took on that faraway look again, "I used to watch you from my window sometimes. Looking so lost my arms ached to hold you. But I dared not. I wanted nothing to bind you to this place."

"I know." No need to mention Edgar. We both knew him for the cause.

The pain was back in her eyes. "Who else did you wish to see?"

"Brychan."

Slowly, she shook her head. "He took exception to some of the ...*works*... of my son." She watched me while I absorbed this, then added quietly. "'Twas not a pleasant death. Annie was overset with grief and died soon after."

I struggled with the bile that rose sour in my throat, "I feared it. Brychan was of the sort to stand up to Edgar. But I had hoped to see Annie." Still lost, searching for something to say, I stammered, "I...I had no idea you knew her."

"I know all our people, Nicodemus." Mayhap at any other time 'twould have been a reproof but she said it gently now, a part of her pride. "I approved of Edgar's ways no more than Brychan did, so you see me..." she gestured round her, "...chatelaine of this room. Three years he's kept me here but still I know everything that comes to pass in Tansley, even to the coming of a wandering friar!" Her lip twitched so I knew 'twas her had sent Nessa. "Kat is in Cooling."

Some of the bile receded, "You knew who all my friends were."

"You didn't have many. She lives in the cottage at the end of the last of the right running lanes." She looked troubled, "You will find her changed."

"How?"

But her head shook denial, "Past time you went, boy. Buss me again."

I didn't push it. She looked tired, even, for the first time in our interview, a little beaten and I would find out soon enough. As I leaned forward to kiss her cheek, the old arms came around me, sudden and fierce, an she could wrap all the embraces she had denied me, and herself, when I was young, into one. I gathered her in and returned it, more moved than I had words to say, and a little shocked to find no weight to her though there was still steel in the arms that gripped. We stayed like that a long time.

"Thank you, boy! Best get you gone." The arms loosed and as I stepped back she said sudden, anguished, "Have a care, Nikki. Go swiftly and don't get caught. He'll be back from his hunting soon and I…" the old thumbs gripped each other across her chest, "…I have no power over him!"

"I'll be careful." I bussed her again on the cheek, then swiftly packed my things. With a hand on the door I turned, seeing her regal again in her chair, her face in the shadow. My thumb found the latch.

"Nikki. Ask Kat about her boy." She would say no more but waved me away.

§

I passed by Farleigh's Snitch and Pudding Hill though there was that in me wanted to ride by Brychan and Annie's cottage at least, mayhap because it would have felt like home. *Foolish, Nicodemus, you spent but a night there.* I clucked at the mule and moved on. Maybe not so foolish, but not important enough to be worth the risk; besides, 'twas a weary way to be setting out so late and I wanted to make it to Cooling.

An the mule was slow it was hardy enough to push steady on throughout the afternoon and all the long summer evening as well, so we managed to get there just at the fading of the light. I stared to see it. 'Twas quite unchanged from what I remembered as a boy, before 'twas sacked by the raiders. Cottage had been replaced by cottage even, so far as I could tell, down to size and how each was placed upon its tiny piece of ground. All the more remarkable in that the inhabitants were entirely new. Riding down the street I found the temple where first I'd thought I might have felt the presence, tucked in its self same spot, timber for timber just like the old. I smiled to see it. 'Twas not the people's doing but Cromart's, who had been nothing if not methodical. *No. Not an apposite memorial.* As conservative as the people he ruled he would have thought it important to put things back exactly as they were, an only as an affirmation of the old pact between serf and overlord, they to serve and he to protect.

The whole place seemed deserted but only because folks were all inside. Happily they'd not yet settled away so not even the dogs commented upon my passing. 'Twas no task to find the cottage, small, a pattern with most of the others, neatly kept, with a wall of stone and a matter of fact little garden of herbs and vegetables but no flowers. Leaving the mule at the gate, 'twas but three paces to the door and then my knock, a dull thudding that hung harsh against the evening still.

I was a long time waiting. At length the door, protesting, shuddered to a crack and one eye, baleful, in a cheek like suet pudding, scanned me bleakly up and down.

"What do 'ee want?" Petulant. The voice cracked.

"I…I'm sorry. I was told I'd find Kat here."

The eye scanned me again then the gap began to widen, farther and farther, until almost 'twas all open and still she filled it. She was vast. Not just the cheek, but all of her one great pudding.

"I be she!" 'Twas said flatly, in no expectation.

"K…kat." I was appalled. The Lady Beatrice had warned me she was changed but this enormous slab of a woman bore no resemblance to the laughing girl I'd known. An there were any, 'twould be in the dancing eyes yet the great face was still averted, the one eye that I could see was flat, devoid of laughter, of anger, of anything.

"What do 'ee want?"

I saw then how foolish was my mistake. I'd thought to ride back into my past and pick up old friendships, but my friends were as dead as my parents, Brychan and Annie in the ground and Kat buried deep in this hulk of flesh. My trip was a waste; I'd risked Edgar for a child's dream. What would Damonryan say?

Time to cut my losses. I opened my mouth to say I'd been mistaken, to turn my back and to go, when the feel of the Lady Beatrice' arms stole around me.

"Can I come in?" She stared at me, unblinking. "The Lady Beatrice sent me."

A long moment more, then she turned ponderously from the door, leaving it open. Taking that as invitation, I ducked beneath the lintel and followed her in. 'Twas full dark inside so I could see naught but her bulk against a back window. She moved and shuttered it, and then the others, saying nothing until she'd done.

"We'll need a light."

'Twas said grudgingly, but she found the flint in the dark and a spark leapt deft enough and caught a wick that flared, smoky, in a tallow dip. Holding it well out and down from her, she set it on a table, then pushed it towards me.

"Sit." 'Twas evident she wanted a good look at me.

She sat herself at the other end, her face up and out of the light though I could see she still held her head turned. The table was perfectly clean I noticed, both to the eye and to the touch, so I folded my arms upon it and leaned farther into the light. Somehow, mayhap coming from Halting, mayhap because she'd let herself go, I'd expected the place to be filthy, part of my reluctance to come inside. But the little of the floor I could see was meticulously swept and the only smell was of sweet herbs she must have set into the tallow. Even the small part of her acres of gown I could see was clean and neatly patched and I felt sudden ashamed. Something of Kat was still alive and I'd no right to judge by her appearance. I turned my gaze back straight at her, across the dance of flame, trying to put my thoughts in order, thinking of what to say, how much to tell her.

"Nikki?" A little girl's voice now, questing, unsure. I smiled as best I could, still not comfortable. "Dear ta god!" The voice was stronger now, "'Tis you!"

In her surprise, she had turned her head full on. Seizing the light I held it up. 'Twas my turn now.

"Dear the god!" Discovered, she held her self steady in the flame, letting me look my fill, her eyes unreadable. The whole left side of her face was a ruin, immobile, puckered with shiny scars, the kind that burns leave. Not in a fire though, caught in the flash of kitchen oil as sometimes happens to drudges. Branded. Over and over again, remorselessly, with what only could have been a knife, the mark of the tip running to the corner of the eye and again to the edge of the mouth.

"Edgar?" Dumbly, she nodded.

"Because of me?"

"Not really."

Only the right side responded, the left stayed frozen so it seemed to leer as she talked. I did my best to keep my reaction from my eyes but she turned the ruined side away again, though not with any resentment I could see. She appeared used to it. Gently, I put down the dip.

"'E come back to ta castle in a t'underin' rage after you and t'arper be gone. There was trouble between 'im and Lord Cromart at once, on account 'e cut one of ta men up something fierce."

"I know. We watched him do it though he didn't know we were there."

"Just as well. 'Twould 'ave been you 'e cut, an 'e didn't do worse. Any road, 'e left everyone strictly alone then. A week later Baldric left for Cooling, but 'e took me with 'im. Ta mistress saw us married first."

Something about the way she said that made me say, "I'm sorry, Kat. That was my doing."

"Was it, now? Took a lot on yourself, you did!"

"I was afraid for you on account of Edgar. I asked Baldric to see an he could get you out."

" Sa. 'Appen Edgar would 'ave done for me anyway. Baldric was ta best thing 'appened to me though I didn't feel like that at ta time. Thought 'e was too old.

"Anyway, year or so later, Edgar sees me comin' 'ome. There was no one else about, so 'e tried to take me. Told me in a voice gave me ta shivers, I was *ta bastard's friend* and that *time 'ad come to pay my shot.*"

I felt my heart sink, "So he *did* do that to you because of me."

Her voice softened. "No, all 'e wanted was a little sport. 'E fair gave me ta creeps but 'twas nothing I couldn't 'andle. Wouldn't be ta first time. Serf women get used to that."

"Cromart!" I was scandalized, "I'd never have thought it of him."

"Nor you should, neither. But some of ta soljers and knights weren't so particular. An Cromart knew, 'e would 'ave given them trouble, but 'twasn't worth our while to report it. Too many ways for it to come back in t'end. Any road, I bit my lip and prepared to put up with 'im." She shivered and her voice grew distant, "'Twas worse than I could ever 'ave thought. 'Is 'ands were cold and they pushed and prodded at me like arms from a grave. Even now, in ta dark of winter, I feel them come upon me. 'E ruined me for any other man."

She was silent a long while, then took up the thread, "Trouble was, 'e couldn't. Nowadays, they say 'e don't try anymore, but 'e still did then." She paused, "I laughed at 'im."

I visualized Edgar as I remembered him on the stair and I knew I would never have had the courage to scorn him so openly. "So he did this to you."

"Aye. 'E was like a madman, beating me and screaming names. I more or less expected that but 'e went on and on so I thought 'e would kill me. Then 'e went all cold, *I've a better idea* 'e said, then 'e tied me 'ands and lit a fire." Her voice went flat, with no expression "'E sat me up and 'e came at me mortal slow. And each time 'e made me wait for it, swearing that, an I moved, 'e'd 'ave the eyes out of me. Four times 'e done me afore I fainted but that wasn't good enough for 'im." She put her finger to her ruined cheek. "Can't count 'ow many more 'e did till 'e got tired of 'is little game. When Baldric found me 'e was gone." She paused a while then added bitterly, "'E left me my eyes but whether 'twas because 'e gave 'is *word* or because 'e wanted me to see 'is 'andiwork I don't rightly know."

She told it all so matter-of factly I didn't know what to say. At length I asked, "What did Cromart do?"

She seemed to ignore my question, lost sudden in the memory. "There's no pain like burning, Nikki." Now the hurt came through, "I was out of my 'ead for weeks and Baldric, bless 'im, never left my side. By the time we could think of aught else, Cromart was dead."

"I heard Lord Blanchard got him in the end."

She snorted, "So they say. Sure, t'ere was no love lost between 'em since Blanchard killed your parents and burnt Coolin' to t'a ground. Funny, though, ever since, Edgar and Blanchard 'as been t'ick as t'ieves." She sighed, then, for the first time I heard an echo of the old Kat, "Never mind all that, Nikki. Tell us about yersel'." The good side of her face bent upwards in a smile, "Look at you, a priest!"

"Not likely, Kat," I smiled, thinking of how outraged Brother Fernand would be at her contention, "I'm a harper."

"Ohhh!" The right side of her face was transformed, "Nikki, you never brought your harp? I'd be mortal proud to 'ear you play it!"

She seemed more aggrieved at Edgar that I hadn't than at anything he'd done to her. She had some things to say about him that would have earned Damonryan's respect so I was sorry he wasn't there. He would have enjoyed her. At length, she ran down.

"I don't need a harp."

I sang for her acappella. You can hear in some of the old songs that they were written that way, with a drone note on the downbeat, to keep the rhythm and to give untrained singers a home to come back to. That's often hidden by the harp, damped down behind arpeggios that sweeten the songs for noble ears. A pity. In her kitchen I sang them as they should be sung, lusty, unvarnished, the only accompaniment her great hands rolling the rhythm on the table, and sometimes her voice, a clear soprano she could raise in a descant would make a Welling choirmaster shiver. Then we did some of the chants, the old ones, still heard on high feast days, so she knew them a little, call and response, me doing both until she got the hang of them, then throwing them back and forth as they should be, 'til the notes stacked up like bells, pealing amongst the rafters of the little cottage.

'Twas not long before the neighbors were in. Tallow dips ran from end to end of the table and on the sills as well, each family bringing their own until the tiny cottage was lit brighter than any hall. Someone brought a bhodran, the great north country drum with a goatskin hide and crossed braces behind that the player held in one hand while twirling a double ended stick with the other. There was a tin pipe and three pairs of spoons, as well as an old wooden paddy doll that the player danced on the table between the tallows, and even managed to paddywhack off his knees and ankles and arms, to the delight of the children bundled in the corner. I sang alone, I sang accompanied and sometimes I just listened, pulling at a mug of homebrew, one of the non musical contributions. Kat held court in the center, her head high despite the light, her good side beaming, her hands dancing rhythms on the table that made the bhodran player sweat to keep up.

It took me back to my childhood. 'Twas a good north country time and it never once crossed my mind that Edgar should hear of it.

Chapter 25

"'E won't," said Kat flatly.

We were both a little bleary eyed, though, truth to tell, folk had gone to bed quite early relative to what I remembered from my childhood. There was little leisure with Edgar as overlord. Folk could not afford the loss of sleep.

"You can't know that."

"Listen to me, Nicodemus. These are my people. Edgar may 'ave them turning on each other at ta castle, I don't doubt it. But not 'ere."

She sat back, massive arms folded, and glared at me. Already I had acquired the trick of reading just the good side of her face, so the other faded back. However careful she was with the outside world, 'twas born on me sudden that here, she was the *madronna*, the glue, the one that all the others turned to. If not of Cooling, at least of her lane. I bowed my head, accepting her judgment.

"All right."

She heaved up and fetched a pan of oaten cakes from the fire, forked three on my plate and whacked down a crock of tashenberry syrup.

"Mmm." With all the blandishments of the south, I hadn't realized how much I had missed plain north country cooking. "Aren't you supposed to be out with the others?"

She sat down to the remaining two cakes, "I minds ta chickens. 'Is lordship would not be best pleased to see 'is 'andiwork out in t'open."

"I didn't know he was so nice."

"'Is friends are. 'E's ambitious, is our Edgar, and there's all manner of fancy folk comes round 'ere. Even ta King! 'E's even got hisself a new coat of arms." She shook her head over that, "'Is da's wasn't good enough, t'ough t'at bleedin' dagger suits 'im. Any road, 'is little games don't look so good. 'Twas bad ta first year or two 'e took over but 'e mostly leaves folk alone, now. Can't hide everyone and run ta fief!" She stopped, a piece of oatcake halfway to her mouth, "Don't want to come up on a killing offense afore 'im, though. 'E gets to 'ave 'is fun and then bury what's left." She popped the piece in and chomped down hard, then shrugged, "I keeps out of sight and 'e leaves me be," she added simply, "I don't mind. I be too fat to work in ta fields!"

She was all of that. 'Twas hard to think of Kat inhabiting this monstrous body. She seemed to know what I was thinking.

"Couldn't stand a man after Edgar," she explained, "'Twas easier this way. Poor Baldric, 'twas 'ard on him, and 'e so good to me."

I thought of what Beatrice had said as I left. I'd seen no evidence of a child, but she'd seemed to think it important I asked.

"So your…son?…is Edgar's?" I asked gently.

"No!" The denial was out of her before she knew it, "'E's…"she tailed off, "'Oo told you?"

When I told her she looked stricken. "Means, sooner or later, Edgar will know," she muttered. "May'ap 'e already does. May'ap 'e's just biding 'is time!"

"Easy, Kat. I had a strong sense that the Lady Beatrice has ways of knowing what's going on in the fief that Edgar knows nothing about."

"'E'll find out!" she wailed. "Edgar likes boys!" she was crying now, great sobs, her words wedged between. "Mostly…'e leaves ta Mutchley ones alone but… C…Carrick be a comely lad. …An 'e knew 'e was mine… 'e'd take 'im, sure." She put her head in her hands, "Ohhhh… Why did I laugh at 'im?… 'Is boys don't never live too long!"

I sat stunned. I'd heard of such things, whispered by the younger boys in the novice cells at the abbey; but, after that, I'd kept my eyes open and I'd seen no signs, not even between boy and boy. Mayhap I was a rustic but it seemed to me that any brother who so violated his trust would have received the shortest of shrifts from the abbot. In the end I had marked it down as a tale. Now here it was in the life and uglier, to judge by her last statement, than anything that might ever have happened in an abbey.

This was no good to Kat. I pushed aside my disgust, reflecting sudden that the Lady Beatrice had never yet said anything that was not to the purpose. I needed at once to settle Kat down while considering just why it was that Beatrice had wanted me to ask after the child. A warning for Kat? To what end?

"Tell me about Carrick. Whose was he?" I looked about the cottage, "How have you hidden him?"

"I'm sorry." I'd brought in a packet of tea from the mule, something she'd not had since she worked at the castle kitchen, so she got up and made some now, to settle her mind. While she did, the story came out. By the time I'd a mug, I knew the boy was Baldric's. Despite the revulsion Edgar had left her with, she managed to lay with him a time or two and Carrick was the result. Content with a son, I gather Baldric never pressed her after that. A fever swept the village when Carrick was two, taking mostly the old and the very young. Baldric had succumbed as well as one of the neighbor's babes. Terrified that Edgar would come for her child when he was older, Kat had talked them into a switch. What steward knows one peasant brat from another? 'Twent down in the annual ledgers, dead, of the fever, one Baldric, forty-nine summers and one, Carrick, son of Baldric and of Kat, two summers. Meantime, Carrick lived on as Crensh, son of Dendyl and of Missy, now ten summers.

By the time she had done Kat was settled down and I suspected I knew why Beatrice had told me. 'Twas a risk but I'd already put myself at hazard. The law was unequivocal, the penalty severe; *but no more than what Edgar would have done to me had he caught me anyway.* What gnawed at me more 'twas no proper role for a harper; we stood for the old ways, for tradition and courtesy and honor. *Aye, and barons are supposed to defend and not prey upon their people.* I made my decision. That defense would stand me no stead in any court, I knew, but it just might do before the god.

"Kat." I looked at her above the mug, "I could take him."

She stared at me for heartbeat after heartbeat, her good side sudden as expressionless as her bad, all except her eyes, where hope fought it out with hurt.

"You could both be killed," she breathed at last.

"No worse than what you fear he faces, an he stays," I countered. "Besides, we're close to the marches. We'd be in Umber by nightfall."

"Runaway serfs are no better treated there."

"An there's no alarm from here, who's to know? He'd go as my servant."

"Oh, Nikki!" her lips worked, "'Tis more than I could wish but 'e be so young! I'd never see 'im again!"

I opened my mouth to deny it, but I could not. I was not like to be back so long as Edgar ruled and now was not the time for empty promises. "All I can say is I'll take good care of him."

She stared at me a long time, before at last her head bowed down in assent. "I know you will," she whispered.

§

It took longer to get away than I liked but who could blame her? Besides, 'twas not all her fault. I saw at once his clothes would not suit.

She had him fetched in from the fields where he watched the goats with other boys his age. That itself took a time. While she was gone, I wondered what I'd got myself into. Quite apart from the business of helping a serf to run away, I'd promised Kat I'd take care of him, without knowing even what he was like. For all I knew he might be a half wit. When at length she pushed him through the door, I could hardly believe my eyes.

"Don't mind ta dirt, Nikki," she said apologetically, "We keeps 'em all like this."

'Twas not just the dirt but the smell. The child was filthy beyond belief, a stark contrast to her spotless cottage. I had to fight to keep my hand from my nose. "On account of Edgar?"

She nodded. "Mostly, 'e leaves 'is own folk alone but it don't do to tempt 'im."

I looked beyond the dirt and saw a well made child, all leg and skinny, as a boy that age should be, with a pair of brown eyes that regarded me steadfastly. At a nudge from his mother he made a little bow.

"Good day to you, 'arper." A line well rehearsed.

"Good day to you, Carrick," I said as solemnly as I might, "But I think it had better be Brother Anstey just now."

"Didn't think you looked like an 'arper! See, Auntie," he said scornfully, "'E's naught but a wanderin' friar...oww!"

Dragged forcefully by the ear, he disappeared and I could soon hear his wails as Kat scrubbed him down in the garden. 'Twas borne on me that mayhap I'd taken rather a lot into my hands.

"They'll never do, Kat." Clean, dressed in his best clothes which Kat kept put away, he looked much better. Indeed, an Edgar had a taste for boys, I could see he had better been kept dirty. But not as my servant. Right now, best clothes or not, he didn't look anything but a serf. "I've got a spare robe in my pack could be cut down an you can sew it."

She could and did, but she claimed her fingers were unpracticed and she made it a slow business. Sa. Mayhap they were but every stitch brought closer the moment when the boy would be gone. While she worked Carrick sat small and still and, I think, frightened, though he tried hard not to show it. She'd told him what was afoot before she'd brought him but I don't think that it came home until I denied his clothes. The world he knew was to be swallowed up behind him and sudden, he didn't know who he was. I saw myself in him and resolved that at least he wouldn't be left to wander round a castle for months on his own. Yet there was naught 1 could say now to make him feel better so I let him be.

When at last Kat was done, it didn't look like much, draping badly where 'twas cut uneven, with the cowl, which she'd been afraid to touch, still much too large. It didn't matter. An he covered his head so no one could see the cut of his hair, he no longer looked like a serf; no one would expect the servant of wandering herbalist to be finely dressed.

"Ye'll stay for supper?"

'Twas truly late by now and I fain would be away but there was such pleading in her voice I'd not the heart to deny her. They'd had few enough suppers together as it was. My nerves were on the stretch and would be until we were clear but there was no real danger. Eastings Wood where Edgar hunted lay between us and the castle. Were he not still at the one he would be at the other, north either way, where we were bound south.

To give her credit, she was brisk about it. A simple supper, jugged coney but with herbs and greens and turnip all pulled fresh from the garden. She'd not wasted her time in the kitchens, was beautifully done, but by rote, so I didn't think that either of them noticed. They both tried to be cheerful and Carrick, child that he was, even managed it a time or two, before he'd remember and taper off. I joined in where I might but the meal was not a success. I felt like I was at a funerary supper and began to regret we'd stayed.

"Thank 'ee, Nikki!" She gave me a gargantuan hug through the tears, so I knew I'd been right after all. Taking Carrick to the corner, she had a few words in private, then folded him up until he was all but lost. He wrapped his arms about her neck, so skinny they looked like strings about her, and I stepped outside to see to the mule.

§

"There's the path!"

He'd not said much since we left. Bidding him pull the cowl over his head, I'd set him on the mule and he'd waved to his mother the little time it took us to get down the lane. Even as we turned the corner I had seen her heave her bulk out the gate and off to the neighbors. An there was to be no alarm there must be a funeral, a box and a grave. No one would see the body. Crensh, son of Dendyl, would die of the pox that very night and the steward would be satisfied. It gave her something to do. An 'twas a melancholy task, she could take comfort that all she buried was some stones, and that Carrick was safe beyond Edgar's grasp. What Dendyl and Missy thought of it all I never did find out.

Since leaving Cooling, we'd picked our way along the old road and I'd talked of my childhood here in these marches, to keep him from brooding too much and to let him know I was not so strange. For some minutes now I had been looking for the path than branched off and ran up to the old croft.

"Can we go see?"

'Twas on my tongue to say no, but 'twas the first real interest that he'd taken. Sudden, I found it in my heart that I wanted to go as well, to see the old place, my mother's garden, what was left of my father's walls, the swelling solitude of the upland meadows. 'Twas pure foolishness, I knew. The garden would be gone, even the stone beneath the grass for all I knew, but 'twas not so very far to go and we could fade straight from the croft into the marches. I turned the mule aside.

I was glad I did. Abandoned places are always melancholy but there was a beauty and a peace there I was pleased to see. The scars were gone, covered by grass and flowers that had tumbled out the garden and ran in rivers about the yard. 'Twas not my mother's order but the sheer abandon of the colors would have delighted her. Amidst the profusion, the one gable still stood, soft gray weathered and mute, standing proof of my father's hands.

I'd told Carrick what had happened and we found the graves, untouched, except the board was gone. He stood there with me a long time and at length his hand crept into mine and gripped it and I was glad. The beginning of a bond. He was trying to tell me that he felt for me, that at least he knew his mother lived.

I smiled down at him. "Why don't we camp here? Morning will be soon enough to move on."

I woke with knife at my throat. As my eyes came open I felt a hand in my hair and I was pulled sharply to my feet, the prick of the blade never off my neck. Though my eyes watered from the pain so I couldn't see, I'd never a doubt of who it was; I felt the cold of the night chill burn clean through me. As my vision cleared Edgar loomed up before me, plain in the edge of the dying fire.

"Well, well," he said pleasantly, "A traveling friar." He nodded to the man behind me who let me go at once. "What are you doing here?"

"Am a doctor and an herbalist, my lord," I replied, affecting a Suthy drawl and bowing with what I hoped was an appearance of brotherly dignity. "I have been visiting Tansley." As I came erect I forced myself to meet him square for even a mendicant would have no reason to shy off. I watched his eyes and began to feel a little easier. There was no flicker of recognition.

Yet something nagged at him, "Why here?" he twirled a gloved finger about him, "'Tis not on the road."

"My stock was low, lord. They said in Cooling was an old garden here once much known for herbs." So far so good, but I wondered frantically what he did here. Had he been following us?

"Who said?"

"I don't know, lord. An old dame. I didn't get her name."

He seemed satisfied and turned to where a third man held Carrick by the scruff. Not seeking us then, I was sure, or he'd either have asked me more or naught at all. Three horses, for himself and the other two, plainly men-at-arms. They were none of them accoutered for hunting. *Blanchard.* The croft was on the direct path back, as I knew to my sorrow. 'Twas our bad luck the moon was out and he'd smelt our fire. But what did he at Lashly that he went in secret?

"And what have we got here?"

Sudden, I forgot all about Lashly. Once I realized that Edgar didn't know me I'd thought to bluff my way through this but, whatever else he might be, Edgar wasn't a fool. Let Carrick open his mouth, and we were wholly undone. Edgar couldn't fail to recognize one of his own in the distinctive Tansley speech.

"J...just my servant, lord," I croaked, striving desperately to bring his attention back to me, "A...a worthless boy."

But Edgar was interested in boys. He waved the man who held him, forward into the light.

"What's your name?" he asked Carrick softly.

The lad stood, frozen as a rabbit.

"Your name?" His voice was a lash now.

Despairingly, Carrick opened his mouth and I slumped, knowing there was naught in the land I could do. Not yet half a day and, already, I was forsworn to his mother.

"U...u...ung...aa...aah!" I stared. He'd twisted his lips around and rolled his eyes, an in pain, but actually at me. "A...ah...aarung," he got out. *Bless the child!* Sudden, I saw what it was he tried to do.

"He's dumb, my lord." I felt the sweat stand out, "Has been from birth."

"Has he now?" Edgar looked at him a long moment, then twisted back to me. "Very nice, friar," he said, and his voice was sudden as it had been that night, all those years ago. "Your kind disgust me. So holy. So righteous. So…chaste." He smiled nastily, "But then, your pretty boy can't talk, can he?" He stared at me, face to face, a long time and something flickered in his eyes but he brushed it off like a buzzing fly. He'd something else on his mind. He stepped back.

"It doesn't do for the brethren to fall from the ways of the god. I think I'll relieve you of your temptation." For a moment more he stood to see how I would take it, then nodded to the man behind, "He can go." His eyes moved back to me, "Now, brother. Before I change my mind."

They stood all still and watched me shamble to the mule, his henchmen grinning, pleased to see even so humble a member of the cloth discomfited. Passing behind the animal, I stumbled, and my scrabbling hand passed over a dozen stones before I found one sharp enough for what I wanted. In my haste to mount the beast it shied around, not once, but thrice, so I heard one of the soldiers laugh. With its head right at them I drove the stone into its rump as hard as I could then sprang back to be clear. Even as I felt my heel catch on a stone, the maddened animal sprang forward.

"Carrick, run!" I managed to yelp, pitching backwards, then my head struck and the blackness took me.

§

I woke with aching head and ribs and my cheeks on fire. My head I understood and even my ribs. Someone had done a masterful job of kicking them. My eyes fluttered open.

"Watch it, fool, he's awake!"

A hand grasped my hair and the shadow slid past my eye, scraping at my cheek.

"'Old still, naow, brother," a voice hissed in my ear, "Lessen you wants to lose more than your beard!"

The blade came away and flicked the curling hairs upon the ground and came back. A knife. With spots of blood already on the blade. I closed my eyes again and held my head rigid.

"'At's ta way ta load ta dice!" The scraping went on and on until the fire had spread to all my face. "Done, me lord!" The hand let go my hair and I found myself seized and pulled to my feet. A brand, newly kindled from the fire was thrust into my face and Edgar strolled up.

He didn't look long. "So 'tis you." His eyes stared, a mad kind of hate in them. "You would have been better to let me have him, bastard. Now I have you instead."

I chose my words carefully, "I have been duly consecrated, by Welling Abbey. You have no right to touch me."

"Welling is it? My, my! You did get far. Still…" he drew his own knife from his sheath and looked lovingly along the blade, "You're only a mendicant. Someone didn't like you, Nicodemus. Besides…" he spun the blade in his hand like a juggler and I felt the edge against my cheek, "I have a prior claim. Your harper friend is still under interdict and you *did* help him escape." I felt the blade begin to cut, "You're mine… *bastard.*"

"No." He stepped back, and I could see my blood gleaming wetly on the blade. "I think…your knife, Arold." The third man stepped forward and handed him his blade and he held the two of them up before me.

"You perceive the difference." He brushed the edge with his thumb, "Not so sharp." Abruptly, he flipped his own and sheathed it. "Not so pretty either. Arold won't mind an it loses its temper. Arold can draw another from out the armory." Dear the god, I sudden saw where this was going and the fear must have flared in my eyes for Edgar smiled.

"Arold." He held out the knife and the man took it with a grin and bent and thrust the steel into the fire. Edgar smiled harder though his eyes were black as wells of night. "Arold and I have done this before."

Then he just waited, the smile fixed there like a mask. I could smell the burning of iron and the gorge began to rise in my throat. Frantically I tried to recall my training, to grasp the calm, to meet this as my father's son, but I could not. Fear had a hold of me, it snapped at my tripes and at my bowels and it shook them like a dog.

Seeing my struggle, Edgar smiled the harder, "Don't shit yourself, bastard. 'Tis such an unpleasant smell."

The taunt hit me like cold water and I straightened and managed to spit him in the face. The smile went out and he wiped it off.

"An eye for that, bastard. An eye at least."

He stooped like a hawk and the blade was in his hand, glowing red. I struggled to break from the grasp of the man behind me but he was powerful, a soldier, and it was futile. Wrapping an arm about my neck, he seized my hair with his free hand, brutally snapping my head back and there was a low laugh to my right from Arold. Edgar stepped close and the knife was up so I could feel the heat begin to sear my cheek. He flipped the knife from hand to hand.

"Which side, bastard?" He might have been talking to his mother. "Choose quick, before the heat goes!" I answered him nothing. "*Choose!*" he snarled, "Or I take *both!*"

"Th…the left."

"You hear that, Arold?" He was back to his boudoir voice. "Always they take the left." His eyes flared and I saw it would be now.

There was a quiet *thump* to my right and abruptly the blade was away. Edgar dived to the left, away from the firelight, and I could hear the cat lithe quick roll of him away in the dark. The hand was gone from my hair and even the grip about by throat let off a little. With all the anger and fear that they had loosed in me I smashed an elbow back. Had he not been distracted I would never have got away with it but as it was I caught him full in the belly. His breath went out with a *whoosh* and I was free. The only way left was the fire. I vaulted it and ran for the dark but as I went, I saw, from the corner of my eye, I need not have worried about Arold. He was stretched cold upon the ground.

"Over 'ere, 'arper." I heard the sound of horses and there was Carrick, already mounted, with two more reins in his hand. "Quick!"

He thrust a bridle at me and before I rightly knew what I was at I found myself aboard a wicked great horse. *Dear the god, 'tis Edgar's charger!* 'Twas well for me he'd been ridden or I would never have held him. As it was, I had my hands full. He reared and wheeled, so I almost lost my seat, and I heard a shout close to on the ground. After that I got him moving but lost Carrick in the dark.

"'Ere I am, 'arper."

"I thought I'd lost you!" He came close and I could just make out his outline.

"Naa!" he said scornfully, "'Ad ta get yer mule, now, didn't I?"

I laughed, though it had a nervous edge to it, even to my ears, "Carrick, you're a wonder!"

Then I looked back. I could see the fire with an edge of my father's gable, just standing out against it, by which I judged the south pasture must be nigh. *Too close.* Behind us was dead silence where confusion should have reigned. Already, Edgar hunted in earnest.

"This way," I urged the charger forward, "There should be a fence close by, and a gate." We found it, but we didn't need the gate. Already, there were sections down. We crossed into the pasture and were away into the night.

Chapter 26

To Carrick's great disgust, I returned the horses. Rather I left them at an inn on the southern edge of Umber with strict instructions to turn them over to the local baron who would see them back to Edgar. I'd no wish to be branded a horsethief and my trip had left me with the firm impression that Edgar held more sway in Umber than any lord of Angleterre had a right to.

He was a funny little fellow, proud as I suppose I'd been when I was that age. After he'd saved me I offered to set him up any way that I could, but he'd none of it. He wanted to be my servant.

"Do you mean my apprentice?"

He considered that. "Can't sing!" he said flatly, "Mam was always telling me to 'old me trap."

Whether he meant Missy or Kat I wasn't completely sure. He'd always had to call the one *Mam* and the other *Auntie* although he'd known who his mother was, right enough. Since he'd been with me, he'd taken to calling them both mam. Poor little soul. He'd been in hiding all his life, not always sure who he was, so he'd come to hold on to the image of his father, *Ta lady's groom!* as he'd announced to me, an that were second only to the baron himself. He'd hung around horses whenever he could and had a way with them, which was how he'd been able to creep up and relieve Edgar of his, all undetected. I thought his face would break when I told him Baldric would have been well pleased with him, but he didn't strut it off. His pride didn't run that way but was a secret thing, held close and deep.

The missile which felled Arold? A stone of course, fired from his sling. He'd brought it with him, without telling me. 'Twas almost the only thing he owned. I tried it a time or two with him, for I'd been no mean shot in my youth, but I was out of practice. Besides he was better than ever I had been. I told him to keep it and more than one coney found its way into our pot as a result, for I did take him as my servant. Damonryan had run his course and there was no better way to keep my promise to Kat.

Besides, it made him feel like he belonged. That was a thing that I could appreciate.

§

"What do you think?" I looked down at him for, now that he'd taken on to be my servant, he absolutely refused to ride while I went on foot. It slowed us down a bit but I didn't mind. We hadn't had far to go and it would have hurt his pride for me to insist.

"Coo!" he said, awed, "Not 'alf bad for a 'arper. I'd a slummed it for a baron's, an you 'adner tol' me." I laughed. Even in Umber, we'd stuck to the byways. He hadn't even seen a castle yet.

"An you want to stay my servant, we're going to have to do something about your language! Come on!"

Only Nlandeth was in the house. She eyed Carrick disdainfully, but said never a word, contenting herself with jerking a thumb towards the back. Leaving Carrick at the barn to take care of the mule and my kit, I strolled out to the field behind. Barth saw me first.

"'Arper," he hissed. "Watch this!"

Bellarus turned and his old faced creased a little more, "Nikki! 'Tis good to see you back, boy," but even he was a little distracted and he quickly turned back. Sa, here, I knew, I was not the main event. Somewhere out on the road with Carrick I had come to terms with that. There's nothing for reconciling one to one's role in life like coming close to losing life itself.

They'd set up a more formal kind of a list with my quintain in front of us and a pole fence stretched down the sward. At the far end, dressed in half armor, lance held high, Damonryan was caraçoling Darksome. Even as I watched, he stopped and dipped before a pole and the lance come down and rang from a hanging shield. At once, he wheeled about, the long way, three quarters of a full rotation, then leaned forward in the saddle. The destrier seemed to know his mind for almost before he was done the hooves were flying, as near to a gallop as a horse, so loaded, could achieve. As they swept by the lance took the wooden man straight on the chest and to my great surprise, the slender wooden shaft exploded as the dummy pitched backwards.

"Five times he's done that!" cackled Barth, "In a row, mind 'ee!"

I was puzzled. "How came the lance to shatter? I've never seen that off a quintain before."

"Ahh! 'Tis the master's invention," said Barth, as proud an he'd done it himself, "Make's it more like the real thing!"

The master? Things were going apace here and I felt my heart sink. *Where would this lead?* "When all is said 'tis still but a quintain," I growled.

"Nikki!" The mare reared to a halt, and he was down and tossing his helmet at Barth. In full armor. I couldn't have done it in jerkin and hose.

As mildly as I could I inquired, "Isn't that a bit showy?"

All three of them roared and Damonryan clapped me about the shoulder. "'Tis the whole idea! Come. Let us hear of your adventure." As we walked off to the house all I could think of was *'Tis?* Sudden, Damonryan seemed larger than life.

§

"And this is Carrick…"

Seeing Damonryan, the boy instinctively ducked his head, "My lord…"

Bellarus openly chuckled at my aggrieved look. "He's a peasant boy," I hissed at the old man, but said nothing to the lad. When at last he came up from his bow his eyes were so wide that I doubted not they had swallowed his ears in any case. He could be excused but my old master seemed as mesmerized. 'Twas in my mind they would not fool the Queen so easily, but I could see they would all of them be as deaf as Carrick to my protestations.

There were just the five of us at supper. Barth was due at his sister's table and, for all I could see he had wanted to stay, he could not well get out of it. Not knowing what to make of the boy, Nlandeth had at last set a place for him, and I'd not the heart to gainsay him. Time enough to take up his duties.

The truth was, I'd not the heart for anything. I let the talk go by me in a buzz, answering only when I had to. Carrick was full of our adventures and 'twas easy to let him have the floor, simply putting in a word or two at need, just enough not to hang a pall with my silence. I felt a deep malaise, though why, I could not find for the life of me. Shock, as sometimes happens, when events are over and one at last is safe? I didn't think so. Had been almost a week since we'd encountered Edgar and I'd had time and to spare for that. Nor was it physical. I could feel none of the signs of sickness. Damonryan and Bellarus' plan? Nothing had changed, 'twas more or less as when I'd left, except the starman had achieved far more than ever I could believe.

And that, of course, was it. I think it must always have been in the back of my mind that I would return from my little jaunt to find my problem had solved itself. Deep down, I had expected that by now the difficulties that lay in the way of Damonryan becoming a knight would have made themselves manifest and he would be on the point of giving it up in disgust. Instead, the three of them were more committed than when I'd left, enthralled by victory over a wooden dummy and the awe of a north country child.

My fears pressed in upon me and the talk around the table receded to a distant burble, then ceased altogether. Bellarus old head bobbed up and danced, disembodied, in my vision, like a boar's head carried in on a platter by lurching servants.

"Nikki, what is it?" Painfully, an drawn together by a needle, I saw his eyebrows gather together, "Another knife in the dark?"

Was it? I tried to remember, but that was so long ago, and I could not focus that far back. My whole being was in the now, trying to push back against the crush of my terrors. Surely I had felt like this. Yet even as I had the thought, somehow, I knew it was not so. So close, so very close, yet with the difference that this came from inside and that from without. An I had so much trouble telling them apart, how should Bellarus? The breath was already on its way from my lungs to my tongue to answer his question *yes* when my head shook him out a *no*.

"The…wine," I stammered lamely, still shaking my head, not now in denial, but trying to clear it, "Nothing more."

He looked at me strangely a moment more, then his features relaxed, "Come to think of it, you haven't been saying too much tonight. Best we get you to your bed."

Absently, I nodded agreement, but inside I cursed my lack of courage. From the god or not, I knew my fears to be well founded. Had I but told Bellarus *yes* he would have set his face against the plan straight away. That might have weighed little with Damonryan at first but the long and short of it was without the old man's support, he had no plan. Only Bellarus could gain him a hearing with the Queen.

Such a small step, yet I could not take it. I was no conduit but I could see how the conduit of the god could come undone. Who is to say at the sound of the god's chosen instrument who it is that plays the strings? When one is anointed, but the god has turned aside, 'twould be so easy to abrogate.

I closed my eyes. Temporizing. As I was when I left for Tansley, hoping somehow that things would have changed when I returned. My conclusions could be no different than they had been then. There was no place for me here, no part for me to play in the little tragedy that was unfolding. I was on the point of taking Bellarus' advice and pushing away from the table, with the clear intent of taking to the road in the morning, this time to ply my proper trade, when occurred one of those small events around which a whole life can pivot.

"So what are you going to do now?" Damonryan was asking Carrick.

The little face lit up proudly, "Be ta 'arper's servant!"

"Are you, now?" The starman grinned hugely, "Good! He needs one. His last one," and here he thumped himself on the chest with his thumb, "Just decided to be a knight!"

Leaping to his feet he hauled Carrick's chair out from under him, "Come on, youngster. No more sitting around for you. You must stand at your master's elbow at table, and serve him." Smoothly, he reached down and deftly filled my wine glass, "I'll teach you all your duties."

Throughout this performance, Carrick was dumbfounded; the thought of such a high lord showing him how to be a servant almost undid him.

"Yo…yo…yo…you, my lord?"

"Who else?"

I had known him for months, lived with him closer mayhap than with any other person save only Bellarus, but I was as surprised as Carrick. An 'twould be fatal to accept the mantle of his nobility, yet I had long ago stopped thinking of him as my servant. Who of our people, in seeking to climb above their station, would pick up with their old as quick as that? Sudden, I realized he was still my friend, that however I felt about what it was he was trying to do, I owed him my support, with no more carping or backbiting. As sure as I was he was on the wrong path, still the fork in the way was far behind us. I reached for my glass, sudden warm in the thought of *us*. As much as anything, I realized, I had been dreading the loneliness of my road. Putting from my mind all thought of leaving, I found the rest of my fears draw off to a more manageable distance.

§

Once I decided to throw in my hand, I found time hung not so heavy. Though nothing would stifle my misgivings, I discovered I could at least watch Damonryan's preparations with a degree of interest. What he really needed was practice against a live opponent, but that was flatly impossible. No knight would ever agree without inquiring closely into his antecedents and they would never stand close scrutiny. That, of course, was the nub of my objections, but I held my tongue and helped Barth rig the quintain so that it would hold a lance—a still lance, with an unwavering tip, that would come up at only half the speed he would see in a tournament—but, still a lance. He fared pretty well with that, even when we started to vary the length so he couldn't always be certain where the tip was. He and Barth were jubilant for a while, then silent. Even they were aware it was a pretty poor imitation of the real thing and the practice sessions began to get shorter and to lessen in intensity. Happily, when I had returned, it was not much more than a month to the tournament, so the day to leave hove up more quickly than mayhap any of us expected.

'Twas helped along by Bellarus' firm determination to get to Estonval early, in order that we might be sure of a place to stay. Thus, a week before the day, we took counsel and declared the starman ready. Indeed, he had done better than I would have believed and I found myself drawn in to the hope that, an he could draw a young and inexperienced knight, he just might manage to acquit himself respectably. What would come after I dared not think. I would just have to trust that Bellarus would indeed be able to talk the Queen around. We agreed, an 'twere possible, to hold off from that until after the fanfare of the tourney had settled down. The next day we departed for Estonval.

Chapter 27

The truth was, I was looking forward to it more than I had anticipated. The Estonval Tourney was more than just a tournament, 'twas also one of the greatest fairs in the land. Bellarus had talked me into entering the Harping, and though I had little hope of winning, a good showing could not help but further my career. Then too, Carrick was ecstatic. True to his word, Damonryan had taken him in hand and he was bidding fair to be an excellent servant. Quick as mercury, even his speech had lost some of his edge. Though the north country was beginning to fade a bit, some of the child still peeped out. He regarded the whole business of going to the tourney as the highest kind of treat. It was hard not to be infected by his enthusiasm.

Barth's horse threw a shoe on the way so we came late to Estonval and had our hands full to find an inn with the Fair about to begin. By the time 'twas done was too late to enter Damonryan into the lists, so Bellarus left early in the morn to catch the heralds before the lists should be fixed.

He returned in some agitation, "The lists are full! A troop rode in from the north, last night, under flag of truce, and enrolled a round score of knights. The heralds are at their wits end trying to fit them all in and they wouldn't hear of enrolling another unknown knight."

"Another?" I asked.

"Aye, the northerners are all to ride bannerless, with blankened shields, as is their right, an they can satisfy the heralds. They are led by Duke Granly himself, and he has given his oath that each is a sworn and noble knight. The heralds have no choice but to accept that."

I stared at him. While 'twas not unprecedented for a knight to joust bannerless, for a vow or some other such reason, 'twas rare enough that we'd had fair certainty that Damonryan would be the only one. For Granly to head up a score of such was unheard of. What was it that the Duke was playing at? I could see the same question on my old master's face.

"All for nothing!" Damonryan swore murderously,

Bellarus tossed aside his cloak and looked thoughtful, "Perhaps not," he said quietly, "There is meaning in all things, an we have the wit to look."

"What is that supposed to mean!" Damonryan was in small mood for the old man's riddles.

"There's a smaller tourney in the autumn. Less public. Mayhap a better occasion to make your mark. Meantime, best you learn by watching this one."

"The hell with the publicity!"

Bellarus regarded him levelly, "No matter how well you manage to acquit yourself, in the end your fate rests with the Queen. And the only chance you have with her is for us to plead your case quietly."

Damonryan wasn't listening. "You said *best*. What did you mean?" He looked at him through narrowed eyes, "You're holding something back, Bellarus. There's another option, isn't there?"

"Aye." The old man sighed, "But 'tis a cold one. At the last day of the tourney the champion will stand against any knight who will challenge."

"He should be pretty tired by then."

"He has half a day to rest. The Champion's Challenge is usually a formality. 'Tis like a battle—the loser's horse and gear are forfeit."

Damonryan whistled at that, "Replacing them wouldn't leave much for a farm." He stared gloomily into the distance, considering, "Damn! Fall is a long way off."

"Believe me, 'tis for the best!" The old man clapped him on the shoulder, glad he'd accepted the inevitable, "You're not as old as you claim," he laughed, "You're too impatient!"

Damonryan managed a grin but I could tell he was still less than pleased. Patience comes with age, not time. For all he had more years than Bellarus, he was yet a young man as his people reckoned it.

§

By the third day of the tournament there were but eight knights remaining. I studied them as they paraded around the ring, two by two, blazing silks and shields paired against silkless somber black, the symmetry symbolic of the fineness of the balance between the bright south and the northern shadow that hung over it. *Over us* I thought, realizing sudden with whom I had cast my lot, *over us*. That there were as many northerners was a puzzle, the more so as the Duke himself had not entered the lists, but sat watching proudly from his own pavilion. The blackened shields kept individual identities concealed but the knights and barons of Umber were known. Most of them had entered the tourney at one time or another. Granly, himself, had been runner-up the year before, going down only before the Queen's Own Champion. To hear the experts talk, he was the only northerner that had a chance. Yet here fully half the survivors thus far were from Umber.

An he would underscore my doubts Damonryan, who had watched all the earlier events, murmured, "There's your champion." The man he pointed to wore the black. Surprising to me was that he was smaller than the rest, though broad across the shoulders and through the chest; it was his horse that drew the eye.

"That's a brute of a beast!"

"And it does more than half his work for him," agreed Damonryan. "He never misses with that lance, but an that doesn't do the trick, the horse veers into the other mount at the last moment. Knocked Sir Gorham of Gore's clean out from under him."

I whistled, "I didn't think that was legal."

"It is so long as he keeps to his side of that line," he pointed to the list line picked out in lime on the dust, "Before they meet. Takes superb timing."

Seeing my look Barth laughed, "'E's become quite t' student of t' tourney."

I smiled, then commented, "'Tis a wonder he does no damage to his steed."

"He's had a special breastplate made," said Damonryan, "See, there, on the left side, where the horses strike. I'll bet it's padded underneath, to spread the force." He added softly, almost under his breath, "Come on, my bucko!"

"You cheer for the northern side!" I blurted out.

"Tisk, tisk," he chided, "I thought harpers were supposed to be neutral." He laughed at my look, "Strictly business. I marked him during the first round, and by the end of the second I was sure. I figured him at three to one, but he's small and he's not a local boy so I still got twelve to one. If he does win I stand to make back all I've laid out to become a knight."

I looked at Barth but he carefully avoided my eyes. So. No doubt he had something riding on the unknown knight as well, probably placed for him by Damonryan. Somehow, I didn't think he had the face to wager on the north himself. Chewing on that, I missed the full import of my companion's words.

All the morning matches had north against the south so the crowd seethed with excitement and we were hard put to find seats in the common stand. Damonryan's man fought last, and by then the tally was two for the south and one for the north. Whatever the Duke was playing at, he'd made a better contest than the locals expected. I found myself wishing that the tourney would serve and have done.

I studied Damonryan's pick and was forced to admit he had made it well, though I found little to admire in the man. His opponent paraded gaily before his Queen, caraçoling his horse and dipping his pennoned lance in elegant salute, his armor bright, his shield blazoned proudly with a boar's head on a field of roses, a crest I didn't know.

"Sir Jarvanon, of Montral," Damonryan murmured confidently into my ear.

By contrast, the unknown northerner stayed stock still at his end of the list, a dark statue, malevolence in taut repose. With a shock, I realized that where all his fellows' armor had been painted black, his was naturally so, the darkness in the very metal, an 'twere simple iron instead of steel.

"I didn't know you could get the requisite strength into metal of that color," I whispered. Why, I don't know. There was no need for such quiet, so far back.

"Neither did I." Damonryan's response was just as hushed, and I realized the whole crowd was quiet. Whatever the betting had been earlier, it seemed the people now knew this was the man to beat. "It's not iron, though. I've seen it take a blow or two yet there's not so much as a bent link."

"It must be worth a dozen ransoms. He couldn't have had it made just for this."

"Squire must like it," put in Barth, "No polishin'!"

I smiled dutifully, but I could see Damonryan had the same thought as I. What kind of a man pays so much extra just to have his armor all in black?

The starman measured him again with his eyes. "If I didn't know better I would say that's the Duke himself."

My eyes slid to where Granly sat. There was naught to choose between the two for pride, though the Duke looked the bigger man. Still, 'twas hard to tell with one in armor. *A twin?* I thought not. Not with Granly's reputation. He didn't look like the kind of man to tolerate that kind of competition. *A man who never lets go!* I'd heard that somewhere. Watching him now, I could well believe it. Whatever my foolish dreams, this was only a preamble, a challenge to precede the real passage at arms. What was it Tanfred had said? *War in the spring.*

I could read only confirmation in the grim, determined carriage. Sudden, Damonryan's money or no, I wanted with all my heart to see his champion on the ground. My harper's vaunted neutrality went out the window for a fight that would, in the end, make not the slightest difference. It made me feel, for just that moment, an I were pitted against the implacable knight myself. *A fancy,* mocked my inner voice, *And safe. No one to know but you and the god.* For the first time in my life I regretted that I could not pick up a sword myself, but my voice would not let up. *So he could whittle you like a fence post?*

Sir Jarvanon reached his end of the list and nodded to the herald, grace on horseback, a master of all such formal movement. The trumpets sounded, and then the herald's pennon fluttered to the ground. At once the knights spurred into a gallop. At least Sir Jarvanon did. The massive horse beneath the northerner seemed to flow from still statue to extraordinary speed without spur or even knee. Grace had switched ends. Where the Dankar knight bounced and thundered, his opponent went like water, all concentrated flow, a spring flood flashing through a canyon.

For all of that, Sir Jarvanon was no pushover. It seemed he knew all about the man's trick for he stood in the stirrups just before they met, leaning forward to catch him before he could veer his horse. Undaunted, the black knight swayed back like a dancer and swerved the steed in any case, catching the lance and turning it with his shield even as his own went home. 'Twas a shrewd blow, full on the helm, though not quite square. Sir Jarvanon's head started to snap back then the tip of the lance let go and slid off. The steeply slanted tourney helm had done its job and you would say they had come off with equal honors but that the horses struck. Off balance already, the southerner was almost flung from the saddle. Only by his splendid horsemanship was he able at once to keep his seat and rally his horse from stumbling.

Now the choice was his. Reaching the end of the list, he spurred back to his squire and exchanged his shattered lance for a long, two-edged horse sword. Seeing this, the Duke's knight did the same, but with an economy of motion that seemed to mock his opponent, the horse cantering, the lance dropped and the sword caught flung by a squire without the beast ever having to break stride. Jarvonan circled and the other knight followed, so that you would say the Dankar man had the initiative, save that the great black horse seemed to match his stride for stride, effortlessly, keeping the distance set at whatever his master wanted. At last the southerner darted in. Steel wheeled, flashed sunlight and then crashed against steel, the block by the unknown almost desultory. He let his horse do the work, rearing and kicking out against the other steed. Again and again they came together, each time a pattern of the last, the unknown using his sword only when it suited him. Then sudden, when the other horse had tired, the black knight went to such savage strokes that I feared for the other's life. Abruptly it was over. Outmatched man pitched from the saddle of outmatched beast, felled by a backhand blow to the helm that drew a gasp from the crowd and not a few cries of *Foul!*

"'Twas a legal blow," commented Barth grudgingly. "He turned the edge and caught him with the flat." Wager or no wager, from the way he spoke I knew he liked the way his champion fought no better than I.

As the heralds confirmed Barth's judgment I mused, "'Tis a wonder he doesn't wear out his horse."

"He's got a matched pair," retorted Damonryan.

That afternoon I'd a contest of my own to prepare so I missed the fights, but I gather it went much the same, with one man each from the north and the south falling from the competition. By now, there were few surprised when Damonryan's champion prevailed, and he told me he could have turned a good profit there and then by selling of his wager. Loyalty went out the window at the betting booths. Lord Bartholemy, Baron of Endinson and the Queen's Own Champion, always the odds-on favorite, had dropped to no better than even.

§

The Harping was held that night and my companions all turned out, even Barth who admitted to no ear. I had no expectation of being one of the three finalists but my piece and playing were mentioned by the judges and I got no few invitations for a winter's hosting. 'Tis as well as an unknown harper can expect to do. The Queen's steward himself had invited me to play at the palace so I considered my efforts well rewarded. My friends were pleased for me and we made a merry night of it, none happier than Damonryan though, to my surprise, he drank but little and slipped early off to bed.

"Sorry Nikki," he whispered as he went, "Don't let me put a damper on things. That sunderling at dinner didn't quite agree with me."

I was surprised. 'Twas a dish he usually reveled in but mayhap he had got a bad piece. At any rate, he was over it by morning. I got to the grounds late, slipping down between he and Bellarus as they squeezed over for me just before the tourney final began.

"Feeling better?" I inquired.

He looked at me and laughed, "Better than you, I suspect."

Sa. He'd hit the mark with that though, truth was, 'twas not so very hard to hit. I had but half an eye for the fight and I remember little of its beginning save that it seemed to me a copy of the one I'd seen before. I noticed more the crowd which groaned or cheered at every blow their champion took or gave, veering back and forth from ecstasy to despair in a way that began to stand for me just how futile was the business anyway. The Baron had a noble horse himself, but even so it was outmatched and though he put up a sturdy fight the crowd grew silent as again and again the unknown antagonist urged their beasts together. To my eye, unpracticed and bloodshot though it was, he seemed strangely reluctant to finish the matter which was at odds with the ferocity I had observed before. At last I began to pay some attention. Even as I did the Baron's horse stumbled slightly, pitching him a little sideways in the saddle, and the dark knight's arm came around in a great sweeping arc. He struck a blow that glanced off the top of his opponent's shield then caught him beneath the chin. Blood ran red from under his helm. He toppled from the saddle, falling badly and laying quite still.

The crowd came to life with an ugly roar and now the screams of *foul* were in good earnest. Ignoring both them and his fallen foe, the dark knight wheeled his great stallion around to face the heralds, then stood it stock still while he lowered his sword and stretched it down in mute and theatrical appeal.

"The bastard's good!" I heard Bellarus' bitter comment. "I'm sure that was deliberate, but he'll get away with it."

"But he used his edge!" I protested.

"Aye, but he caught the shield first, so they must rule it an accident." I turned to Barth for confirmation but he and Damonryan were away already to collect their winnings. I just caught a glimpse of them, plunging through the crowd. To make it worse, Carrick, who had strutted like a cock at my success the night before, had now abandoned me to go with them. My disgust of the man below spread to them, who could see only money in the destruction of a human being.

The heralds made a show of conferring but, an they did not like it, yet there was little they could do. In due time they confirmed Bellarus' opinion. By then, they had the Baron's helm off and were carrying him from the field. Though they had not covered him so at least he lived, yet the stillness of the form told its story. Indeed his neck was broken. He lived out his life between his bed and his chair.

Contemptuous of the crowd, having gotten his verdict from the heralds, the figure below rode slowly up before the Queen, then stopped. For the longest time he just stared at her and she, as unmoving, back at him. Then at last, as slowly as he'd rode, he inclined his head at her in the veriest sketch of a bow. Ironic, or merely insolent, I couldn't tell from that far up, only that it had naught of fealty in it. As the heralds blew for silence, he wheeled his horse aside and cantered again to the end of the list. The noise rose angry at that while the herald's blew again and yet again, to no avail. Indifferent, the black knight ignored the crowd, just kneeing his horse to a statue and waiting until it should subside. The Queen let it run a time then stood and held out her hand. At once the crowd went quiet.

Only then did his squire bring him out his banner. Whoever he was, 'twas not his own. The cloth, unfurled as plainest black, snapped defiance of identity in the tugging breeze. 'Twas as good as a gauntlet thrown down before the Queen, her champion a broken man, leaving the Duke and this unknown man the two best upon the field.

An he would underscore the point, he seated the banner like a lance, then spurred his great beast into the victory ride, not the slow canter of tradition, but a headlong gallop about the ring, once, twice, then thrice without slowing. At the end of the third sweep he dismounted at the full gallop, swinging his horse in behind him to a halt even as he grounded the haft of the banner at his heel. 'Twas a superb performance that should have had the crowd upon its feet but that they could feel the contempt for them came with it. As it was, there was only sullen silence.

"What now?" I whispered

"Is there any here would take the field against the Champion?" cried a herald in reply.

"The Challenge is issued three times and then the tourney is declared at an end," said Bellarus grimly.

"An 'tis answered," I inquired.

He snorted his derision, "Then they fight in the afternoon."

We tried to leave but the press would not allow. Hoping yet to see this dismal Champion in the dirt, the crowd hung on past all reason, forcing us to wait. The heralds kept their trumpets grounded in a stillness so complete I fancied I could hear the great beast crop the grass, while its master sat easily, arrogantly in the saddle. After what they considered a decent interval, they brought them up to their lips then sounded the call again. And again there was no answer and now the crowd grew restless and I saw at last that people began to trickle from the ground. Yet the heralds disdained to increase their pace so by the time the trumpets came up for the third and final call, the trickle had swelled into a stream and the crowd noise grew so that even the commanding voice of the herald came but thinly through the roar. Moving now, I saw across my shoulder the dark champion wheel his horse and start for the gate, two motions going opposite, he and the crowd two counterflows in a painter's composition. Then, unbelievably, an caught by the artist's brush, they froze, pinned to the canvas of the grounds by the soaring call of a single trumpet.

From the far end of the grounds, from the People's Gate, there came a single knight, blank again of all devices, trotting slowly in to meet the ragged cheer that rose from the turning crowd. There was a buzz as people wondered who he was, that grew sullen as they realized his lack of crests and colors bespoke yet another northerner. Bellarus and I looked at each other and I felt my heart turn over in my chest. The crowd was wrong. We knew the solitary figure below us all too well.

Chapter 28

"What in the land is he playing at?" I gasped, "That's not even Darksome he's riding, but Jenny. Dear the god, that brute will bowl her over!"

"The mare's worth a good deal less than the destrier," Bellarus observed grimly.

Reaching the shield that hung to the side of the Queen's pavilion, Damonryan struck it with his lance. "I would take the field," he cried, and turned to face a bemused Elinor.

Against the hush that fell, Elinor's voice rang clear through the stadium, "And may We know, Sir Knight, whether you are from the north or from the south?"

"Neither, Madam. Yet, an You will, I would ride in the name of the south."

Elinor looked at him gravely, having no wish to see the south go down before the north again, but knowing also it would cost her as much in face to refuse. I saw Bellarus bite his lip. Was not a position she would relish and she would not thank Damonryan for putting her there however nobly he might acquit himself. She temporized.

"Consider well, Sir Knight. All your gear and horse are forfeit an you lose!"

"An I ride in the Queen's name and go down before the Queen, what boots it my horse and armor?"

"You've been giving him lines!" I accused Bellarus.

He shook his head majestically, "Certes I taught him how to talk to a Queen, and to carry a bold front, but this is his own doing. I knew naught about it." He smiled, though I could see the strain of worry behind, and dropped back from courtly speech, "Haven't you noticed, Nicodemus? He's a player born."

"He'll get himself killed, and then all will be for naught!"

Bellarus gripped my elbow and said fiercely, "Not for naught, Nicodemus. 'Tis well I like the lad, but he's just a man when all's said. Best you remember, 'tis himself he rides for down there, not for you, not for the god, only himself." He dropped his voice, "'Twas not for him you were sent to the wilderness."

I shook him off, "The infocom," I said bitterly, then turned and stared unseeing a the field below, "I've been afraid of that for a long time. So now he gets spitted like a capon merely because he has outrun his use."

He ignored my tone, merely rejoining me mildly, "Nay. 'Tis simply that his fate is his own and not the god's. As most men would prefer."

He left unspoken, *And you should know the truth of that!*

§

The Queen made up her mind and her voice rang out, "We are pleased, Sir Knight, to have you ride in the name of the south." She was so contained, 'twas hard to tell an she was pleased or merely being politic against her will. Coolly, she turned to withdraw until the afternoon.

"She might at least have let him carry the colors, " I commented bitterly.

Bellarus snorted, "Would you, in her place?"

Before the Queen could leave, the champion called out, "Your Majesty, let me but change my horse, and I can save you the trouble of coming back this afternoon." The voice rang strangely from out his helmet. He'd not as much as opened his visor.

The Queen turned to Damonryan, "And would you be willing to move this contest forward, Sir Knight?"

Damonryan bowed his assent and Elinor signaled to the heralds, who blew another fanfare. As the crowd settled back into their seats and the knight had his other charger brought out, the starman rode slowly around his end of the field. Bellarus watched him a while, then muttered, "He does not seem so easy in the saddle."

I noticed it too, a thing I could not precisely put my finger on, but palpable and quite new. Then I saw the unknown studying his would-be opponent with the same contempt he had shown the crowd. I nudged this to my companion, whispering back, "Mayhap he doesn't wish to."

Too soon was the man ready and the knights both in their place. The trumpets flashed up and blew their final call. The pennon fluttered and there was the thunder of hooves against a deadly hush, then a quickly rising sigh. The mare was a pretty thing, and it was like she would soon be crushed bloody in the dust. As they came together, Damonryan raised up in the saddle for an early thrust. His opponent again swayed back while still managing to take dead aim at the center of the starman's helm. The old fashioned pot had not the swept back sides to shake off the tip. Somehow Damonryan got his shield up and turned the blow inside, but his own lance went wide outside in the process. The black knight kneed his stallion, the great steed swerved left, and I shut my eyes. There was no way in the land that Jenny could stand up against the coming crash. The Duke's man had won in a single pass and Damonryan might easily get crushed in the collision. It seemed an eternity, something of Damonryan's time-standing-still; when at last it came, it was amazingly quiet, leaving me wondering stupidly an the mind when it speeded damped down the ears in the process.

"Dear the god, she just danced aside!" exclaimed a delighted Bellarus.

I opened my eyes to find the riders had passed each other. To my surprise, the unknown was reeling back, fighting to stay in the saddle.

"What happened?"

"The mare is nimbler than Darksome. She sidestepped and then the other rode into the sweep of Damonryan's lance."

A sweep! I felt like laughing and crying at once. The surest blow in jousting but you seldom saw it. While a lance held to the side cannot miss the sweeper was generally hailed from the saddle by a well aimed tip long before his blow could land. I was sure Barth hadn't even taught him the stroke but by missing wide, Damonryan had inadvertently delivered it.

It wasn't much, but even as the other wheeled back his horse, the heralds signaled the pass a draw. The choice fell to

Damonryan and he was not slow to take it. At once he swung clear of his mare and lighted on the ground.

For a terrible moment, I thought his opponent would ride him down where he stood, but his ambition outweighed his temper, for not even the champion of the Duke of Umber could survive such disgrace. Wrenching the beast aside, he brought it to a halt but stayed in the saddle, considering his waiting opponent. Eventually, he wheeled away and rode over to the herald.

"I claim right to change my weapon," he called.

The herald seemed on the point of protest, but he was a man bound by protocol, and so barked out formally, "You have that right!"

I looked wonderingly at Bellarus, who shrugged "Lance against lance, hand weapons on horseback, hand weapons on foot. Damonryan has chosen the last, but knights are not obliged to carry every weapon for every kind of combat with them. He can now go back to his tent for any appropriate weapon he has."

"He has a sword. What's his game?"

He stroked his beard thoughtfully, "I don't rightly know. Nothing good, I fear."

His fear was justified. Already, in response to some unseen gesture, his squire was bringing him out a brute of a club, a ball of steel on a steel handle.

This time the herald did protest, "That is no Knightly weapon!"

"Indeed it is, Sir Herald," he responded, handing him the club for his inspection, "'Tis a Morning Star with the points removed, thus blunting it for tourney use as the rules require." The heralds conferred, passing it back and forth between them, most requiring both hands to do so.

"He's seen how light is Damonryan's shield," said Bellarus. "He's going to batter it to pieces!"

"He won't stop at the shield."

The thing was massive. I could see no way that Damonryan's old helm would stand as much as a single blow from it. Reluctantly, the chief herald handed back the club.

"'Tis within the rules." He turned and called formally across to Damonryan, "Sir Knight, you may also change your weapon an you wish."

"Nay, Sir Herald, I am no fishwife to be saying, *Now this one, now that one.*"

Laughter rippled a little through the crowd and I saw even the Queen smile, but his opponent went very still. Damonryan ignored him.

"But since my helm will not avail me against yon *club,* why I will dispense with it."

The audience gasped as he waved forward the no less astounded Barth. Coolly, he tossed him both helm and gauntlets, then made an elaborate bow to the herald, without ever once looking at the stock still knight. Though the herald looked grim there was naught he could do but have the trumpets sound commencement.

The man's rage had no wise cooled. As the last flourish blew away in the breeze, he closed, almost an he were afraid Damonryan might change his mind and call for his helm. The starman simply waited, sword and shield at the ready. Once in range, the knight sprang, sweeping the club forward in a whirling, head-high arc. Damonryan wove back, thrusting his shield to catch the blow square on the top. There was a fearful crash and a rending sound, followed by a groan of dismay from the crowd as the shield buckled where it had been struck.

"Even a squire knows to turn a blow like that at an angle!" groaned Bellarus. "The god! What have I done to make him think he had a chance?"

Even I, who had seen him fight before, thought that he was finished at a single blow. Indeed, with a broken shield, he could have sued for peace without dishonor. Instead, he cast the useless thing aside and circled back. The great club whirled again, chest high this time, a rib-crushing stroke even armor wouldn't stay. It didn't have to. Damonryan danced back flowing like water before the blow that passed so close you would have thought the wind of it would have knocked him down. Then he did an extraordinary thing. Quick as thought while the club finished its swing he danced back in and out again, and while in he rang the flat of his sword off the side of his opponent's helmet. A bee sting, less, a gnat but the knight stumbled a little. In a blink he'd recovered, cat quick despite his armor, more surprised I think than dismayed. The two circled, the unknown more cautious now and more dangerous. He moved the club about, weaving it slowly, like a cat that lashes its tail. Then he swept in again, leaping and swinging, and again Damonryan sprang back. This time, though, the blow was a feint, as the club came down he turned it round and brought it up and down again and then again in a series of swinging motions any one of which could have felled the starman like a struck ox. Five times the great club swung and five times the starman avoided it, giving ground steadily, managing not a single return stroke, not that it mattered. Dulled for tournament use as it was, his sword would make little dent in that armor.

After a circling space the northerner repeated the tactic, with the same result except that this time Damonryan waited for the last stroke then leaped in and rang another blow from off the helm. Just the flat again, sideways, against the temple, so the helm rang like a bell through the arena. The crowd cheered but it had no effect on Granly's man. He could shed blows like that all day, whereas he only needed to hit Damonryan once. He gave up the circling and bore straight in on his opponent, driving him back with the ferocity of his rush, wheeling in blow after blow. Damonryan went backward, flowing before the great club so it never touched him, but giving ground. Now it seemed, the knight shepherded him, not so much trying to land the club as weave a net of brutal steel through which his opponent could not pass. Damonryan saw his danger, but so skillfully wove the knight, that he could neither turn nor break through, but must steadily give back. He fought it, giving ground as slowly as he might, but the northerner was inexorable, more like one of Damonryan's *machines* than a man: step, sweep, sweep, step, sweep, sweep, so the starman could not even bring his sword into play. At last, Damonryan was backed hard up against the arena wall, and now he'd no place he could go. The great club went up, higher this time, not a containing stroke but a killing one.

Before it could come down, Damonryan ducked beneath the arm with that impossible speed of his and was behind. The club swung at nothing and the starman's sword rang twice, each time sounding the bell of the other's helm. With a bellow of rage the tormented man spun around swinging, a furious backhanded uppercut that went clumsy wide. Deftly, Damonryan stepped in and out, leaving the helm ringing again. To the vast surprise of all who'd expected their unknown champion to be bloodily crushed, the fight began to seem a farce. Again and again, the knight would charge with a flurry of blows, but the weight of the massive black armor and the club began to tell. Increasingly, they were awkward swung so Damonryan would dance easily away, then in again and ring his sword again from off the helm. Always he used the flat, staying well within the rules, and always he struck against the ears. The effect must have maddened the man who was so close to being champion but he grew circumspect, striking no longer, circling, blocking, on the defensive now. The crowd began to jeer him and cheer for every hit of Damonryan's. The figure in black ignored them, just blocked, and circled, and blocked again.

"He's searching for an opening," Bellarus hissed.

And so he was. However much it may have galled him, however weary he might be, still he needed but a single blow to land. The starman knew it too, darting in and out, using all his advantages now, his marvelous speed and his lack of encumbrance, his sword weaving back and forth until it seemed all the air about the other knight was slashed with steel; but the shield came up and out, so every sparkling silver arc was caught against a boss of flattest black; and still the unknown circled, gathering his resources.

Sudden, Damonryan's heel seemed to catch upon the grass, pitching him backwards to the ground. 'Twas just what his opponent had been waiting for. For all the weight of his armor, he sprang like a stooping hawk, the club whirled high. As he landed, with all his remaining strength he brought it down. Time stood still, just as Damonryan had described it. The great club at the top of its arc, the starman prone on the ground. *Roll. Roll!* I seemed to scream with every whiplash nerve, though naught came out my mouth. Instead, incredibly, he coiled from off the ground and flowed in to meet the blow. Driving his sword up like a stave, his left hand on the blunted point, he caught the black armored wrist just outside the hilt as the club came down. There was a crack could be heard all round the ring and a scream from the unknown knight as his weapon flew from out his fingers to the grass. From where he clutched his arm, I was fairly certain that his gauntlet had saved his wrist. The steel cuff must have snapped the bone above instead.

"Come on, Nikki. We'd better *move!*"

Chapter 29

Without ceremony or waiting to see an I would follow, the old man pushed his way down through the crowd. By the time I'd the wit to follow him they were on their feet and roaring and it was all I could do to get through at all, much less catch up with him. Happily, they were too enthralled with what had taken place on the grass below to mind overmuch the odd shoulder or elbow. To my chagrin, when at last I had vaulted the parapet to the turf below, the old man was half way across, the great green cape of the master harper billowing about him.

Already, the knight and Damonryan stood before the Queen and the Duke who had ranged himself beside her. The other's squire was there, behind his master, holding his gauntlets. pushing him behind. Despite he was before the Queen, the man kept on his helm. Beside him his right arm hung straight down, the only sign that would admit of his injury. Somehow, even from behind and at a distance, there was a quality of stillness, of containment, like a sail that bellies with great forces but so guyed down it never stirs itself.

At some cost to my dignity I managed to catch my old master before he arrived across the arena. A grim faced herald had started forward but Bellarus had waved him away. Seeing my harper green he had let me through as well. No others had had the temerity to flow across the barriers.

As we came up, Elinor flicked a pair of gray flecked eyes our way and then back again. An she recognized Bellarus, she gave no sign. 'Twas the first time I'd seen the Queen up close and I was startled to find her so short. Yet, though they hadn't turned our way a second time, I could still feel those eyes; her height didn't diminish her presence by a jot. I couldn't imagine how her lords had ever made the mistake of discounting her.

The Duke bulked massive beside her. Black hair, black eyes, a great black beard and an expression of simmering wrath that looked somehow an 'twere a permanent part of his features. No wonder he dressed his people in black armor. He glared at our arrival, causing the other knight to twist his torso and so bring us in the range of the very limited vision granted him by his tourney helm.

He froze when he turned round to us, an eerie feeling. I'm no knight but I've been around the breed enough to know good armor when I see it. That helm alone would be worth the best part of Bellarus' beloved Warely. 'Twas cunningly made, all sweeping curves back from a great, predatory beak, no place for a lance to catch, not even the eye holes. The latches were all at the back, invisible from where I stood. The whole was so constructed that you could tell exactly where he looked, despite you could not see his eyes. The beak was pointed straight at me.

He had that stillness again. Of a sudden, I knew who it was, just from the way he stared. *Edgar.* Somehow he'd aligned himself with Umber. Some of the pieces fell into place. The unmarked knights. How he'd stumbled across Carrick and I when he'd been supposedly hunting. He's been coming back from Umber. Secretly. My mind whirled. The beak broke back. There was much here yet that I couldn't see but already the Duke was talking.

"What are they doing here?"

'Twas the herald who answered. "The master harper, Bellarus," he intoned formally, "Who, four days agone, gave surety for the challenger."

The Duke looked Damonryan up and down. "Who are you, knight? I know you not."

For answer, Damonryan waved back to the People's Gate, where stood Barth. The old man of arms beckoned behind him and, to my horror, determinedly carrying a shield, out stepped Carrick. Unlike the one he had carried so briefly in the fight, this one was blazoned, with some kind of great war bird.

All around, the Queen, the Duke, her attendants, who included some of the highest nobles in the land, were looking stunned. The chief herald's choler ran from his high brocaded collar clear to the top of his bald head.

"An eagle!" he exclaimed wrathfully, "But none such as is carried by Chelemonth of Westernesse! There is no such device in the land!"

I remembered the Westernesse crest now. Certainly its poor bird looked like a half wrung chicken compared with the magnificent creature Carrick was now advancing so proudly. An the herald and the Duke were angry now, 'twas nothing to what passed with Damonryan's next statement.

"Quite right, master herald," he bowed, "I am not of the land."

The Duke exploded first, "This is a farce!" he stormed, "Why should my knight turn his arms over to one not gently born. Arrest this impostor!"

The herald was only too happy to oblige. He swept his hand back at the guards and pointed to Damonryan. To a man, they swarmed forward.

"I am still Queen, I believe?" Elinor's voice was quiet but it held all the frost of a clear winter's night in the Fastness. The guards froze. "My lord Duke?"

She knew the Duke was determined to replace her as soon as he could, but now was not the time, in her lands, surrounded by her people.

Slowly, fractionally, the black head bowed; reluctantly, the black bushed mouth growled out assent, "Your Majesty." The eyes, when they came up, were on Damonryan, and they said he would pay for this injury as well.

Elinor ignored him like a lackey. Coolly she turned to Damonryan but before she could speak Edgar called, "A moment, madam, an you please." Without giving her time to answer he signed to his squire who reached up to remove his helm. The Duke made to protest but he held up his good hand, "No point, now, my lord duke," he said easily, "I fear I've been recognized." The voice, even muffled as it was, erased any doubts I might have had. Sure enough, his squire took off his helm and it was Edgar, but an Edgar now I was hard put to know. He bowed slightly to me, smiling, urbane, "The harper, Nicodemus, and I both come from Tansley." You'd never know that he'd called me *bastard* or sought to burn my eye out merely weeks ago, or even that he'd just lost a battle he ought to have won. He ranged himself beside the Duke and nodded at the herald. "Edgar," he said quietly, "Of Anglesea."

'Twas all the cue the herald needed. He rapped the ground with his staff and proclaimed, "The Lord Edgar, Baron of Benson and of Tansley, Right Knee to His Majesty, King Bantrus of Anglesea."

There was a deep muttering went through the crowd of courtiers at that. There was significance here that I should grasp but the bile rose up in my throat and they all seemed sudden very far away. I felt an arm at my elbow. "Easy, Nikki," Bellarus whispered, "I thought you knew."

My grandfather's honors! Whatever all this really meant, it seemed obscene that Edgar should be the one to have them. Not only Right Knee, which presumably had to be held by someone, but Benson as well, which Cantor had sowed under decreeing the title should never again be held. I felt physically sick at the thought. 'Twas all I could do to look at Edgar. Strangely, what I saw in his face cured me better than any physic. You could say he purred, like a cat that lies quite still with a mouse between its forepaws.

Elinor silenced her court with a twist of her head. An she saw the significance she chose to ignore it. Instead she continued to regard Damonryan. "Well?"

Carefully, he bowed to her. He'd taken her measure and knew she was no one to trifle with. Her desire to put the Duke and Edgar in their places did not mean that he'd won. He'd a hearing, that was all. She would make up her own mind.

Beside her, the Duke protested again, "This is a farce!"

Loosing his belt he turned to the pair and let his scabbard drop, "Not so, my lord."

Nodding to Carrick he had him come forward and help him strip off his armor, revealing beneath the strange outland garment I had seen him in when first he stepped from off the ship. The colors rippled as he moved, like sunlight off gently breezy water. The Duke was unimpressed, and said so. Beside him, Edgar said nothing nor gave any sign of what it was he thought. Having made his sensation, he appeared content to wait and let the matter play itself out. Elinor knew better than her rival. She'd first lulled her lords to sleep with her interest in artists, cooks and tailors. She'd shown her first mastery over them by dressing them all like the popinjays they were now. She knew her fabrics. She knew at once there was nowhere in the land could have made up this. Bellarus recognized his cue.

"Your Majesty," he stepped forward, "Allow me to present the Lord Damonryan, Baron of Danforth, Ambassador from His Majesty, King Johnthompson, of Unity!"

"This is outrageous!" fumed the Duke. I tried to school my face after the Queen's, hoping desperately it did not give away how right I thought he was. Beside him, Edgar's eyes glittered dangerously, but he continued to say nothing. Somehow, I had the feeling he was a step or two ahead of the Duke already.

She held up a tiny hand. "I know Master Bellarus of old, my lord," she said. I was glad her eyes were on him and not on me. She kept them there a long time but he never flinched. At length she seemed satisfied, "He has never served me before with unseemly tricks." Her gaze shifted to Damonryan. "Certes, we have never seen such garb before."

The Duke snorted, "A clever tailor and a jongleur's imagination!"

The gray eyes went to Edgar now and dropped deliberately down to the costly black armor, "In fine, my lord, the clothes make the man," she murmured.

The Duke flushed, more angry now than ever, though beside him, Edgar kept his half smile, for all the land unperturbed. I could feel his anger kindle, but he hid it well. I'd the feeling that some part of it at least was directed towards the Duke. A master at keeping those about her off balance, Elinor was already back to Damonryan. "Well?" Whatever pleasure she took from baiting the Duke, she was punctilious in her forms towards him. The starman was accorded no such honors.

"A further demonstration, Your Majesty." He waved Carrick forward and whispered to him, then stood with arms crossed, every inch the lord, while the lad tore back to the gate. The stance, I noticed, was aimed at the Duke, though he kept his eyes on Elinor, acknowledging the one as the challenger, the other as the judge. I'd no idea what it was he had sent for and thanked the god 'twas not the infocom. Surreptitiously, my fingers went to my wrist. 'Twould not be beyond Damonryan to pull another of what he called his *fast ones*, but I found it safe enough. To my, and everyone else's surprise, Carrick returned with his riding boots.

"Give them to the Duke."

Carrick took them over, but that lord just dropped them in the dirt. "A strange cut," he sneered, "It proves no more than the clothes!"

"My sword has been dulled for the tourney, my lord, and my lord Edgar used a …err… morning star, was it not?" Damonryan's smiled contempt, "However I would wager that your sword is sharp." Damonryan waved at the boots on the ground. "Cut them, my lord," he invited, "They should not prove too much for you."

A little baffled, the Duke glared at Damonryan but he could see no trap. Realizing he would look the more foolish for refusing he drew his sword and took an awkward backhand swipe. A boot flew twenty feet through the air and Carrick ran to fetch it. When he returned, Damonryan held the boot before the Queen.

"No cut," he said, "Surely, my lord, you can do better than that."

Enraged, the Duke went at the remaining boot with a will, striking down at it against the ground like a blacksmith at an anvil. When at last he had done, Carrick ran over and picked up the crumpled wreck, blew off the dust and straightened it, then returned to Damonryan. Wordlessly he handed it to the Queen. I knew those boots. How not? He had worn them every day since I had rescued him. They were as supple as the finest leather, yet they took no mark, no matter how he abused them. She would find no cut, not so much as a single scratch. The boot was as good as new. Damonryan repeated his claim.

"I am not of the land."

Elinor turned the boot over carefully, examining it with great care. "'Tis certain this is not, at all events," she pronounced at last. She said it calmly, an she were passing on a turnip found in the royal flower garden. "Best we hear your story, fellow."

So he told them, right there on the floor of the arena, and a strange audience it was, too: the Duke, frothing at every word, the herald not so very far behind him in outrage and the little Queen and Edgar like still water in between. There were others, of course—I've heard the tale from many more lips than could have had ears in hearing—but Elinor was in charge, and whatever they may have claimed later, they were merely backdrop that day.

He didn't tell them he was from the stars. That would have been too much on such slender evidence, besides being a thing none of us really wanted known. Instead he fell back on the Tales and said his people had been in another of the five boats that left the great land and that they had come to their own land they called Unity. And that lately, he had taken ship to go exploring, and it had gotten caught by a storm and swept for weeks across the great ocean until it foundered on our shores. By inference, his ship was a sailing vessel. He left much to inference. Indeed, his tale was largely true, in much the way the Old Tales are true. Our Great Land was undoubtedly the mother planet, Earth, and Unity was settled from there as well. The only real lie was that his people left with ours in one of the original five ships.

The questions came thick and fast, most from the Duke, and Damonryan had to get a bit more inventive. We heard of the Great Boar of Unity, a beast with a hide so tough neither axe nor spear can mark it, so it must be killed with a thrust through the eye. A hazardous affair one would infer. At least, the people of Unity seemed to think enough of the deed that a lad was given a pair of boots made from the hide of his first kill. When the Duke asked how boots could be made from a hide that couldn't be cut, the starman replied airily.

"A guild secret, my lord. Not to be shared with a mere baron."

I held my breath at the sheer bravado of that, but it was the right answer. One they could understand. I might have thought of him as just Damonryan, but never for a moment did he let them see anything other than the baron he claimed to be. An they accepted he was not from the land, he wanted there to be no question he was noble.

There was anyway. From the Duke. But Damonryan was not playing to the Duke, but to Elinor and her court. He explained that his ship was wrecked and he the sole survivor and I stepped forward and confirmed I'd seen the ship. Following his lead I told as much truth as I could, speaking of a great ship, far larger than any we made, colored all in silver. An in their minds they saw a scaled-up, silver painted trading lugger, why that was as close to the truth as I wanted to take them. I confirmed the ship had been wrecked and that Damonryan was the only survivor. At that, the Duke made a final throw.

"And how do we know he's not just a simple sailor?" His look said he'd like to put the question to Damonryan in his dungeon at home.

"Do sailors in Umber commonly wear armored boots?" asked Damonryan.

"Sailors commonly steal anything they can get their hands on!"

Damonryan smiled thinly, "And do the sailors of Umber commonly defeat the Duke's own champion in single combat?"

Through all of this Edgar had said nothing, content apparently to let events play themselves out. Now, with the Duke on the point of making a hot retort, he made a little bow at Damonryan and said, so graciously I was hard pressed even to know him, "They do not." Then he gave the Duke a look and at last I saw the old Edgar.

The Duke ground his teeth. Edgar had just made it very plain that he would rather by far lose the tourney and all his gear than have it put about he'd been defeated by a peasant in masquerade. Though her face showed nothing, Elinor must have savored the irony.

"Well, my lord?"

After all her efforts to rein in Granly, she was leaving it up to him after all. I held my breath. On the face of it there was no reason the Duke need be as concerned for Edgar's pride as was Edgar. From what I'd heard, he was a man with scant regard for his underlings. He cleared his throat and looked at Edgar who simply looked him back. I quietly let go my breath. What it was I couldn't fathom, but there was some hold there.

"I yield the tourney." 'Twas rasped out, the barest minimum, without a bow or any actual acknowledgment of title. It was made with a look of purest hatred for Damonryan that boded ill for him an they should meet in future. But it was sufficient.

Granly stamped off with no further word. For a wonder, Edgar sketched Damonryn an elegant leg then made his bow to Elinor before he also withdrew. For all his urbanity, I'd no doubt he shared in Granly's feelings.

§

The spoils of the tournament were substantial. The herald who, despite his earlier outrage, was a stickler for accuracy, had ruled that, in addition to Edgar's armor, both his destriers fell to Damonryan. Umber had roared at that but the old man was implacable. Both horses had been used in the Tourney so both were forfeit. Edgar had complied with a grace I'm sure he was far from feeling. Still, they were of little immediate use to Damonryan. For her part, Elinor acknowledged his own, wholly bogus title and granted him a room somewhere in the outliers of the royal castle. It was tiny, suited to a representative of some minor and barely respectable principality, but of course he had to take it. He was a seven day wonder, questioned furiously, fêted everywhere for a week and then forgotten. Much of that was by design. On Bellarus' advice, he made Unity seem as commonplace as he could, so they came to think of it as much like Westernesse. He also made it plain that the prevailing westerly gales would make his return impossible—he'd come a staggering distance *with* them as it was—and that further visitations from Unity were in the highest unlikely. With the exception of a lady-in-waiting or two, the court quickly lost interest. He was disappointingly ordinary. More importantly, he had no power base. He was just one more royal hanger-on and Estonval had no shortage of those. The ladies, of course, were interested in other things but even they he put off, as gently as he might. He had no wish for dangerous entanglements.

One or two persisted, Lord Ralven in particular, and a fat little brother in a greasy cassock who oozed a distasteful and wholly false charm. Lord Ralven, on the other hand, had the real thing, the most innately and gravely courteous man I have ever met. Barth was too abashed by the palace to serve Damonryan while he was in residence so Carrick and he had switched places.

The boy reported that not only was Lord Ralven the only noble to bother with his name but he even remembered it when he was far from their quarters running an errand. "And greeted me," he added breathlessly, "Though I was no more than a servant running through a hallway!"

Hearing that, Bellarus had smiled, "'Tis his job to know everything, young shatterbrain. He is the Queen's Ear!" He repeated the warning more soberly to Damonryan, when the lad was out of hearing.

"I'd suspected something of the sort. Still, it's Brother Rastius that worries me more."

The old man pulled at his beard in annoyance. "I should have thought of that. Your tale touches the temple very closely. I take it he's official?"

"So I suppose. He hasn't said. But he's asking a lot of questions about our beliefs on Unity."

"How have you answered him?"

"Put him off, mostly. Told him I haven't detected any real differences between our beliefs and those in the land. That sort of thing."

Bellarus raised his brows, "And he believed you?"

The starman shrugged, "So far, I've managed to avoid seeing him for very long. That may prove more difficult, now that I'm not in so much demand."

"Mmm. Nikki, time to see an all that training at Welling did you any good. Take him through the preparation for Second Rites. I'll see what I can find out about this Brother Rastius." He stood up, and stretched his back like a stiff old cat, "Though I doubt but 'twill confirm what we suspect."

Damonryan looked suspicious, "What are Second Rites?"

"First Rites take place at birth," I explained. "Second Rites at eight or nine, when a child is old enough to accept the god of his own knowledge and volition. An Unity is as like here as you claim, Brother Rastius could reasonably expect you to know your catechisms."

"With some differences, Nikki. Small ones, that will not offend the good brother. I leave it to your creativity." With that, the old man waved airily, and was gone. Leaving us to sweat.

Damonryan had an appointment with Brother Rastius the following day so we'd little time to soak into him what a child imbibes at its mother's knee and then learns formally in six months of instruction. Happily, he'd picked up enough of the main outlines during our wanderings to stay out of serious trouble, so 'twas only the details we need worry about. Still, an official inquisitor of the temple, for such Bellarus found out he was, was no mean opponent. My only consolation was that no noble in the land would have much more than the bare catechisms. The deeper mysteries the temple reserved for her own initiates. We spent a hard day and night at my room at the inn, with Carrick posted outside against over curious ears, but in the end I was satisfied. Damonryan reported the next evening that Brother Rastius appeared to be as well. At any rate, he was demanding no more interviews.

Strangely, 'twas Edgar that advanced his fortune. I had not understood how high he had risen in Anglesea but Bellarus brought me up to date. We'd never talked of it before, nor had Beatrice mentioned it, mayhap because both knew how I would feel about Edgar usurping my grandfather's honors. For that's what he had done, in effect. Bantrus was a drunkard and a voluptuary. He and Edgar had served as squires together and now suddenly he was king and his old childhood friend one of his closest advisers. Where others in his council tried to make him measure up, Edgar pandered to him. He was the king's drinking companion and his pimp. While he kept Bantrus in his cups, he was beginning to run the Kingdom of Anglesea. His appearance at the tourney did not bode well for Dankar. Umber, by itself, should be manageable. Add Anglesea to the pan and 'twould be nip and tuck as to which way the scales would come down.

With the uproar about him all died down, Damonryan received a discrete feeler. His lordship, the Baron of Benson, for such Edgar now preferred to style himself, was prepared to ransom both his gear and the two chargers from his former opponent. A considerable sum was proffered but Damonryan scorned gold. Land, he said, was what he was after. Then, before Edgar could mull that over, he went to Elinor and told her what was afoot.

"And you think that he'll offer it you?"

"I do, Your Majesty. The Lord Edgar cannot readily replace that armor. I understand he is well placed in Anglesea."

"Will you take it?"

"A baron without land, Madam, is like a fish without water. Yet I confess a distaste for the good Baron. I would rather, by far, pledge my fealty to Your Majesty."

She considered him. "In plain speech, you want me to give you land, or else you'll take it with my enemies."

"Nay, Your Majesty, I'd not be so big a fool. Edgar has no love for me. Say rather, an you would grant me lands, I could afford to make a present of his gear to the crown."

"Including his horses?"

Damonryan just bowed.

Elinor bestowed one of her rare smiles upon him, "Art a bold rogue. I have a feeling we shall be in need of such before so very long." Her humor may have been as much tickled by the Duke's predicament as the starman's proposition. For would be with the Duke her people would deal over the matter of ransom. It suited her purpose to treat Edgar simply as the Duke's man— as he had been presented—rather than his ally. 'Twould discomfit His Grace greatly to have to deal with the crown. Besides, she could get from him in the end more than any fief was worth. She turned both sides of the whole affair over to her chancellor.

Thastus was a vulpine man who treated each of the Crown's assets an they were his own. He and Damonryan apparently bargained like fishwives, with the opening offer being but a manor, a knight's portion, not much bigger than Bellarus' beloved Warely. Mayhap the chancellor hoped to take advantage of the newcomer's inexperience, but he missed his mark. Damonryan had made discreet inquiries and knew to a copper piece the worth of what he had on offer and in the end he got what he wanted. Indeed, he could have had a bigger fief, for Mutchley was small for a baronial domain, but it was in the west. With luck, 'twould be less affected by the coming war. For a bonus, 'twas hard by Bannering, so Bellarus would not be far away. Indeed, I was never sure that the pair of them hadn't it in mind from the first, though neither would ever admit it. At any rate, Thastus must have had Damonryan's measure by then for he turned sudden effusive in his praise of the domain, pleased, I think, to get off so cheap. Whether he'd had his eye on it all along or not, Damonryan took it.

§

It took two days longer to sort the documents out and for Damonryan to swear, in a brief ceremony, his formal oath of fealty. In the hiatus, I had more requests to play than I could well honor. I'd turned them all down. 'Twas impossible to distinguish the genuine from those who simply wanted to pump me on my companion. But now one came I could not well refuse, though I was under no illusion was a desire for my harping was behind it. Ralven, after all, was the Queen's Ear, but for exactly that reason, I could hardly put him off.

He'd a suite of rooms in the palace, small, but richly furbished, full of elegant, lacquered cabinetry that displayed the distinctive Suthy marquetry, rarely seen in Dankar. Here and there were pieces, a shimmering egg of thinnest porcelain, a graceful silver chalice, it's surface worked swirling in blue, the Dalshiel arms, hung in the window, stained in glass with colors deep as still water. There were others, each superb and each unique, a single expression to proclaim each craft's art, yet none out of place and none clashing, despite the smallness of the chambers. I could have spent the evening in individual admiration, but Ralven's man waved me through. No doubt he was used to such reaction.

The inner chamber was simplicity itself. For a wonder, 'twas paneled, that Suthy marquetry again, with but a single tapestry, though old as the tales, as the hawkers would have you believe of any piece sufficiently threadbare. The real thing, in this case, an I were any judge. In contrast, the carpet on the flags looked an it had been shipped straight in from the Caitlon workhouses, with a pile deep as grass. A harper's dream. I didn't need to sound a note to tell the chamber had superb acoustics. The only furniture was a table at one end, big enough mayhap for twelve. Ralven sat at the head in a beautifully carved chair. Beside him was set a single other place.

Admiration turned to apprehension. I'd expected others. The invitation had been to play and while any harper would claim a place at the table, 'twas most unusual for it to be the only one.

He smiled, discerning at once my confusion, "The invitation was genuine, Nicodemus. Though, an you would not take it amiss, I would be pleased to hear you play *before* we take our meal, rather than after."

I understood Carrick's fascination. He was all grave courtesy. Even as I unslung my harp I knew I could demur and have it accepted with unruffled grace. 'Twas slightly unnerving, playing for an audience of one, but I quickly got used to it. He was an attentive listener and I'd been right about the acoustics. Mindful of his collection, I discarded what I'd planned for the night, and reached to the corners of the land. I even gave him a little Welling plain song. 'Twas the right thing to have done for after I had finished he indicated the seat beside him and we talked of music. His appreciation and depth of knowledge was rare amongst the nobility, bearing out the promise of his chambers. Nor did he simply hold forth, dispensing his knowledge, as so many great lords do; rather, he discussed, so I felt I might have been talking craft with another harper over a pot of ale. A great gift, and useful in the Queen's Ear. Even as it occurred to me I would label him that for his knowledge of music alone, I had to bring myself up with a start and mind me to go carefully.

Yet, when the dinner was served, he came round quite openly to the subject of Damonryan. No effort was made to disguise what he was or why he asked. He lost not one jot of his courtesy but he questioned shrewdly, pressing gently for detail, and then gently for more and then more again. Nothing passed his notice. He wanted to know about everything, the ship and how I left Welling, our journeys, mine across the barrens and the two of us afterwards. I had the sense that he knew most of it already, but that he would always sift for more. That impression was heightened by a trick he had of doubling back to a subject after I thought we had left it.

"Tell me about the ship, again."

"I told you. It was wrecked, I didn't see much of it, before the waves took it finally. I was too busy getting Damonryan out."

"Both of you said it was silver. Painted silver, or the metal itself?"

"Metal. But not silver itself. More like steel."

"Hard to believe, that a ship of steel could float."

I remember wondering to myself what he would think an I claimed it had flown, but I made no comment. Instead I called for his man and whispered what I wanted. He was not long gone and Ralven had the patience to wait. The cup he brought was silver, but no matter. The bowl was another of his exquisite pieces of porcelain, too delicate, it seemed to me, for all that water. I took good care not to tap it with the cup as I set it floating in the middle.

Ralven regarded it thoughtfully, then flicked it so it rapped against the side. The porcelain held. "Of course," he murmured, then stood up. The evening was over.

"Thank-you, Nicodemus." He nodded at the harp, "'Twas a gift worth the hearing, you gave. Let you give me one in return."

I schooled my face but was surprised he'd be so crass. I would have expected a man as deft as he to let his servant deal with any honorarium, but I had him wrong.

He smiled, "Don't poker up. 'Tis for your ears, which seems to me wholly appropriate in the circumstances." He stared at me a long moment. "Your brother Andrea," he said at last, "Has not forgotten you and now he has taken a great interest in your friend. 'Twas he sent brother Rastius and I doubt me he is satisfied." He steepled up his fingers, considering carefully, "The good brother is an ambitious man. Already he is high in the temple and like to go higher. Let us say that he is not as neutral in matters secular as he should be. Best you go very careful of him."

As I left, the servant slipped me a purse but I barely noticed, so busy was I wondering at what he'd told me. Not the what of it, for that rang true enough. The why. Then, walking back to our inn, I seemed to recall Bellarus saying once that Brother Andrea haled from Umber. Was Ralven identifying him as a mutual enemy?

At last I looked at the purse. A hand of golden marks. Generous, but not overtly so. The word that leaped to my mind was *deft*. I found myself laughing softly to the night.

§

We rode out the next morning, blithe to leave the court behind, Damonryan's warrant for Mutchley fresh in his saddlebag. The breeze set from the west, blowing clean in our faces. Sudden, I realized, in all the attention, the maneuvering and the questioning, I had never gotten a chance to ask him about the fight.

He told us that he'd used the mare, not because she cost him less, but because she could dance from side to side so much better than his charger. "It's the oldest trick in the wrestler's book, to use your opponent's weight against him," he commented. Money had played a part, for by winning his wager on Edgar, he had made enough not to worry about hazarding his gear. As for the club, he was simply contemptuous, "There's not a bouncer worth his salt on Unity that couldn't have thrashed him," he snorted. "I've seen one of them take on three haulers with hydro-wrenches, which aren't much different. Once you get them moving, they're committed by inertia." He laughed, a deep rich sound of pure delight, "Edgar would profit from the learning of a little physics!"

About the Author

Michael Bruce-Lockhart was born in Edinburgh, Scotland in 1947 and emigrated to Canada with his family in 1954. He holds degrees in electrical engineering from M.I.T. and had a short career in industry (as chief engineer of Newfoundland's first high tech start-up) and a long one in academia. He is never happier than when creating things. After forty years designing hardware, then software, he has now come back to his first love: books.

He has been married to Carole Peterson since 1981. They have one son, Cullam, who is both a musician and an engineer. All hands live in St. John's, Newfoundland.

Extract from
The Baron of Mutchley

Chapter 1

The Lord Damonryan, self-styled Baron of Unity and now, by royal decree, Baron of Mutchley, stared morosely across the stubbled fields of his new domain.

"This is what Thastus calls a tidy little fief?" He blinked back the flying rain that crashed down in wave upon cold wave, "What the land needs is some honest realtors!"

"Nay, 'tis good land," I rejoindered, "'Tis just the season and that it has been somewhat neglected." It had that. I saw stretches of wall half atumble and water running free in places from where weeds choked out the ditches, runneling the stubbled fields.

He shook his head, "It all seemed like such a good idea. What am I going to do, Nicodemus? I don't know the first thing about farming!"

I sighed to myself. Ever since we'd left Bellarus' little stead that morning, he had grown steadily more morose, but there was no point in commenting upon it. "That's supposed to be your steward's job. We'll have to see why he isn't doing it."

The castle did little to improve his mood, for it was dank and dirty, the lord's chambers shockingly neglected, with only the steward's quarters having any semblance of order. The man himself, Betemus, was old and as sparse as the acres he was supposed to tend. He was stunned to see us, as well he might be. Damonryan gave him what must have been the worst five minutes of his life when he saw the contrast between the old man's rooms and those that were supposed to be kept for the Baron. 'Twas all he needed, on top of a long, cold, wet day in the saddle, doubting himself all the while. His rage was truly towering. I feared for the steward and would have been surprised to see his feet turned straight to the road. I should have known better. The starman's sense of justice was deeply innate and not even for Betemus would he overturn that; but the steward walked soft for many a day thereafter.

In truth, there was little wrong could not be set to rights. The walls were sound, the barns still provendered and the people basically content. The steward knew his business and was honest, his books in proper balance; but he was old, with little fire and less imagination, and had gotten into the habit of doing only what he thought strictly necessary. Within a day or two, the worst faults had been amended, and within a week, the servant's sullenness at being made to work had turned to a cheerful bustle and the castle came to life, even Betemus marching about with a brisker step.

"All that was needed was a little leadership," I commented to Damonryan, over our nightly jar, "'Tis a measure of the cost of this strife that such places go untenanted."

"Seems to me, Nicodemus, that the less castles are tenanted, the better for the land."

"That's no way for a new baron to talk," I twitted him.

"Hereditary baron, and I'll thank you to remember it or it's off to the stocks for you, my lad," he retorted, holding his hands out to the fire. "Brrr! Castles are overrated! How you could ever live through the winter in a castle in the north is beyond me."

Such a simple conversation. Yet it caught the essence of those early days of Damonryan's baronhood. Being made a baron himself had changed not a whit his objections to the whole idea of privilege; though he had reached for it, he wore his mantle lightly, believing always in himself and not his title. And vague plans about what might or might not be done with the infocom were swept away in the press of what he considered necessary to be done then and there.

He was aghast at the castle fireplaces, castigating them as too large and inefficient. The day the first snow flew he got after the problem in good earnest. In vain I pointed out he'd plenty of fuel in his woods.

"Not enough to keep me warm," he shivered, "Not with these medieval monstrosities!"

For two days he delved in the infocom, then designed a central furnace which, to the steward's dismay, he intended to put in the dungeon beneath the keep. This plan, as was to happen so often, fell apart when he found he could not get enough tin in all of Tamus to make up the ducts he required to lead the heat about the castle. Nothing daunted, he delved again, and decided to

Rumfordize each fireplace. A mason was duly engaged from town, but happy though he was to get the work, he could only scratch his head at the plans sketched out for him by the Outlander, as he had begun to be called even before we left Estonval.

In the end I took a hand, and between cajolery and threats to turn him back, I managed to get the old tradesman to accept my help. It took three tries and a week to get the first one right but by the third attempt we at least were working smoothly, though what with the old man's obstinacy and his peremptory treatment of me as an apprentice, I found myself sorely out of temper. Stiff legged as cats, we both would have been pleased to see the whole thing fail, he for the satisfaction of told-you-so and I to be simply shut of him. In the event, we were disappointed, but that quickly turned to wonder and then enthusiasm as the room come to a cheerful glow with but three or four sticks of wood. Even Damonryan's insistence on tearing out part of the work to add an external air supply, an idea he'd dug up while we labored, did not diminish our newfound well-being. In three days we had completed two more conversions. At that point, tired of the mason's overbearing ways, I packed him back to town. We'd Damonryan's quarters warmed to his satisfaction. I could train a pair of men from the estate to do the rest at their leisure.

The man had grumbled every step of the way but within a year he'd made a good thing of his new found skills, though several times, to my great amusement, he must come, hat in hand, to have me work out the necessary dimensions. Likewise, the Mutchley men I trained found themselves after in great demand to convert cottages around the domain.

"Such a simple technology," marveled Damonryan, observing what he called the ripple effect with no little satisfaction, "Maybe I've been looking in the wrong places!" Indeed, within half a score of years, Tamus fires, as they came to be called, were widely used in Estonval and even in Anglesea; and though there was little impact on the woods of Mutchley yet it eased the pressure on the forests about the towns. Even at Mutchley, it meant less work to cut and split the wood, which was just as well. Damonryan had other plans.

With scant appreciation of how a baron's life was to be ordered, he would change whatever fell beneath his eye with little remorse. He scandalized Cook by chasing her from the kitchen one morning and cheerfully cooking himself an omelet, then swearing like a soldier when it stuck to the pan.

"Iron!" he said in disgust. "What a mess." He tossed the pan in the great sink, then went and retrieved it and started to scrub it out. "I had the most beautiful set of polycerams aboard the *Loribel*," he mourned. "It would almost be worth mounting an expedition just to retrieve them."

"Could you do that?"

He stopped for a moment, considering, "No. She's down too deep." He started in again but Cook had crept back.

"'Tisn't fittin', sir," she said firmly and relieved him of it. For a wonder she started in on it herself instead of handing it to one of the scullery maids.

We left, but he was back next morning, and between the two of them they managed to work it out. Thereafter there was a special pan for My Lord's omelet and the god help the scullery maid who touched it, for she must answer to Cook, herself. Needless to say Cook was a personage feared in the kitchens a good deal more than the Baron himself. Though adamant about changes, these were few enough and ordered with enough charm and tact that Cook adored him, declaring to any and all that the Baron was the only man she'd ever met who understood a kitchen.

For his part, he confessed to me his surprise at what he'd found. As much as he could, for there was less than he liked so he bemoaned the loss of his Joshuah, he had made a study on the infocom of what he called medieval times on the mother planet Terra. "You know, Nicodemus, your society is such a pattern of those times that I'd fallen into the trap of expecting it to be identical. But it's not. That old dragon downstairs understands both hygiene and nutrition." By which he meant that we bathed and washed our dishes and knew what foods to eat to keep our health, apparently not the case with his people in the times he mentioned. He swore again that even the nobles bathed but once a year!

Yet baths annoyed him, as did the constant stream of servants to his quarters every night, bearing water from the kitchen boilers. On the road, he had been able to use the bathhouse, but he quickly discovered he was not welcome in the one at Mutchley. No one, of course, said anything, but their constraint shouted at him louder than words. The Baron bathed in his quarters. That was all he needed to become obsessed with the idea of one of his showers. Constantly, he closeted with the blacksmith in an effort to achieve his ambition, setting out to plumb the whole castle. The cost defeated him in the end so he settled for a bathing room in his quarters, with a cistern and boiler above for pressure and heat.

Even with this, he taxed the distracted smith almost past his abilities. Disdaining our simple stoppers, Damonryan demanded what he called *a decent tap* and Alsted's failure to produce led to a deal of unhappiness. For all that the starman claimed to be able to repair most of what was on his ship, he always used parts that were ready made; he'd never had to actually make one. Pressed into service, I at last managed to help the smith concoct a tap that served. In some bemusement over all the fuss I tried the thing myself and found there was something very pleasant about warm water coursing across my body. Before long Damonryan was laughing at me that I was more addicted than he.

Sa. To be fair, his efforts were not just directed at his own comforts. Within a week of our arrival he had ridden all about his fief and, to their everlasting astonishment, introduced himself to each and every one of his villeins, shaking them by the hand as though they were the very gentry. There no few who thought him soft in the head, but, an he knew of it, he never let it bother him. Watching him as we rode about, I realized of a sudden he lacked completely any sense that there should be something due his consequence.

He was also unafraid to show his ignorance, asking the farmers straight out why they did such and such a thing, and bombarding the steward and myself with questions 'til I saw the old man's lip begin to curl and his answers took a patronizing turn. His first night with his new lord should have warned him better, for in a week he was asked a question wiped the curl away.

Thereafter he began to sweat. The questions became shrewder and Betemus found he must defend his own performance. By the time the new Baron had his improvements at the castle well in hand, he had a score of plans for things could be done about the estate.

He didn't wait for spring. 'Twas a mild winter anyway, with little of snow. On any day that was passing fair he had his people out, putting to rights what never should have been let go in the first place. An they complained of the cold he did not hesitate to join in and see for himself, to the deep chagrin of the old steward. He learned to rock a wall that way, finding first that the stones were not so bad on the hands as they complained, then getting interested. By the end of that day, he could do it as well as most of the field hands. They, no more than Betemus, knew what to make of that.

Once the basics were back in order, he went on to the new. First there were the windmills, simple enough devices, though, as usual, we had an awful time trying to get one working. I had seen such things before—they were used somewhat in Suthy for grinding corn—but the one in the infocom we thought looked best bore little likeness to those. Steadily we had fallen to a pattern, where Damonryan, knowing better what had been done and could be done, would decide what next to try and something of the way, while I would work with the smiths to discover the how. Well it suited us. 'Twould never cross my mind to use a mill for lifting water, but given a sketch from the infocom of how it might be done, I was away; 'twas a process I found not so different from writing a song—cutting and patching and polishing, and always trying, casting out whole verses at times, until at last you have the fitted whole. But it took him to look at the well and see the mill. He could sort through the cornucopia of infocom mills and say this and not that because 'tis slow enough or could be geared or might be built with what we had on hand; but though I saw him work for hours when the end was firm, he could never try and cast away and try again. It did not matter. Though I knew I must take the road again, lest I cease to be a harper and my own man, yet I was in no hurry. I found great contentment in the workshops. It was like being back at Welling.

Damonryan had talents in other directions. Had it not been for him, the mill would have been just a castle curiosity. Once we had a satisfactory *prototype* (as he called it) pumping up the castle's water, he ordered three more be built and called in the headmen of his four villages, offering each a mill for their water. To his amazement, for he knew nothing of the countryman's resistance to change, they each refused him when they found they would have to build a cistern to assure supply when there was no wind. He pulled his beard at that, for change was what he wanted; but he dismissed them, without resorting to his full baronial authority.

Two days later, he struck a deal with the least resistant man, building the cistern with labor from the Baron's corvée, and giving them the mill for a six week trial. When the time was up, he simply ordered it dismantled, the cistern as well, but only after the mill. Long before the castle men had got to the bricks, he received a hasty suit to leave it in its place. An the headman was not convinced, his wife and the other women who had to haul the water were. In the bargaining that followed, the Baron got his corvée back and half as much again for the mill itself. 'Twas not long before the other headmen came to terms and when they complained he charged them more he retorted that next time they should think ahead a little further.

There were other things, some new and some not. When the summer came we developed solar dryers could reduce a whole tree's fruit to a hand of jars for journeying or for winter. He had vastly extended the network of drainage ditches and irrigation canals. Not everything worthwhile had to come from the infocom. He was not above learning from the meanest of his peasants, and whatever he took, he held, and sifted against what he already knew or could glean from elsewhere, and gave it back. Always he cajoled and bargained and dealt, and some of the labor he gained he used at the castle, but most he would turn and use to improve the land and the villages.

"Labor is capital here," he laughed, "And I simply do what any good business man must and plow my profits back into the business!"

But he did more than that. I at first had thought his bargaining nothing more than the hallmark of the trader, which of course it was, and he relished it. Betemus was dismissive of it, though he took care not to show it when his master was about, but I soon saw that Damonryan could command, an he had to. Rather though, he would build his people up, getting them to believe in what he was doing and even more, to believe in themselves. Leadership, in the end, is not telling people what to do but getting them to do what must be done themselves. Finding that much of what they did, they did ultimately for their own benefit, the corvée began to be more productive. The serf's age old habit of going as slow as could be gotten away with dissolved in the face of anger, not from the steward, but from his fellows. To Betemus' utter outrage, his lord hurried the process along by forming a council of the headmen and turning over to them a portion of the corvée, to use as they saw fit.

"Sir, you spoil them!" he wailed, "Mark my words, soon you'll be able to do nothing with them."

"Sirrah," he replied, and I was amused to see he could talk like the haughtiest of barons an he wanted, though where he got a word like that was more than I could say, "How much has been done in the five months of my rule compared to the last five years of yours?"

The steward bit his lip and said nothing.

Damonryan smiled, though I don't think it made the steward's heart glad to see it. "Mark my words, Betemus," he added softly, "You will learn my methods or we will have done." The old man was in a quake after that and tried hard to comply. In the end he became useful enough that Damonryan could leave him on his own for weeks at a time without he fall too far back upon his old ways.

Carrick thought the world of him. They were alike in some ways. The lad had Damonryan's quick ear for language but also his lack of interest in music. He had become an exemplary servant, more under Damonryan's eye than mine, for the Baron was quick to notice any lapses and was not above twitting the lad that he could lay my shirts out or clean my boots far better. He was never unkind about it but Carrick would take it to heart and try all the harder.

Though the lad took pride in our engineering accomplishments, he had no interest in them himself. Emerging from the workshops late one afternoon, I found him with Barth in the practice yard. Somewhere in the armory they'd found a small sword, some lordling's of long ago, no doubt, and the old man-at-arms had the lad hard at it.

"Cut down, now cross-parry. Cut left," the boys arm flew down and cut a small notch out of the board Barth had mounted on a practice post, just at his height. "'At's it. Back parry, back parry! Wrist 'igher! An 'e comes at you from the third position, yer mincemeat!"

Noticing me, Carrick came to a panting halt. I shook my head, "Don't let me interfere."

He resumed, but with a wary eye on me, so I moved thoughtfully on. Though the wood on the board was fresh, it had seen much use already. And to my eye, Carrick had a knack. Before supper that night, I sat him down.

"Carrick, would you like to transfer to the Lord Damonryan's service?"

He was on his knees in an instant. "Oh, sir, "he wailed, "I didn't think you'd dislike it. Indeed I didn't. Why, the Lord Damonryan himself learned to use the sword in your service."

"Be easy, child. I don't dislike it. I just though you might be happier with the Baron. I'll be going back to the road one of these days again, you know."

"I *do* know, sir. And in these times you'll need a swordsman to protect you." His face still wore his anxiety like a mask, "Please don't turn me off, sir. I'll give it up an you want."

Did I want? I didn't know. People who wear swords, it seemed to me, are more likely to end up on the wrong end of one. Still, "'Tis your choice, lad. You do your work well and have a right to use your own time as you will. Either way, I'm not about to turn you off." I grinned at him, "Not unless you keep calling me *sir,* that is. It makes me feel too old."

He was on his feet in an instant. "Thank-you, si…,Nicodemus," he corrected. "I'll keep it up, then. I think a sword would be more use against someone like Edgar, than a sling. Now I must be about my duties or I'll hear of it from the Baron!" He was gone like quicksilver.

§

'Twas the grinding mill gave the outlander his greatest pleasure. Though the upper reaches of the Apson bounded the fief to the north, 'twas too far to be useful. There being no other stream on the fief large enough to support a mill, all the wheat was ground by hand. He thought little of it until we rode over to pay a visit to Bellarus and Damonryan saw that Lord Tanfred had a mill large enough for all the flour on his outsized domain. With Tanfred's bemused permission, we studied the mill and agreed we could adapt it for wind. Once suitable stones were found and shaped, the work went easy enough, though the gears, far larger than any we had essayed before, took longer and with more castoffs than we had thought. Used to that, Damonryan was puzzled far more by how slow the mill itself went up.

"They're up to their old tricks," he said, in disgust, "It's as if they didn't want it."

"The mill is ever the Baron's," I responded.

"What do you mean?"

"Did you ask Lord Tanfred how much he took for the milling?" He shook his head. "One bag in four is the normal portion and some take one in three. And once the mill is there, the serfs must use it and pay his price, whether they will or no."

He frowned at that, then laughed, "Well I've a little surprise for them and they'll damn well regret they ever went slow on one of my projects." By then, I knew him better than to worry for the serfs, but for once he wouldn't tell me what it was he was holding up his sleeve.

The mill was done at last, just prior to the harvest, and he decreed a feast, asking every serf on the fief. 'Twas Halting Castle all over again, with the kitchens going full blast for days, except that he built no special hall, but held instead what he called a *buffet*. Neatly did this solve the problem of the serfs seating in his lordly presence, for he had all tables cleared from the hall but for the ones on high which he had loaded with food and plates. People then served themselves, and sat where they chose upon the rushes, for all the land like a picnic at a fair, but held indoors. 'Twas a form they knew and quickly they grew comfortable, helped by ale going round in plenty, making for a festive eve. There was the usual mummering, with a splendid baron lolling about the hall followed close by a gray stick of a steward with a steady wagging finger and a large red woolen tongue. I was played by a man with a wooden harp and a hammer and a great broken gear that he constantly mixed up.

They watched us slyly, anxious we would take it in good part, and ready to break off should we seem displeased. The steward was not amused as his charicature wagged his tongue instead of his finger behind the Baron's back whenever he wasn't looking, but as Damonryan and I took care to laugh as hard as any at their antics and those of the would-be harper trying to play his gear, they cared little for Betemus' frowns. Then, leading them in chorus, I played most of the well-known songs of the season, celebrating the harvest and the chance of winter rest. When at last I had done, Damonryan rose and held for the silence which pooled around him then spread to the farthest corners of the hall. He said all the words were called for, gravely accepting the accompanying applause, then held again the silence.

"And now we come to the matter of the mill," he said lightly, once he got it. The silence took on a deeper note. "I had in mind to pass the mill on to the council," there was an outburst at that, but he held up his hand, "But…it seems, despite you've come to know me, you've decided 'tis to be the Baron's mill." There was no response but only staring eyes, as they all wondered what was coming next. "Betemus. What's the Baron's Portion?"

"One sack in four, my Lord," came the satisfied reply.

"Dost concur, Neddle?" he asked the oldest of the headmen.

"Ay…aye, my Lord, 'tis usual, but…"

"Come, Neddle, surely 'tis a fine mill? Why, there are Barons would charge a bag in three!"

"My Lord!"

His victim was ashen now, as were most of his fellows, and Damonryan relented, "I'll tell you what. I'll set the Baron's Portion at one in four, or…" he looked around, building the drama as much as he could, "I'll let the council have it and you may appoint a miller who may charge one in twenty for his portion. In return, you must put back into the corvée twice the hours I spent on the mill."

It was a generous offer, for it gave them what no serfs had anywhere else in the land, control of their own mill. They were quick to accept, but their faces grew very long again when he presented to them the exact total of the hours they had taken to build the mill. Then there were rueful smiles at his shout of laughter, and by the time they had drunk on the bargain and were shuffling into the night, no few were laughing at themselves and swearing not to stint on their Baron again.

I watched them go, content. 'Twas hard to believe, but we'd been there a year. A good year, a wonderful year, one I would treasure for the rest of my life. Despite Tanfred's predictions there'd not been so much as a rumble of the war we thought had been brewing. Just across the river, Umber lay as quiet as we did. Looking at them leave, I could believe that this is the way the god had meant for things to be. Then I saw the mummer's broken gear, abandoned in the corner, and glanced down at my harp, still on my knee. *'Twould be too easy for me to get comfortable here.* A sergeantry might be all right for Bellarus, he was already harper. An I would be one, 'twas time to take to the road again. I would have to go in the spring.

The Baron of Mutchley is scheduled for publication in the fall of 2010

www.ingramcontent.com/pod-product-compliance
Lightning Source LLC
Chambersburg PA
CBHW060156260626
47160CB00001B/292